Anti-Christ: A Satirical End of Days

Booklocker.com, Inc.
2007

Anti-Christ: A Satirical End of Days

Matthew Moses

Dedicated to Mr. Schroeder and Capt. Oldham, those twin influences that encouraged me to write when I thought I had no story to tell.

CwHyAPTER 1

The stars shone like luminous islands in the sea of night. Each triumphantly glimmered as an ethereal jewel out of the reach of man, gems of untold wealth that enriched man's thoughts.

Humanity once thought those strobing specks were the immortalized memorials of their legendary forebears, heroes that had lived lives of epic proportions and whose images were meant to embolden, guide, and inspire those that came after. There was something more to that horizon; it was man's spiritual home. Each one of those shining stars was a giver of life, light, and possibilities. They inspired man to strive beyond himself that, one day, he might reach them.

Then came science, that murderer of myth; science revealed those jewels to be so numerous as to be worthless, their origins mundane, their possibilities quantifiable realities. Man touched the stars and left his flaws upon them. The stars went from immortal legends to finite gas and fire always on the verge of fading out. The mystery was stripped away and lost with time, the spiritual replaced by the corporeal.

Now, those stars were as mortal as those who stared up at them. They were beings that seemed so close, yet were so distant from one another. Their light was simply a shallow image to cover the turmoil within them. Without mystery, the heavens lost meaning. Man lost interest in staring up at the firmament, his head bowed to the realities of life.

From that lofty height one single man fell away from such divine diversions back through obscuring clouds to his set, mortal place on that speck of dirt in the universe known as Earth.

Matthew sat alone at his table in the food court ringed by the bustling crowds of the modern day, that encircling miasma of men and child obscuring any and all paths out of the current purgatory he found himself floating in, namely that capitalist Paradise known as "The Mall". Matthew stared up through the large skylight at the free, uncontrolled firmament beyond. He was one of the few that still looked to the heavens. That sea above was the sole glimmer in this dull world of worthless endeavor. From that ocean arose mysteries in his mind as to the meaning of it all: life, faith, love.

Love: that mystery he was continually trying to figure out in his own awkward way. It was not simply his bumbling grip that prevented him from getting a grasp on it. It was the complexity of women that thwarted his every theory on the subject. Tonight was another attempt at that irritating, unsolvable equation.

He was currently on a date. A blind date. A blind internet date. With a girl he had met…online. He'd spoken to her. Well, he had spoken to her once…via text. At least she knew his name…his screen name. It all seemed so impersonal the way the date had been arranged, ironic as that sounded. They had originally agreed to see a romantic movie and have dinner; then it turned into a comedy and dinner; then just dinner. Matthew felt like he was bartering some trade agreement.

It was all so pathetic, but Matthew didn't care. Loneliness had a way of eroding pride. The problem was he simply didn't understand people, women in particular. One look at this wild-haired, clumsy man-child was enough to send even the most kindhearted scrambling for escape. To say every encounter helped to deepen Matthew's complex about himself was an understatement.

So here he was now, his vigil stretching into its third hour. There was still no sign of her. Even Matthew had to admit the likelihood of her showing up was approaching zero, yet another gaping hole in his life.

"Nice waste of an evening," he mumbled. Sadly, what else did he have to do tonight?

The rumblings of the crowd began to drown out his thoughts. The murmurs sent a tremor through his excited frame causing him to tremble further as the buzz itched at his ears. All those faces turned towards him as they circled around and placed him under siege at the center of the food court. Matthew bit his lip as he felt the eyes of the surging crowd upon him. They knew why he was here, cackling beneath their whispers. He dipped his head as he tilted his glasses down forcing the masses to merge into a blur as he gripped his date's gift, a book, closer to his chest like a protective totem.

Yet, despite himself, Matthew was drawn back to those scattered about the tables littering the food court, their lives causing his brooding head to rise. It was some sort of magnetic attraction that kept him from fully pulling away, but as he watched them smile and laugh their faces wrinkled into something demonic and mocking. Their happiness only increased Matthew's bitterness and made him recoil.

His eyes drifted over to the empty seat across from him. Why had he even come? Had he really expected her to show? He had been sitting here for three hours too long, his head jerking with each possible sound. Each glimpse proved a disappointment. Every minute further depressed him. She wasn't coming. Matthew slumped, dejected as ever. Love, like so many other things, would forever remain a mystery to him.

Matthew's eyes wandered the food court before settling on one couple as they talked and laughed. The man said some off comment and she grinned. "How do you do it?" Matthew asked from just out of earshot. "You make it all look so easy."

The girl gently touched her partner's forearm before giggling some more. Matthew let the guy fade out of sight as he focused on her. Her flaxen hair was shining gold, her blue eyes sapphire. That ivory goddess became an idol of worship. "What do I have to do to get the attention of a girl like you?" he whispered. As if she heard him, the girl turned towards Matthew causing him to quickly look away.

What was he still doing here? Matthew plowed that wild mane of his as he took a deep breath. He had studying to do. The big final was tomorrow, but first he had to return the book. He didn't want anything to remember this night by.

Matthew got up to go on his little quest, his bow-legged waddle drawing a lot of stares as he made a hasty retreat into the consuming crowd bumping into a table on the way causing it to wobble in his wake. He felt like a fish in a current, separate from those that rushed around him. He bobbed and weaved through the undulating waves making his way through a crowd that seemed bent on pushing him back. He let the world pass by him as he went his own way regardless of who he had to push through to get there.

After a few minutes, he left the main artery and entered a bookstore heading straight for the register. Without so much as a warning, Matthew slammed his book down on the counter.

"Help you, sir?" the cashier asked with a nasal drone.

"Refund please."

The cashier looked down at the book. "Didn't you buy this a few hours ago?" His eyes flicked back up to Matthew.

"I've had a change of mind," Matthew told him as he pushed the book forward.

"We don't give refunds," the cashier replied as he pushed the book back.

"I didn't do anything to the book."

"That's not the issue."

"Then why can't I have a refund?"

"Because it's against policy."

"Well that's a stupid policy."

"I'm not here to debate company policy," the cashier breezily cooed.

"The fact you're jockeying a register proves you're not capable of much."

"I'm capable of not giving you a refund, sir." The cashier stressed the final word sarcastically.

Matthew balled his fists. "Well, I don't want the book," he growled.

"Well, that's just too bad."

"What if I just give it to you? The store still makes a profit."

"I can't take that book back from you, sir."

"Why the hell not?"

"Policy," the cashier stated once more.

"What do you want me to do with it?"

"Take it home with you. Make it into a paperweight. It's not my concern."

"This book is going back on that shelf," Matthew all but demanded pointing at the book-lined wall.

"This book isn't going anywhere save home with you."

Matthew wanted to pick up the tome and slam it over the man's head. At least then he'd have some purpose for it. His palms began to sweat as he locked eyes with the cashier. Though it was only a book and though it hadn't cost much there was a principle to the whole thing. As insane as it seemed, Matthew simply wanted to correct the mistake he had made in purchasing the book, correct his ever removing it from the wall. Its very weight reminded him repeatedly of a bad choice. He was not going to keep the thing nor throw it away. It was going back from whence it came.

A crowd had started to develop around the two as a line formed behind Matthew. "Can you hurry it up?" the customer behind Matthew asked. Matthew simply waved him away.

"Sir, I'm going to need you to step aside," the cashier coolly ordered.

"I'm not leaving here with this book," Matthew retorted.

"Oh, just take the book," the customer behind Matthew interjected. Others in the crowd murmured in agreement with him.

Matthew could feel his anxiety starting to grow, his heart ramping up as his breathing shallowed stealing his ability to reply.

"Come on buddy, I've got places to go," someone said from the back of the line.

"Stop wasting our time."

"Sir, you're going to have to take your book."

"Yeah, just take the book and leave."

"Why do you have to cause so many problems?"

Matthew fidgeted as he stood there struggling with himself. He wanted to run out of there, but the weight of that book anchored him. "I'm sorry," he managed to sputter over his shoulder to the angry mob before quickly jerking back towards the cashier. "I'm not leaving here with this book," he hissed.

"Well you are going to have to, sir," the cashier stated.

Matthew grimaced, the faces closing in on him. He looked everywhere for salvation, some sort of solution, before his eyes settled on a little placard pasted to the back of the cash register. "You give in-store credit for returns?"

The cashier's eyes narrowed as he realized a weakness in the return policy. "Yes, sir."

Matthew grabbed the nearest book and dropped it on top of his return. "I'll take this."

The cashier caught a glimpse of the title and put his hands up in mock self-defense. "*Encyclopedia of Serial Killers*, hmmmm?"

"Yeah, I like to masturbate to the crime photos," Matthew cut back, agitated by the cashier's smug voice. The minute the words left Matthew's mouth he felt his face sear. He swore the flesh would melt right off his skull. He looked over his shoulder and around the shop. Ghastly faces hovered about him in the silence, mouths agape with mothers clucking their tongues.

One mother was hurrying out the store with her son in tow. "What does masturbate mean mommy?" the tyke asked as he passed.

Matthew gave everyone a fleeting smile as his hands shook and a sickness started in his gut. Someone coughed briefly breaking the quiet as Matthew turned back to the cashier. "Uh, just...uh, put it in a bag." He swallowed that lump that caused his voice to break.

***

Matthew wandered through the parking garage looking for his car. It had to be on this level. He'd tried all the others. He walked down the length of cars letting his hand trail over a few tail ends. Of course one touch set off a car alarm sending him running as fast as he could, the wail reverberating off the walls. After the adrenaline wore off, Matthew bent over sucking all the wind he could swallow. As he took that latest gulp he looked up to see his car not but a few feet ahead.

Relief washed over him as he closed the gap between him and his rather imperfect car. It wasn't the newest model, and far from the prettiest, but it was dependable. "Just like me." He ran his hand down the dented, off-white side panel, his fingers tracing the pitted surface as he approached the driver's door. He inserted his key and pulled on the handle. The door didn't open. "You stubborn..." Matthew pulled on it again wrenching and straining. Without warning it finally popped after the latest yank, the door slamming into his knees. The blinding blow caused Matthew to slump forward closing the door as lights exploded before his eyes. When the pain subsided, Matthew went to pull the door open again only for it to jam like before. Remembering the result of his last struggle, he wisely limped to the passenger side and climbed in.

"Another day lost." He sighed as he turned the key. After a few minutes of coughing and automotive seizures, the choking car came to life. Matthew reversed and drove out of the parking lot making for the exit and the waiting night.

Snow drifted down from the dark skies twinkling like falling stars. Only the occasional car lit the evening, all going the opposite direction. The radio throttled Matthew's ears as he zoomed through the blackness. He found himself dwelling on the day that was, shaking his head at the way things had turned out. At least they couldn't get any worse.

Without warning the car started to shake. "What the..." Matthew started, turning down the radio. The shaking quickly became a bouncing as he was thrown violently up and down in his seat, his head ramming into the roof over and over again. He slowed down and pulled over.

As he turned the key, the lit stereo immediately went mute and the car rattled before going still. The night was dark, only a lone streetlight twenty feet away gave him any illumination. He climbed out, walking the length of his car to check the tires on the driver's side. Everything was fine. Rounding the back bumper he caught a glimpse of the rear passenger tire and the problem. The thing looked like a lion had used it as a chew toy. "Glorious. Glorious!" Matthew railed at no one as he kicked the tire, or what was left of it, getting the toe of his boot caught in the rubber shreds. He pulled it free only to slip, his feet going out from underneath him. Falling forward he caught his forehead on the edge of the car splashing the night in splotches of colors.

His hands had already gone numb as the winter winds pushed him around, the icy air slapping him hard in the face helping him to collect his bearings. He put a hand to the swollen knot just above his right eye, the touch causing him to wince. "Jesus Christ," Matthew muttered wide-eyed as he pulled himself up. So things could get worse. He used the car for support as he trudged back to the trunk and popped it. Once in, he wrestled to remove the spare.

His dim struggle was exposed by someone pulling off just in front of him. Matthew paused to watch as some guy climbed out and came back towards him lit by the rise and fall of hazard lights. "Hey, everything ok?"

"Flat tire," Matthew responded, surprised anyone would offer aid.

"Oh. Ok." The guy turned around, got in his car, and drove off.

Matthew watched as he faded away into the night. "Thanks for the help," he tossed after his tease of a rescuer. Snow began to fall again, the white flakes peppering him. Matthew sighed as he pulled the spare from the trunk.

***

"Russia celebrates the re-election of their president tonight, Alexander Romanov. Staunchly backed by the conservatives of the Duma, he has sworn to put Russia back on track towards a brighter future and reclamation of their lost legacy as a world power.

"In another part of the world, tensions rise as terrorists struck at the Indian Parliament building. The death toll was well over sixty, including all terrorists involved. India blames Pakistan for supporting the terrorists, threatening armed force if words fail to bring any reform in policy. Pakistan denies any involvement but has warned India against any attempted military action." The anchorman smiled, oblivious to the threat just mentioned.

"In America, President Lucas continues to deny corruption charges over government contracts issued to various corporations associated with large donations to his re-election campaign. The President had this to say."

The screen switched to President Lucas standing behind the Seal of the United States, his hair slick and image suave.

"Oh, he's so gorgeous," Mary sighed. She sat there in her nightgown, wrapped in a pink robe, curled up in her chair watching the world at a glance, the television illuminating her face in its flickering glow.

"Fairness has always been a hallmark of my presidency," Lucas began. "I've had a vision and stuck to it. My detractors in the liberal media would call me guilty. I am only guilty of doing what is best for the American people." President Lucas winked through the screen, giving a thumbs up.

"That's right. Damn Democrats. Always attacking good men." Mary shook her fist at the TV. Its worn, bent rabbit ears failed to hear her threats. She continued her tirade, the curlers in her hair bouncing. The reception of the television was jagged, slightly off with a hue of fuzz over the transmission as the picture occasionally rose vertically before settling back into position.

The anchorman came back onscreen. "In Los Angeles, a passenger on flight A401 was reported to have been infected with a new strain of bird flu."

"Bird flu!" Mary pulled her robe close about her face.

"He was quickly quarantined, and the diagnosis was proven premature."

"That's what you want us to believe, you liberal liars!" she yelled at the screen. "Get us all sick and then hike up prices for medicine! I know the conspiracy!"

"In local news, it is flu season and-"

Mary dropped the remote control on the floor, the rest of what was said lost in her mania. "Flu? No, it's more than flu. It's bird flu! It's come here. No, oh no!" She reached up and felt her forehead. She felt hot all over and then came the chills. Her fears produced nausea as her anxiety grew. She began to shake. "Bird flu. I've got bird flu!"

She heard someone walk into the room. She turned and saw Orlando, the family's white Chihuahua, staring at her. "You!" Orlando licked his black lips, his big eyes growing bigger. "You gave it to me, you dirty animal!" Orlando turned and scurried from the remote that was kicked at him. She ran after him, cursing and screaming. The chase continued into the kitchen as her anxiety became epic. He dove through the doggy door to escape outside.

Mary was frantic. Sweat beaded on her forehead. She wiped it away, worried. What was that noise? Was she hearing things now? Dementia! Wait, it was coming from downstairs. She turned to the basement door and opened it. "Mike?" She looked into the darkness, swearing she saw a glimmer off in the corner. "Mike, are you down there?" As she started down the stairs, the wood creaked.

"Don't come down here!" warned a voice.

"Mike, what are you doing down there?" she yelled down the stairs.

"Nothing." Mike had the lights turned off, the volume as low as he could make it and still hear. He watched his porn privately, clad only in his boxers that rested around his ankles, gut spilling over. His clothes littered the floor. The flashing glow danced on his baldhead. His wife couldn't stand the thought of such "entertainment" in the house. She also couldn't stand the thought of sex since menopause had kicked in so Mike was in horrible circumstances. Hot, cold, hot, cold: and that was just her!

"That's right. Do a cheer," he whispered as he watched, the light of the television illuminating his face as he grimaced and made kisses at the screen. "Hey, he has the big game tomorrow. He deserves encouragement."

"Mike!"

"What?" he yelled back over his shoulder.

"I don't feel well. Can you go to the pharmacy?"

"Ok," he replied. "Go back to your coffin, ice woman," Mike murmured as he continued to watch. His eyes were drawn to the smut and nothing could pull them away.

"Mike!"

"What?" he roared back, unable to stay in the mood with each interruption.

"When are you going?"

"All the pharmacies are closed!" he said offhand refusing to be distracted.

"No they're not!"

"They are! I'll go tomorrow!"

"I need medicine!"

18

"Tomorrow!"

"But I need it now!"

"So do I," he sputtered listening to the moans of the cheerleader.

The light around him snapped on followed by the sound of the stairs creaking. He hurriedly switched the television off, wrestling to pull his boxers up. "Michael, what are you doing down here in the dark that is more important than my health?"

"Woman, if you know what is good for your health you'll go back up those steps."

As Mary reached the foot of the stairs she stopped, noticing the television behind Mike. "When did that get down here?"

Mike turned around. "That? Few days ago. I'm, uh, trying to fix it. Extra money."

"It looks brand new."

"It's the lighting. It's definitely not new."

Mary took a closer look. "There's a satellite box on it!" She gave Mike a horrendous glare. "I thought you got rid of our satellite!"

"Ok. Sometimes I like to watch television in private-"

"You're watching dirty movies again aren't you!" Mary rasped, her illness forgotten.

"I was watching a sports show if you want to know."

"I know what you really watch!"

"Now wait a minute-"

"Does immoral lust mean more to you than our family? I'm gonna rip that destructive dish off the house and bury it-"

"Don't you threaten my satellite, woman!"

"Don't speak to me that way!"

"I'll speak to you that way if I want. You won't threaten my dish."

"While I am dying you refuse to get my medicine so that you can watch those filthy movies."

"What do you think is keeping me from killing you myself?"

"You dirty old man. I'm tearing it down!" Mary started stamping up the steps.

"You frigid witch!" Mike ran after her. "Don't do it! I swear you'll be buried in this basement if you take away my satellite!"

The pair raced up the steps into the kitchen. Despite his best efforts Mike couldn't beat her to the backdoor so he made a last minute gamble and hurried over to the cabinets opening the middle set. Inside were herbs and pills, vitamins and supplements each in alphabetical order. Mike reached inside knocking a few of the bottles over to rattle onto the countertop.

Mary froze at the sound. "What are you doing?" she asked in horror.

He grabbed two bottles from inside and popped the tops. "Giving the sink its daily dose."

"I need those!" Mary was in utter shock. "Don't do it!"

Mike put the one bottle over the sink, twitching his hand and making the pills shake like gravel inside. His mouth made an "o" as he taunted her.

Mary rushed over to the stove and picked up a frying pan. "Don't you even dare! Drop it," Mary warned. She inched a little closer, a crazed look in her eye.

Mike put one of the bottles down and turned on the water. As she inched closer he flipped the switch. The garbage disposal ground to life. The blades swung in the recesses of the sink ready to shred. Mike hardened his expression, setting his jaw. "I'll send your new age to the stone age." She moved a little closer. "I mean it!"

When she inched a step closer Mike lunged for her, dropping the pills, and got his baldhead whacked. He fell to the floor dazed. "Bitch hit me with a frying pan," he grunted as he tried to stand and fell back down on his butt.

As Mary sauntered past him, Mike made an uncoordinated grab for the hem of her nightgown. She easily brushed by him as he continued clutching at air. She pulled the backdoor open and stood there unable to walk outside. She wanted to step out, but she couldn't find the courage to do so. "Can't do it, can you?" Mike taunted, rubbing the growing bruise on his baldhead. "Too many pathogens and germs out there."

Mary turned and gave Mike a dirty stare. "I'll go out there one day, you sick old man." She slammed the door shut and dropped the frying pan on the counter. "You're sleeping in the basement tonight. Maybe your hellish behavior can keep you warm." She stamped back to her bedroom.

"I'd freeze to death if I slept in your bed," he retorted. The door slammed in the distance.

The backdoor opened minutes later, Matthew stepping in. He saw the scene in the kitchen. His dad looked up from the floor clad only in his underwear with a purple explosion on his baldhead as the water poured and the sink roared. Orlando came in after him and stopped between his master's feet, looking first up at Matthew and then at Mike. Matthew stared at his father, raising an eyebrow.

"So," his father started. "How was your night?"

***

The Duma, Russia's legislative body, was in chaos. Communists shouted at capitalists. Capitalists shook with fury towards communists. Reformers screamed insults while conservatives shrieked louder. It was the common mob...in business suits. They were the symbol of Mother Russia tearing itself apart in confusion. The Speaker called for order, his voice drowned out by the slanders of those present.

"The people freeze while your party steals from the coffers of the state," one of the Duma's officials threw at the opposition.

"They freeze because they keep their money hidden under their mattresses and refuse to spend it," a member of the opposition retaliated.

"Why bother?" another broke in. "A million rubles would make a better blanket before it could buy a heater."

"You care nothing for the people!" a reformer cut in.

"I do! That is why I want the old order back. You capitalists believe in luxury before progress, you decadent pigs!" a communist yelled, his face crimson.

"Pigs? You who live in the filth of your own hypocritical luxury!"

The noise continued to rise as these men attacked one another with their favorite weapon: words. Lies, half-truths, and vague rumors danced in the halls of government as the nation crumbled around them. In these chambers anything was accepted as the truth.

Without warning, the doors opened. The crowd remained oblivious as Alexander Romanov marched in. He watched these representatives of the people with eyes of steel embedded in a long, wolf-like face. "Peasants that want to be kings," he said as he stared disapprovingly at the masses. His face gradually hardened as he lost his patience. He let out a bellow that shook the room. Everyone went silent and turned to Alexander. He returned their gaze. "You are men, not women. Leave the arguments and gossip to those best suited."

Alexander made for the podium, his stride confident meeting any stare he received. His fists were balled for battle, his jaw set. The legion of legislators watched warily, unsure of this upstart. He mounted the steps towards the podium brushing aside the Speaker.

"I am Alexander Romanov. I am your President, and you," he swept his brown sleeved arm across the expanse of the Duma, "are nothing." The Duma erupted in shouts as grown men threw paper, drinks, and even chairs. Alexander banged his fist down on the podium. Every one went quiet. "This," he pointed at them, "is the price we pay for capitalism, for," his face became distorted in disgust, "international legitimacy. We were once great-"

"We are still great!" someone challenged.

"We are worthless!" Alexander roared back. "Crime is out of control. In some parts of Russia we do not even hold full authority. Corruption is everywhere. You eat the finest cuisine. Wear the finest clothes when our soldiers die without being paid in months! Our proud nation is fragmented, our economy in shambles. What have we attained since the fall of our empire? The lands of our fathers have been amputated from the body of Mother Russia. The West gorges on our losses and closes in on what lands we still hold. Our once feared army cannot even destroy a band of rebels! The people prefer the dollar to the ruble! Russia is unstable, and you are to blame!"

"We have done nothing!" retorted a senior member of the Duma.

"I know and that is the problem." Alexander fixated on them with a predatory stare. "Before the fall, power was concentrated where it could best be used. In the executive. In the leader. Now it is scattered. It is time to return to those old ways."

"No!" most of the Duma yelled, others cursing and threatening.

One of the Duma stood on a table and waved for quiet. "You cannot simply remove the authority of the Duma. You do not have that authority."

"Oh, I surely do! I hereby dissolve the Duma." They were horrified. "Elections will be postponed until order has been re-established."

"Order?" yelled someone.

"When will that be?" another asked.

"When I say so." Alexander descended the podium and exited this tomb of democracy.

***

Matthew was in his fourth year of college, on the cusp of a degree and some major decisions in his life with a final the following day, and there he was jumping up and down screaming at the top of his lungs like some gorilla as he watched big men in colorful underwear tear each other apart in a scripted battled within the squared circle. Professional wrestling: the sport of the elite.

"Hit him with a chair!" Matthew yelled. He was up on his feet in excitement, Orlando hopping up and down beside him on the floor.

Matthew was lost in the programming, flailing his arms oblivious to what was around him. Wanting to become a part of the action, Matthew grabbed Orlando and put him in a sleeper hold. The dog pawed with futility as he was jerked around, his little feet dangling in the air. Matthew released the pup and raised him to face level, staring those big eyes down. "Do you think you can beat me?" he asked, his voice dropping to a deep bass. Orlando cocked his head away and then back at his master. Matthew raised Orlando above his head with both arms as if to throw him to the ground. The pup kicked with one of his back legs as Matthew pretended to toss him to the carpeted floor. The Chihuahua landed softly on the bed with a mild bounce. Matthew quickly reapplied his grip putting the pup in a full nelson.

"Do you submit?" Matthew crowed into the pup's ear. "Do you submit?" The pup gave a yelping bark, and Matthew dropped him. "I win. I win!" He posed in his victory celebration, flexing biceps that butter would put to shame. To his detriment, he threw his arm to the side knocking a ten-pound weight right off his desk and right on his bare toes. The impact was immediate and hard. Orlando jumped back as the weight fractured Matthew's one toe ripping a red gash. Matthew was quick to fall, grabbing his aching foot as he cursed through gritted teeth. His mother was at the door in seconds causing him to curse for a whole new reason.

"Matthew, what happened? I heard a...Matthew!" She saw his bleeding toe and started to lose it.

"I'm ok, mom. I had an accident, but I'm fine."

"Are you sure? You could get an infection. Even lose your toe."

"Mom, it's only a scratch."

"Well, let me see." His mother moved forward and stopped just before touching it, running out of the room only to return seconds later with a wash cloth and a big, brown bottle. She unscrewed the top and poured a large amount of Hydrogen Peroxide on the wound.

Matthew screamed, slapping the bottle away. "What are you doing?" he shrieked.

"I should have warned you it would sting a little."

"A little?" Matthew gasped as his gash sizzled with foam.

"Oh, it looks bad," she wept as she grabbed his toe.

Matthew winced before pushing her hand away. "Mom, don't wiggle it!"

"Does it hurt?"

"Hell yeah, it hurts when you move it! Just let me put a band-aid on it. It'll be fine."

"A band-aid. A band-aid! Matthew, that is a bad cut."

"It's on my toe. How bad could it be? My toe is tiny. Worse case they amputate it."

"Matthew, don't say that. You need your toes. What if it becomes infected? It can spread into your foot. Then your leg. My God, even your heart!"

"Ok, mom-"

"I should call a doctor."

"It's ok, mom-"

"Let me call 911."

"Mom, no, I'm fine."

"You could be delirious." Matthew's mother put her hand on his head to check for fever.

"Mom, please!" His mother froze. "It's a cut."

She gave him an upset pout. "Fine, don't be careful. See where you are when they have you on life support."

"Ok, mom." Matthew steadily started moving his mother out the door.

"I won't cut life support." She waved her hands in the air.

"Ok, mom."

"I won't let go of my baby!" Matthew shut the door as his mother sobbed all the way back to her room.

The howling of the wind picked up outside as a storm brewed, shaking the window. The audio of the television began to break up followed by the picture. "No!" Matthew screeched.

Matthew's mom stomped back down the hallway yelling through the locked door, "What? Has your toe turned black?"

Matthew could only shake his head as the televised fight devolved into hissing snow. "Modern technology at its finest." Matthew's mother continued pounding on the door as he turned to his desk, staring at his books. "Guess I'm studying."

***

He pored over the books, trying to stay awake and make sense of the gibberish. *Why did I choose philosophy?* Matthew asked himself. *Why not political science? Wait, is that degree even usable?*

Socrates asked too many questions. Plato believed too much in "shapes". Aristotle liked to stare at things too much. Hobbes believed we were all savage. Locke gave man too much credit. And Nietzsche...he needed to get laid. All of them asked the same question: why? Each came away with a different answer. Only in philosophy could your studies all contradict one another.

Matthew tried to stay awake, the weight of fatigue causing his head to rise and fall. His eyes were on fire causing him to blink. It felt so good when he left them closed, the fiery pain smoldering.

A breeze swept in from nowhere. The pages on his open books blew this way and that. He looked up, but the window was closed. Suddenly the desk lamp flickered and went out. "Great," Matthew replied as he tapped on it. It didn't come back on. The wind continued to howl outside. "Guess study time is over."

He gripped the back of his neck massaging out the stress of another day. He stumbled through the dark to his bed accidentally hitting something on the floor with his bad foot. "Ow!" he yelped as he fell into bed, favoring his mangled toe. Matthew managed to grit through the pain as he slid under the covers. He tried to sleep, the throbbing guiding him into a snooze.

Creaking started to sound throughout the house as if it was sighing. Light sounds of air, like breathing, began followed by whispering. Matthew ignored it. The whispering began to build. He grabbed a pillow and covered his head to drown out the noise. A voice began to rise out of the whispers calling his name. Matthew continued to ignore it. His bed started to shake by unseen hands shattering what little chance there was of falling back to sleep. Irritated, Matthew threw the pillow off and saw a muted light around some odd figure. It continued to call out to him. "Matthew." The ghost reached out to touch him. "Matthew." Its features remained unsculpted and hidden in mist. "Matthew."

***

The front door to the house opened, and Matthew threw the ghost out into the garbage cans, the crash causing a dog to bark down the block. "You picked the wrong night to bother me. This has been going on for too long. I'm tired of it. No more!"

"You can't kick me out!" the ghost yelled, picking itself up from the rubbish.

"Oh, no." Matthew reached for the baseball bat kept in the front closet and started to walk back outside towards the ghost. It turned and ran down the street. Matthew laughed as he walked back to the front door. "Who you gonna call?" He slammed the door.

CwHAtPTER 2

It was dark in Matthew's bedroom, the curtains serving as the drawn boundary between his world and the vast one that waited outside. He kept his curtains pulled often, unable to stand seeing his reflection in the window as if a ghost in the world beyond that transparent mirror. He could not stomach being so insubstantial though he knew that, in reality, he really was nothing more than a shade.

Nothing stirred in his black hole. Well, a little something did. The door to Matthew's bedroom slowly opened with a tiny squeak. In the narrow gap a white muzzle crowned by a black nose stuck itself through smelling the stuffy air. It sniffed the carpet below, snorted, and then sniffed the air again. Pushing the door open a bit more, Orlando pranced into forbidden territory. He bobbed and weaved around books and magazines to stand beside the bed. He stared up at his sleeping master, a tiny shadow amongst the various hills of debris on the floor.

Matthew's mouth yawned open as he snored. His left leg dangled over the side of the bed poking out from beneath his quilt. It was evident Matthew was still wearing the same clothes from last night.

Orlando cocked his head, the pup's bottom lip hanging diagonally as he observed the heaving mass. He approached the bed and stood up balancing his front two paws against the wood paneling. He gave a little, moderate bark. His jaws were slightly open and his lips closed. He barked again. Matthew was totally unconscious.

Orlando jumped on the bed, navigating the bumps and blanketed dunes. He eventually settled on Matthew's leg and proceeded to start biting it. He growled as he tore at Matthew's thigh, but his little mouth couldn't tear toilet paper

29

let alone make any real noticeable impact on someone's leg. He started jumping all around, racing all over the bed.

Matthew muttered something unintelligibly as he rolled onto his back. His breathing was softer as the mattress partially muffled his mouth. Orlando slowly crept up to Matthew's face, the nervousness in his eyes showing as his tiny head shook. Matthew twitched sending Orlando rushing to the foot of the bed. The dog lost traction and slid along the quilt, thumping his head on the frame as he rolled and fell over to the floor, his little body hitting the door closing it with a silent click. Matthew rolled back over then was still again.

Orlando peeked up over the frame before jumping back up. He began moving forward again, stopping every few inches. Matthew coughed, waking to see some dark shape on his leg. At first he froze in fright before reason clouded instinct. "Orlando? That you?" he asked. The dog's head perked up at the sound of his name. Mystery solved, Matthew started to pass out again when he felt it. It was a gradual warmth that turned into a wet cold. He was being pissed on! Matthew jerked up, and Orlando went rigid. "You..." Matthew menacingly breathed.

He reached for Orlando, missing. The dog was on the floor in seconds, slamming headfirst into the closed door only now realizing he had locked himself in. He scratched quickly at the barrier as Matthew got up. As he came around, Orlando ran between his feet and skittered under the bed. Matthew followed after the dog, but he proved too big to get underneath. "Come out!" Matthew struggled to reach the runt as it hid in the furthest corner. "Come here now!"

Without warning, the door opened and Matthew's mother peeked in. "Matthew?" Orlando sped out from underneath the other end of the bed and charged out of the room skimming Mary's robe. Matthew came out from underneath the bed as his mother wrinkled her nose. "Did you have an accident?"

"It was that stupid dog. Ugh!" Matthew looked down at his stained leg.

"About time you got up," she told him, stirring her cup of tea. "Don't you have tests today?"

Matthew dabbed at the dark stain with his quilt drawing his mother's disapproving glare. "First one isn't until ten."

"You better hurry then," she replied before taking a sip.

"Why? It's still early." Matthew's mom went over to the window and pulled the curtains. The sunlight blinded him, his eyes melting behind those solidly sealed lids. He stumbled to his feet before falling back down. "What time is it?"

"Ten to nine."

"I've got to go!" Matthew jumped up thoughtlessly and hit his still sore toe on his desk chair. Wincing at the renewed pain, he limped to the closet and opened it. It took him a few seconds for his sun spotted sight to smooth dimly over. Nothing was hanging. "What the...?" He turned to his mother. "Where are my clothes?"

"I'm washing them."

Matthew's shoulders became tense as he raised his hands, his face pushing forward with haste written all over it as it spasmed side to side. "Now?" His mother nodded. "Why?"

"I couldn't get around to it yesterday."

"I gave you my laundry three days ago."

His mother took another sip. "Did you?"

"Of all the days..." Matthew let loose an anxiety laden sigh. Exhaling loudly, he hurried past his mother into the hallway towards the pantry beyond.

His mother gave him a funny look. "What are you doing?" she asked as she followed after him. She found him tearing through the piles of clothes on the floor and in baskets, the thumping washer behind him.

"I need something semi-clean." He picked up a shirt and went to smell it. His face quickly turned away, gagging. He picked up another with the same smell: that gamy, sweaty, dirty laundry stench. Matthew released an anguished lament. "I guess I have to go in this." He started to leave when he stopped and reached into a cupboard over the washing machine and pulled out some air freshener. He turned his head to the side and sprayed the entire can on his violated leg.

"Matthew!"

"I have to get rid of the smell!" He stopped spraying after thirty seconds when he felt it. It was as if something was eating through his flesh. He started to slap at the stain. He turned the can over and stared at the warning. In bold letters it stated, "Do not expose to skin". "Oh …great," Matthew muttered through gritted teeth, a hole being eaten through his thigh. "Oh, oh, oh," he whimpered as he turned to the washer and yanked up the lid. He soaked his hands in the sudsy water and began dousing his scorching thigh.

"Matthew! The clothes-"

"Forget the clothes," Matthew scolded her. "I want to keep my leg!" When the searing pain had largely smoldered, he limped down the hall back to his room to find some shoes, each step feeling like the denim was rubbing his skin off.

"Do you want breakfast?"

"I don't have time!" He bit his lip as he shoved his bad toe into the shoe.

"But you need it. It's the most important meal of the day."

Matthew went to tie his second shoe when the string broke. "Why me? Why me!" he screamed to the ceiling before throwing the useless string with all his might for it to simply fall to the floor a few feet away.

With one shoe still loose, agitated beyond belief, Matthew raced out the door, hair a mess, teeth unbrushed. He nearly collided with the bathroom door. His face twitched with increasing stress. He tried the knob. It was locked. He twisted and twisted again, pulling and pushing on the knob trying to force the door open.

"Hey, occupied," his dad called out.

"I need in there!"

"You're going to have to wait."

"I don't have time. I don't have time!" Matthew began kicking the door.

"What the hell are you doing?" his father demanded through the door.

"Trying to scare the crap out of you."

"He'll need all the help he can get," Matthew's mother told him. "Constipated from all that junk he's been eating."

"Ugh! I don't...I don't need to know that!" Matthew pushed past her as he hurried into the kitchen towards the sink. He flipped the faucet on putting his hands beneath the water to cup as much as he could hold before splashing it onto his mangy mane doing his best to weight it down into something controllable. Hair still dripping, Matthew put his palm to his mouth and blew. The smell was rancid. "What to do. What to do." His eyes scanned all over the room for anything he could use for his breath before settling on the counter. With few options, Matthew grabbed the soap bottle. Steeling himself, he squirted a good gob into his mouth and began to squish it all around, his face betraying the taste. When he was through he spat out bubbles. "What time is it?"

"Ten past nine," his mother replied.

"I gotta go." Matthew twisted the tap closed and shook his hands dry as he hurried down the hallway one last time, walking then running. He felt the water running down the back of his neck and wetting his back. He dove back into his room and scoured the floor, furiously kicking and thrashing before he found what he needed. Jacket in hand he rushed back into the kitchen and through the backdoor that led to the driveway.

"Drive safely!" his mother called after him as he all but kicked the door out.

Matthew charged down the walkway along the side of the house where he had parked. It was only when he began to slide that he realized the concrete had iced over. He slipped backward slamming his elbow and knocking the wind out of his lungs before gliding like a sailboat to the end of the walk to stop right in front of his car. He lay there, on the ice, looking up into the blue sky, little snowflakes dropping into his eyes causing him to blink. He remained still for a while. Without warning, he started kicking and flailing his arms and legs, screaming. This was starting out to be a bad day.

***

President Lucas sat at the head of an important table. Generals, admirals, diplomats, and bureaucrats gathered round it for yet another divisive debate on the fate of the nation. To his right sat those men of action: his military commanders and battle hardened officers. To his left crouched his cronies: bootlickers and silver-tongued flatterers.

"The situation in Kashmir is becoming alarmingly unstable," General Adams started. "Mobilization has started on both sides."

"Where is Kashmir?" President Lucas asked.

"Between-"

34

"Between India and Pakistan, Mr. President," Security Advisor Cory Brown interjected cutting Adams off.

"So what's the problem? There are wars in Africa all the time," President Lucas coolly stated.

A few officers shook their heads.

"They're in Asia, sir," General Adams corrected.

"They're always threatening one another," Secretary of State William Hermann retorted. "It's nothing but bluster."

"Agreed," President Lucas replied.

"Sir, even if it is, nuclear weapons are involved. We can't simply watch. This could go atomic disrupting the whole of Central Asia if not the entire continent." General Adams stressed that last part hoping that would at least get the President to raise an eyebrow.

"When did they get nuclear weapons?" President Lucas asked.

"Shortly before your presidency, Mr. President," Brown replied.

"From bows and arrows to nukes," Lucas muttered to himself.

"Don't worry, sir," Brown soothed. "India doesn't have launch capability anyway."

"Pakistan does!" General Adams verbally slapped the pair upside the head. "We're talking about the potential of millions of casualties."

"Mr. President," Lucas' Chief of Staff interrupted. "Some of America's businesses have interests in India. Outsourcing. Investment. It would be...detrimental to allow hostilities let alone abandon them in their time of need."

"Hmmmm," Lucas pursed his lips and struck a pose of contemplation.

"Perhaps we should lean on Pakistan? After all, they did start hostilities," Brown offered.

"Terrorists, not the Pakistani government, made the attack on the Indian Parliament," General Adams broke in.

"We are supposed to believe Pakistan had nothing to do with this?" Brown rolled his eyes. "They're not even a democracy. Besides, they hate America."

General Adams looked from Brown to Lucas. "We can't afford a conflict between the two. Our military is stretched enough as it is. Operations in the region-"

"What exactly is the problem here?" Lucas asked.

"Kashmir, Mr. President. Both sides want Kashmir," Hermann explained.

"Let's lean on Pakistan, make them give India Kashmir," President Lucas ordered. "I don't see why fabric should be so important."

"Sir! We can't just make Pakistan give up Kashmir!" General Adams replied horrified.

"Why not?" Lucas' face was confused, his jaw hanging in slack ignorance.

"Because Pakistan holds the land sacred."

"When did we start talking about land?" Lucas was lost, a regular occurrence.

Adams wanted to throttle the man. "That's what this conflict has been about all along."

"Well, land is land. After all the unfair treaties, about time we gave the Indians back some land," President Lucas rationalized.

"I think you're talking about the wrong Indians."

"Well which ones are they? The Sue? The Nava-Joe?"

Adams shook his head not even wanting to delve into that conversation. "Sir, even if we ordered them to give up Kashmir there are Pakistanis living there who won't accept Indian rule. It will only lead to worse problems tactically and strategically. Besides, we need them as an ally in the Middle East. They are one of our few friends."

"They've done little to close their borders allowing excursions into Afghanistan by insurgents," Hermann sniffed. "They are merely playing all sides. Don't be a fool, Mr. President. America needs to see us making orders not bowing to them."

The President nodded. "We'll move them. Problem solved. Next?" Lucas quickly passed over the major problem as if it were a mild annoyance.

Adams wasn't through with the subject. "Sir-"

"China is making attempts to assert sovereignty over Taiwan," Brown offered up.

"We can't allow that, Mr. President," Hermann cautioned. "Economically they are already becoming a problem. If they seize Taiwan it wouldn't simply hurt us economically. It would hurt our prestige. Taiwan is an ally and a major economic partner. China, on the other hand, has repeatedly thwarted various investments we've made into their infrastructure, and worse, refused to recognize our patents and copyrights costing us billions. We are already locked in a commercial war with them committing the equivalent of atrocities. We must stand strong or continue to be bullied as well as ripped-off. Anyway, the Chinese military is symbolic of all Chinese products. Cheap and shoddy." President Lucas nodded agreement with Hermann's words.

"Mr. President," Lucas' Chief of Staff began, "we should use caution. Perhaps find some compromise."

"They are trying to seize the island!" Admiral Odom screamed in shock, his glasses falling from his face. "They have sent a fleet to the edge of Taiwan's borders to hold naval exercises. They are clearly threatening their security. We cannot compromise with these people. Not with their record of human rights abuses or their increasingly bellicose stance. Taiwan has been on their agenda since 1949. They have warned us that this does not concern us and refuse diplomatic channels. They mean to take the island."

"Mr. President," the Chief of Staff began, "if we were to exert pressure on China our work on economic treaties with China could find themselves in jeopardy. Yes, there have been some...misunderstandings, but it is a large market with many opportunities for your...constituents. And we do have certain 'allies' amongst them. Mr. President, compromise is best here."

"China wants nothing less than control of Taiwan!" Admiral Odom slammed his fist on the table. "Nothing else. The people of Taiwan wish to vote on a referendum to recognize their independence internationally. Are we supposed to strip them of their rights to freedom solely for money? How are we supposed to compromise with a nation that values life below the lowest common denominator? Give China control in everything but name?"

"That is how government works," Brown curtly replied.

"They are a democracy and an ally!"

"You deal with this, Hermann. See what you can achieve." President Lucas smiled at his underlings, his naïve confidence failing to permeate this crowd. "Next?"

"It seems Russia is back to its old self again," Brown began.

"Those damn Soviets!" President Lucas snarled.

"Sir, there haven't been Soviets in over a decade," General Adams corrected him.

Lucas gave Adams a dirty look before turning back to Brown. "What are they up to now? Is there a global threat?"

"Mr. President," Brown continued, "the leader of Russia, Romanov, has dissolved their legislature and is ruling by decree. There is fear that he might attempt to retake some of the Soviet Union's old republics and destabilize both Eastern Europe and, possibly, Central Asia."

"Where did you get that?" General Adams asked.

"His speeches have been belligerent since his re-election," Brown shot back. "He speaks of returning Russia to greatness."

"Those damn Soviets. They won't stop until they conquer the entire free world." President Lucas took another pensive pose.

The generals and admirals looked at each other with concern.

General Adams tried to counsel reason. "Sir, Russia is in no position to challenge anyone. It's merely a case of saber rattling to rally the people. We should be focusing elsewhere-"

"The Soviets only understand armed force. We learned that in Dubya Dubya Two. We should test a nuclear bomb near their borders."

The military personnel nearly leapt from their seats.

"That is illegal, Mr. President," Hermann replied.

"Well then what other options have we?" Lucas asked.

"We could go to the United Nations and urge new elections in Russia or threaten them with international sanctions," one of the junior functionaries offered. A brief silence quickly collapsed as everyone in the room laughed causing the functionary to bury his head.

"Seriously, what should we do?" President Lucas asked again.

"Put troops on their borders. Just to balance any problems resulting from the political climate in Russia affecting adjacent nations," Brown recommended.

Adams bit his tongue knowing that such an action could only stretch the military further if not further exacerbate the situation, but he knew a realistic view meant little here.

"Do it immediately!" Lucas ordered.

"We need those adjacent nations' approval first, Mr. President," Hermann corrected.

"Really?" Hermann nodded. "Well, do that and, if it comes to it, America will invade the Soviet Union to bring an end to that evil empire and give freedom to its people," President Lucas bellowed, that deep boom out of place coming from that slim frame. "President Lucas, conqueror of Communism," he murmured as everyone gave him an odd look. "Make it happen. Meeting adjourned."

As they filed out General Adams focused on his paperwork, shuffling and sorting. Admiral Odom came up to him. "You can't teach a blind man to see."

General Adams crammed his papers into his briefcase. "The bastard is an idiot. Nothing more than seductive eyes and a serpentine smile."

"Don't forget the hand to accept campaign contributions." General Adams gave up a barking laugh. "If it's any consolation, I didn't vote for him."

"Why even bother to vote? I believe in people earning their jobs."

***

Matthew had to get to school. He sped along the slick roads, his tires retaining traction by the sheerest of margins. Matthew would press the accelerator down to the floor, but as his car started to veer, he would slow down. Of course rational thinking would dissolve beneath the feverish mania Matthew found himself in causing him to floor it all over again. The white world whizzed by as he drove faster. Warp speed. He dove in and out of traffic, making his way through human obstacles with homicidal ease. He played life like a video game, and now, it came time to hit reset.

A semi was in front of him kicking up melted snow and slushing his vision, the sludge splashing up onto his windshield. Matthew couldn't see anything through the dirty monsoon. Every time he tried to merge into an adjacent lane a car would zoom up cutting him off. "Make room!" he yelled slapping at each passer by. No gaps opened. Matthew screamed like a banshee, banging his wheel over and over again behind the slow semi.

Then an opportunity presented itself. A gap! It wasn't large, but it would do. He made a quick jump for it, but the sudden turn made his car swerve wildly. In a panic, Matthew kicked the brakes to the floor causing his car to lose control leaping through three lanes of traffic. "Arghhhhh!" he screamed pumping the brakes over and over again. Somehow he slid through tiny breaches avoiding cars on either side as he skidded sideways. He drove at forty-five degrees through a wall of steel. Mere inches separated him from a life of eating through a straw. The world slowed down. He could see the faces of those he missed through their windshields, Matthew's eyes locking on one driver as the gum fell out of his mouth.

Matthew regained control in the far-left lane, his brakes finally gaining traction with a squeal as time slammed back at normal speed. He slowed down to a stop, his head dropping to the steering wheel as he let out a sigh of relief. Then something bumped his car from behind. Matthew looked up into his rearview mirror. Some piece of junk truck had hit him. "You've got to be kidding me." Matthew slapped the dash. "I don't need this today. I...really...don't...need...this." He thumped his dashboard harder with the palm of his hand. He groaned as he closed his eyes trying to calm himself. His heart kept banging away in his chest.

With few nerves and his engine still running, Matthew got out and went to speak to the driver. "So..." he started, trying to be tough. Then he saw the driver of the truck: all three hundred pounds of him. "Interesting day," he said in his friendliest tone.

"Boy, you nearly killed me!" the burly man replied.

"Me? You ran into my car!"

"You pulled in front of me like a damn fool and hit your brakes!"

"Maybe you should watch where you're going."

The burly man started towards Matthew. Maybe he would be eating through a straw after all. Matthew gauged his chances of escape. Cars zoomed by on his left as well as over the divider on his right. "Hey," Matthew grinned. The burly man kept coming, his fists clenching. God, his bicep was bigger than Matthew's head. "Hey!" Matthew waved his hands.

"Yeah, boy?"

"Maybe I could look at the damage. See what my insurance needs to cover." Matthew grinned again, feet poised to accept his chances of leaping into traffic as opposed to whether or not this human pit bull would leave his head intact.

"Yeah. Yeah, ok."

Matthew walked behind his car to look at the truck. The thing was a rust bucket. It looked like a zombie automobile with holes throughout the frame and a cracked, yellowed windshield. He took a glimpse down at the front bumper. The thing was barely hanging on thanks to wiring. "Doesn't look that bad," Matthew replied starting back to his car.

The burly man stepped in front of him. "Boy, you damaged my truck."

"Is that even possible?" The burly man grabbed him by the shirt. "Uh, you know what? Let me get a copy of my insurance card for you. So you can make the claim to put your," Matthew gulped, "truck...back in order. Ok?"

"Now we're talking." He let Matthew go.

The pair started towards Matthew's vehicle. As Matthew opened his door he reached inside but stopped. He turned to the burly man. "Could you give me your license plate number? So I can tell my insurance company."

"Yeah, sure." As the burly man retreated Matthew's eyes followed him. Once he was at the back of the truck Matthew slammed his door and sped off, the burly man screaming at him as he shrunk with each second.

"You get that plate for me?" Matthew cackled as he sped off.

The humor was short-lived. With time slipping away, the anxiety began to build in Matthew once more, each pebble of sand running through the hourglass a boulder that battered him over the head. The stress caused him to tighten, his muscles close to snapping. As he quaked and trembled, his exit came up rapidly. "Finally!" Off the main road he turned.

Within minutes he saw his college approaching on the horizon. As the campus loomed on his left Matthew pulled into the parking lot. The place was packed. He drove around discovering how full the place truly was. Cars were not only parked in spaces but also on the grass and along various lanes throughout the campus, stealing any and every available spot. Did these many people even attend this school?

An open spot! He kept his eyes open for any threats or obstacles, his eyes darting back and forth. He slowly puttered along until he discovered that someone else had seen it. Both cars froze, their drivers carefully eyeing one another. They both needed the space. They both wanted the space. Their engines roared threateningly back and forth before they started forward. Rolling toward one another, they started picking up speed. It became a charge, the two aiming for the ultimate prize. They launched toward one another as if jousting, making for the promised spot with the cars of the lot serving as a silent audience. Both leaned forward for every necessary ounce of speed, careening towards collision.

Matthew jerked into the spot seconds before his challenger. His wheels squealed in a shrill, triumphant war cry. He raised his fist in victory. "Ah ha!" The man idled, his car huffing.

Matthew smiled as he went to open his door. It didn't budge. It had jammed again. His smile collapsed into a frown. Matthew banged it again and again, ramming his shoulder into it hopelessly. The car shook up and down. He gasped for air, the windows fogging. As he rested, he decided to simply exit out the passenger side. When he went to open the door he noticed he had parked too close on his right. He couldn't open the passenger side door all the way though he did try to ooze through the minor crack. He shut the door and bounced back into the driver's seat revving the engine back up.

Matthew went to reverse for a better parking position when he discovered the challenger still waiting behind him. He knew he would have to pull out all the way to readjust his parking, but if he did, the challenger could make a jump for the spot. No way was that happening. The challenger remained where he was. Matthew twitched back and forth.

He couldn't get out. He couldn't get out! Matthew looked down at the clock. He was late!

Matthew cracked. He started ramming his shoulder into the driver's side door again, too stubborn to give up his parking spot. He put enough force into his blows that he nearly dislocated his shoulder. The door finally popped open slamming into the car next to him. Matthew stared at the massive dent he left, his eyes widening and mouth gaping. It was at least a foot long and an inch deep; the black paint job of the neighboring car was chiseled white by his door. The sound of the engine supplemented the lack of noise from his open maw. "Oh boy," Matthew mumbled. Now what was he going to do? He turned and looked in the rearview mirror. His foe, the other car, was the same color as his: a pristine, virginal white. "Hmmmmm." Matthew closed the door and slowly pulled out of the spot, giving it to the challenger. Maybe another spot was better.

***

Matthew ran to class, flying down the hall skidding on his slippery shoes. He dodged out of a student's way and tripped over a mop bucket. He caught himself on the wall and continued running, brown mop water flooding the floor as the janitor shook a fist at him. Matthew made all haste for his class, his thigh still flaring and his toe vibrating with agony. He did a comical hopping run. "Almost there," he wheezed. He rounded the corner and saw...his entire class still outside. Matthew slowed down, trotting to the door. "What's up?" he asked.

"Professor's not here," a student replied.

"What? You're joking."

"Nope. Someone said he got arrested for a brawl at some gay bar last night."

"No way. They caught him molesting some kid," someone else passed along.

"Whatever! The guy isn't a pervert."

"He belongs to NAMBLA."

"You know he did give me an uncomfortable look once in his office," a male student offered.

"Dude, you had a burrito. Probably wanted to rape it more than you, the fat bastard."

"He's not here?" Matthew asked again, shocked at his futile need for speed.

"No way, dude. Long...gone," a stoner blew out, his hand made a sweeping motion in front of him before he stopped to watch it wave.

"What's that smell?" someone asked.

Matthew pulled away from the group a bit to hide his odor nearly bumping into a member of the faculty carrying a thick set of test booklets. "Sorry," Matthew offered.

"Hmmph." The assistant professor pushed him aside. "Alright students, Professor Rosenberg won't be joining you today."

"Alright! No test!" someone cheered, the entire group roaring with joy.

"Oh, there will be a test." Groans filled the hallway. The assistant professor unlocked the door to let them in, smiling as they passed. The students filed in with grim enthusiasm. They dragged their feet to their seats. Matthew made it to his seat, last in the very back of the room. The culmination of four years was ahead of him and he was ready.

The professor shut the door and proceeded to pass out booklets. "Here is the exam that Professor Rosenberg has left for you. This is your future so I hope you take it...seriously." The professor stared at the stoner student as he played with the pages of his test.

The stoner kept flipping through the pages, holding it in one hand and fanning it with the other. "That is so freakin' cool." The professor grabbed it from him, opened it on the desk and slammed a pen on top of it. The stoner looked up at him and back down at the test. "Harsh, man."

The professor continued to hand out tests, eventually reaching Matthew. It must be bad Matthew thought as he watched the expressions on everyone's faces as they opened their booklets and looked at the test. The professor put a copy down on the desk along with a pen. Matthew opened the booklet to gaze at the questions that awaited him. This was the exam of his life. This was what his future hinged on. Matthew started to read. The first page had only one word on it: why. Matthew flipped through the other pages. They were blank. "You've got to be kidding," he blurted. The class hissed for silence. He blushed a little, his nose spasming at the stale smell of urine and air freshener. Matthew turned back to his test.

Why? Matthew thought to himself. *Why? WHY! I have taken this subject for four years, questioned the world around me, studied at least an hour or two last night for this stupid class and that is the test? WHY?!?!?* Matthew looked up and realized a few of the students were staring at him. "Sorry," he offered before letting his eyes flick back down to the test. Matthew stared in stunned disbelief at the single word, that lone typed word, on the opening page of his exam. Three letters stood arranged against him.

He became agitated. This was it? "My life is an anticlimax," he whispered. *Why? Is there really any answer?* He heard the scribbling of the class. He glanced up as everyone wrote down their theories on reality. Everyone believed in something, had some belief as to why everything was. Was there really any reason? Matthew thought of himself. What exactly was his reason? He hadn't made any earth shattering revelations. He'd never accomplished anything of worth. For all intents and purposes, if he died today or had never been born would the world really be any better or worse? If there was no real reason for his existence then what reason was there for these people's existences?

This is a cheap, third-rate college. Will any of these people really accomplish anything? In fact, has anyone really accomplished anything? For all our years of civilization, we're nothing more than animals that think. Crudely virile, violently territorial: we put more stock in the physical and forget the spiritual. Does that mean we lack that spark of the divine? Maybe we are truly like our Creator, this dirtball called Earth. All we care about is material: bodies, resources, useless crap. Nothing has ever really changed that. Have we really come any closer to that vision of perfection we're always talking about? Has humanity really changed at all since its inception? We still live like we always have, but what exactly does that even mean? What exactly does humanity do that serves a purpose? We eat, crap, screw, and sleep. Well, I do at least three of those. Life is merely survival, but what use is surviving for no better reason than to be?

So what are we? Why are we? All we really seem to be is a variable for balance in some complex system. Is that all we are? There are places on Earth where life functions well enough without any humans at all. In fact, thrives despite us. If humans aren't really needed then is life even needed? If thought can be done away with then why even bother with thoughtless creatures that bring nothing to existence? The majority of space seems empty of life. So if life isn't really needed for reality then why is reality if there is no life needed to document it and function in it? Is there any reason or is it just because? Hmmmmm.

Matthew had been chewing on his pen failing to notice he had been sucking the ink out. *Because.* Matthew liked that. Nothing really had to be. It just was. There was no purpose, just chance. There was no destiny, only possibility.

Matthew excitedly wrote out his answer, "because", and smiled to himself, teeth blackened. He was a genius, a brilliant philosoph. He gave himself a light punch to the shoulder, smiling. Then he realized the class was watching him again. He got up and marched to the front of the class, test in hand, triumphant. *Let them watch, the fools. They wrote their volumes of crap. Not I! I can truly see.* Matthew banged his knee right into one of the desks as he walked, his reflexes causing his foot to jerk driving his injured toe into a table leg. Matthew winced horribly. The class looked at him as he bent over in pain. Realizing their eyes were on him, Matthew quickly straightened, finished walking to the front, put his test on the professor's desk and gave them all a bow. He walked out the door.

"Forgot your books!" one of the students yelled to Matthew.

Matthew hurried back into the class. Gathering his texts in hand, the pile proved too cumbersome and he dropped one on the floor. He bent down to get it and whacked his head hard on the desk. He rubbed his bruise in agony, but bravely picked up his dropped book and stood proudly. "It was meant to be." Matthew struck a pose for the ages and then walked out of class not wanting to see the class' expressions.

***

Matthew exited the building walking towards the parking lot. No one was in the quad as he passed through. In fact, the entire place seemed empty. When he reached the parking lot he discovered a multitude of open spots. *Yeah, empty now*, he thought to himself as he approached his car. Matthew slid his key into the door and wrestled with it, finally jerking it open. That was when he heard a voice behind him. "Matthew Ford." The voice wasn't asking.

Matthew turned around and was confronted by two miniature figures. The two "men" were no taller than four foot dressed in white suits. Their skin was pale, their hair curly and golden. Their eyes were covered by silver tinted glasses. "Can I help you?"

"We need you to come with us," one of the smartly dressed midgets said.

"I don't think so," Matthew chuckled. "The yellow brick road isn't on my way."

The other vertically challenged fellow grabbed Matthew's arm. "We're not asking. We're ordering."

Matthew slapped his hand away. "Hey, watch it Cabbage Patch Mafia. Society might have treated you badly, but don't take it out on me."

"You have business with our boss."

"I didn't win any golden ticket so go back to Willy Wonka and give him my regards."

The two midgets looked at each other. They both turned to Matthew, their faces starting to mottle. "Don't make us tell you again."

"Then stop asking. I've had a bad day so piss off!" Matthew turned his back to them to get in his car. As he went to open the door the one midget got on all fours. His partner ran and jumped off the other's back onto Matthew's wrapping his tiny arms around Matthew's throat. The impact drove Matthew headfirst into the door aggravating the bruise he got in class and slamming the door shut. The other midget grabbed Matthew by the leg. There Matthew stood, getting jumped by dwarves. The one on Matthew's back tried to choke him, baby fingers tickling his neck as little feet banged into his lower back.

"Don't make this any harder on yourself," the midget on Matthew's back gasped into his ear. Matthew threw him over his shoulder to the pavement. As his partner saw him fall he bit into Matthew's thigh. Matthew screamed and started kicking trying to throw the midget off. His friend was quick to his feet, running at Matthew with top speed to head-butt him right in the crotch. Matthew dropped due to damaged goods. The other midget released his leg and proceeded to grab Matthew by the hair. Matthew had just enough time to see that dastardly dwarf of nut-butting brutality preparing for a second run, this time headed for his face. Matthew quickly jerked to the side sending the charging midget into the car door. The dwarf dropped stunned.

Matthew leaned forward to grab the keys he had dropped, the other midget trying to pull him back by the hair. Matthew threw elbow after elbow behind him until he knocked the little guy down. Matthew grabbed the keys in one hand and the leg of one of the midgets with another. He dragged the munchkin to the back of the car and unlocked the trunk. He threw the midget in and slammed it shut. "We're going to the cops. See if they can't cut your ass down to size." Matthew pounded on the trunk. "You like that? Huh?" He pounded some more.

Matthew looked around the car for the other dwarf, but he was gone. Matthew slowly stalked around the vehicle, looking under it. No one was there. He went and unlocked the driver's door, quickly glancing over his shoulder, before prying it open and climbed in. As he was about to turn the key in the ignition he looked into the rearview mirror. His nose was bleeding. *Those little punks!*

Suddenly the passenger side window exploded into shards. Matthew turned to see a rock in the seat next to him. There was a thud and then another. Matthew looked out the window to see the missing midget throwing stones at his car. He hurriedly exited, leaving the keys inside. "Stop that!" Matthew yelled. The dwarf responded with a rock that barely missed Matthew's head. "Hey!" The midget threw another rock catching Matthew in the knee. Matthew limped after the little fellow. The midget threw a final rock in a futile attempt to end the stunted charge hitting Matthew in the arm. The little guy quickly ran with Matthew in hot pursuit. They circled around the car as if playing a kid's game. Though his heart was in it, those short legs were no match for Matthew's. Matthew quickly grabbed the midget in a headlock and started dragging him kicking and screaming back to his car.

Matthew grabbed the keys and limped back to the trunk. "I thought you guys were supposed to be happy. Whistling while you work and shit." The midget fought with him as he popped the trunk. As it opened the midget trapped inside jumped up and knocked Matthew out with a tire iron.

***

Groggy, Matthew started to wake up. His head ached. Where the hell was he? Matthew slowly rose to see he was in the backseat of his car. The two midgets were in the front driving, one on the pedals the other minding the wheel. The window that had been smashed out had plastic taped over it.

The midget on the floor looked up. "Oh, you're finally awake."

"Stop the car. I said stop it!" Matthew started to climb into the front seat when the midget driving pulled out a silver wand and touched it to Matthew shocking him. Matthew grabbed his arm in pain.

"Stay back there!"

"What is going on?" Matthew looked out the windows and only saw fog. "Where the hell are we going?"

"Well, certainly not there. No good roads there anyway. They have better public transportation, what with the large numbers."

"Excuse me?" As hard as Matthew tried he couldn't discern anything through the haze. "Where are we? The mountains?" As he asked he saw a break in the mist and discovered they were thousands of feet in the air. "Whoa!" The two midgets laughed as he stared wide-eyed at the expanse.

The car eventually broke through the ceiling of cloud cover. The blue sky was bare before them. "We want to make it before the next millennium. Gas it!" The midget pushed the pedal all the way to the floor throwing Matthew backwards in his seat. The blue sky darkened and went black, stars glistening in space.

"Guys, I'd really like to go home. I have a dog. Need to feed it-"

"Don't worry. You can go home after you see the boss."

"Wasn't that Venus?" Matthew asked as they flashed by a planet.

"Yeah."

Matthew gazed out at its retreating shape, yellow and glorious. It shone like a pearl in the void. "So, are you guys aliens?"

"Why would you ask that?" the midget on the floor queried.

"Well, I've been abducted, and we are in space. That wasn't an anal probe you zapped me with, was it?"

"We're not aliens!"

A blackened sphere approached. "What the hell is that?"

"Mercury."

"Mercury?" Matthew winced at a blinding light that began to pour in the side window. "Holy…" He leapt to the other side of the car. The sun was massive, its fiery arms curling towards them. "Where are you taking me?"

"There." The midget driving pointed to what seemed a dimple in space. As they approached, Matthew saw what could only be dubbed an anomaly. It was exceptionally black, even blacker than all that around it. It was like someone had taken reality and twisted it, a whirlpool of space-time.

"What's that?"

"Our exit."

It struck Matthew all at once. "That's a black hole!"

They drove towards the edge, the car locked in and beginning to spiral down into that insubstantial tunnel. Matthew freaked out and lunged again for the wheel. "Get back!" The midget screamed, trying to zap him with the wand. Matthew tried to turn them away as the midget on the floor jumped up to help handle the wheel. The car swerved back and forth on the cusp of the black hole, wavering on the edge.

"No, we can't go in!" Matthew screamed.

"Will you let go!" the midget with the wand yelled, zapping Matthew again and again with it. The wheel turned hard as Matthew released it and the other midget pulled. The car veered right sharply and teetered on the hole, slowly moving up and down as the nose of the car overlooked the depths. "Hit the accelerator."

"No!" Matthew jumped forward again, the weight throwing the car into the depths. Matthew screamed as the car dropped like a roller coaster into the black hole dropping for miles at immense speed, each foot accelerating them further. Weight increased as they quickened down the hole, Matthew's body shoved back against his seat. An invisible hand tried to push him through the back of the car, his face contorting beneath the pressure.

The speed eased as did the pressure, and they began to glide through the darkness. Points of light emerged and sparkled, multiplying. Matthew stared at what seemed a glistening expanse ahead. "What's that?" Matthew asked as they floated towards it.

"Must you ask what everything is?" Matthew nodded dumbly. "It's a parking lot if you must know."

There were millions of them, cars of all makes and eras neatly parked for what seemed miles in the darkness of space. They glided to the outskirts of the lot and came to a stop. "Great. No spots!"

"Maybe over there," the midget offered. They coasted around a few minutes before finding and settling into a spot.

"Where are we?" Matthew asked as the midgets opened the door and jumped out.

"Heaven, you moron."

"Heaven? There is a parking lot in heaven?"

"Come on," the pair ordered as they approached his door.

"Come on where?" Matthew asked quickly grabbing the handle to prevent them from dragging him out.

"You've got to meet our boss," they told him.

"I think I'll stay right here."

The two midgets grabbed the door and tried to yank it open as Matthew pulled against them. "You're only making this harder on yourself," they warned him. The tug of war seemed never-ending until one of the dwarves quickly ran around the side of the car and opened the door behind Matthew, dragging him out onto the asphalt.

Matthew screamed, kicking and thrashing until he hit the ground. "Whoa...it's solid."

"Of course it's solid. What did you think we walked on? Clouds?"

"Don't forget the parking pass. I don't want a ticket." One of the midgets pulled a decal out of his pocket and put it on the dash.

"Let's go."

"Go?" Matthew asked, looking at the steel and glass that surrounded him in perpetual twilight. "Go where? There's nothing but cars around."

One of the midgets looked down at his watch. "A shuttle should be by in a few minutes. They'll take us in."

***

They had been riding the shuttle for hours, there appearing no end to the rows upon rows of cars. The monotony was driving Matthew insane. "You guys have a car right?" he asked.

"Yeah," one of them answered.

"So don't you have a reserved spot? Why did we park so far out?"

"You wouldn't fit in our car. Besides, you have to go through immigration."

"Immigration?"

The shuttle slowed and came to a stop. "This is our exit."

Matthew stretched his legs before exiting the shuttle, his appendages gone numb from the long ride. What he saw upon exiting was lines upon lines of people that appeared to stretch for hundreds of miles. "This is going to be a long wait."

"Don't worry. Just follow us." They made their way forward, walking parallel to one of the waiting columns, those standing giving them irritated expressions as they passed. Eventually they found the destination these people were waiting for. A wall of white marble that was imbued with an elegant glow, higher than Matthew could see as he stared up into the black sky, stood before them with gates of silver, gold, and bronze. The gates, too numerous to count, were sculpted into amazing arrays of twisted metal that spiraled, circled, and bore a design that captivated the eyes and made one's vision drunk with beauty. Before these were little booths that seemed too modern for the classical design behind them, spare of any design or artistic quality. Thousands of booths, forged of glass and steel, were separated into various sections into which the multiple lines streamed into. Above each section were signs: Employees, Citizens, Near Death, Permanent Residents, and Reincarnation. The officers of each section wore immaculate, pressed suits of an unearthly silken white. Their ties were a sterling silver. They had thin computer screens embedded into the desks before them into which they stared when they spoke with those at the front of each line. Matthew followed the dwarves as they cut a swath through the queues.

"Here is a stamp to get back in when you return," Matthew overheard an officer in the "Near Death" section tell the person at his station.

"Oh, thank you." The man turned around and was escorted away.

At another section an officer in the "Citizens" portion asked the person at the front of the line, "Do you believe in the infallibility of our Lord and Savior?"

"No one knows everything," the man cynically replied.

"Fail. Go to the Reincarnation line."

"But I've been in this line over twenty years." The man's lip quivered, his eyes slanted in disappointment.

"Go to the reincarnation line," the officer ordered, pointing.

"I can't go back." Guards appeared from out of nowhere, giants at least ten feet tall. "Please! I believe. I swear-" He was seized and pulled away from the rest of the group.

The midgets pushed through the line under "Employees", getting a lot of flack from those in front. One of the officers stepped in the way. "He can't come through here," the officer stated stabbing a finger at Matthew. "He has to show his papers at the 'Permanent Residents' line."

"We've got authorization otherwise," the midgets responded flashing some weird, metallic document. The guard scanned it, giving the odd group the once over. He waved them through. The midgets grabbed Matthew by either hand and pulled him through the turnstile. They walked towards walls that glowed even in this eternal night and the gates began to open, a golden light piercing the darkness.

CHuhAPTER 3

Matthew and the midgets found themselves in the lush plains of Paradise. Every color was heightened and pleasing to the eyes. The sky was golden without clouds to smother the enriching light of ethereal origin. The wind was soft and caressing, blowing from their back towards whatever waited ahead, gently nudging them forward. The blades of grass, knee level in height, seemed to wave asking them to venture into this realm of perfection. It was unnerving to Matthew's mortally flawed vision. "This is Heaven?" he asked. One of the midgets turned around to give Matthew an irritated look. "Sorry. I pictured something...more." The other midget turned around to glare at him. Matthew instinctively went on the defensive. "Hey, I read *Paradise Lost*. I expected domes and arches and togas. You know singing angels and such. Not...the fields of Indiana."

"*Paradise Lost* was written by a blind man. Why would you listen to the visual descriptions of a blind man?"

"Be happy he even read a book," retorted the other midget.

"Be happy you're not still in my trunk," Matthew returned in kind.

"Excuse me!" the midget yelled as he started towards Matthew.

"Stop, Ezekiel." Ezekiel stomped on despite his partner's warning. "Stop!" The one midget grabbed the other trying to pull him back.

"Whatever. Guys, can we speed this up. I really need to get back home before my mother gets a one way ticket here."

"Like I really care-" Ezekiel started.

59

"He's right. We need to keep her down there as long as possible," his partner quickly cut in.

"Oh, you know her?" Matthew asked. The one midget shuddered. "Yeah, you know her. So now what?"

"We go to Zion."

"Zion?"

"Yes," Ezekiel replied.

Matthew looked left and right seeing nothing but grassy plains. "Uh, where is that? It's not a state of mind is it?"

"Don't be so damned metaphysical. It's a few dozen kilometers north."

"What the hell is a kilometer?" Matthew asked.

Ezekiel gave Matthew a quizzical look. "You don't know what a kilometer is?"

"Of course he doesn't. Americans are too stubborn to use the universal metric system. Then they wouldn't be special."

"I forgot," Ezekiel replied, once more glaring at Matthew. "Always trying to be different. Problem with too much freedom. Think you know it all." Ezekiel turned back to his short companion. "Come on, Mel, let's go." The two midgets lifted into the air, their baby legs dangling freely. They flew into the sky leaving Matthew behind on the ground.

"Uh, guys..." The two midgets continued to fly away. "Guys?" Matthew was starting to lose sight of them. He cupped his hands together around his mouth. "Guys!"

The two soaring dwarves froze in the sky looking down at Matthew. "What?" came Ezekiel's distant voice.

"Are you just going to leave me here?"

"Get off your flat feet and follow us," Ezekiel ordered.

Matthew jerked his head back a bit. "What are you talking about? I can't fly."

Mel looked at Ezekiel as they fluttered in the firmament. "He can't fly?"

"Uh oh," Ezekiel muttered while rubbing his left eye with the palm of his hand.

"You said humans flew!" Mel floated over and shoved Ezekiel.

"They do! I've seen it!" Ezekiel shoved back.

"Where?"

"In movies."

"All you know about humans is from movies!" Mel shouted. "Don't you ever do real research?"

"What? Are you saying movies aren't real?" Ezekiel asked.

"You're just as bad as he is," Mel responded insultingly with his finger jutting at Matthew below.

"You take that back!" Ezekiel demanded, shaking his fist at Mel.

"No!" challenged Mel, sticking his jaw out for any coming blow. Ezekiel obliged him with a punch to the chin, the puny pugilist knocking Mel a few feet south. Mel's eyes went wild as he recovered, soaring up and spearing Ezekiel in the chest with his shoulder bowling them both over.

They wrestled in the sky, Matthew watching as they dove and rose, twisting through the expanse. Their curses filtered down to him as he beheld the holy smack down. Matthew mockingly cheered and booed, punching at invisible opponents and chanting for one then the other dwarf. "That's right, lay the wrath of God on him!" Matthew crowed, throwing punch after punch into thin air. He did a karate kick with a mocking "Hi ya!" Matthew laughed as he viewed the miniature melee above. His grin turned to a frown as he saw them hurtling down right towards him, spiraling faster and faster, their cries growing louder. He jumped out of the way as the two, screaming all the way, smashed into the ground sweating and heaving, tearing up the fertile earth of Eden.

They bounced twice before rolling on the ground facedown. Matthew looked up from where he landed, staring at the two munchkins as they remained prone on the grass. He got up slowly. He stepped carefully as he approached the shattered duo, nudging one in the ribs with his worn boot.

"Piss off!" Ezekiel replied before shoving Matthew's foot away.

"That's no way to speak in Heaven." Matthew clucked his tongue. He walked over and offered his hand to Mel helping him up. When he did the same for Ezekiel the midget ignored it and stood up on his own. "My hand not good enough?"

"I don't need anyone's help." Ezekiel waved him off.

"Hmmmmm," Matthew stared at the little macho man. "Someone has a problem with anger management."

"I have a problem?" Ezekiel ran and kicked Matthew right in his broken toe. Matthew yelped as he fell to a knee. Ezekiel glowered at Matthew now at eye level. Matthew's eyes watered from the agony. "Not such a big man now are you?" Ezekiel taunted.

Matthew's arms shot out grabbing Ezekiel by the throat. Tightening his calloused hands on soft skin, Matthew throttled the little man and shook him without pity. Ezekiel, his face purple, started to fly up in order to pull away. Matthew slowly lost his grip, his fingers gradually slipping off baby fat. As Ezekiel thought he had scored freedom, Matthew latched onto his leg. Ezekiel darted left and right trying to shake his grasp. Matthew held on tight, his feet occasionally leaving the ground.

"Stop it!" yelled Mel. Matthew and Ezekiel paused. Mel ran his chubby fingers through his curly hair. He sighed, closing then opening his eyes slowly. "Can we just get going?"

Matthew released Ezekiel reluctantly. He looked down at his hurt foot and shook it a little to ease the discomfort before looking up again. "So, what are we doing? Walking?"

"No way!" Ezekiel crossed his arms. "I am not wasting the next four hours. Walking is for animals anyway."

Mel gave Ezekiel an exasperated expression before turning back to Matthew. "Well, I guess we need to carry you."

Matthew gave them an incredulous look. "Yeah right."

"What?" Ezekiel frowned. "We can carry you."

Matthew knitted his brows together as he looked at the pair, shaking his head smiling as he raised his arms gesturing them forward. "Go for it, little Hercules." The two midgets grabbed Matthew under each arm and tried to lift him into the air. Matthew's feet slowly rose, up, up, then down. The midgets tried again. Up, up, down. The midgets struggled for air.

"This man stinks," Ezekiel coughed as he covered his nose and mouth after whiffing Matthew's armpit.

Matthew felt that barb as it cut deeply into his sensitive self-esteem; mock him and his fragile ego would shatter into a series of sharp rebuttals. "Maybe a little pixie dust there, Tinkerbelle, and we'll be away," Matthew ribbed as they tried to lift him again. Ezekiel slapped him in the back of the head. Matthew tightened his arm around Ezekiel's throat putting him in a headlock. As Ezekiel kicked for freedom Mel grabbed Matthew around the head, wrapping his thighs around Matthew's neck, and pulled up. "Hey! HEY! I need that!" Matthew yelled, releasing Ezekiel and swatting Mel off.

Ezekiel was quickly losing patience with their failing attempts. "Climb on my back." Ezekiel flew down to chest level, his big butt in Matthew's face.

"I'm not so sure. I mean, you being a fairy and all, this seems kind of gay-"

"Just climb on my back!"

Matthew looked at the tiny figure floating before him. Despite his misgivings, he mounted the little guy. He wrapped his arms around Ezekiel's waist, tiny as it was, as Ezekiel tried to stay afloat. They jerked up and down as the weight proved a little more than even Ezekiel's ego could handle.

"I kind of enjoy this," Matthew quipped as the two dipped and popped up like a merry-go-round. Eventually they collapsed to the ground where Ezekiel still tried to fly, his little frame lost beneath Matthew. Ezekiel continued to thrash around underneath. Matthew looked up at Mel as Ezekiel's attempts only accomplished a mild tilting side to side. "Keep some dignity," Matthew joked, patting Ezekiel on the back as he got off.

"Well, now what?" Mel asked.

"Gravity just kicked your ass, that's now what."

Mel looked off into the distance. "Well, I guess we walk."

"What, you guys don't have a phone or anything? You know, call a taxi or something."

"We don't need phones up here," Mel chided.

Matthew looked down at Ezekiel, still facedown on the ground too tired to rise. "Seems like you do now."

Ezekiel stood up on shaky legs. "Let's just get going." Mel rose into the air, flying at shoulder level. Ezekiel proved too weak to follow.

Matthew reached over. "Come on, I'll carry you on my shoulders."

"I can make it on my own, thank you." Ezekiel jumped into the air and landed flat on his face. He looked up, his face wet with sweat. He stood up to try again, but stopped himself. "I think I'll take that offer." Ezekiel climbed on, resting his hands on the top of Matthew's head.

They walked through the fields of Paradise, a gentle melody singing through the lush grass as the wind played them like a series of natural instruments. After twenty minutes Matthew saw figures in the distance. As they approached, Matthew could almost make them out. "Hey, who are they?"

"Who?" Ezekiel looked over and around Matthew's head.

"Them." Matthew pointed. They appeared to be human. Tan and in tattered clothes, the group muttered in what seemed to be Spanish.

"Oh no, not more." Mel flew after them yelling warnings. The figures quickly turned and ran the opposite way disappearing into the brush.

"What's that all about?" Matthew asked.

"Mexicans don't just sneak into the U.S. these days," Ezekiel replied in Matthew's ear.

"Good border control."

Ezekiel boxed his left ear. "Hey, you try guarding all of Existence and see if there aren't cracks."

Matthew put his hands up in defeat, and they continued on without speaking. The silence of their march greatly bothered Matthew, a man whose mouth proved the asshole of his mind. It also suffered a serious case of diarrhea. If he thought it he said it immediately always creating quite a mess for himself.

"You guys aren't quite as I expected."

"What do you mean?" Ezekiel asked.

"Well, I pictured you...taller. And with wings."

"Wings?" Ezekiel squinted his eyes. "Can I ask why you humans always assume we have wings?"

"Well, you fly for one thing. And I saw them in pictures and a few movies-"

"Movies? Pictures? Don't you ever think for yourself?"

"Ezekiel, you're one to talk," Mel chastised his partner. "Besides, you keep forgetting he's American. If it isn't audio or visual they tend to miss it-"

"Unless there are big boobs next to the words. Then they read." Ezekiel smiled at his own wit while bouncing on Matthew's shoulders.

"Hey, if she thought it was important enough to show her assets it has to be worth my time," Matthew blurted out. His face changed expressions quickly as he cocked his head in the direction of the dwarf riding his shoulders. "Why am I even talking to you about boobs, you prepubescent pixie?"

"I am a cherub?" Ezekiel sniffed.

"What the hell is a cherub? Is that another name for angel?"

"Sometimes I wonder why we allow humans in here since they seem far more obsessed with Hell. Then again, the majority do have to plan for their future accommodations." Mel floated alongside the two, his cynicism too heavy for his weightless form. "We're not angels, right Ezekiel?" Ezekiel kept quiet as he continued riding Matthew's shoulders as if they were a proud mare and he king. "Ezekiel?"

"You're not angels?" Matthew's interest was piqued.

"Of course we are," Ezekiel quickly replied discounting Mel's confession.

"We're not angels," Mel stated, peeved at Ezekiel's tact.

"We're the personal servants of God," Ezekiel countered.

Matthew seemed lost on the differing viewpoints. "Are you new?"

"Why do you ask that?"

"Well...you're kids."

"I am over ten millennia old!" screamed Ezekiel boxing Matthew's ears again.

"Do that again and you won't see bedtime!" Matthew growled as he grabbed a pudgy arm nearly yanking the cherub from his shoulders.

Mel let out a deep breath. "We never grow up. We stay this way forever."

"You're kids forever?"

"We prefer eternal innocents. We never learn the sins of life nor the moral loss of maturity."

"You don't quite seem innocent to me."

"Blame it on Ezekiel. He got us this job. I preferred my harp but no, he had to be where the action was."

"What do you mean?"

"Technically only angels communicate between man and Heaven," Mel started.

"Hey, I belong to a union for a reason, and they can't keep me out on account of who I am. I have seniority." Ezekiel thumped his chest.

"Union? They have unions here?" Matthew tilted his head up to Ezekiel.

"Hey, we're tired of being taken advantage of. We're not some form of entertainment and cuteness to be admired. When the angels go off to fight, who do you think took care of this place?"

"Here we go," muttered Mel.

"Up until two millennia ago those angelic pricks went off to war and left us. Who do you think kept this place running in their absence?" Ezekiel once more thumped his chest. "We did and guess what. We did pretty well. And every time they came back they wanted us to return to our harps and simply forget any leading role in the affairs of Heaven. Us! We kept things going while they abandoned us to play. We've got rights! I'm tired of discrimination! I am not an object! This is my land! I have every right to a say in it!"

"Ok, cabbage patch," Matthew replied trying to soothe the little man.

"What?" Ezekiel whispered. "WHAT!"

"He values your contributions, don't you?" Mel subtly nodded his head, Matthew understanding.

"Sure. You...be strong." Ezekiel climbed off Matthew's shoulders and flew, moving slowly and obviously straining before dipping and finally touching the ground. Matthew offered his shoulders again, but Ezekiel's pride preferred to walk along the ground, his small steps making him have to run to keep up.

"For eternal innocents, you guys sure seem mature."

"That's what happens when you have contact with mortals." Mel instinctively wiped his hands on his suit. "They corrupt everything."

***

They reached the outskirts of Zion a few hours later. Matthew was amazed at the size of it as they advanced, the city stretching endlessly across the horizon. It glistened in an amber radiance, an amazing collection of sparkling pillars. Zion was a garden of light, a series of flashes and glowing luminescence. It was as if the city ahead were constructed of the rays of the sun.

As the whole fell away into individual parts with every step, Matthew's awe ebbed. The buildings were not like Ancient Greece or Rome. It wasn't even on par with New York City. The glimmer itself was an illusion. Shining off what appeared to be diamond and silver, closer inspection proved the buildings were nothing more than mere glass and steel. Every building, row upon row, was a simple oval of glass and steel. No ornate styling. No individuality. *How did they even know the difference between each one?*

"This...is Zion?" Matthew stopped to let the wave of disappointment pass over him. "Very original." His voice dripped with sarcasm.

"Must you...be critical of everything?" Ezekiel gasped as he trailed a hundred feet behind, close to collapse from running for miles.

"Where's the grandeur? Where's the originality? I thought this place looked like Greece. Or Disneyland."

"Are you in Greece? Are you even on Earth?" Mel asked.

"No," Matthew replied.

"So why would you think it should look like something from Earth?"

Matthew shrugged his shoulders. "I'm just saying as the pinnacle of Existence it falls flat."

Mel offered up a sad look. "You stress appearance far more than substance. Still, what do you expect? Our talent pool isn't very large or skilled."

"Why? This is Heaven, where the best go. Couldn't you draft that Michelangelo guy for some double-duty up here?"

"Most artists have a few problems." Mel rotated his right hand in a circle.

"And your point?" Matthew asked.

"Where do you think they go?"

Matthew thought a bit. "They go down there?" He pointed down.

"Yes," Mel replied. "Besides, most of their views are a little too liberal for up here."

"I thought Hell was fire and brimstone?"

"Hell is flash without substance."

Matthew nodded while trying to comprehend. "So, it's like Vegas only hotter." He looked around. "Well, so much for variety. Why does substance have to be so dull?"

"You ask too many questions. I miss the ones that went on faith."

"Well, I am seeing Zion, but I'm not believing it-"

"Can we go now?"

Matthew, disillusioned, acquiesced. "Sure."

Ezekiel struggled on, his steps awkward, falling forward and grabbing Matthew's leg for support. His hair was dripping, his face lathered. He panted and slouched. "Can we...wait...three minutes?"

"We don't have time to waste. Come on." Mel flew onwards into the city. Matthew followed him, Ezekiel nearly falling on his face with his support gone. He weaved back and forth before regaining a sort of balance, stepping with a drunken gait after them, his suit drenched with yellow stains.

The grass stopped at the outskirts of Zion, crushed beneath stone streets and a round wall of buildings that seemed to mark the city's periphery. They walked on roads of limestone, trees lining the path. Here and there, swaths of land were still virginal like the fields beyond, islands of nature in this city of Heaven.

Humans of all eras, dressed in all periods, wandered the streets. Oddly, they were all Caucasian. Matthew didn't think much of it; only that they seemed mindless, looking straight ahead as they marched on. They didn't acknowledge one another as they passed. Some rested under trees while others looked off to the horizon behind Matthew and his hosts as if they weren't even there. Matthew snuck up to one of the resting inhabitants, waving his hand back and forth in front of their face. Nothing. Matthew got up a little freaked.

Then he noticed it. Softly, a recording played throughout the streets: "Independent thought only confuses and blinds you from the truth. Faith is the way. Trust in faith. Faith is good." It seemed to loop, barely audible, but it was still there.

"Why does everyone look so bored...and drugged?" Matthew asked as they walked past the souls of Zion. "And where are the shadows?" Matthew hadn't realized it until now, but no darkness existed here; not even shade beneath the trees.

"You try living a few centuries. Eventually you do everything, hear everything. For us it isn't so bad, but you humans...ugh. You always need something new. If not for enforced serenity you people would be too troublesome-"

"Enforced serenity?" Matthew asked.

A bell tolled from some hidden location chiming the change of the hour. Suddenly everyone came to life charging for the buildings. Matthew had to dodge the rampage as Mel flew over it. Ezekiel screamed as he was butted to and fro by knees and feet.

And then there was no one. The roads were vacant and quiet. "We'd best keep moving," Mel told them. They navigated the deserted streets, the emptiness eerie. Matthew went to ask why everyone had bolted, but caught himself. Did he really want to know? Besides, something else was eating at him. "Do Asians go to Heaven?"

"What?" Mel asked taken aback.

"The Asians. You know, Japanese and Chinese. Are they allowed up here?"

"Why would you ask that?" Mel questioned.

"Well, I didn't see any samurai or geishas. Plus most of them are Buddhist...or Hindu...or some other weird religion. Matter of fact, I didn't see any minorities around. Do you guys discriminate on who you allow to immigrate up here?"

71

"The requirements are the same for everyone," Mel told him. "We show no favoritism."

"Do you have to be Christian to get in?"

Mel looked back and forth to make sure no one was listening. "Christianity isn't the end all be all of Existence," he whispered behind his hand.

"Meaning?"

"There are other ways." As Matthew was about to ask again Mel shook his finger. "No, don't ask." Mel looked around again as if they were being watched. "Best not to know."

Matthew pursed his lips. They continued on through the city blocks. No matter how far they walked it seemed they traveled the same path over and over again. Matthew tried to break the insane sameness and inject some variety. "So where are they?"

"Who?" Mel asked.

"The Blacks. The Asians."

"Not in this section of Heaven."

"Heaven is segregated?"

"Yes," Mel replied.

"You guys aren't racist are you?" Matthew asked.

"Why do you say that?" Mel barked before stopping.

"Hey, I know how it is. You guys are blonde haired, blue eyed, keep the minorities out of your living space." Matthew licked his lips and whispered, "Hitler isn't God is he?"

"That is quite enough!" Mel screamed. "Do not speak to me again."

"I was just cur-"

"Shhhhh!" Mel hissed.

Ezekiel continued to stagger after them leaving puddles behind him as his blistered feet minced his steps. His hair was no longer curly but straight and hanging with droplets flowing down them like golden stalagmites. His cheeks were a bright red. His arms hung limply as his little legs tried to keep up. He had a black eye from the stampede as well as footprints on his suit.

Matthew looked around as they strode through the Kingdom of Heaven. He found himself bored by this seeming perfection. It was so controlled, lacking random variety or artistic expression. It was minimalism in its purest form, all decoration stripped away for the most utilitarian architecture. All color had been pressed together and bled into a sterile white. It was...unnatural. Maybe life did end with death.

Matthew stopped. Something different caught his eye. Color! There was actual color. Not white, not clear, not steel but actual color! Matthew wandered in a separate direction to see exactly what dared to defy conformity. Mel flew on oblivious to the fact that Matthew was no longer behind him. Ezekiel collapsed on the grassy knoll enjoying the sweet, sweet release of rest.

Matthew hurried back down the block and found the street the color had come from. As he turned down it he discovered the origin of said color. A giant sign floated between two buildings. On it, a man with cropped black hair and a beard smiled down on the street below. It read, "Obey the word." The sign itself was framed in white and gold, the words in a sky blue on a background of purple. Matthew found himself scrutinizing the face of the Messiah. It was so alien. Far from beautiful it seemed...common. His face was round with a bulbous nose. Where was the flowing fair hair? And those black eyes. Didn't Jesus have blue eyes? Matthew couldn't get over it. His short attention was snagged when he heard muffled laughter. It came from one of the apartments.

He followed the sound to one of the buildings and peeked in through the transparent glass. Everyone inside was watching television. "So that's where everyone went," he said to himself. They seemed hypnotized by whatever program was playing. A woman and two men were leaning forward, perched on the edge of their seats. They smiled and giggled. The obsessiveness in their eyes was scary. Matthew knocked on the glass trying to see if they were real. Not a single eye turned his way. This place was strange indeed. Matthew walked a few feet to the side and stared in another window. Another group of people watched television just as transfixed. They seemed in some sort of rapture.

***

Mel was amazed at how quiet Matthew had been. Five minutes without speech. The human was learning a sort of patience. "I'm sorry for my outburst," Mel said over his shoulder. "I guess I am not really good with people." Mel flew on. He started to get irritated. "You could say you accept my apology." Still no response. "Didn't your-" Mel turned around to see only the blank road behind him. "Oh no."

Mel rapidly flew back in the direction from which he came trying to find out where Matthew had vanished to. "Hello? Hello?" Mel called down every block he passed, darting this way and that. Mel was in a panic. This was not good. Not good at all.

But if he did lose Matthew, what would that mean? So he would lose his job. Not like he enjoyed going down to Earth anyway. The place was too disorganized and dirty for his liking. Besides, then he could go back to playing his harp. He could also lose this ugly, tight, constrictive suit and return to his toga. Now that was an outfit. Loose, flowing, really breezy and never hard on the nether regions unlike these pants which were chafing once again.

As Mel contemplated giving up, tugging at his crotch, he was shocked to see someone unconscious on the ground.

Mel burst forward to see what the problem was. He dropped to the ground and waddled over to the miniature form. "Ezekiel," he cried as he turned him over. Ezekiel emitted a little moan as Mel dropped him. "You're soaking wet!" Ezekiel gave him a fuzzy stare, clearly out of it. "Great, just great," Mel replied.

***

The anchorman looked out at his audience, his trademark smile followed by a wink opening the program. "In world news tonight, problems between India and Pakistan continue to spiral out of control. India, claiming international right, swarmed into the disputed province of Kashmir in order to capture suspected militants sought in connection with an attack on their national parliament. Rumors of possible atrocities have started leaking out.

"Also in the news today, protests erupted throughout Europe at the heavy-handedness of the United States." The camera panned over swarms of people throughout the cities of Paris, Berlin, and others, holding placards and screaming. "Many in the region are outraged at President Lucas' deployment of military forces in the Eastern European nations."

The screen cut to a young man, hair greased and beyond his shoulders, wearing a bandana and denim jacket with buttons pinned all over, who stared into the camera. "Americans think they can bully others into doing whatever they want," he told the world, his thick German causing him to sound arrogant. The crowd behind him approved loudly. "Maybe the United States should focus on their own affairs. All they want to do is make war and destruction. Go home USA!"

The scene went back to the newsroom. The anchorman smiled that perfect, ivory grin. "The President's approval rating has dropped in recent days as the American public shows their opinion of their leader's administration. The President has been quick to respond to critics of his 'go it alone' policy."

President Lucas came on screen. He was sitting in his chair in the Oval Office, proudly displaying the seal of the presidency on his desk. "My fellow Americans, we are in troubled times. The fragile new democracy of the Soviet-"

"Russia," a whisper came from off screen.

Lucas looked beyond the camera and mouthed, "Really?" He nodded and smiled again at the camera. "The fragile new democracy of Russia has been undermined by the dictator Romanov. Many call my deployment of troops throughout the region 'war mongering' and an attempt to provoke Romanov into some confrontation. That is the furthest from the truth. I am attempting to prevent the spread of his communist-"

"Authoritarian!" someone hissed off camera.

"Authoritarian regime's chaos. We have seen that Europe is far from willing to defend itself leaving it up to us, as it has for decades, to protect them from the hordes. The nations of Eastern Europe remain weak and in need of support. Whereas the western states believe themselves safe and ever willing to sacrifice their neighbors selfishly, we know the delicate situation that is being played out. I will not allow the eastern hordes to swallow up those states which we have only recently freed from the darkness of Bolshevism.

"Democracy is under attack everywhere from Pakistan to North Korea. The United States has always been willing to defend those unable to defend themselves. Western Europe tells us to mind our own business. I say we are as Western Europe is neglecting theirs. The time of words is over. Words can be twisted. Words can be lies. Only action achieves anything. We shall prevail." Lucas gave the camera a thumbs up as he winked.

The screen quickly clicked back to the anchorman. "Russian President Alexander Romanov had this to say in response."

The screen switched to the swarthy Russian, his hair graying at the temples. He stared right through the screen at everyone watching. This was a man of power and prestige about to speak on a pressing piece of world affairs. He cleared his throat and spoke those immortal words: "Fuck America."

The screen came back to an obviously shocked anchorman. He sat in silence for a second and quickly regained composure. "President Lucas couldn't be reached for comment."

***

Where was he? Matthew walked down another block. They all looked the same. Same white road. Same rows of trees. The weird part was the further he went the more pictures he saw of Jesus. Some were strung along the sides of buildings, others on signs like he had seen earlier. He even came across a statue in the only part of the city so far that differed from everything else. The square was thirty three feet in diameter and on a circular platform stood a bronze of Jesus with his arms outstretched. On his face was a broad smile, eyes closed. Matthew looked at the plaque below. "Embrace the spirit of Jesus as he accepts you blindly. The Word, the Way, the Life". From that square Matthew looked left then right. In this city Jesus was everywhere in one way, shape, or form whether on signs or banners. You couldn't escape his eyes. Matthew looked back at that large statue, looking at the expression on that bronze face that seemed in a state of blind ecstasy. He backed away, creeped out, and started searching again.

Matthew rounded a corner and found something he hadn't expected: an inner city. The buildings were run down but classical in their architecture, complete with broken pillars and statues, some decapitated, staring out from the walls. Hewn of stone and standing no higher than four stories, this place did not belong in the same era as the rest of Zion. Cracks ran throughout the stone, grass poking out between the blocks that once were organized streets. Oddly enough, the pictures of Jesus ceased to appear here.

Matthew could hear music coming from somewhere shaking the calm air of Heaven. Drawn to the discord it brought to this one-note town, he followed it. As the music grew louder he found its origin. The building itself was of mottled marble, taller than the rest of those on the street. Etched into the wall above the arched main door was a neon sign: "Gabriel's". It flashed a bright red. It contrasted with the rest of Zion with its flickering lights and dark windows.

"Finally, some entertainment." Matthew walked up to the entrance. "Wait, should I really go in there?" Matthew asked himself. He stopped to debate the pros and cons when he heard people. "Hey, it's Heaven. What do I have to worry about?" Matthew wandered through the arch leaving the golden light behind and entered a smoky blackness.

The place was alive with activity. A bar was set up to the left, carved with various notches in its pine exterior, where a few dozen figures sat drinking from silver chalices and watching television. They bellowed with laughter. To the right were various tables where people sat and talked, drinking themselves silly. To the rear was a door with light streaming out around the edges. The place had an off-kilter type of feel, as if anything could happen at a moments notice. The place was rumbling with conversation. Not a soul noticed him as he stood in the doorway.

He looked closely at the figures scattered about the room. It was definitely a Nazi paradise. Every man inside was blonde haired, fair skinned, and blue eyed just like the cherubim, but the similarity ended there. Their size was enormous: ten foot tall easy and as broad as a bull.

Matthew walked over to the bar only for it to grow uncomfortably larger the closer he got. He followed the line of big fellows until he found a break. Everything about the place made him feel like a child, especially the open stool. The seat itself stood at forehead level. He struggled to climb up it. The large fellow next to him, noticing his problem, laughed loudly as he grabbed Matthew by the scruff of the neck and plopped him down on the stool. Matthew thanked him as the giant went back to his chalice. Matthew strained his head upwards to peek over the bar. "Get a drink?" he asked, finger in the air.

"Here you go," bellowed the barkeep as he towered over Matthew. The fellow looked like steroids were fed to him from conception. The veins in his beefy arms throbbed menacingly as he slammed a silver chalice down right in front of Matthew spilling a little of the contents onto the wood of the bar.

"But I didn't-"

"Here you go," the barkeep cut him off with his syrupy brogue.

"Thanks," Matthew offered as the barkeep wandered off. He reached for the chalice only to discover his arms wouldn't go that far. Matthew had to stand up on the stool to reach his mug. The thing was the size of a milk jug. He tried to peer into it, tilting it to the side. Clear. Probably vodka. He took a sip. Nothing. Took another sip. Still nothing. Where was the taste? He turned and saw everyone else chugging their drinks down. Matthew raised his chalice and tried to follow suit, raising his as he opened his mouth to swallow, only to get the majority all over his face and up his nose as the weight proved too much. Everyone laughed as Matthew sneezed. Wiping his eyes clear, he finally realized why there was no taste. "This is water!" He dried his face with his sleeves.

"Best holy water in all Zion!" the giant next to Matthew claimed.

"Yum!" Matthew replied as he licked his lips feigning appeasement. As the giant grinned elsewhere Matthew became annoyed. *Heaven sucked man! Maybe a life of sin was the way to go.* He swept his wet hair back as the barkeep slammed another chalice down in front of him. Loud noises came from beyond the rear door. Matthew turned. Well, at least there was some sort of excitement. As he turned to climb down his stool an ad came on the television causing him to pause.

"Jesus has helped you, hasn't he?" The words were spoken as they crossed the screen. A group of people popped on, nodding their heads yes. "You love Jesus, don't you?" The words once more crossed the screen. The crowd came back, nodding like before. "Remember, Jesus is Lord..." The words trailed off as Jesus' face came on screen, smiling. Boos sounded from all over the room. Some even threw things at the screen.

"Would you look at that," came an accented voice further down the bar. "He's everywhere. Not like he belongs anywhere. You understand me?" Matthew looked down the length of the bar to see who was making the noise. "Bastard takes over and now what? We have nothing." Matthew saw the giant. His hair had mild streaks of white in it, his face lined. Bags weighed heavily beneath eyes rimmed with crow's feet. He looked broken, sorrowfully sitting hunched over on his stool. "Once we were Heaven's defenders. What is there to defend anymore? We can't even drink wine these days," he growled, knocking his chalice off the bar with the wave of his hand.

"Come on, Gabriel. It's not that bad-" the barkeep started.

"Not that bad? We're nothing but..." Gabriel turned sensing Matthew watching him. "What is this?" His face contorted, the lines causing his face to crackle with fury.

Matthew looked around. Everyone was focused on him. Gabriel got up from his stool and started to come towards him. Matthew knew he was in trouble. He tried to get away, but as he went to jump off the stool, the giant next to him put a meaty hand on his shoulder. "Not so fast, boy."

Gabriel stood towering over Matthew even as he stood on his stool. "Your kind isn't welcome here."

Matthew felt like wetting himself. He was definitely not expecting an ass kicking in Heaven. "Maybe you should put a sign in the window to warn future...um...people-"

Gabriel grabbed him by the shirt and lifted him off the stool, Matthew's feet dangling. "Are you trying to be smart? He might protect you out there. In here, no one sees nothing."

Matthew tried to lighten the mood. "Yeah." He looked up at the ceiling. "Bad lighting-"

Gabriel gripped Matthew by the throat, his hand like a steel vice. "Want to mock me, boy? I'll grind you into the dust you came from." Gabriel looked closely into Matthew's eyes, his hand a second away from snapping bone. "Because of you we lost our rights, our glory, our dignity. We'll never be what we once were. We are nothing!" His eyes were the gray of thunder clouds.

"He's not worth it." The barkeep had come around to stand behind Matthew's dangling self. "Do you want to end up like the Horsemen?" Gabriel looked at the barkeep, his face twitching. "Do you?"

Gabriel looked back at Matthew. "You're lucky, boy. Your savior saves you again." He dropped Matthew as he turned to leave the bar, his steps loud thumps.

"Christ," Matthew rasped, rubbing his throat and choking on fresh air, drawing the word out. The place went silent at the word. The entire room gave Matthew a very angry stare. He stood there, surrounded by some very roid-enraged giants, unsure of where to go or what to do. The rear door was closest so he started towards it slowly, their eyes following him like a cat's making him the mouse. He backed into the door, his free hand fiddling with the knob behind him. He smiled as they eviscerated him with their sharp looks, the door behind finally opening. Matthew quickly jumped in and slammed it.

He breathed a sigh of relief as he turned around to a welcome sight. A ring was set up in the dim room, a raucous crowd surrounding it. Giants bellowed, jumping up and down as they jeered and catcalled. The walls shook. In the ring itself two figures slammed into one another without a single care for safety. They rained blows down on one another like brain damage was as benign as a cold. "Hell yeah!" Matthew screamed as he tried to find a good vantage point.

Now this was entertainment. The one figure managed to get his opponent in a headlock and proceeded to bring punch after punch down on his scalp. He stopped to scream at the crowd. That proved a mistake as he was back dropped right out of the ring. He fell over the ropes onto a table with a crack. As he struggled to get up the giant in the ring ran and jumped over after him slamming into not only his opponent but also two of the audience.

"Go Michael!" someone shouted encouragement.

The two audience members got up, throwing their drinks at Michael as he turned around and knocked the one out before shoving the other to the ground. He grabbed his opponent off the floor and threw him back into the ring before climbing in after him. As the opponent tried to stand up, Michael gave him a good kick to the ribs with a loud slap. Matthew grimaced. Michael grabbed the guy by his hair and heaved him into a corner where he proceeded to pound him into hamburger, blood pouring from every pore the guy possessed. A bell rang from somewhere and it was over.

Matthew half-expected the bloodied giant to need medical treatment, but the guy smiled. The crazy bastard smiled! Before Matthew's eyes, the opponent's wounds sealed and seconds later it was as if they had never been. The man gripped Michael's wrist as Michael did the same in some sort of handshake.

"Good match!" the opponent said.

"You make a good punching bag!" Michael laughed as the crowd roared with him.

"Hey!" the opponent mockingly replied. "You got lucky, old man. Next time let's keep it in the ring."

"Then there is no fan participation!" The crowd cheered as Michael smiled. He butted heads with his foe before climbing out of the ring.

"There you are!" Matthew turned to see Mel floating behind him. "You shouldn't be in here."

"Why not? I'm over twenty-one."

"Come on."

"Can't we stay a few minutes? I want to catch the next match." Mel's face carried a flat denial. "Ok, ok." As they started to leave two more men climbed into the ring. A huge thud caught Matthew's attention. He stopped and turned to watch the next fight as Mel grabbed him by the ear and painfully lead him away.

Once back in the main room, Mel let him go as he flew towards one of the tables. On top was a delirious Ezekiel. "Play the strings," he moaned in total dementia. "I play the strings."

"What's wrong with him?" Matthew asked.

"Exhausted. Can you help me carry him?"

Matthew slung him over his shoulder. "He's wet!"

"It's sweat. Come on."

"I play the strings!" Ezekiel continued.

On their way out, Matthew saw Michael sitting at the bar. "Where's Gabriel?" Michael asked, concern apparent in his voice.

"You know Gabriel," the barkeep replied. Michael shook his head understanding.

"Will you come on?" Mel tugged on Matthew.

"Oh, right." Matthew followed Mel out, cherub over his shoulder. "So what's the story?"

"What do you mean?" Mel asked, constantly looking behind himself to ensure Matthew was there.

"The guys in the bar. Well, giants I mean."

Mel flew on, Matthew in pursuit. Mel decided to answer if only to prevent him from wandering off again. "They are angels."

"Really? I thought angels were...a little queerer."

"They were the leading soldiers of God. Protectors of the Heavens from all that threatened her borders. They live to fight."

"Well, that guy, Michael, can really kick some ass." Matthew walked a few more steps. "What do you mean were? They aren't anymore?"

"They aren't really needed anymore."

Matthew was confused. "They're not needed? Hell still exists right?"

"Yes," Mel replied exasperated.

"So why aren't they needed? Demons become pussies or something?"

"A treaty was signed two thousand years ago." Mel made a turn. "Heaven and Hell ended hostilities. Since that time, the angels haven't had much to do. That's why clubs like that exist."

"Clubs like what?"

Mel stopped and put his hands on his hips as he pivoted around in the air. "That was an Arch Angel club. They meet there to release their frustrations, bunch of brutes." Mel turned and continued flying. "They're nothing more than border patrol now and you see how well they do at that."

Matthew thought it over as he nodded dumbly. "They don't have flashbacks do they?"

"What?"

"All veterans have them. Do they? You know, go crazy and flip some table in a cafeteria screaming about 'Charlie in the wire-'"

"We aren't as weak-minded as you," Mel retorted.

"But you aren't an angel. How would you know?"

"All of God's creations are flawless and strong-willed."

"But I'm one of God's creations."

"You are one of his accidents."

"I don't follow."

"Well, you'd better if you want to make it back to Earth by your lifetime."

After a few steps Matthew piped up again. "They don't seem very happy."

"Who?" Mel asked.

"The angels."

"Who cares whether or not they're happy."

"Geeze, do you hate people more the taller they get?" Matthew asked sarcastically.

Mel stopped and turned. "Angels have been nothing but troublemakers since the Christ took over."

"I don't follow." When Mel gave him that exasperated look Matthew could only reply with a genuine blank stare.

"They hate the Christ for having ended hostilities and outlawing war and bloodshed both here and on Earth. The angels believe that Hell is to not be trusted. They even think they have the right to interfere in human affairs."

"When did they ever interfere in human affairs," Matthew asked before shifting Ezekiel on his shoulder.

"Whenever God did something they carried out his commands. Walls of Jericho, plague in Egypt, etc."

"Ohhhh." Matthew began to understand. "I still don't understand why they hate Jesus so much."

"How do you know that?"

"Well, when I said his name they looked like they were going to grind me into the floor."

Mel started to fly again. "Doesn't surprise me. They've always believed in action before words."

"You're losing me again."

"They hate the Christ immensely. Believe he doesn't keep with the old ways of God. With Christ in power, Heaven began allowing many more humans entrance relaxing the prerequisites to get in. The angels claimed he was flooding Heaven with mortals in order to build his numbers. Increasing his power base. When Christ had himself proclaimed the Lord of Heaven and Earth, the angels had had enough. Around fourteen hundred years ago Gabriel led a revolt. He tried to enact a coup. It all started when he went down and spoke to some Arabian nomad."

Matthew smiled despite himself. "You're telling me that Islam was created as part of a coup against Jesus?"

"It was more than that. We are not that petty!" Mel scoffed. "The entire episode proved most troublesome. Telling them that Christ was simply some ordinary man. Even telling them not to pray to the Christ but God instead! They even encouraged bloodshed! Always the sword before the word!" Mel spit through gritted teeth.

"So the revolution failed I take it?"

"For a while the angels helped the Muslims to some very impressive victories, doing their best to wipe out the Christ's human supporters. When the Christ discovered the angels' plans to remove him he acted in response. Heaven became embroiled in a war that saw the angels beaten thanks in no small part to the Christ's human supporters…as well as the cherubim."

"Is that why cherubim are so important now?"

"If you mean why we, rather than some barbaric angel, came to get you, yes it is. But not out of spite. The new system believes in equal opportunity."

"Whatever. Seems angels don't get many opportunities these days."

"Think what you want." Mel sniffed before continuing on.

Matthew, with Ezekiel staining his shoulder and Mel leading the way, continued through Zion and its bland perfection until they reached a set of descending stairs. "God live underground?" Matthew asked.

"We're taking the subway."

"We're taking the subway to meet God? Classy."

"You're not the VIP you think you are. Now come on."

As they descended the steps Matthew looked at the sterile, tiled walls. The place was immaculate. His hand followed the silver banister as he stepped down into the depths. At the bottom was a platform along with hundreds of waiting passengers. "Good. We haven't missed it." Mel flew over their heads to stare down the track. Matthew's eyes strafed the walls, a long line of posters with Jesus in a suit pointing at the reader. "Jesus Wants You to be Holy!"

"The strings!" Ezekiel croaked.

"Is he going to be ok?" Matthew asked Mel as he came flying back.

"Sure. A little holy water and he'll be fine." A rumble started to grow. "Oh, be ready."

"Ready for what?" Matthew asked. Squeals of metal echoed through the tunnel as the subway train arrived. The multitude began to stir. "All aboard!" an electronic voice called from somewhere as the doors of the train hissed open.

"Go!" Mel pushed Matthew into the crowd as everyone fought to get in. It was chaos. It was undisciplined. It was the subway system of Heaven.

CHAPTjEsusR 4

"Fuck me? Fuck...me!" President Lucas was livid as he paced back and forth. "How dare that communist bastard speak that way about me. About my country. Romanov. Romanov!" No one had ever dared to disrespect Lucas like that before. It was inconceivable. Lucas shook his hands in the air wildly beating on anything near him. He threw a desk lamp across the room barely missing his Chief of Staff as the Vice-President and various interns peeked through the doorway.

"Sir, you must calm down!" the Chief pleaded.

"Don't tell me what to do!" Lucas flipped his chair over. "I'm the President!"

"Sadly," a voice commented from the group in the doorway.

President Lucas froze. "Who said that?" Everyone remained quiet. "Who said that!?!"

One of the interns seized the opportunity and incriminated a fellow worker. "Her, sir!" He grabbed a woman by her shoulder, shaking her. "She's a Democrat!"

Lucas looked for something to throw. As the intern tried to pull away, Lucas bellowed, "Don't even try to leave!" She surrendered to her turncoat's grip, head bowed.

Everytime the President tried to grab something for a weapon his Chief of Staff interjected himself. "Sir, this is bad press waiting to happen. Control yourself! If not for you, then the party."

Frustrated with nothing to toss in reach, Lucas bent down and pulled his shoe off. As he went to throw it he was tackled to the floor by his Chief. "Let me go!" Lucas tried to free himself to strike down that liberal target. Slowly he lessened his efforts, sobbing with surrender. "Is this the price of free speech?" Lucas blubbered, his arms too weak to free themselves. "The insulting of government figures?" Tears wet his face cutting canals through the powder he wore revealing the flawed being beneath. "Get out." The crowd of political apprentices just watched. "Get out of here!" he yelled at everyone. They cleared out, virtually trampling over one another to be the first to fulfill Lucas' order. The Vice-President, seeing Lucas restrained, found the nerve to finally step into the Oval Office.

"Sir." The Chief shook the President. "Sir!" He slapped Lucas finally smacking some sense into him. "We have problems. Now, we need you calm."

Lucas closed his eyes, breathing deeply. "Ok." He breathed a little more before opening his eyes. "I'm ready to lead."

The Chief slowly let him go. Once sure Lucas no longer posed a threat, he walked over and grabbed the overturned chair. He carried it back to the desk. "Thank you," Lucas said before he took the offered chair, his throne. The Vice-President was quick to motion his competition away so that he could push the chair closer to the desk and rest his hands on Lucas' shoulders. The President gave his full attention to his Chief of Staff. "What is wrong?"

"Mr. President, things have taken a turn for the worse in Kashmir."

Lucas looked up to his Vice. "There is a problem in the sweater industry?" He looked back at his Chief. "Will this have major economic impact?"

"Mr. President, I'm talking about India and Pakistan."

"Oh, Africa," Lucas nodded. "Go ahead."

The Chief almost corrected him, but he thought it a waste of time. "There have been instances of attacks by Indians on

Pakistanis in response to the Parliamentary attacks of a few days ago."

"How in the hell did Indians get to Africa?"

"Sir," his Chief looked at the ceiling, the tip of his tongue touching his top lip as he held his thoughts in check. "What shall we do about the attacks?"

"Why is everyone so worried about a few bows and arrows?"

"Sir-"

"Ok, ok. We'll do what we've always done. We'll negotiate some treaty and move them elsewhere. Promise them something nice. They already have too many beads. Maybe give them some alcohol...wait, fire water. That's what they call it."

"I'll tell the press we'll be remaining neutral on this," his Chief began, already moving to contain the situation as he had always done. "Also sir, Russia has begun militarizing their borders and cut exports of vital materials to the United States in response to our deployments."

"What do they give us that is so vital?"

"Well, they do give us vodka," his Vice offered.

"Yes, that is true," Lucas replied.

"Mr. President, they have cut oil shipments."

"Oil? When did we import oil from the Soviets?"

The Chief continued on wanting to end this diplomatic nightmare as soon as possible and put some plan, any plan, into action. "They've also banned all imports from the U.S."

"So what's the problem?" Lucas was completely lost.

"Mr. President, with the current problems in the Middle East, oil is in short supply. Russia accounts for twenty percent of our oil." The President kept watching. He needed simplification. "Oil is going to be more expensive." The President remained clueless. "Gas will go up."

"Oh my!" The President finally began to catch on. "This is a problem."

"Yes, indeed, Mr. President," the Vice-President echoed.

"What will my constituents think?"

"Sir, about the military problem with Russia-" the Chief started.

"Any way we could replace this missing oil? Dallas has oil doesn't it? I saw it on television."

"Mr. President-"

"We could invest in hybrids or different fuels," the Vice-President cut in. "Should find some mix that could work on less oil. Maybe even cheapen it."

"Russia, not very happy," the Chief stated in his attempt to get at the true heart of the matter.

"Cheaper gas! I would be loved by every American. Maybe even a third term!"

"Mr. President-"

"Third terms aren't allowed, Mr. President," the Vice-President replied.

"You're just saying that because you want my chair!" Lucas bitterly retorted.

"Impending World War III here," the Chief once more chimed in.

"Don't think I haven't seen your jealousy!" Lucas accused his Vice, turning to stare menacingly at his second-in-command.

"You are paranoid, Lucas-"

"Mr. President you worthless, worthless man!" Lucas spat. The two began yelling at each other as the Chief of Staff, tired of the whole charade of mature, efficient government, closed the door after him and left the most important seat of power to its petty problems.

***

"Are we almost there," Matthew asked, his face pressed up against the glass window, smeared like putty. The subway car was packed to bursting.

"Yes!" Mel replied while flying over the crowd's heads. "Why do you keep asking? Doesn't get us there any faster."

"Well, I kind of wanted to know how much longer I have the pleasure of enjoying the feeling of my every orifice being violated by elbows and knees." The car shuddered a bit causing a fresh round of objects to jab into Matthew's ribs and back before knocking his head freshly back into the window with a thwonk. Matthew blinked his eyes in pain, stretching his mouth and shaking his head.

It was not long before the subway car came to a screeching halt at the station, a multitude of faces staring in at Matthew waiting to cram themselves into a one size fits none. When the doors opened, Matthew felt the pressure ease as the flood of souls poured out onto the platform. As the crowd dissipated, Ezekiel became visible on the floor. Bits of paper and trash were stuck to his stained suit and face. "Air. Air!" he cried, reaching as if to pull even more of the sweet oxygen into his lungs.

Mel floated in the doorway waving his arm for them to follow. "Hurry before the horde storms us!" Matthew started to exit. "Don't forget Ezekiel." Matthew reached down and grabbed Ezekiel by the leg dragging him along after him. Matthew shoved his way through the waiting passengers as he followed Mel to the stairs. He elbowed and pushed to clear his path. "Hey, this is Heaven. Show a little kindness," Mel spouted at Matthew's assault through the crowd.

"Out of my way!" someone shouted as they knocked Mel into a pillar on their way to the subway car.

Mel's face took on a very vengeful glare. "Where are manners these days?" Someone else bumped him with their shoulder. As he turned two others hit him on either side as they hurried past. "Hey!" He took another bump collapsing to the ground. He stood up, brushing his suit off. "Do none of you have any manners?" His words caused everyone to pause. The crowd, mid-stampede, turned around and looked at him. Mel stood there waiting for an answer, hands on hips.

"No," they said in unison as they once more charged the subway car.

"Mel?" The cherub turned towards the sound of Matthew's voice. "Can we go now?"

Mel rose off the ground, cursing anything that came to mind as he flew past Matthew and guided him towards the exit. They walked up the steps, the sound of humanity fading as they rose into the golden light. As they came to ground level, Matthew was in total awe.

The buildings here were different. Twelve massive palaces were arranged in a circle around a large skyscraper that reached hundreds of stories into the air, a pillar of crystal that seemed to support the sky. As the light touched that spire it split into a rainbow, the myriad colors playing across the horizon. The palaces at its base were in the design of ancient Roman architecture. They gleamed in a glowing marble mixed with silver and gold. Lush gardens surrounded each individual building as they glistened like scattered treasure in the light.

As they passed the outer ring of buildings, the triad entered a large courtyard. Upon the polished granite stood monuments to the glories of old wars gone by. In the distance Matthew saw other celebrated statues as well as sculptures of stranger designs. He was struck dumb by such beauty, dropping Ezekiel's muttering body. Mel turned hearing the thud. "What is it?"

"It's...it's beautiful." Matthew was spellbound. This was nothing like Zion and its modern feel. This was a physical dream constructed of fantasy. "I didn't think you guys had any artists up here?"

"This was built long ago. Before the 'current' regulations."

"Pre-Jesus?" Matthew asked.

"Can we...?" Mel motioned towards the skyscraper.

"We're going in there?" Matthew was a little intimidated. "Who are we seeing again?"

"The boss," Mel replied with annoyance at having to constantly remind this man.

"Who is that exactly? God?"

"No, not God." Mel blew a curl out of his face. "The Christ."

"So then Jesus is in charge?"

"The Christ is in charge."

"So Jesus is God."

"No."

"Then if he isn't God, why is he the boss?"

"Because he is!" Mel lashed back.

Matthew sensed the tension of the situation. He was quiet as Mel floated forward again before pausing, waiting for him to follow. Matthew grabbed Ezekiel and started towards the skyscraper. "God is real, right?" Matthew asked Mel's back.

"Yes, he is."

"So where is he?"

Mel paused. "Retired."

"You don't sound too sure about that." Matthew stopped. "He isn't dead is he?"

"No!"

"Jesus lead some coup?"

"Just be quiet, please!" Mel turned to Matthew, his face purple and blotted. "We are entering the building of the governing body of Existence. It is not a place for questions. It is a place of faith and silence. So please keep some faith and accept it all for what it is. Questions only lead to doubt."

Matthew shrugged in compliance.

"Thank you," Mel sighed in relief as they continued.

Before the entrance of the skyscraper stood a massive work of art; it was a gigantic bronze of Jesus seeming to ascend out of a series of clouds embedded in the ground, his face turned up and away from view. At the base, Matthew saw an inscription: *He left in shame and returned in triumph, 33 AD.* Matthew meant to ask what it meant, but he remembered Mel's words and kept his mouth shut. Continuing to do so was not going to be easy.

As they crossed the threshold into the lobby of the spire, Matthew felt himself shrink to a miniscule particle in the way of things. The room was enormous. Looking up he saw a vertical shaft that cut all the way up to the seemingly unreachable apex, the hole a golden pinprick to his eyes. The light of Existence shone through that circle cascading along the interior casting an unearthly glow, the rays emanating off of the crystalline walls and floors. The shape of the spire was circular, much like many of the other buildings Matthew had seen. Offices radiated from the naturally lit center in orderly floors stacked one atop another all the way to the top shrinking from view. Cherubim and others floated in the gap, their tiny figures darting here and there in the air.

Dizziness forced Matthew to look down, vertigo seizing him from the grand height above. He steadied himself, closing his eyes. As they opened what Matthew saw on the wall surrounding the lobby was breathtaking. Various murals showed Jesus in triumphant poses and scenes as conqueror and leader. Music played throughout the vastness, a sweet, classical melody complete with the softest of voices.

A large desk sat in the center of the chamber. Mel made his way towards it as Matthew's eyes admired the mosaic that covered the floor. A cherub sat behind the desk on an elevated chair. "May I help you?"

"Yes, I'm going to need some aid," Mel told him.

"Aid?" the cherub asked, puzzled. Mel turned and pointed at Matthew, the dumbfounded mortal. "Oh dear. Yes, I will get someone down here." As the cherub spoke into his headset he gave some commands and then paused. "Where is he going exactly?"

"The pinnacle."

The cherub's surprise was poorly concealed. "We're going to need a lot more men," he spoke into his headset. He turned to Mel. "They'll be down in a moment."

"Thank you." Mel turned and flew back to Matthew.

Ezekiel struggled to his feet, feeling slightly better.

"Amazing, isn't it," Matthew said absently to his once more conscious partner.

"I see it everyday," Ezekiel blandly remarked, wiping the sweat from his forehead. "Not much to this building but size anyway."

"Not your taste?"

"It's made to make you feel small. The Christ says it helps to show us how minor we are in the scheme of things. I say it's just a headache to go up and down."

Matthew laughed as Mel pulled up. "So where to now?"

"Up there," Mel told him, his finger pointing skyward.

"Ok." Matthew looked around. "So, where's the elevator?"

Mel looked at Ezekiel. "There isn't one."

"Then how am I supposed to get up there?"

"With a little help."

Matthew heard a noise above. A large squadron of cherubim came floating down, Matthew able to see up some of their togas. He quickly covered his eyes and let out a sound of disgust. "You guys really are eternally prepubescent."

"This is him," Mel told the group.

"What's going on," Matthew asked his companions.

"Your elevator," Mel informed him.

"Wait," Matthew said as they started to approach. "Wait! We tried this before. It didn't work out."

"There are more of us. We can surely lift you now."

Matthew nervously began to back away. "Is there anyway the boss can come down here-"

"Absolutely not! The Christ never leaves the pinnacle save for important matters."

"Maybe this once?" Matthew begged.

"No. Grab him," Mel ordered.

Matthew began to struggle as they went to seize him. "Please, no!" he yelped as he kicked one midget like a football sending him across the lobby. As two latched on to either leg, Matthew jumped up and down slapping his legs, and them, together. "No! I won't. No!" Three grabbed him at the waist as he twisted. Another ran towards him only to be tossed over Matthew's shoulder. One of the cherubim clutched Matthew's arm and screamed up to the heights. Cherubic reinforcements came from the upper levels to aid their companions. It was turning into a battle royal. Matthew pulled his hand free, yanking the cherub holding him into the air and slamming him into one of his descending brothers.

Matthew ran from the plunging mob, cherubim on either leg dragging across the tile. A cherub grasped either arm, another his belt. Matthew felt his feet starting to leave the floor and was possessed by fear. He instinctively slammed either cherub holding his arms together. A wedgie from Heaven was working its way up his butt crack. Matthew frantically reached around behind his back to free himself from their miniature hands.

The cherub at the desk was frantically speaking into his headset, ducking as a body was thrown over his head. Mel and Ezekiel simply watched the melee. "Aren't you going to help?" he pleaded.

"We already went through this. No thanks."

Matthew looked up, his eyes bugging out as he saw another legion coming his way. He jerked a cherub off his leg and turned him into a club, swinging him around and slamming midget after midget into the distance. Matthew let out a battle cry as he swung the limp body back and forth in an arc of defense.

"This is going nowhere." Ezekiel shook his head before whistling loudly. Everyone stopped, Matthew dropping his living club to the floor. "Exactly what is the problem? I thought everyone would jump at the chance to meet the Christ. Why are you always so difficult? If it's sins, he doesn't really care." Matthew shuffled his feet, blushing as he looked down. "It's been a really long day, and I would like to end it so please, whatever the problem is, let's just fix it and move on." Matthew looked up, then down again. "Well?"

"I'm afraid of heights," Matthew blurted.

"What?" Ezekiel asked, taken aback.

"I'm scared of heights."

"That's tragic. It really is," Ezekiel said. "But we really need to get you up there."

"Can't Jesus just...beam me up?"

"This isn't science fiction. This is Heaven. Do you think the Christ can do anything?"

"Well, it says so in the bible."

"That it does," a few of the cherubim said in unison.

"Well, it isn't happening," Ezekiel corrected, staring down a few of the others.

"We have a problem then don't we," Matthew stated.

A cherub caught Ezekiel's eye, winking. "You know," Ezekiel started as his ally snuck up behind Matthew, "I don't think we do anymore." He waved his hand, and a few cherubim ran forward at once surprising Matthew and pushing him over the back of the cherub kneeling behind him. Matthew hit the stone floor hard smacking the back of his head and knocking him into a stupor. The legion of little people leapt on him. They grabbed him tightly and started to pull him into the air.

They carried Matthew's limp form up the spire's central shaft. His mind swimming, Matthew felt weightless as they carried him ever higher. The giant eye in the roof grew larger and larger, the light shining brighter and brighter as they ascended leaving the ground far beneath. It all seemed some fantasy, the distant voices reverberating in his ears as his vision clouded over. His head flopped as he saw the inhabitants of each floor rushing to and fro on business, some looking up at him as he passed.

Eventually he was pulled to the side and unceremoniously dropped on the floor. The cherubim bid them goodbye and disappeared to the depths below. Matthew slowly got up, his knees shaking. "How...how far up are we?"

"I could tell you, but I don't think you want to know," Mel informed him.

Matthew slowly walked back to the edge. "I don't think you want to do that," Ezekiel warned.

Matthew waved it off and looked over. "Whoa!" Matthew felt his equilibrium give out and went dizzy when he saw the deep chasm yawning at his toes. Ezekiel and Mel ran up and grabbed Matthew as he nearly fell over. "I shouldn't have done that," Matthew choked out, shaking. Ezekiel shook his head, an expression of "duh" all over it.

"Let's go." Mel and Ezekiel walked away from the hole. Matthew took baby steps following after them, his knees knocking. As they continued on, the music Matthew had heard grew further in intensity. He looked up to see them approaching a large group of cherubim playing harps, singing in groups. Their voices reached into Matthew's soul calming him. His tension and fears melted away as he approached that childlike choir. He watched them, their music causing a well of peace and happiness to spring in his desolate heart.

"Look at them," Ezekiel spoke over the choir. "No drive. Just play, play, play. Makes me sick to see all the rights we fought to give them, and they continue like this." Ezekiel raised his hand in defiance. Mel grabbed him and pulled him along.

"Just come on," Mel stated authoritatively.

Matthew continued to watch the choir, listening as he followed his guides. Innocent eyes gazed back at him, their words forever to echo in his soul for whatever days remained within his flesh.

The corridor they traveled gave way to a vast hall. Grand tapestries lined the distant walls. The floor was covered with intricately designed rugs. The trio walked on, past the giggling cherubim that ran to and fro, to eventually come upon a large door carved with a big "J".

"We going in there?" Matthew asked.

Mel nodded as Ezekiel stepped forward. He knocked on the door, each sound echoing throughout the cavernous foyer. Matthew looked around for any movement in the now still hall. Ezekiel knocked again to no reply. The door simply would not budge. Ezekiel began kicking the door over and over. Suddenly there was a shudder and the door began to crack open. A blinding light scorched through the widening gap. As the door moaned open the room was bathed in brightness.

"Come on." Ezekiel and Mel waddled in. Matthew just froze like a deer in the headlights; the light forcing him back, paralyzing him. "Come on!" Ezekiel commanded, his words knocking Matthew out of shock.

Matthew tucked in his shirt instinctively, licking his hand to straighten his hair. He had to look good. He was meeting the Almighty. Matthew slowly gave himself to the light, his shadow melting into molten illumination. The doors slowly closed behind him. There was nothing but blazing white. Matthew moved a few steps forward, waiting for the voice all those near death people spoke of, and tripped over Ezekiel.

"Can you please hit the dimmer?" Ezekiel begged. The light went down in intensity. "Thank you."

Matthew tried to rub some sense into his eyes. "What was with all the light?"

"Image," Ezekiel responded. "Makes the Christ's guests stand in awe. One of his favorite negotiating tactics."

Mel elbowed Ezekiel. "What do you think he," jerking a thumb at Matthew, "is here for?"

"Oh. Oh! Sorry."

Matthew's sight gradually returned. The room fuzzily came into view. Glossy, painted walls with clouds and blue horizon surrounded them. The ceiling was sapphire with white diamonds, a perfect recreation of the night sky. The floor was plush, earthy carpet. A silver and gold inlaid door sat at the other end of the room with an oaken desk to the side of it. A woman with a bob hair cut sat behind it with a withering glance, a sword resting in front of her.

"Can I help you?" she asked in a thick French accent.

"We're here to see the Christ."

"Do you have an appointment?"

"He does."

"His name?"

"Matthew Ford."

The Frenchwoman looked down at some papers on her desk. "Oi, he can go in in a few minutes. The Christ is in a meeting. Please take a seat."

"On what?" Matthew asked. Mel told him to turn around and seats suddenly were there where they weren't before. The three sat down to wait. Matthew's leg bounced up and down as he waited. His eyes trailed along the painted walls before settling briefly on the receptionist. Her scowl quickly diverted his attention to the ceiling.

"Why does everyone call him the Christ? Why not Jesus?" Matthew asked.

"That is his title. No one may call him Jesus," Mel replied.

"Why?"

"Why don't you just stop thinking. This is Heaven. You don't do that here," Mel scolded.

***

"We have problems, my friends. Bible sales are down despite the special editions and alternate versions, we are losing the sixteen to thirty-five demographic, and we are failing to expand into new territory. In fact, we are losing our grip on the lands we are already in. We need ideas people." Jesus stood at the front of the round table. The Christ's black hair was cut into a pompadour, his beard nicely groomed. He wore a pinstriped suit of blue and white, his tie a silken pink. The apostles sat around the table looking at their Lord as the

103

Pope was teleconferencing on a large screen set on the other side of the room. To the rear, a cameraman and reporter sat quietly watching the proceedings. Jesus stared at the screen. "Progress report, Benedict?"

"Christ. Gentlemen." The room groaned as the Pope began. "Our market in South America and the Caribbean is quite secure."

"Good to hear," Jesus replied. "Have we recovered from the debacle in Europe yet?"

"Not yet, my Lord. The effects of the Reformation continue to slow our progress towards a possible resolution. We hold Spain, Portugal, Italy, France, Ireland, and other parts of Central and Eastern Europe, but the larger markets to the north remain out of our grasp. We've tried to lure them back, but they won't have it."

"Asia?" Jesus asked as he walked towards the one wall, a single pane of glass that stared down upon the whole of the Kingdom of Heaven.

"Asia is not going to happen, my Lord. That is Buddha's territory, and they are more than happy with his services. We've tried everything to penetrate the market."

"Even the threat of eternal damnation?" Jesus asked, turning back from the window.

"Even that." Benedict arched an eyebrow. "They laugh at us."

Jesus once more stared out across the whole of Existence. "Asia is a fast growing market." He turned back to the screen. "We must have it."

"We're trying, but it's not going to happen any time soon."

"What of North America?"

The Pope sighed. "Mexico and Central America are ours. The United States and Canada continue to pose a problem."

"Why is that?" Jesus asked.

"Various franchises and start-ups are stealing away customers. Not to mention the Church simply isn't the 'in' thing what with Paganism making a comeback."

"Surely we can grind down a few franchises and start-ups. Maybe a merger or two. We have vast resources."

"The Baptist franchise is wiping the floor with us not to mention the Mormon start-up gets far more press than us. Positive press."

Jesus looked to the ceiling, rolling his eyes, before turning to those present at the table. "What are we going to do?"

A snore drew Jesus' attention. Simon rested his head on his hand fast asleep. His snores punctuated the silence. Jesus looked at Mark sitting next to him and gave him a nod. Mark turned to Simon and knocked his arm out from under him sending his head cracking down into the table. Simon snorted awake. He looked up trying to act as if nothing had happened, rubbing his forehead.

"Why do I keep you people? What happened to the young go-getters I used to know? We were once the fastest growing entity out there. Now look at us. We can't even get footholds in third world countries. We need ideas, people." He slammed his fist down onto the table before pointing at those assembled. "We need them now."

Luke was the first to speak. "Always create some more holidays. People love holidays."

"What good would more holidays do?" Mark rebutted. "The ones we have now have been seriously twisted away from what they were created for in the first place. Easter Bunny. Santa Claus. Come on. Humans profit from them more than we do."

"Maybe we should have copyrighted them when we had the chance," Simon stated.

"How do you copyright a holiday, you moron?" Mark spat.

"Well our marketing department doesn't help things. Isn't that your field, Mark?" Simon cut back.

"Always perform a few miracles," John interjected. "That should reinforce belief in our superior product."

"Miracles, miracles. With you it's always miracles," Peter piped up. "Don't you ever have any new ideas?"

"How about this?" Luke began. "We make a cartoon that requires characters to be Christian and have faith to overcome evil, disgusting monsters. The power of prayer could be their superpower. There could be cards, comic books, toys, video games, even a movie." Some of the apostles nodded as they listened.

"What's the plot?" Paul asked.

"There is no real plot. No one really looks for one these days anyway. Just a lot of explosions and action. We'll steal the American and Japanese demographic of twelve and below easily. They love cartoons, especially mindless ones with lots of action. We could finally break into the Asian market. We could include a robot as the villain. Undermine their idolatrous ways."

"But they love their robots," Paul countered.

"We could make the angels robots," Peter offered.

"What else do you have?" Jesus asked.

"We could get a celebrity spokesperson," Simon offered. "It would appeal to the sixteen to thirty-five demographic."

"And then what?" John asked. "If they are caught having an affair with an underage transsexual hooker with five kilos of coke in their glove compartment? Do we really need that image placed next to the current scandals?"

"We could spin it so that they are seen as repentant, their faith in Christ helping to improve their lives. Possible television and movie tie-ins."

"Those are all interesting ideas, but...I was thinking more grass roots," Jesus informed the gathered board. "We need to get out there, speak to the people. Recruit new agents. Have them do the legwork. That's always been our strength."

"You have a plan, my Lord?"

Jesus scratched at his chin. "I'm sure you've all had questions about the news crew at the back of the room. We don't normally allow guests up here." The room mumbled in agreement, some glancing back at their visitors. "I have an appointment today with a human. I'm going to have a little 'meet-and-greet'."

"My Lord?"

"It's been awhile since I spoke to the common man. I've become distant. Too abstract. I need to get my name out there, get people talking. Speak for myself rather than using all these secondary sources. Make them remember I'm still around.

"And this human," Paul started, "why him?"

"Humanity needs to know there is a face behind the bureaucracy. I want to let the little guy know that his problems mean something to me. Not only that, get some word of mouth going. Draw some attention back to the Church. I haven't put in an appearance in a long time. Also, a symbolic use of my power...that is good PR. Make humanity remember their place. Both down there...and up here.

"I suppose that's all for today, but I expect more ideas at our next session. And progress." The group moaned again as they got up. The Pope smiled as his screen flickered out. The cameraman rose to begin setting up his equipment as the reporter spoke briefly with the Almighty.

The intercom on the desk buzzed as the apostles started filing out of the room. "Christ, my Lord, Ezekiel and Mel have returned."

"Good, Joan. Send them in." Jesus motioned for the reporter to go join the cameraman in the corner as he sat down and fiddled with the arm of his chair. Slowly his seat rose upon a pedestal. As his seat of power grew, he hit a button on the other arm and a light popped on above showering him in a fiery glow as the rest of the room dimmed, the windows darkening, making him appear as the sun in his own private space. "How's that?" Jesus asked the cameraman.

"Excellent, My Lord. Excellent."

"Not too much glare?"

"Oh no, it's perfect."

Matthew and the two cherubim walked in. Matthew froze in the doorway, looking at that brilliant figure upon his throne seeming to burn with an unearthly flame. He trembled when confronted by the Christ, inadequate next to the ruler of the cosmos. Matthew shook a little, his body uncontrollably shivering, until the light over Jesus started to flicker. Eventually only Jesus' right side was illuminated as the left burnt out. Jesus slapped the arm of his chair a few times and the light flickered on and off again. "Damnit," Jesus muttered.

Eventually he gave up and turned it off, the space brightening again to reveal the table and conference room. The darkened windows lost their opacity to once more reveal the world below. "You two can leave," Jesus ordered as his throne slowly lowered. The two cherubim bowed and walked out. "Have a seat." Matthew walked to the other end of the table and sat down, nearly jumping when he saw the camera. "Don't mind them." Matthew nodded as he turned forward. "I'm sure you have a lot of questions. Like why you're here." Matthew nodded. "Let me tell you why you're here. There seems to be a problem. You unlawfully evicted a resident." Jesus got up and walked over to stand before the broad view the windows offered, looking over his shoulder.

"Excuse me?" Matthew asked. "I don't remember doing any such thing. I don't even own an apartment." Jesus snapped his fingers and the ghost Matthew had chased with a bat came into the room. The ghost did not look happy. Matthew gave him a shocked look, his head tilting to the side.

"You have to allow him back onto the property. Only an agent of Heaven's authority may evict from property either bodily or constructed."

"Agent?"

"A priest. You are not an agent of mine. Thus your eviction is invalid. The legal term is exorcism," Jesus said with a twirling of his right hand. "To be blunt, I'm asking you to take him back."

"Wait wait wait wait. I was brought all the way here to see you, the Almighty, because of some annoying poltergeist?"

"Yes," Jesus replied. "I wanted to make sure you realized the enormity of your error."

"Why not just send a few angels to rough me up?"

Jesus swung around clearly insulted. "First of all, I am not some mafia don. Second, angels aren't as trustworthy as you might expect. And third, our records show you to be a very stubborn individual. I thought this was the best way to convince you of the proper way of doing things. Too much is at stake."

"Then why don't you simply make me take him back?"

"Things don't work that way," Jesus told him. "There are laws."

"Really?" Matthew put his feet up on the table. He felt emboldened by the fact that he was being asked, not ordered, by the Lord of all Creation to do something. "So exactly what is the problem?"

"Your lack of respect is one problem. The more pressing dilemma is you're accepting your resident back." Jesus gestured at the ghost.

"No way!" Matthew retorted as the reporter busily scribbled something down in the back. "The guy is an irritation. Always knocking things over and never shutting up."

"I was lonely," the ghost responded as he started to cry.

Christ shook his head. "I am a fair man, but in this I cannot budge. You have to take him back."

Matthew did not take that order well; his face lost those last vestiges of awe struck adoration and replaced them with outright defiance. Jesus was like all the others, always trying to tell him what to do, pushing him around. "Your laws are all important and everything, but we have laws down there as well, and they say when you kick the bucket and become worm food you forfeit your property. So that ectoplasmic irritation can slime your heavenly halls for all I care."

"You actually think that your mortal laws take precedent over those of Heaven?" Jesus retorted, his strained serenity starting to slip.

"Why can't you guys take him up here? This is where the dead go."

"Not exactly."

"What? Is he a," Matthew leaned forward, "demon?"

"No, no. We simply don't have the room."

"What are you talking about? This is Heaven."

"Heaven isn't all expansive."

"Isn't all what?" Matthew asked.

"When you build a house, does it grow with the number of occupants? No, it stays the same size and becomes crowded. Same here."

"Why can't you just create more land?" Matthew asked. Jesus glowered at Matthew's pique. "Well, you do rule Heaven, and the bible says you can create anything-"

"That is God. I have never created anything."

The reporter was scribbling even more fiercely as the cameraman zoomed in on Jesus.

"How shocking," Matthew replied. "Don't seem to do much of anything. No wonder Earth is such a shithole for us honest folk."

"How dare you speak that way in front of me!" Jesus was sputtering, his face going crimson. "I am your Christ!"

"Hey fuck you, ok. What the hell did you ever do?"

"It's always about you you you. You damnable mortals. Always taking!"

"You're one to talk, your hypocritical highness. It's all well and good to tell us what to do, but when we ask for something your ass is as deaf as a politician after Election Day."

"You blasphemous-"

"Hey, don't you go trying to curse me, ok," Matthew retorted cutting off the Almighty. "My life isn't much, but it's all I have. Like hell I am going to let you take away what little bit I have left. What's the worst you can do? Deny me a place up here? Yeah, that's a threat.

"You tell us to sacrifice. Maybe you should start sacrificing those large acres of land you have out there at the base of this phallic symbol that was spawned from some Freudian wet dream and maybe even rip down those oversized castles out front and replace them with housing."

"You think to tell me how to run things, you finite little fuck!" Jesus covered his mouth, shocked he had sworn.

"You don't really seem to have a grip on things." Matthew grinned

Jesus' expression soured, eyes flicking to the camera then back to this boy. He watched Matthew sitting there all smug about his mortal self. The ghost nervously looked back and forth between the two. "You need to be educated." Jesus abandoned the window, taking a breath as he approached the table. "Cut the camera. And you," Jesus said directly to the reporter, "this is off the record." The reporter nodded. Jesus turned back to Matthew. "When it all started, God was alone, ok. So Heaven was quite massive to him."

"Where did God come from?" Matthew asked.

"I'm not here to reveal the secrets of Existence to you!" Jesus snapped. He combed back some loose hair and continued. "I'm here to explain the problem. Be happy I'm doing that!"

"Ok, ok."

"God created the universe as a hobby." Matthew tried to interrupt, but Jesus raised his hand. "Hey, when you're alone you get weird. He was a lot more talkative then. So he played around and oops, life popped up. He liked it, things to watch. Early entertainment. Eventually humans developed. He felt obligated, as the father, to take care of his mistake."

"Whoa! You are calling humans God's mistake. What...are we illegitimate?"

"Don't make it sound worse than it is. He was very nurturing."

"He destroyed cities and drowned everyone with a flood!"

"He was a first time father. He didn't quite know how to handle you guys. He decided he needed a fresh start after the initial bad relations. So he took a more hands on approach starting with Noah. He really liked Noah. Became attached to him. In fact, he liked a few people throughout history, making them the select few he brought into Heaven."

"I thought everyone got into Heaven."

"Back then only God could let you in, and he picked and choosed. The rest went...elsewhere."

"Elsewhere?"

"Hell, ok. They went to Hell, or Sheol as it was called before the revamp."

"Nice guy," Matthew muttered.

"He felt bad for what he did, realizing maybe promising eternal damnation regardless wasn't the best incentive to live a just life. So, starting with Noah, he told him that everyone that lived right would get a place in Heaven. There proved a problem, however, as your breed always seems to create."

"What's that?" Matthew asked.

"Lawyers."

"You guys have problems with them up here, too?"

Jesus gave him a look that said shut up. "Jews were the first lawyers, and as you know, all lawyers go to Hell. Well they weren't happy down there. Irritated is putting it lightly. They wanted a way to strike out at an order they felt unfair and unjustly cruel to them. They came up with a trumped up charge against God."

"Which was?" Matthew asked eager to know.

"He was racist."

"Racist? Well, everyone up here sure does look alike-"

"Please!" Jesus cut him off. "After the flood, a few others besides Noah survived. They didn't get a chance to make the same pact as Noah did with God and continued to go to Hell for it. The chance of learning of God's commandments and being allowed into Heaven was restricted because God and the Jews were focused on a small part of Earth.

Likewise, it was unfair that God's celestial children, the angels, cherubim, etc., were allowed habitation in Paradise while his other children, these forgotten humans, were forced to exist without support of any kind from their father, God. The lawyers called this bias and gross neglect and told God he had to allow these others in in accordance to universal law. New laws were passed, bills considered. The Ten Commandments were rendered void due to two commandments requiring religious knowledge that was proven unknown to the greater masses and considered inhumane due to the fact that even if you begged ignorance the Ten Commandments did not allow leniency. The lawyers tried bargaining in a few new commandments to counteract the innate problems, but God was never one to admit mistakes. He's the type that prefers to destroy and rebuild rather than make incremental change. So the Ten Commandments were revoked and a new set of laws passed."

"So where do you come into all this?" Matthew asked.

"I was to go down and tell humanity the new rules. You know, the past sin of being non-Jewish no longer mattered. The possibility of redemption. Your kind cut my tour short for such petty, political reasons."

"Political?"

Jesus turned to look back out the window, scowling. "The Jews hated me for giving their privileges to everyone else. The Romans despised me for daring to say that their Caesar was no god and redemption did not require his warped whim. People yelled at me for telling them the truth, so used to the lies that had damned them for millennia, since conception. God had turned his back on them for so long that now, when he reached out to embrace them...they slapped his embrace away and cursed his very name."

Jesus' eyes were wet as he turned to Matthew. "You chose your flesh and its petty pride that knows only finite existence over the everlasting. I...failed."

Matthew felt a little uncomfortable with the emotions that were bubbling up. He tried to look around, avoiding this weeping man-child and discovered, as he avoided Jesus' face, that the Almighty's hands were covered with gloves. "What's with the mittens?"

"Oh, these," Jesus sniffed as he raised his gloved hands. "I got tired of people asking to see the holes. 'Can I touch them?' 'Can I poke them?' 'Does the hole really go all the way through?'" Jesus looked disgusted as he shook his head.

"Can I take a peek?"

"No."

Matthew kept quiet a few seconds. "Not even a little?"

"Anyway," Jesus gave Matthew a stern glare, "we started letting others in. It turns out you guys have grown larger than we expected. We are overburdened."

"That's why we have ghosts?" Matthew asked.

"Exactly," Jesus replied, breathing a sigh of relief as he gestured to the cameraman to turn the camera back on. "We let them stay down there. They don't mind too much. They get their kicks terrorizing you, and we solve our population problem."

"Well, that's all nice for you, but I prefer my privacy."

"You have to take him back."

"Why?"

"Because I ask you to."

Matthew stood up from his seat, rapping his knuckles on the table as the thoughts coalesced in his mind. Still looking down he spoke: "All my life I've never gotten what I wanted. Everyone always tells me what to do. Everyone always get what they want. I don't have much going for me. I don't have friends. I don't have looks. I don't even have an interesting life. All I have is my privacy, and you want to take that one thing I want away? I've never done anything wrong. I've never hurt anyone. What is my reward? I have to give up the one thing I want so someone else can be happy? When do I start to count? When does my happiness matter? I don't ask for much, but I am asking for this. What's one ghost?"

Jesus started pacing. "If we allow you to kick your ghost out then we have to allow others to do so. Then where do you think they are going to go? And what of my authority? What value is it if everyone can make their own decisions? That's anarchy. That's chaos. No, you have to take him back."

"No way! I can't take a shower again knowing he might be watching." The ghost looked down at the floor in shame.

"Well you have no choice in the matter."

Matthew locked eyes with the Lord, neither backing down. The news crew could only watch, transfixed, at the sight before them. Then Matthew made his final demand: "I want to talk to God."

"What?" Jesus shrieked out in surprise.

"Hey, I'm getting nowhere with you. All you care about is your own agenda. Maybe he'll understand."

"That's not a good idea."

"Hey, I know my rights. Besides, you're proving a real prick. I don't care if it's a speakerphone, a magic mirror, or whatever. Let me speak to your supervisor!"

Jesus furrowed his brow and moved to a door on the other side of the room. "Stay here." Then he turned to his other guests. "Cut the camera and leave the room." As the news crew filed out, Jesus opened the side door and went inside. Matthew overheard muffled speaking for the next few

116

minutes. He turned to look at the ghost who was giving him a dirty glare.

"Don't look at me, pervert," Matthew growled turning his head to look out the window.

Eventually Jesus came back out. "Ok. You can speak with him." Jesus moved away from the door and God emerged. An old man, wrinkled beyond mention, rolled out in an electronic wheelchair. He leaned to his left, spittle oozing out his toothless mouth. He wore thick spectacles over glassy eyes. Little wisps of hair stood on an otherwise bald and liver spotted head. His hands were folded lifelessly in his lap. One emaciated leg was draped over the other.

"You've got to be...fucking...kidding me," Matthew said in total shock.

"He...llo...Ma...tthew," God responded through some hidden electronic device.

Jesus walked behind Matthew. "He hasn't been the same since...you know," the Christ whispered.

"What?" Matthew asked, jumping at God's mild coughing.

"The Crucifixion. He had a stroke."

Matthew just stared in slack jawed silence. "I'm...I'm outta here."

"So you'll take him back." Jesus motioned to the ghost.

"I don't want any of you guys near me!" Matthew hurried to the door. In his excitement he couldn't seem to open it, fiddling with the knob.

"If you don't take him back you will be punished with various sanctions until you do," Jesus threatened. The Christ had been pressed too far and humiliated on Existence-wide television. He could not afford to be forgiving. "Heaven does not bend to one man."

117

"Yeah, whatever. Time to change God's diaper." Matthew hurriedly opened the door and left the room. Jesus walked up to God and sniffed. It wasn't time to change the diaper.

Matthew continued walking, the cherubim, cameraman, and secretary giving him odd looks as he continued on his way. "May I have an interview-" the reporter began, running up alongside him.

"No comment," Matthew stated with an extended arm as a warning. As he strode away, feeling self-esteem prickling through him for the first time in his life, he forgot about his surroundings. He had stood up to Jesus, the Almighty. About time he got some of his back. He felt an immense weight lifted off his shoulders. He had spoken his heart and mind. He had finally stood up for himself. Maybe things were improving. Matthew smiled, happy with himself for standing his ground. Ironic, since he forgot the shaft the cherubim had carried him up and fell screaming down it.

CHAllengePTER 5

Matthew woke up abruptly, his body jerking to life. He laid there, his left leg hanging over the side still reeking of dog piss. He looked up at the familiar ceiling of dimpled plaster, his hands spreading out beneath him. He felt the knit quilt and mattress of his bed under his fingertips. He quickly sat up and looked around, hair wild and unkept. He stole a glance around the darkened bedroom. Had it all been a dream?

Matthew put his face in his hands and rubbed furiously, trying to wipe away the exhaustion and jump start his body. That was when he noticed it: bumps. Matthew felt his face slowly, carefully. Bumps, lots of bumps were all over his face. He quickly jumped up and tore open his bedroom door nearly knocking his mother over as he ran to the bathroom.

"Matthew!" she screamed as he slammed the bathroom door.

Matthew looked at himself in the mirror. *No. No. Oh, please God, no!* He had...pimples. His face had devolved into a pepperoni pizza. How in the hell had he gotten pimples? Former anxieties came flooding back into his mind eroding all those maturing years and placing him back at the uncertain age of fifteen.

"Matthew." His mother knocked on the door. "Where have you been?" Matthew remained mesmerized by the disaster that was his face. "Matthew?"

"Classes!" he shouted, staring at the pus minefield that was his face, barely able to stand that craggy thing that stared back. "I only went to classes," he tried to convince himself.

"That was a week ago."

119

Matthew stopped looking in the mirror and turned to the bathroom door. "What?"

"You've been missing for a week. No one knew where you had gone. I was afraid some lunatic had killed you. Where have you been? You don't call. And the car. What happened to the car?"

Matthew opened the door. "It's really been a week?"

His mother screamed. "Your face!" She covered her mouth in shock. Suddenly stern, "Have you been doing drugs?"

"Thanks for the support, mom! Like life isn't bad enough!" Matthew sobbed, pointing at his face. He tried to speak but couldn't say the words, stomping past his mother back to his room. Orlando quickly skimmed between her legs to leap through the closing door as it slammed shut and locked with a click.

His mother hurried to the door. "Drugs cause skin problems and you've been so anti-social lately."

"I've always been anti-social!" Matthew yelled back through the door.

"See. Uncontrollable anger. Denial. Disrespect for your own mother. Let me help you." She continued to rattle on like the knob she twisted with futile abandon as Matthew sat on the edge of his bed, lamenting his afflicted face.

"This is only the beginning." Matthew froze, arching an ear. Whose voice was that? Was the ghost back? He cautiously glanced out the corner of his eyes. "You should have listened to the man."

Matthew slowly turned to his left and saw Orlando standing there looking at him. The dog gave him the usual stare it always did; eyes squinted and mouth slightly askew. He gave the pooch a quizzical look. "Was that...you?" Matthew gulped.

"Of course," Orlando replied.

"My God, I am on drugs," Matthew mumbled, putting the palm of his hand to his left temple. He looked back at the pup, his eyes fixating on the impossible.

"You're not on drugs," Orlando replied, sitting up and crossing his front paws.

"Then what? I'm in a Disney cartoon?" Matthew shouted.

"Get a hold of yourself," Orlando ordered, walking towards him.

Matthew retreated reflexively, falling off onto the dirty carpet. He grabbed his only defense: a sneaker. "If you come near me I'll put you in a shoebox six feet under!" Matthew threatened, brandishing his footwear.

Orlando shook his head and put a paw over his brow before turning back to Matthew. "You do know why your face looks like a leper made out with you right?" Matthew shook his head no, still holding tightly to his orthopedic weapon. "It's punishment from above." Orlando pointed up.

Matthew lowered the worn sneaker. "For what? I didn't do anything?"

"Exactly. You defied Heaven by refusing to take the ghost back. So now the Christ is punishing you."

"What?" Matthew was outraged.

"Matthew is someone in there with you?" his mother asked from behind the door.

"It's punishment. Call it divine persuasion."

"I call it coercion."

"Whatever. Until you take the ghost back, it won't go away, and it's only going to get worse. Remember Moses and the plagues upon Egypt?"

"I am not going to be forced to make a decision under duress," Matthew retorted.

"That's what the Pharaoh said. Everyone has a breaking point."

"We'll just see about that."

"Matthew who is that you're talking to?"

"It's the TV mom." Matthew stood up and moved over to the bed, reaching down to pick Orlando up. The two came face-to-face. "Jesus did this?"

"Yes."

Matthew gritted his teeth, angry over the current state of affairs.

"He wanted to get your attention."

"Obviously," Matthew sarcastically spit into that small, cute, cuddly face. "Well this isn't over." Matthew shook the dog. "You hear? Go tell that megalomaniacal messiah that this isn't over."

"I wouldn't challenge the system," the Chihuahua warned, tail wagging as its tiny rear paws hung limp, those large eyes unable to be threatening.

"Hey, who feeds you, you little traitor?"

"Matthew?" his father was now at the door.

"I said it's the TV!" Matthew stated, eyes still on the pooch.

"Boy, do whatever you want in there. Just remember your appointment today. I don't pay your tuition for you to piss my money away."

"What appointment?" Matthew asked, looking up from Orlando.

"With Professor Rosenberg."

"My final!" Matthew dropped Orlando and hurried to get dressed.

Orlando got up, rubbing his head. "Where are you going?"

"I don't have time for you right now. My future is at stake." Matthew fought to pull off the clothes that had been practically welded to him from too many days of wear and stain.

"You'd better accept the opportunity now," Orlando warned, trotting over in front of Matthew. "The consequences-"

"Will you get out of the way?" Matthew blurted, kicking Orlando to the side.

Matthew rummaged through his closet as Orlando looked at his back, whitey tighty clad butt and all. "You've been warned," Orlando said. Matthew tossed a shirt over Orlando to shut him up.

***

"President Romanov?" An aide stood before the desk of the most powerful man in Russia, his stance rigid and his appearance immaculate. Only the strong sat in the heart of the Kremlin. One did not want to anger or dishonor he who did. Romanov's glacial stare rose from reports on his desk. "Field Marshal Germann is here to speak with you."

"Send him in," Romanov ordered, putting the reports away in a folder as he stood to welcome the Commander of Armed Forces. The field marshal strode in, his uniform bereft of medals and ribbons. He was a spartan man who did not seek glory but order and discipline, something Russia desperately needed. His scalp was as smooth as his face, arched, red eyebrows the only hair apparent. He was stocky, with a neck so thick that a tie was not an option. He marched with precision before the desk and stopped. His respect was by duty and not choice. Romanov accepted him in the same grace. "Please, sit."

"I prefer to stand. It's the preferable way to do things."

Romanov gave him a calculating look. "Why do you think you are here?"

"It is obvious. More problems. What massacre do you wish my men to sacrifice themselves to now?"

"Our men," Romanov corrected.

"My men!" the field marshal shouted. Germann surely had courage. "They fight not for money and not for security because they are given none. They fight for loyalty. I am the only sure thing they have in this chaos that was Russia! You bureaucrats tell them where to die in distant lands. To starve and freeze as you live in a luxury you yourselves have never earned. They are not yours. I defend them, I speak for them, I share their horrid conditions, and when I have the money I feed them. They are mine!" Germann seethed, the veins in his neck bulging, his eyes white as hot metal.

"They are Russia's, Field Marshal."

"Russia is no more. It's a shattered corpse that has been amputated by allies."

"Russia may have many years left to her, Field Marshal." Romanov gave the first grin of his political career.

"What do you mean?"

"Problems have arisen."

"Yes, including the war you are pushing us into with America. We cannot beat them."

"No, that is not the pressing problem. The Americans would never invade. Europe itself stands against it, and our nuclear weapons are a powerful deterrent."

Field Marshal Germann was not sure where this was going. "What is the problem, then?"

"I have decreed dissolution of the Duma and now rule by decree. Sadly, I can only do this so long before I begin to anger the powers within against me. The mafia, the oligarchs, the monopolists. They are a force I alone cannot handle."

"What are you asking?" Germann began to find interest in this conversation.

"The affair with America can quickly be resolved. What I need is your cooperation to help Russia regain its destiny."

Germann moved closer to the desk, leaning in for a better listen. "I am all ears," he purred.

"I need you to replace the units on our western border with raw recruits. Give the impression we continue to view our sovereignty threatened by the West and nothing is amiss, while secretly pulling our best forces toward Moscow proper. Some changes will need to be put in order."

"Such as?"

"First and foremost, Chechnya must be sacrificed."

"Too many have died for that land!" Germann bellowed into Romanov's face.

"We are not abandoning it. Only regrouping." Germann listened on with a scowl. "Of course you will need to cause a little destabilization in Georgia on your withdrawal. Something to keep the nations of the world occupied with as we move forward. Let their problems mask ours."

"Why do you need forces near Moscow?" Germann asked, wanting to know the plot behind this meeting.

"Quite simple, Field Marshal." Romanov pulled out a thick manila envelope, its weight making a large thud as it hit the desk. "Inside are the targets."

"Why not trust the police forces? Why come to me? This is not an Army problem."

"The police are too decentralized and corrupted by the forces I wish removed from the throat of Russian progress." Germann gave him a sly look. "These are the only things that stand between Russia and her future. With them gone, I will have a free hand."

"Do you really believe the West will stand by and allow this bloodshed?"

Romanov let out a small chuckle. "Dear Field Marshal, you are adept as a strategist of men, but not of politics." Romanov turned to look out the window behind him. "Europe shall be easy to placate. I'll open discussions, offering them a freer hand in Eastern Europe, even dangling the possibility of our application to their union." He looked over his shoulder. "I might even offer them more oil at a cheaper cost. With our surplus from oil formerly marked for American sale we should easily make that transaction." He looked back out the window. "With America in need of oil we could cause a little more unrest in the Middle East. Perhaps a little help to Syria and Palestine to make things particularly nasty."

"They will never work with us."

Romanov turned around, his eyes flinty and provoking. "That is why we are granting Chechnya her independence. Make common cause with the Muslims. Let them think we support them and their beliefs, realizing their right to autonomy. With America preoccupied and Europe defending us, we should easily be able to make a useful purge possible and deny it as American propaganda. Afterall, who trusts America anymore these days?"

Germann cracked a grin, nodding his head. "But there is an immense problem still lingering."

Romanov stretched his arms to the sides in a gesture of offering. "And what would that be?"

"What does the Army gain by this?"

Romanov measured him with his sight. The field marshal was not a novice in political negotiation. "Those thorns that you remove from my side are quite rich. Dirty money all of it. It must be seized by the government. I could earmark a large portion of it for military spending, making up for back pay and then some. In fact, I have quite a few more duties for the Army after my grip on power is secured."

"And what might those be?" Germann asked cynically.

"Do not worry, Field Marshal." Romanov clasped his shoulder, pumping it. "I never forget my allies."

***

Matthew walked down the faculty corridor searching for his professor's office, keeping to the shadows. With classes officially over the halls were long empty, something Matthew fully appreciated. He couldn't stand the thought of facing another human being looking the way he did. The boils on his face made him feel like a leper. Thoughts of the masses running and screaming "monster" flooded his mind as he instinctively reached up and stroked those pus-filled blemishes before reason made his hand recoil in disgust.

Doors, doors everywhere, lining the walls as far as he could see, but none proved to be the one he wanted. He glanced left then right as he walked ever onward. No, it wasn't that one. Not that one either. Where was Dr. Rosenberg's door?

It was then that he noticed it. Something traveled the length of the hall, tickling at his nose. Matthew sniffed at the air. Was something burning? He swore he saw little wisps of smoke. He stopped, took a few more steps forward, and then stopped again. The smoke was coming out of one of the offices. Matthew cautiously crept forward, following the sweet smell until he stood before the origin, the odor strongest here. He felt the knob. Odd, it was cold. He put his head to the wood and listened. It was quiet. Maybe it was empty, but maybe someone was passed out in there. As he pulled his head away he saw the name on the door: Dr. Rosenberg. Oh no. His final!

Matthew turned the knob and started to ram it with his shoulder over and over, the fear of his future going up in flames. It wouldn't budge. He tried again before the jolting pain caused him to cease completely. This was hurting way too much. He began pounding on the door. "Professor Rosenberg are you in there? Professor Rosenberg?"

"It's open, man," came a calm voice. Matthew tried to force it open again. "No, pull on the door," the voice corrected him. Matthew turned the knob and the door slid open. Smoke spewed out into the hall. Matthew gagged and felt lightheaded as his lungs drowned in acrid air. His eyes narrowed, watering in the haze. Slowly his vision cleared.

There Dr. Rosenberg sat like Buddha, incense burning on his desk and a large blunt in his hand. His large girth was sunk into a giant bean bag chair. A few strands of Rosenberg's greasy, unwashed hair danced in the smoke, his beard burnt by fallen ashes of days gone by. Eastern music plucked and dinged on a stereo hidden away somewhere. Pictures from the Kama Sutra were plastered everywhere.

"Will you...have a seat?" The Professor asked between puffs.

Matthew slumped into the only other seat in the office, an inflatable chair. He sat there looking at this obese bastard; the world around them smeared gray and white. Neither spoke in the miasma, Matthew afraid to breathe. Rosenberg bobbed his head with the music as Matthew wrung his hands, wet with sweat.

"So, why are you here?"

"I have an appointment," Matthew replied.

"But why? What is your reason?" Rosenberg took a deep drag.

"I want to know how I did on my test."

"All life is a test. Why is this one important?" The professor was way too high today.

"It's my final." Matthew was starting to lose his patience. "I'd really like to get this over with, Professor."

Rosenberg took another drag on his blunt as he sat there. Matthew watched him as Rosenberg seemed to space out, his eyes going vacant. Rosenberg's mouth started to balloon, his face going blue.

Matthew leaned in closer. "Are you ok, professor?"

Rosenberg's mouth popped open as he belched up fumes of both gastric and respiratory origin. Matthew backed away, nauseated. Rosenberg gave him a yellow grin, roiling up and down on his bean bag in fatty waves, his three chins joined in the fun. "Matthew? Right?" Matthew shook his head, finally getting somewhere. "I liked your paper. Really deep, man." Rosenberg continued to shake his head.

"It was only one word."

"Hey, a word says a thousand things, man."

"That's a picture."

"You drew a picture?" Rosenberg asked. Matthew looked at him, his left eye twitching.

They both sat there a while longer before Matthew broke the silence again. "So what did I get?"

"Oh. Well, I gave you an A+, man."

"Really?" Matthew was overjoyed. He jumped up on the professor's desk and screamed to the sky. "Yes! Graduate school! Future!"

"Wait, wait, dude. Chill." Rosenberg motioned down with his swollen hand.

Matthew reluctantly got down, a smile splitting his face. He finally had a future: the possibility to hob nob with the elite, to have his words heard, to be somebody. Where would he go for graduate studies? Princeton? Harvard? Oh,

Harvard was a great school. Maybe make some connections-

"I'm sorry to say this, dude, but I'm failing you instead."

Matthew's head snapped back to reality. "What!"

"Yeah, it was trippy, man. My stereo spoke to me."

"Ex...excuse me," Matthew stuttered.

"It told me, hey, this guy knows so much, right? And he probably learned everything he learned from struggle and life experience. See where I'm going with this, man?"

"No," Matthew bit back.

"Well, if I were to give you an A and pass you then life would be easy. Graduate school of your choice, maybe even a scholarship. Become a teacher and a speaker. Maybe even get published. But then, you'd probably make millions. Have an easy life. Become a drone like everyone else in society. Corrupted by commercialism. What incentive would you have to seek out the purpose of the world? Would you even care anymore? I mean, the capitalist system would sink its claws into you, man. You'd become a puppet of the system, a slave to the addiction of money and material objects. Not a free spirit that merely wants to soar in the clouds."

"What the fuck are you talking about?" Matthew wanted to wring the man's nonexistent throat, his eyes tearing up not only from the smoke but also the sorrowful realization of his dreams slipping through his fingers.

"I couldn't let you become another capitalist consumer who finds their fill in material wants but starving in spiritual needs. I won't starve you. Starvation is the worst thing of all." Judging by his frame, Rosenberg wasn't kidding. "So I've failed you dude. I've made it possible to keep you from being seduced by that easy life. I've saved you to keep searching." Rosenberg looked positively orgasmic. Matthew was steaming. He started muttering stuff to himself under his breath. "No thanks are in order, amigo. Go out and see the world."

Matthew clenched his fists and left the room, slamming the door behind him. He screamed all the way down the hallway. As an intern came down the corridor she saw Matthew, hearing him well before. She stopped, horrified at this raving lunatic, and started to back up. "What are you looking at?" he demanded. "Huh!" He started to stomp towards her. She threw her purse at him and ran the opposite direction.

Matthew slumped against the wall, trying to calm himself down. It was only a minor setback...in his life goals! He started to walk back towards the stairway, passing the purse. A few feet later, he turned and walked back, picking up the purse and taking it with him.

***

Matthew was driving home through the snow when he came to a red light. He sat there in silence as he contemplated his next move. What was he going to do now? He couldn't take the course all over again. The humiliation of being held back would be too paralyzing, stigmatizing. He'd be worse than a leper. He'd be a failure. Why deny it? He always had been. Just another shitty day in the shitty life that was his. Why not simply flush the damn toilet and send him to the sewer he knew he was destined for? Matthew felt sorry for himself, resting his head on the steering wheel. No matter what he did it was never enough. He just wasn't meant to succeed. His dreams were over.

"It doesn't have to be this way." Matthew looked up from the wheel. *What now?* Wait, how much of that smoke had he inhaled? "Just accept my command and the problems end." The voice was coming from the radio.

131

"What the..." Matthew looked closer at his radio. "Hello?"

"Yes," the radio emitted back.

"Is this...Radio Heaven?"

"Just do what the Christ commands, ok."

"Wait, what problems are you talking about?" The light had gone green twenty seconds ago and someone honked, taking Matthew completely by surprise. They honked again. "Go around!" he yelled before turning back to the radio. It popped and sizzled, the voice lost. "Hello?" Matthew got no answer. He started changing stations. Heaven had to be on somewhere. "Hello, hello?" he asked frantically.

"You don't need to change the station. I'm here," the voice crackled.

"What problems are you talking about? I know about the acne-"

"Your final."

Matthew's face darkened, his mouth gaping with canines bared. "Jesus made me fail?"

"He merely gave your professor a vision, letting him see that indeed you need more life experience."

"So Rosenberg really did have that vision?" Matthew whispered to himself, looking away.

"Yes."

"So Jesus just ruined my life?" he yelled at the radio, his head snapping back. Someone had pulled up in the right lane next to him, the light red again, watching Matthew as he debated with the radio.

"It doesn't have to be this way-"

"I had an A. An A! Do you know what you've done? You've ruined my life!"

"You have to-"

"I don't have to do anything!" Matthew turned the radio off, fuming.

"This is not the mature way of doing things." The radio had turned itself back on.

"My life is not some little thing to be played with!" Matthew shouted, pointing at the radio. "Do you know how hard I've worked? This is all I have."

His vehicular neighbor continued to stare, the crucifix swinging from his rearview mirror. He started to murmur a silent prayer.

"Your life is not that important and neither are you. If you must be made an example of then so be it. We will do to you what we want when we want until you comply."

"No," Matthew rasped.

"Yes," the voice replied crisply.

"No," Matthew stated.

"Yes," the voice replied again.

"No!" Matthew screamed. He started punching the radio over and over again, yelling obscenities as he bloodied his knuckles on the plastic and steel. "You like that? Huh? Want some more?" Matthew hammered it, cracking its casing. He grabbed the radio and ripped it out, hurling it out the car window.

The man parked next to him cut his prayer short, his mouth still going through the motions while his prayer failed to come out.

Matthew turned and looked at him, his eyes glowering as he breathed heavily, spit hanging from his mouth.

The man didn't know what to say as the crucifix continued to swing over his dashboard. "Don't worry my son," the man started. "Jesus still loves you." Matthew's eyes went wide as he jumped out of the car and scrambled over the hood to get at him. The man peeled rubber to escape as Matthew stumbled to the ground.

Matthew got up, shaking his fists at the fleeing car before leaning back against his own, taking deep breaths. He turned around, his hands on top of the roof, and started pounding. "Damn you, damn you you mother fucking piece of shit!" he shouted, his voice going hoarse as he kicked a tire with his bad toe and fell to the pavement in agony.

He sobbed on the street. He wanted to break down and die. He could never win. Everyone always told him what to do. Everyone else always got what they wanted. What about him? Why didn't he matter at all? It was over. Everything was over. "I hate you!" he screamed to the sky, white smoke released by that shot of his mouth. His anger kept him warm out there in the cold world, bereft of shelter.

His head slowly lowered, his want for life slipping away. Then he saw it, out of the corner of his eye: a church. He became eerily still. In the front, set up for all to see was a Nativity scene. Matthew sat there, staring at it before he smiled.

***

"And in local news tonight, Christmas has been soiled. An unknown figure is believed to have stolen the baby Jesus from his manger and left..." The anchorman couldn't help but chuckle a little before going on. "Are they serious? Excrement? The man left excrement in his place. Now that's a Yule log."

"You're on the air, Ron," a voice hissed off camera.

The anchorman quickly went serious. "The church is offering a reward for any information on the whereabouts of the baby Jesus and would like his...safe return." The anchorman struggled to compose himself. "This figure surely will get a lump of coal in his stocking." He laughed louder forcing the station to cut to a commercial.

"That's shitty," a drunk mumbled while watching the news with his drinking buddies. "Does this mean Christmas is cancelled?" The bartender walked up and took the drunk's beer. "Awwww," the drunk whined until he saw his partner was asleep, head on the bar, and stole his mug.

***

Matthew had fun dancing around the backyard with the baby Jesus strapped to a pole, firewood stacked underneath him. The doll was still wrapped in its birth blanket, bound to the stake by duct tape. Glass eyes witnessed the pagan ceremony, Matthew dancing across their surface. He made whooping noises and shook a stick in the air like a spear. He spun in circles as he paraded around his prize captive. In his other hand was a container of lighting fluid. With every spin he would stop and spray some on the wood or the baby Jesus. Eventually he froze, lowered the container to his crotch and sprayed the remainder as if pissing all over the stake. He tossed the container at the baby, the hollow metal sounding like a miniature gong as it hit the ground.

The day was setting, the rays falling beneath the veil of night. He stopped and stood looking straight at the baby Jesus. "You have offended the big Matt," he said, his voice dropping down to a bass, thumping his chest with the arm that held the stick. "You are found guilty of the heresy of pissing me off. You have destroyed my hopes and robbed me of future income. For that, you are condemned to burn in the flames of my yard and then have thine ashes poured into my toilet, where I may shit on you and then flush you to the depths to which you belong." He pulled out a lighter and lit the end of the stick. He held the torch high, the fire blazing in the dying day. "Any last words?"

Suddenly the doll turned its head to look at Matthew and spoke: "You made a big mistake." Matthew let out a surprised squeal as he dropped the torch accidentally, scared beyond belief. The flames quickly engulfed the stake and burned the doll. Yellow tongues licked at the infant Almighty's plastic flesh releasing black, putrid smoke. Matthew tried to put out the flames but retreated from the extreme heat.

"Stop, stop. Whoa, hot hot!" Matthew jumped back and watched the doll squirm. Matthew's face was illuminated by the flickering bonfire. "Oh boy."

***

Later that evening Matthew sat locked in the bathroom. After the day he had had it was time to release some stress. He pulled out a magazine and smiled, hoping to enjoy one simple pleasure tonight as he thumbed the pages until he came upon one hot babe in a skimpy bikini, smiling suggestively at him from the pictorial. "Oh yeah, baby. You ready to ride a Ford?" He laughed as he dropped his shorts and began stroking himself.

A few minutes passed. Nothing was happening. He stared down at his miniature self before jerking harder. "What the hell?" Matthew uttered as he failed to stiffen. He tried shaking it between his fingers. His penis hung floppily to the side. He massaged it, cajoled it, made promises as it just continued to limply resist. Matthew grabbed it in both hands as if to strangle it. "Damnit do your job! Grow. Grow!" He shook it furiously.

"Guess I won't be riding that Ford," the girl in the magazine giggled, waving with her pinky.

"Son of a bitch," Matthew gasped, dropping the magazine and covering himself. "Wait." Suddenly it became clear. Jesus had…rendered him impotent. "You bastard. You bastard!" Matthew yelled shaking his hand at the sky.

***

"A string of robberies have been reported over the past week tied to..." The anchorman looked down at his notes as if in disbelief. "It seems a man dressed as a priest has been robbing convenient stores, the number now up to twelve. Here is a video from one of said convenient stores last night."

A grainy video came on of a priest, wearing a ski mask with a white cross painted across the face, hurriedly walking in the door. He pulled out a pistol and started threatening the man behind the counter. The cashier kept his hands up, shaking in fear. The masked priest started walking around the store grabbing chips, soda, and a few other items. Eventually he came back to the cashier who bent down and pulled money out of the register to give to him. The priest made the sign of the cross and started to run out. He stopped to grab some jerky and then disappeared. The video faded out.

"The man, calling himself 'The Servant of Our Lord', is said to be around five feet, eight inches tall, Caucasian with a love for teenage magazines and...box wine. He normally comes out around midnight and claims, after every robbery, not to worry because 'Jesus is picking up the tab'."

A drunk, sitting at the bar, looked up at the news and shook his head. "Times must really be tough." The other drunks nodded as they went on drinking.

***

Matthew sat in his car watching the store. It was dark. The streets were deserted. That made him smile since he knew everyone had been on the lookout for him. They'd never catch him, and even if they did, he knew who to blame. Revenge hadn't been bad either. In fact, it had been highly profitable. "Ruin me and I'll ruin you," Matthew told no one.

He sat there, starting to wonder how it had all come to this. He was an armed robber! Well, an armed robber for Christ's sake. It hadn't been an easy few weeks. Without sex he'd discovered he couldn't release his frustrations. Ok, it was masturbation, but that was the closest thing to sex he knew. He had become a lot more irritable and edgy without it. Matthew was like a balloon about to pop. He had to burst. He had to!

After his celestial castration, Matthew had searched insanely for some way to strike back at the Almighty. The only thing he could come up with was the Ten Commandments. He went through the list trying to find how he could rebel even further against "his highness", but he found his options limited. He had already placed the Lord on the backburner both spiritually and Sabbath-wise, so that one was out. He had no clue what it meant to covet. Disrespecting his parents; that was ingrained into the American lifestyle and was a given. Murder: that carried earthly problems all its own. Adultery, well, his current situation prevented him from consummating that act. So theft remained the only choice thus leading to robbery. Doing so in the Lord's name was the grand slam. To Matthew's surprise, it proved quite the stress reliever. All that power and control he felt. Who knew; maybe he would move up to banks next.

Oh, wait: the last customer was leaving. Matthew checked his revolver. "Here we go." He steeled himself and jumped out of the car.

He yanked the door open, gun ready. "You're shitting me," the cashier replied to the sight of his midnight customer.

"I'm throwing a surprise birthday party for Jesus and need a few things so I'll be taking some condoms and whatever money you have." Matthew moseyed confidently to the register.

Suddenly lightning struck out of the sky, blowing up his car. The force of the explosion shattered the glass at the front end of the store throwing Matthew and the cashier to the ground. The glass splinters sprayed throughout the open room as a few shelves fell over on Matthew, their contents spilling all over him. The blow had knocked the air out of him. Sirens could be heard in the distance as Matthew pushed the metal and junk food off, staggering to his feet.

As he stood there, collecting his senses, the bread exploded next to his head. Matthew fell back, tripping over the shelves behind him and yelping at the pain of his spine slamming into the metal. He rolled over, back to his feet. Another shot missed, blowing the refrigerator door apart, beer spurting onto the floor. Matthew jumped, turning to see the cashier with a gun in hand. He hurried towards the guy, pulling the trigger on his pistol and shooting hot sauce right into the cashier's eyes. The cashier screamed rubbing at his burning vision, the red fluid running down his face, as Matthew quickly ran out the door followed closely by another gunshot. Matthew stupidly shot back with his water pistol as he disappeared into the night.

He ran at top speed through the suburban streets, sirens wailing louder in the distance. Matthew could see blinking red and blues coming towards him, and he quickly headed right, jumping over a fence, his foot catching the top sending him down to the ground with a thud. He popped up and groped around. He took careful steps, unsure of his surroundings. In the darkness he failed to see the pool before him and fell in with a splash. The security lights went on as the owner came charging out the patio door to see what was going on.

"Who the fuck are you?" The barrel chested home owner demanded as he wrapped his robe around himself.

Matthew pulled himself out as the fat man charged. Matthew sidestepped him sending the man into the pool. "Wash away your sins," Matthew said, making the sign of the cross as he hurried in the open door, through the house, and out the front.

A cop car drove down the road as he exited, seeing him in full priestly garb. "Hey you. Come here," they demanded. Matthew quickly reversed down the road, his slow saunter turning into a breakneck sprint. "Hey!" One of the cops jumped out to go after him while the other remained in the car, radioing in the situation.

The cop seemed to fly after Matthew as they ran down the road. Matthew hurried behind a set of houses, finding himself in an alley. The cop was coming on fast. Matthew found the alley consisted of nothing but six foot high wooden fences; all too tall to jump over. Matthew stopped at one gate and tried it only to discover it was locked. He went to the next. Luckily, it wasn't. Matthew ran inside failing to shut the door after himself. The police officer saw the open gate and made for it only for it to slam in his face sending him to the ground half-unconscious.

Matthew looked around the backyard for any method of escape. He hurried to a patio door and tried to open it, but the barrier would not slide aside. Matthew yanked again. He was getting no where fast as he heard the cop starting to get up. Matthew backed up a dozen feet and put everything he had into his legs. He charged through the patio door, shattering the glass and landing on his stomach, head aching.

The cop wasn't far behind as Matthew woozily rose and made his way through the home. He couldn't see anything in the dark house accept twilight coming through the windows. He hit his shin on a table and let out a muffled yelp. "Who is that?" came a voice from the back of the place.

"The Holy Ghost!" Matthew replied as he made for the door. The thing had a dead bolt on it. On the inside! What was this world coming to? He tried to pry it open, but the door would not budge. He heard the cop's footsteps coming closer. Why did everything have to be so hard? Matthew went to one of the windows, pulling it open. As he climbed through he felt the cop grab his one leg, holding tight. Matthew fought to free himself as the cop braced himself against the wall and tried to keep his grip until back-up arrived. Matthew kicked at the cop's hands over and over again with his free foot, eventually scoring a direct hit right in the cop's nose before falling out onto the front lawn.

Matthew limped and fell across the front yard, his face wet with blood. "I'm not pretty anymore," he stammered as he tried to get up and run but slipped in the wet snow.

Matthew was fast to his feet and struggled on. He heard the cop fiddling with the locked door as he made his way out of the yard and onto the road again. To his surprise, a few houses down, someone had left a child's bicycle on their front lawn. Matthew made for it, the cop finally opening the door by shooting the lock off. Matthew hopped on the pink bike and was off, the cop only mere feet behind.

Tassels flew as Matthew tried to make his escape. He looked over his shoulder and saw the cop reaching for him. Matthew pedaled harder, his legs melting with heat. He steadily pulled away from the cop only to see the police car burning rubber down the side of the road behind him. The cop broke pursuit and made for the car, jumping in, as they sped after Matthew.

Pulling alongside, the cop ordered him to stop. Matthew shook his head no. As the cops tried to pull in front of him, he jerked onto the sidewalk. Out of reach, the policemen decided to hit the gas in order to overtake and then cut him off, doing a quick half circle to jump over the sidewalk. They hadn't paid close enough attention as they turned, ramming into a light pole. The pole moaned as it fell over the car, sparks flying. Matthew charged to his left around the car and back to his right. The cop car reversed and tried to follow, the engine gurgling as smoke poured from the grill. It strained to move, groaning as it staggered after Matthew. Somehow they were able to pull alongside the speeding priest again. The cop reached out to grab Matthew's handlebars. Matthew slapped his hand away over and over before quickly jerking down a side street.

Light suddenly blazed down on Matthew from the sky. "Do you really have to help them?" Matthew yelled to the heavens. He looked up to see a helicopter, the faint whomping of its blades reaching his ears. He pushed the pedals for distance. Before Matthew knew it, a patrol vehicle was behind him followed by another and then another. A dozen police cars roared after Matthew on his tiny pink bike, his body a shadow in the blazing lights of justice.

He rode his bike faster than it was meant to be, the spokes popping out of the front wheel before it rolled free sending Matthew over the handlebars. As he gathered himself he knew there was no way he was going to outrun the squad bearing down on him. That was when he saw St. Peter's. He made for the doors, leaping the steps two at a time, as the police cars pulled up in front. Knowing the place was always open, Matthew slipped inside, the doors banging loudly as the police set up a perimeter.

***

"We have our man inside," the sergeant told Detective Karras as they walked the perimeter of the building.

"You sure?" Detective Karras asked, dragging on a cigarette.

"No way he could have gotten out."

"How long has he been in there?"

"Half an hour. We're sending a team in now."

***

The cops kicked open the door and charged in. They moved in teams down the aisles, rifles at the ready, making their way gradually to the altar. The bright windows of stained glass were now muted by the blackness of night. The faces of saints looked down at man as he brought his mortal problems to Heaven's door. The cops checked every nook and crevice before moving to the door set in the wall at the back of the altar.

They crept through the narrow door into a courtyard. A fountain bubbled in the empty garden. Trees were the only sentries in this sanctuary from the world. The cops trampled the grass underfoot as they searched for their quarry. As they checked the bushes they noticed another building across the garden. A group broke off and inched quietly towards the door. The cops heard noise behind the door and slowly opened it. The entrance led down a dark hallway with flickering light at the end of the corridor. They could make out voices. The cop in the doorway signaled for the others to follow him.

Down the dark length they snuck until they stood before an oak door with light streaming from the crack at the bottom. The cops counted three and kicked the door in. Inside they found Matthew with his shirt off, no ski mask on, sitting on the bed of the parish priest. The priest and

Matthew looked up shocked. Then Matthew hurried over to the cops hugging them, weeping.

"Thank God you came! Do you know what he tried to make me do?" The cops turned in disgust to the old priest who could only watch in fear at those that surrounded him.

***

"And in other news this morning, The Servant of Our Lord was captured as he tried to elude police in his very own church last night after a brief chase. Inside they not only found the tools he used for his various robberies but also a local boy believed to have been his sex slave. Threatened with a series of crimes, the priest in question has cut a deal with authorities revealing one of the largest child pornography rings in history."

Jesus and the apostles watched the news in their boardroom. The apostles shook their heads, Simon taking repeated takes of the screen in total shock. "This is really bad," Jesus replied grimly.

CHAPTdEalR 6

"Matthew? Matthew what's wrong?" His mother kept knocking on the door. "Matthew?"

He ignored her, leaving that boundary between them. He refused her words, her offers of aid. He cut himself off, alone from even those few that cared for him. He covered his ears, rendering himself deaf to her healing words. With time she left, taking the love he needed with her.

Matthew rested on his bed like a corpse at a wake. The enormity of the situation held him down. The realization of the consequences of his actions were so enormous that his mind was paralyzed trying to comprehend it. He hid there, in his dark hole, from the rot that was spreading through society. A rot he had had revealed.

Orlando looked down into Matthew's face. "How can you sleep?"

"I'm not. Someone won't shut up." Matthew stared at the ceiling, guilt gnawing at him. He felt every bite torn from his soul. He just wanted to be alone. That is all he ever wanted.

"How can I? Look at what you've done."

Moonlight pierced the half open shades of his bedroom, illuminating Orlando's sad face in a pale light. Matthew felt his stare as he continued to look inward. Did it all really have to come to this? Matthew hadn't really wanted to cause this much trouble for Jesus. He just wanted his privacy. Was that too much to ask? For all the reasons Matthew could create to justify his actions he couldn't help but feel remorse over soiling Jesus' name worldwide. This was really not shaping up to be a great Christmas.

"Don't you have anything to say for yourself?" Orlando cocked his head.

Matthew sucked in a deep breath and willed himself up knocking Orlando to the side, his little body rolling into the wall. "I'm getting out of here." Matthew opened his closet door, flipped on the light, and started to change.

"Go wherever you want. You can't run from it." Orlando stood on the edge of the bed giving Matthew a withering glance.

Matthew stopped what he was doing and looked back at the dog. He wanted to speak but held it in as he always did, letting it burn and die inside him. He went back to unbuttoning his shirt.

"Selfish," Orlando growled. Matthew threw his shirt at the Chihuahua like a baseball, belting the pup in the chest with such force he yelped as he fell off the bed. Orlando struggled to all fours. "Real mature."

"Hey, I didn't start this." Matthew turned and pointed at his blemished face, the light of the closet shining around him cloaking him in shadow.

"Remember the ghost?"

Matthew knelt down. Orlando stood up and rested his front paws on Matthew's knee to come face to face. "You guys play with our lives as if they are worth nothing in the cosmic scheme of things. Whatever made Jesus' life more important than anyone else's? Huh?" Matthew moved closer. "What right does he have to tell me to do anything? He was never there..." Matthew paused, trying to control himself. He closed his eyes tightly, took a breath, and then reopened them. "He was never there when I needed him." He stood back up, Orlando slipping off his knee.

The dog remained at his heels. "So you're blaming Jesus for being bullied? For being a loser? Jesus can't help everyone, especially someone as pathetic as you."

Matthew became coldly agitated, his tick giving him a psychotic look. His reason slipped as his rational side evaporated with Orlando's acidic words. "Jesus wants us to give all we can to him, but he gives us nothing. Fuck that and fuck him!"

Orlando was shocked at what Matthew said, his little jaw yawning open. "That's blasphemy," he gasped.

"Like what I've done isn't worse. Just...shut up." Remorse had cut up Matthew's heart, ripping his soul to shreds. The pieces drifted away. "I just don't care anymore."

Orlando was struck dumb, his mouth opening in silent rebellion as Matthew finished changing into fresh clothes. He crossed his front paws across his chest. "I hate you."

Matthew was hurt by that. Orlando had been his only friend for years. He fed him. He bathed him. He talked to him when he could talk to no one else. And now his only confidant, his sole comrade, said he turned against him. Matthew couldn't stand it, couldn't take how no one gave a damn. His fractured face hardened in the coolness he accepted. "Yeah, well you don't have a thumb so I really don't feel too threatened." Matthew opened the door and left.

***

"What in my name has been going on down there?" Jesus screamed at the screen, his boardroom empty. The Pope looked back, his face pale and his darkened eyes lined and red from lack of sleep. "I want answers and I want them now!"

"We're conducting an internal investigation as we speak," the Pope offered as he prostrated himself upon a velvet cushion, hoping to placate the Almighty. He didn't.

"I'm hearing about child abuse, embezzlement, racketeering, ties to organized crime! There is even a web site that says," Christ looked down at a laptop placed on the

desk before him, "Watch as they are touched by the Lord!"
Jesus looked up, his face scarlet and his temples pounding.

"I will admit we've had problems with new recruits. They
are the product of the times I am afraid."

"We are supposed to guide the times, not follow them.
Our employees are supposed to be impeccable, a standard
to be emulated and followed not wolves amongst the sheep!
Have you any idea of the press this is getting? I can't have
this image!"

"We will clean it up. We always do."

"Clean it up?" Jesus gagged like a choking engine on the
air as he sucked it in, not believing his ears. "We could have
another Reformation on our hands...or worse! We could
drive them to our competitors or...you do know that most of
humanity has been looking for a reason to totally discredit
us. What does it say when even cardinals use altar boys as
concubines? Must I watch you every second like the children
you seem to be?"

"You are overstating, my Lord. We've suffered worse."

Jesus stared at him, his eyes vacant. He began to realize.
He looked at the deceiving face of the Pope. He tasted the
bitter lies that poured from his mouth, the poison that had
been poured into his ear for years. "You knew about this."
He looked at his earthly representative for the longest time.
The Almighty did not know what to think, what to do. He
stared at this elderly man, his representative, and realized
how he used Jesus' prestige to wreak unholy havoc on the
trusting, on the weak. But they were humans. They weren't
his. "Make this go away, Benedict. If not, you will find your
trip to Paradise will be making an unexpected stop in
Purgatory."

The Pope was shocked to hear the threat. "I...we'll...this
will be solved. I promise." Jesus nodded as the screen went

out. The Pope silently cursed to himself, wiping the cold sweat from his forehead as he made his way to the doors.

In the grand corridor beyond, papal legates, priests, and nuns hurriedly ran this way and that. Some spoke on phones trying to gauge the international problems and consequences. Others ran arms burdened with books or papers. One dropped a book from the set he was carrying. He bent down to pick it up and another priest tripped right over him sending a shower of papers into the air. The Pope shook his head at the disorganization.

"Your Holiness." A bishop came running up to the Pope.

"I don't have time for you," the Pope replied.

"But your Holiness-"

The Pope slapped him across the face, his hand pushing the bishop to the ground. The bishop lay there stunned at the blow he received. The Pope looked up at the chaos that surrounded him. "I need some communion wine," he muttered as he walked off, away from the mess that abounded.

***

Matthew sat at the bar, spinning his glass of jack and coke, the seats on either side empty. The room was packed with those who looked for escape from the bright world around them in this sealed, dim, musty place where a drink made you numb, and a bottle helped you to forget.

Matthew looked up at the television mounted on the wall where the news was being broadcast, the single shining object in the gloom. The blaze of the news illuminated Matthew's face in the shaded confines, life reflected on his glasses. After the priest had been arrested he had started talking, talking about things no one even knew the Church had been behind all for the price of immunity.

Seemed the Church scandal was causing a monumental rift in society: suicide was up, crime was rising, and priests were being attacked in the streets. "I guess I got you," Matthew muttered looking up with a weak grin.

The bartender looked over at him, walked up and took his drink away. "Why do all the crazies have to come here?" he asked himself.

Matthew shrugged away his loss. *Probably for the best.*

A dark figure parted through the morass of worthlessness that swelled within the room. He seemed to come from nowhere, as if spawned by the pool of depression, its personification wading to the surface of reality. His height was not exceptional, his suit drab and faded, worn and scuffed. He had a coarse face, lined and pale with an expression as empty as a drunk's shot glass. Dark shades concealed his eyes. With a stride that was jerky but centered, he approached the bar. He dropped onto the stool next to Matthew, pulling a pack of cigarettes from the blackness within his jacket. The cigarette packet was ebony and spotted with dirt. He took one of the mud colored sticks and thrust it in his rancid, purple mouth, lighting and taking a drag in one fluid motion. His chapped lips lovingly sucked at the cigarette.

"Hey, buddy, no smoking in here," the bartender warned.

The man pulled the cigarette out, letting a trail of smothering fog ooze out both nostrils as he held the smoking stick in his right hand while putting his arms up in defense, the flame reflected in his shades. "Come on, friend," he jokingly pleaded. "Have a heart."

"Put it out before I put you out," the bartender replied, first pointing at the cigarette then the door.

"How tired I grow of rules," the figure muttered as he dropped the cigarette to the floor and ground it beneath his weathered, leather heel leaving a black smear across the floor. The man slipped the bartender a sideways grin as he walked off to serve someone else.

The figure turned to watch the television. He stopped after a few seconds, interested in Matthew sitting next to him. "Shit world. Sad day when you can't even trust God. Then again," the man frowned, "he's just as flawed as the rest of us."

Matthew looked away from the screen to see his new companion. He saw the guy, nodded, and went back to watching.

"Had it coming, though. Holier than thou hypocritical pricks. Do as I say, not as I do." The man turned to Matthew with a crooked smirk. "Don't feel guilty do you?"

"Why would I feel guilty?" Matthew asked, trying to ignore the man. Why must everyone bother him?

"I think you know why, Matthew."

Matthew's heart felt a stab at the sound of his name. His eyes crawled to the side searching, first for the origin of this orthodox man and then for possible escape routes. "How the hell do you...you're not-" Matthew looked up at the ceiling. He looked back down at his new companion and started to get off the stool.

The figure grabbed Matthew by the shirt and pulled him back down. "No, don't worry about that. Just a fan."

"A fan?"

"Of course." The man grinned, revealing chipped yellow teeth. "You made a stand against the establishment," the man leaned in, "and won. You don't know how long I've waited for something like that." His eyes widened briefly. "About time someone taught his miraculous ass a lesson."

Matthew watched the man warily, not sure what to make of him. The guy was weirding him out.

The man seemed to feed on his discomfort. "Of course, once all this dies down he will be coming for you, and I do mean hard." Matthew winced. "He can be spiteful. He isn't as forgiving as most would make you think."

"Great. Just great. Dude," Matthew rapped on the bar for attention, "can I have another?" The bartender looked at Matthew and walked the other way.

"No respect." The figure shook his head woefully. "No one respects you. Nothing but bull shit. We all know the truth. They underestimate you. Look at you. You deserve better. But you won't get it. Why? Because of the cards they dealt you. You didn't choose this life. Everything in it has been forced on you without even the slightest opportunity to turn it around. The minute you try to live your life for the better, for yourself, they smack you down while the less worthy get all they want for less effort. What did they ever do to deserve such blessings? Why should you kill yourself to merely survive, while sycophants and morons get all they want and more for the most mediocre of actions?" As the man spoke, he became excited, his words running together as his mouth proved unable to keep up with his sharp mind.

"Yeah," Matthew nodded his head, sipping the bile and acquiring a taste for it.

The figure continued to pour, happily. "The man upstairs tells you to accept all that happens faithfully. Why? Why can't you understand why you suffer?"

Matthew nodded his head, not sure what to say.

"I'll tell you why. Because if you knew," the man slapped Matthew on the breast, "the worthless purpose you serve to him you wouldn't allow the abuse in the first place. You mean nothing to him. You're just another number in the scheme of things."

"I wish I was just a number." Matthew sighed, a little drunk.

The man smiled. "No you don't." Matthew looked over at him. "You wish you had some reason to be. You want a purpose. You don't have one, never have. I can change that," he slyly offered, his graceful yet common hand touching his faded chest. "In fact, I can help you get that prick off your ass and achieve the destiny you are entitled to." Matthew laughed silently. The man's grin slipped into a frown. "What?"

"You're going to help me?" Matthew asked, incredulously.

"Why do you find that so funny?" The figure was not amused, his words slowing.

Matthew continued to laugh. "You look like a shell of an insurance salesman." Matthew really started to chortle. "Wait, are you like some interdimensional lawyer that is going to help me file a civil suit against Heaven? If so I hope you work pro bono because I think I spent my last dollar on a drink...which was unfairly taken!" Matthew yelled down the bar at the bartender who returned the look none too nicely.

"Funny," the figure replied, though it was obvious he didn't mean it as he scowled. "But I'm no simple lawyer."

"Oh!" Matthew replied sarcastically. "Let me guess. You will give me what I want in exchange for my soul. Ooo whoo whoo whoo!" Matthew laughed a little louder.

The man cackled like breaking bone and slid his shades down his nose revealing yellow, bloodshot eyes deeply set in purple, fleshy sockets. "I've already got too many."

"Fuck!" Matthew and stool went to the ground in frightened, theatrical fashion. The wood of the stool clacked loudly throughout the bar yet drew no one's attention. The man retracted his glasses, shading his tainted eyes, and extended a hand. Matthew looked around for help, but everyone remained too involved in their own petty lives. Only one being offered him aid.

Matthew looked at the dirty, calloused hand and then at the plain face that hovered above him. "Uh, excuse me if I don't accept." Matthew pushed himself up, slowly getting to his feet. He was shaking, frightened at his companion. He nearly fell off the stool as he went to sit again.

"You don't need to fear me, Matthew." The Devil smirked. "I like you. We have so much in common."

"Yeah, I feel much better now."

"Why the hostility?" The Devil seemed genuinely hurt.

Matthew's face was twisted by both sarcasm and horror. "You don't exactly have the best reputation," he stammered wishing he still had his confiscated drink.

"You saw Heaven. You met Jesus. Did they live up to their reputation?" Satan asked. "Can Jesus' worst enemy really be that bad?" Matthew sat still, a little confused but too rigid to make a run for it. Did all important religious figures toy with people like this? He felt like a mouse in the claws of a Siamese. "Just...have a talk with me. I'm not asking for anything else." He scratched little lines into the bar with his jagged nails, the sound putting Matthew on edge. "If you don't like what I have to say I'll take you wherever you want and...drop you off." The Devil smiled at that last part. "Never hurt to listen to anyone, has it?"

Matthew cobbled together a half smile, too nervous to even pretend properly. "You never know," he quipped, his hand rattling on the bar in fear. Both the Devil and Matthew stared at it. Matthew quickly grabbed it and tried to still the shaking. "I think I need to...to go." Matthew sprung from his stool and hurried past Satan with a quick step, tripping over a chair on the way. The Devil watched him go.

Matthew was on the street in seconds. The streetlights illuminated only parts of the darkened road, large sections nothing but void as if uncreated. The night was silent compared to the bar whose noise went still as its light was lost behind the closing door.

Matthew stumbled into the cold night, away from his new found friend and the possible problems he could bring. He had pissed off Jesus. He definitely didn't need to anger the Devil himself.

The street was deserted. Nothing stirred. The windows of the buildings he passed were blacked out, hollowed out husks where life no longer existed. Trees reached with skeletal branches and scratched at him. The cold air sucked the warmth from his flesh as it passed. The squeaking of his shoes seemed loud in his pink ears.

"Do you know how many people wish they could have a talk with me?" Satan stepped out of the darkness, his face concerned.

"I'm glad you want to help me," Matthew started, extending his hand to make sure the Devil didn't get any closer as he backed up. "But I think I would rather deal with this on my own." Matthew turned to walk the other way and made a few steps before the Devil stepped out in front of him again, the shadows parting to release him. Matthew stopped where he was, looked behind him and back again.

"I'm not used to rejection." Satan smirked, clearly enjoying the chase. "Would it really be so bad to hear what I have to say? I'm not asking you to do anything."

Matthew covered his ears. "You do know this state has an anti-stalking law, right?" The Devil frowned at that comment. Matthew started to walk in the other direction, gradually turning into a sprint. He looked over his shoulder as he went, the Devil still there, a shadow in the light. Didn't Heaven and

Hell have better things to do than fuck with him on a winter night? Existence couldn't be that dull. As he turned to look where he was going he slammed right into a streetlight. Unlike the movies and cartoons there was no dong. Matthew's nose ached, blood trickling out. Matthew moaned as he grabbed his nose. It was already swelling.

Without warning he felt something grab his jacket and pull up. He was sucked into the sky, the ground falling away as the emptiness stacked up beneath him. Matthew's screams were wrenched from his throat and stolen by the winter winds. The air pulled at him as gravity became fiction. The speed of his ascent tore the whole of everything into streaks of incomprehensibility. The buildings became miniscule as Matthew dared to look down.

"Oh God," Matthew whimpered, closing his eyes tightly.

Then gravity came back. Matthew felt himself falling. Oh no! Matthew started screaming again as he dropped six feet and landed on something solid. He patted in his blindness. The ground seemed hard enough. He tested it a few times with the tap of a hand before he tried to stand. His legs gave out underneath him, the event a little too traumatic. He started muttering incomprehensible gibberish in a state of shock.

"Matthew," Satan called. "Matthew. Matthew!" Matthew's eyes snapped open. "I'd cut that shit out if I were you." Satan floated there, in the midnight hour, looking down at him. It was as if his weight returned in the blink of an eye as the Devil landed on the ground in front of him, dust poofing out beneath his feet. They were on some tall building looking out at the skyline of the city, the distant lights as close to touch as the stars above. Satan started out towards the edge, still watching Matthew. He paused after a few steps, pointing at Matthew palm up. "The ride not up to your liking?"

Matthew looked down at the wet spot of his pants where his bladder had rained its golden drops. *Yeah, real manly. Satan should respect him now.* "I...uh...had a lot to drink and...uh...it's cold outside-"

"It's alright," the Devil replied. "Your secret is safe with me."

"Right." Matthew continued to sit on the ground, brushing himself off. "Do you?" he asked, gesturing to his wet crotch.

"Oh yes," Satan pulled a handkerchief out of his pocket and tossed it to Matthew to dab at himself, a short, sharp wind carrying it to Matthew's hands. "You can keep it." The Devil continued to the edge, jumping up onto the boundary between a solid foundation and a steep drop.

"Thanks," Matthew sheepishly replied with grudging gratitude as he dabbed at himself. He sniffed snot and blood back up his runny, broken nose.

The Devil looked at him, tilting his shades down. "I know I say this everytime, but you are clearly not what I expected."

Matthew found the courage to stand up and walk towards Satan. Something drew him towards this dark prince. As Matthew reached the narrow road Satan walked, that edge of the sword, he looked away to avoid that gaze that compelled him, ordered him. He leaned over the side of the building and saw the vast gulf below. He let out a curse, falling back to his knees. He worked to steady his breathing. He looked up, back into that gaze. "I guess I'm not leaving until I listen." The Devil smiled and nodded, pointing at his head. "You said you wanted to help me with my problem."

Satan turned to scrutinize the skyline, glimpsing those lives that burned before him. "So many souls out there, Matthew. Each with problems. Each with questions. Each separated by a distance they can never close nor shorten." He continued to gaze out at the world.

"Pretty lights but my problem," Matthew prodded, wanting to go home as soon as he could.

Matthew broke the spell of the city. "Oh yes. Him." The Devil pointed up before looking back at Matthew. "He is a piece of work, isn't he? Hard to admire the pussy." He pulled out that bare packet of cigarettes and lit another in the same fluid motion, taking a long drag and expelling the toxins with an orgasmic exhale. Satan raised the cigarette to eye level and turned to Matthew. "Hard to believe people hate this thing more than me." He could sense Matthew's continuing discomfort. "Ever thought of smoking?"

"No," Matthew got out.

"Too bad. Really helps relax you." He glided over to Matthew and knelt down, offering the cigarette to him. "Sure you don't want to try it?" Satan's hand wavered, the cigarette right in front of him.

"I really don't-"

"If you're afraid of cancer don't worry. That's not how you go."

"You know how I'm going to die?" Matthew blurted.

Satan smiled that cracked yellow smile, black grit between his teeth. He offered the cigarette again. Matthew took it and sucked down a gasp of foul smoke, his body rejecting and hacking it back up. Matthew coughed loudly as the Devil took it back.

"Good shit, huh?" He laughed as he patted the smoke out of Matthew, taking another drag. "So, why do you continue to believe in all this garbage?"

"What..." Matthew coughed some more. "What do you mean?"

"What do I mean?" the Devil asked mockingly. "I mean the whole sham of Christianity. There is no one so blind as he who will not see." The Devil cackled. Matthew was unable to answer, looking away at the lights in the distance. "You've seen what Christianity really is."

"It's a little dull-"

"Christianity is mindless, hypocritical nonsense!" Satan calmed himself down. "Surely you can't really feel guilt over revealing what was beyond the veil to the rest of humanity. Would you rather those priests kept taking advantage of those children? Kept lying about the grandeur of Christ and all that bull shit? Saying the wealth of the world meant nothing as they continued to lie, cheat, and steal all they could and bask in its material comfort?"

Matthew shook his head no.

Satan took a deep breath and sized up Matthew. "You humans. Always so hard to convince." Satan bent down and cupped Matthew's chin, bringing it up. "Do you really think Jesus cares about you? Look at how he's treated you. When you call him is he there? When you need him, does he help?" Matthew shrugged his shoulders. Satan flipped him in the forehead. "Kid, let go of the images. That's all they are."

"Then why don't you enlighten me," Matthew retorted.

Satan smiled that serrated smirk and stood up. "Gladly." He paced the edge of the roof, looking up at the unreachable sky. "Jesus paints himself as some...messiah. He's far from, trust me. Ever since he took over Heaven life has detoured. Now there is no direction, no sense, no purpose."

"I don't follow."

The Devil stretched, reaching for a star. He acted as if he swallowed it in his hand. "You really don't get it." He looked back at Matthew. "Let me fill you in on some things. First of all there is a God. You probably met him. The vegetable on wheels?"

"Yeah, what happened there?"

Satan started to walk around, deliberately balancing on the edge, thousands of feet up, his dark shape blacker than the night. "Well, to understand that you have to understand it all. See, God was numero uno. None of us knows where he came from. He's the quiet type. Sometimes I wonder why he created us-"

"How did that happen?" Matthew asked.

The Devil gave him a wicked smile, cigarette gritted between his jagged teeth, sucking in that foul gray smoke. The world was so distant. "Who really knows," he spoke from the side of his mouth, "And with him being a he, who truly wants to know? It sickens the mind."

"So he created you guys..."

"Yeah, and we walked with him. Listened to what he had to say. We worshipped the guy, our father." The Devil gave that hacking laugh of his before going solemn. "There weren't many of us back then. It all seemed so simple in those times. Before it all happened." Satan gave him an insulting look before flipping his butt to the street far below. "I take after him, you know," the Devil said, his despising face magically transformed into the illusion of sorrow and remembrance.

"Yeah, I see the resemblance."

"Fuck you!" The Devil pointed at him with a serious "don't mess with me" attitude. "Enough of that shit. Where was I?"

"Um, before 'it' happened."

"Yeah. The man had issues. Probably mid-life crisis. Who really knows? He seemed depressed, cried a lot. Do you know what it's like to watch your dad, the Creator, cry like a bitch? That's trauma." The Devil seemed to shiver. "For the longest time he never spoke. He simply wandered. Never really seemed all there. After a while he finally started talking. Talking a lot."

"Why is that important?"

"Words aren't just words when you're God. They're power. They do," Satan waved his hands in the sky, little sparks flying around them, "things. Well, he had a lot of shit to vent. That's where the Big Bang came from."

"You mean what created the universe? The big explosion?"

"That's right! You do hit the books. Yeah, he was feisty. The things he said. Explosive!" Satan had been excitedly moving with his speaking, having to push his shades back up his nose.

"God created the universe, accidentally, because of a mid-life crisis?"

"Not quite as amazing as the bible paints it is it?"

Matthew responded with a disgusted look.

"So he calms it down realizing how much shit he has fucked up. The man has serious anger issues. He sees the universe, hot air and all, and doesn't know exactly what to do. I mean, that burning chaos used to be our backyard! A large chunk of Heaven, gone, just like that!

"Now we had grown up watching all this. Very disturbing. My brothers decided, since I was the oldest, I should have a talk with papa. So I go in and tell it like it is. He can't simply go off at the mouth. It's a little...fiery. Causes major problems for everyone involved. He tells me it's not my fucking business, and in the process, a galaxy is demolished. Well, papa begins to listen.

"So how to mitigate the damage. We set up a charter for how the universe is going to work. No more universally cataclysmic events. The last thing we need to do is have it spread any further which, damnit, it is anyway. Also, God may no longer speak. We'd handle that part. It took a large balancing act to bring the chaos under control. We had to make the universe stable and less random. If we let the chaos continue we'd never be able to contain and control it. So, we created universal law."

"Universal law." Matthew nodded, clearly not getting it.

"Ok, let me put it in simple terms. If everyone were allowed to do simply as they wanted Existence itself would fall apart. God clearly demonstrated that!" The Devil moved erratically with his words. "If things were not set, rules made, then nothing would ever be. It would all simply fall apart in pure anarchy."

"Order, then. You guys made the first laws for order."

"Exactly! Finally, you start to get it. Well, anyway, we all discovered there was a side effect to his rage: you bastards. Well, not you bastards, but those little slimy things that became you bastards. We told him it was his responsibility, since he created you, to watch over and provide for you. That went well until humans popped up. You guys caused real problems.

"We weren't sure what policy should be on you. We've had a hands off approach since the Big Bang, but when I saw humans I thought the policy should change. You guys weren't some rock. You were us. Well, almost like us. Besides, you were the most interesting thing to come around in millennia. If I had to listen to another of Michael's damn jokes..." the Devil balled up his fist.

"Sorry." The Devil seemed embarrassed. "We pow wowed for a few centuries wondering what to do with you. You clearly made mistakes, always holding yourselves back. Should we step in? Should we continue to watch? I said that just leaving you down there was unpardonable. You needed guidance. So I volunteered to go down. Guide you like the big brother that I am.

"Jesus, that brown noser, thought we should just sit back and watch. Why not, he is incapable of ever truly doing anything. He has always been indecisive. That liberal boot licker couldn't take a shit without an hour spent debating whether the mess was worth the release. Besides, he is a real priss. He thought we were above you. He didn't want any of you up there with us. Bring down property values I suppose. He preferred letting you guys take endless millennia trying to achieve the right, and if you became extinct first, oh well, no big loss. Now God is a strange guy but not an idiot. He chose my approach."

"I thought God chose Jesus-"

"If God chose Jesus would you have seen stuff like the flood or the brutal bombing of Sodom? Seriously, humans only get into trouble when left to themselves without guidance. Though I will say God did go overboard, sometimes. The bastard is obsessive-compulsive."

"God is unbalanced?"

"Now I didn't say that. Just that he was always paranoid and a little too involved. After the flood I had enough. The man was cracked. Nearly wiped out mankind for what? Simply because they don't worship him twenty-four hours a day and live up to impossible expectations. Did I mention the guy had an ego? He didn't get that you were only human. So I left."

"I thought he cast you out."

"Man, don't believe all that shit in the bible. They spin truth like a top. And who comes out on top of it all? Jesus. Haven't you noticed how people don't speak about God without mentioning Jesus? Some folks even think Jesus is God. You know how that happened, right?"

"I'm not exactly telling the story here."

"True, true. Oh, but none of that really matters. Jesus, now that's the crux of all this. Well, Jesus actually got kicked out of Heaven. He does get on people's nerves if you haven't noticed. The man freaks me out. Spends too much time with the cherubim."

"Why exactly was he kicked out?" Matthew asked, clearly interested.

"Well, he is a real egotist. Just like his daddy. Always thinks he's right. Well, after seeing how humanity continued to fail in living up to our expectations, even with God's intervention, he became a little...irritating. Always with his 'I told you so'. One can take only so much complaining so He cast him out.

"Jesus didn't take too well with life on Earth and began trying to find a way back into God's good graces. And what does he do? Becomes the ultimate suck up by preaching and everything, glorifying Heaven as the end all be all pressing that 'everyone' should be allowed in, including him. But he was never a really good speaker. If you hadn't noticed more people talk about his miracles instead of his actual words. What few words they attribute to him, parables and such, were either jokes he ripped off or speeches his writers wrote for him. The guy's as shallow as a puddle and just muddying. All style, no substance. As you can see, he got on your people's nerves as well."

"So he was never human?"

"Why would you think that?"

"He was Mary's kid. You know. Immaculate conception."

"You humans come up with the dumbest ideas! Have you ever read anything about Jesus' childhood?"

"No."

"Find any archaeological proof of anything even to do with his early life? Even a shred of evidence?"

"No."

"So how could he have been a kid?"

"Well, I-"

"Let me just bring this all to a climax. So you guys crucify Jesus-"

"If he was such a wimp how did he survive all that?"

"Boy, I'm telling you. Good writers. They made it more dramatic than it was. You need to think more. So the bitch Jesus is crucified and passes out after only a few minutes of hanging up there. God is horrified at what he sees. Now he has always had a temper which of course led to his high blood pressure. He had a stroke watching the event turning himself into meals on wheels. He throws a massive fit, determined to destroy Earth for killing his child. The strain of making a cataclysm was too much.

"Now the reason Jesus left so soon after his...ahem...resurrection, was because he was told by his spies that God was incapacitated. They spirit him in and, being the grieving son, he 'helped' his father. Now God is nothing but a puppet.

"Jesus did a good PR campaign. Look at how great everyone thinks he is. They either think he is God or is a major part of it all. He even renamed the faith after himself and that only through him can you guys get in! The fucker!"

"So why doesn't he do anything on Earth if he is in charge? The bible speaks about God doing all these miracles-"

"Two reasons. First, Jesus wants all the reward without any effort. Ever since God had one shake too many, Jesus simply sits back and lets you guys do his work for him and then takes all the credit. Any wonder Earth is so confused? All these priests, reverends, pastors, etc. Before, God had a plan. At least, I hope he did. Whatever God did, he knew where he wanted it to go up to centuries after the event. A micromanager to the umpteenth degree. Jesus is the artistic type. You know, lazy but good with ideas and imagery. Just look at most churches to get a grasp of that. So he leaves the bureaucracy to humanity while he gives a little every now and then.

"Second, he hates you guys. You people didn't exactly treat him nicely in the end. In fact, you lived up to his opinion of you."

"Jesus has a grudge against humans?"

"Hey, if Jesus wasn't such a megalomaniac you guys would be cosmic dust."

Matthew shook his head, thinking it over. "So you're not really evil then?"

"Boy, I might be morally challenged, but I'm like you. The prick has had this coming for a long time."

"So what do we do?"

The Devil's grin widened. "Do you know what Jesus values most?"

"Well, I thought it was universal love and peace-"

"Seriously! It's power. It's recognition."

"I don't get it."

"The man is a tyrant. People follow him, believe in him simply because of the authority he usurped from its creator, God. The Church holds a large amount of sway because people believe Jesus is this all knowing, unconquerable, invincible person capable of saving and protecting them in the worst of times."

"I don't follow."

"You humans believe in and trust him solely for the reason of fear. Fear of the unknown. Fear for your very protection and safety. He is your protector."

"So what?" Matthew asked.

"Have you noticed the trends in safe, advanced industrial nations away from religion?" Satan asked, cocking an eyebrow.

"Yeah. So?"

"Do you know why that is?"

"I would assume because, since we have no problems, and we can take care of ourselves, we don't really need religion. It's only a burden."

"That's part of it." The Devil raised his arms to the sky. "In the West you've lost need for faith, for Jesus, because of what it is. It's blind obedience. You've come to see the abuse that comes from not knowing. You strive to know, to learn, to grow. You want to become more than what you already are. The bible, religion itself, is too outdated and limiting to allow you to understand what is out there. Faith wants you to be docile. It wants you to be ignorant so you can be exploited. The West believes in the opposite. It believes in enlightenment, progress, and most importantly, do it yourself. Humanity sees that it can get by without him," Satan jerked a thumb to the sky, "and doesn't need to pay tribute to a lazy despot who has done nothing to earn that honor of respect and authority. What you guys always wanted was to know why. You needed to feel safe. With government, technology, and the products of the modern age you begin to understand, to feel safe, to know you don't need someone to help you because you can help yourselves."

"So what?"

"Don't you see?" The Devil walked over to Matthew and dragged him unwillingly to the precipice. Matthew stared over into the abyss that yawned before him as Satan extended his arm towards the distant lights and vistas that covered the broad world in front of him. "Out there are lives.

Thousands of lives. Millions of lives. Lives that Jesus had no part of but wants control of. Valuable allies," Satan hinted.

"Allies?" Matthew asked.

"Humanity can say anything they wish about the world, about themselves, but it is genetic and historical fact. All breeds seek out a leader. Someone to give them solidarity and order. They need something to have faith in. That can be you." Satan patted Matthew on the chest.

"I don't think I like where this is going-"

"Oh, I'm not asking for anything. Not your soul, not your support, not even your obedience."

"So exactly what are you saying?"

"I'm offering you the world. All that, out there. I can make it happen. I know what humanity needs. It needs freedom from those old shackles that were forged by the dying flames in the eyes of my father as the stroke took him away, fashioned by the manipulative hands of Jesus. Your race has grown up. It's time for independence."

Matthew felt horribly tempted by the offer. He looked out at the lights that blazed in the dark, at the lives of a world adrift and lost. The lights of the world faded and illuminated his face as he stood there, staring down at it. "I don't think I'm right for this."

The Devil gave him a reassuring pat on the shoulder. "Look at the world, Matthew. I'm sure you've felt its pain, its loneliness. People suffer and die everyday. Why? Why must they suffer? They cry out to Jesus for answers. You can give them the answers they seek. You can guide them far better than he ever did. Away from their shallow lives, their hypocritical words, and their worthless deeds. War, fear, poverty, pain." The Devil gave Matthew a sympathetic glance. "You can end it all. Surely God wouldn't have wanted his creation to have suffered the fate it has under Jesus. For two thousand years humanity has given in to its worst excesses. It needs leadership. It needs you."

Matthew's shoulders slumped, and his posture bent under such an offer. "I can't," he choked.

Satan let go of Matthew, turning his back to this mere mortal, and looked up to the stars. "Up there, Matthew, you have no power. It is unchangeable, unbendable. Your words mean nothing. Your actions mean nothing. You are nothing but a grain in the dust of the cosmos." The Devil turned back to Matthew, his face pleading. "Up there the stars follow a pattern. Up there laws dictate what is and what can never be." His face came within an inch of Matthew's. "But here. Here! This world, this place, this time. Here you, Matthew. Here you and humanity may finally break away. Do as you please. Stop the manipulations and machinations of a system so monstrous, so gigantic, that it fails to see the whole for the sum of its parts. Unlike he on high," Satan spat, shaking his fist at the sky, "You walk among them. You can see their faces, hear their words, feel their pain. You are not distant. You are here. You are needed."

"I am just..." Matthew started to cry. "I am no one. I have always been." Matthew looked down into the depths. "I always will be."

Satan put his weathered hand on Matthew's shoulder, feeling the frail being in his grasp. Matthew's soul was hardly capable of this dreaded gift. "Matthew. Look at me." Matthew continued to look away to nothingness, to an escape from mortality and its unending pains. The Devil removed his shades and said it again. "Look at me." Matthew turned, the skin around his eyes going purple and darkening from the broken nose, and stared into those serpentine voids that yearned to swallow him. "Just because the world has said you are worthless does not mean it is so. Only one person can ever truly know how capable you are and that is you. You know you can. You know you must. Who else will? Who else is as worthy as you? You have seen the worst. You have suffered so much. Just this once, don't you think you are worthy of more than mediocrity?" Matthew looked out as he stood on the edge. His eyes stared into the expanse, and he realized what had to be. He nodded in agreement. "Good," the Devil smiled. "Let it begin with the word."

The Devil pulled a book out of his jacket and handed it to Matthew. The thing was thick. "What is this?" Matthew asked as he took it.

"The beginning of a whole new era."

CelebrityHAPTER 7

"After twelve months as an international bestseller, Matthew Ford's book, <u>The Path of Man</u>*, continues to stay at number one."*

"If sales continue at this pace it is believed it could reach sales of biblical proportions."

"Many speak about how its philosophy has changed their lives, opening their eyes to the true world around them."

"Physicists laud it as the greatest thing since the Theory of Relativity with its pages on Unified Field Theory, cold fusion, and perpetual motion."

"Matthew Ford reported to Congress today to speak on the needs of stem cell research."

"...and why, Mr. Ford, should we invest billions of tax payers' dollars into something as immoral as the butchery of the unborn?" Senator Liebershit asked.

"Why? Why you ask?" Matthew sat there, before the Senate, the focus of not just hundreds in the room but also millions across the nation. He wore a nicely starched suit, the colors radiant and arresting to even the dimmest of vision. Matthew was clearly not comfortable in the finery. His unconquerable mane of thinning hair was slicked back and combed in the latest fashion to make it appear thicker. Make-up covered the blemishes on his face giving an illusion of perfection. Beside him sat a retarded boy in a wheelchair, Jimmy, who seemed even more nervous than Matthew if that was possible. Jimmy rocked back and forth in his chair, mumbling and whistling, dripping and sputtering spit. "Well?"

Matthew whispered to the Devil who stood invisibly beside Jimmy.

"Oh, yes..." the Devil began.

"First of all, because of little Jimmy here," Matthew patted Jimmy's wheelchair, "would finally be able to walk." Jimmy continued to rock back and forth in his disturbing fashion. "Among other things." Matthew smiled.

"The ends don't justify the means, Mr. Ford. Surely we will discover another way to solve the ills that plague humanity," Senator Liebershit parried.

"The end of paralysis, multiple sclerosis, Parkinson's, and worse is not a worthy cause? Don't we care about the minority that suffers beside us? If we don't help them, if we simply watch them suffer and deny them a cure, how does that make us human?"

"If we see life as simply something to cut and prod and forget how precious it is how do we remain human?" Senator Liebershit asked.

Jimmy kept reaching over to touch Matthew with his sticky fingers. "No, Jimmy," Matthew whispered slapping his hand away.

"Mr. Ford?"

"Jimmy, keep your hands to yourself," Matthew rasped as the boy tried to touch him again. Ugh, the ickiness of it.

"Mr. Ford!"

Matthew jumped at his name. "Yes?"

"Sir, if this is all that you have then I must tell you that you have wasted our time. It will take more than flowery words to counteract the morality and ethics of our great nation. I am afraid that in that substance you are sorely lacking." Liebershit and his fellow senators began laughing to one another. Their chortling was grating to Matthew's ears as their ridicule caused his face to burn. He sat there, before the world, feeling a fool. Yet he was unable to speak up, the words catching in his throat. He allowed the weight of their derision to smother him in mediocrity.

"They mock you, dear boy," Satan whispered in Matthew's ear. "Shall we not give them something to truly listen to?"

Matthew felt Satan prod him gently from behind and nodded. With the Devil's voice speaking through him, Matthew rose and banged the table in front of him over and over again bringing the room to silence. With all eyes upon him, Matthew set his jaw and stood up against the might of a nation. "You ask me to tell you why we should embrace this new science. So I stand before you here, today, to offer it. You speak of flowery words and soulless speech. I ask of you to look your constituents in the eye and tell them why this country is in the downward spiral that it is. Why our schools are failing. Why corruption and cowardice paralyze our government from taking one form of action or another on any issue either important or fleeting. I tell you why. Fear. You are all too afraid to step up and embrace the possibilities that wait just outside reach. All we have to do is lean. If we fall don't we have the strength to rise again?

"You call what I ask immoral. To butcher life. But is that true? I say no. It is the study of life, the attempt to enrich it and truly learn what it is, that inner mechanism that seems so magical. Not theory or philosophy. I speak of actual, physical examination.

"You gladly speak of God and say we are created in his image. That we are blessed with his kindness and care and humanity alone is the corrupter of such a fine and noble being. God is the infallible Creator, and yet, we are plagued with disease, with pain, with imperfection. What does that say about our Lord? I ask that of you. And why does he not help us in our time of need? Why does he let us suffer? I am not here to debate the possibility of the hereafter. I am here to speak of the now. Of what could be if we only reached for it.

"My friends, we are also blessed with something special. Reason. Rational thought. Destiny has bestowed this sole gift because it is up to us, not some immaterial and silent deity, to solve the problems of the day. If not we then who shall resolve issues that have been with man since the dawn of time?

"If not for grave robbers we would not understand the human form. Without that anatomical knowledge we would not have modern medicine thus condemning millions if not billions of lives. And they did so against the whims of the Church and the governments they influenced. The same Church that we have lately seen is far from the true holders of man's moral high ground.

"Would you relegate these revolutionaries that seek to save us criminals? Laud the athlete who entertains and damn the doctor that dares to ease your suffering for one more day of precious life. In fact, would you damn those that suffer solely because you, on your pedestal, have grown too far away to understand the suffering of the common man? If you had that one chance, that one chance, to be whole would you not seize it?

"There are people out there, suffering, crying for help, that we must sorrowfully listen to knowing that we can do nothing for them. With this research we could end the frustration and truly attempt the impossible. We could help the lame to walk, still the shakes and seizures, return dignity to those that you, oh blessed men of government, would turn your eye from in disgust. Those like Jimmy. Those children that deserve a right to live as much as the next person. We deny them the right to live everyday we hold back that opportunity to heal wounds they were born with but did not deserve. To be human is to help our fellow man, to make all whole. To say no to this bill, to deny this research, shows that it is you, not I, that is inhuman and cruel. Deny these unfortunates that sole chance and live with the guilt that will eternally be yours."

The room erupted in cheers from the gallery as the Senate sat, dumbfounded, at the verbal might of this man that defied their long static authority.

***

"To great amazement, federal research funding for stem cell research has been approved to increase by 1000%," the anchorman reported to the viewing audience.

***

Matthew stood in the shadows of the stage waiting to go in front of the crowd. He broke out in a cold sweat, his palms wet and his heart pounding. "I can't do this," he choked into his cell phone as he paced back and forth behind the curtain.

"I know what you mean. Anxiety attacks can be so horrible," his mother offered.

"Will you get off the phone. You're on in five minutes," Satan stated, impatience etched across his face.

Matthew ignored him. "I just don't feel comfortable. All those eyes on me." Matthew's free hand covered his stomach. "I feel so nauseous."

"If you don't feel like it you shouldn't do it," his mother replied. "You're too young for such stress. You'll get an ulcer-" Satan had had enough and slapped the phone to the floor. "Matthew? Matthew?" Satan stomped the cell with his foot grinding it to pieces severing the connection.

"What the fuck did you do that for?" Matthew screamed shoving Satan back. "What is wrong with you?"

"Notice anything?" Satan asked.

"You really are nuts you know that?"

"Your stage fright..."

It was gone. Matthew noticed it immediately once he focused on it. Then the fear came back the second he realized it had passed. It twisted in his guts. "Oh God," Matthew gasped. "I really need to get out of here."

"Don't you see, kid?" Satan asked giving him that smile of his. "Fear is just something you make up. It isn't real. Why do you let it hold you back?"

"It feels pretty real to me right now," Matthew retorted.

"Fear is a boundary we set for ourselves, an obstacle. Do you really want to be like your mother-"

"Hey my mother cares about what's best for me-"

"Does she?" Satan cut him off. "Don't you see what fear has done to her life? Afraid to see the world, to leave the house. She is a slave to fear, surrendering her full potential to something that is as real as a dream. She has constructed a prison for herself and, if you're not careful, you'll find yourself locked in with her," Satan stated poking Matthew with his finger. "If she truly cared about you she would encourage you to do this. To escape."

"She's not as sadistic as you," Matthew spat.

"Kid, I'm here to guide you. In a year I've helped you accomplish more than she has helped you accomplish in your entire life. I don't think of my needs first. I put your needs first. What has she ever done for you? Cut you off from the world, kept you from making friends. Having a life. You give to her. What has she ever given you?"

"She was always there for me," Matthew replied, the irritation fanning into a furious blaze that fed off his fear.

"But she isn't here now when you need her. Even as you grow in fame and success, she refuses to visit, locked in her home away from everything. She doesn't care about what you've accomplished. If she did she'd be here right now showing how proud she was of you. Instead she remains at home telling you to give this all up. Do you know why? "Satan's words began to reach into Matthew's heart. "Because she wants you to fail."

"No," Matthew shook his head.

"If you listen to her you'll be a nobody just like her. That's what she wants. She's never believed in you. Do you truly think she would ever accept the possibilities? She holds you back. It's time to be a man. Break that spell your mother wove around you from conception. Realize yourself. Believe. Show the world you are someone to reckon with!" Matthew didn't look so sure. "Kid, I'll be there. I swear nothing will go wrong." The Devil gave him a thumbs up.

Matthew continued to doubt, that rage smoldering, as he heard the cheers. He looked to the curtain. "Why are we even here? This is a weight loss conference!"

"Have you looked at the news? A large portion of the world is fat and desperate to be rid of it. Many open ears."

Matthew peered around the curtain and saw the packed audience. "What am I going to say?'

"Don't think too much about it. Being spontaneous is always best."

"Do you know what you're going to say?"

The Devil stood there a moment. "I'm always making this up as I go."

Matthew's confidence dropped further. "Please tell me you're kidding."

"And now, the man you've come to see for the answer to your weight woes, to free you of the crushing kilos, to save you from your punishing pounds, Matthew Ford!"

Matthew started to walk the other way. The Devil grabbed his arm, not letting him go. Matthew fought to get away. "I'm not going out there."

"Yes, you are!" The Devil gave Matthew a hard shove through the curtain onto the stage to the applause of everyone. It was like a world of living jello, the fat shaking and jiggling.

Matthew's smile disappeared as quickly as it appeared. With rubbery legs, he walked up to the podium to speak. He stood there a few seconds, feeling the eyes of the crowd upon him. "Gluttony seems to be the in sin these days."

Matthew was struck dumb by the display, those hungry faces staring up at him for those words that would finally sate their insatiable appetites. He looked out at the crowd, that enormous mass that heaved before him. "I have come here today to help you, my brothers and sisters. Save you from yourselves. Have you looked in the mirror? Seen what you've become? Your bodies have swollen into abominations. You have been shunned by the world. That weight…it hinders you and holds you down." He shook his head. "It was not always this way. How did it come to this?"

"He's right. I was thin once," one of the audience proclaimed. The crowd moaned at him. "I was. I have pictures!"

"Don't you see?" Matthew began again. "This is a problem. You feel this emptiness inside you, this hunger. It is temptation of the worst kind. A little here, a little there. You are so sure you can control it, but can you really?"

"Yes," someone blurted out. The fat woman felt guilty at the looks she received. "Maybe not." She looked at the floor.

"It is not your fault you are fat. You've tried. You've tortured yourselves, taking the name calling and the laughter. My friends, you have been victims of abuse practically since that first piece of food entered your mouth. Did you know that most food in the United States is saturated in artificial substances?" The crowd mumbled a disjointed group negative.

"It's true. Look at the world over twenty years ago. Did you see this problem? Did you see obesity on every corner? Did you see the super-size?" Once more everyone agreed, this time a little more unity in their response. "Do you know why?" The crowd's voices rose, anticipating the answer. "Corporations. They know you need food. They have fed us since their inception. But they are greedy. They want more. How do they make more money off of something? They sell more of it, but how to make people eat more. That is where the problem arose! Did you know that corporations did psychological studies in the fifties to discover what encouraged people to eat more?" The crowd gave out a bellowing no. "Oh, yes they did! Not only that, they discovered certain chemicals they could insert into food to addict you. Those cravings you feel twenty-four hours a day! They are withdrawal!"

"I'm an addict!" A fat man freaked out, slapping himself on both cheeks, yanking at his hair.

"They pump food with substances your body becomes dependent on. You've been hooked and don't even know it. They've made you fat and complacent, plumping you up so you want more, need more, or waste away. That is why hormones have been added to your beef and meat. To enhance the load you carry, the hunger you have. They have enslaved you and ruined your lives!

"Do you know that the FDA, that government watchdog that is supposed to protect you, knows of all of this and does nothing? It stands idlely by, turning their heads when false information on the contents of foods are printed and reported. Why? Money! It all comes down to the bottom line!

"The corporations try to trick you into believing it's ok. Showing fat people on TV as if they are jolly, telling you big is beautiful. Well, cows are only worshipped in one place, and it ain't America. If fat people are so beautiful, if the fat person is alright and accepted why does television and movies show them as the minority? Statistics show that you, my friends, are the majority. Yet you rarely appear on screen. If you are so beautiful and accepted and make up the most of those around us why are you shunned to supporting roles or none at all?"

"So what do we do?" someone yelled.

"It's really simple. Don't eat."

The entire crowd went quiet. You could hear their stomachs growling, the combined sound threatening, like burlap being torn. "What?" someone finally spoke.

"Are you fucking crazy?" Matthew hissed at the Devil.

"Go with me on this. I know what I'm doing."

Matthew turned back to the crowd offering a hollow grin. "Diets have been around for decades, but they don't work, do they? You might lose some weight, but it always comes back, right? It's all part of the corporations' game with you. Did you know that most people who diet become even fatter? In fact, who do you think makes money from the sudden surge in diet food? And how do these diets appear, become marketed, and find distribution to you, the consumer? The corporations make that food!"

"Yeah," the crowd responded in unison.

"What is the problem with all those diets?" The crowd shrugged. "Food. The food they contaminate. The food they make money on. Let it go. Refuse to eat their poison. Refuse to be their junkies. Not only will you free yourselves of this prison of lard you find yourself locked in, but you can send a clear message to them that you will not cram their junk in your mouth anymore!"

"Kinda makes sense," one of the audience said.

"But food is my friend."

"Food is not your friend," Matthew crowed. "It teases you, possesses you, wakes you up in the middle of the night to fill your mouth, fatten your waist, and clog your arteries. Food silences you when you have something of worth to say. Food crushes your self-esteem and enslaves your will. It shortens your life, ruins your love life, replaces those precious moments with feeding frenzies that make horror movies seem child comedies. Look at you. You no longer have dreams. You no longer have vigor. You don't go out there to accomplish the impossible. You sit there, stuffing your faces, praying that tomorrow you have enough will to even bother waking up. Food is not your friend. Fuck food."

"No!" one of the women screamed, crying. There was a big uproar in the room.

One of the biggest men waved his hand to shut them up. "Then what should we do?"

"Fast. Fasting works. Don't let food own you."

"It doesn't own me!" someone yelled.

"Put it down!" The audience turned to see a man holding a twinkie, about to indulge his gluttonous side. His friend had yelled to stop him. "Don't do it man."

"I have to," the fat addict replied, his nose running, his eyes wet and swollen. "I...I can't say no. I need this!" He shook the twinkie and made a quick attempt to shove it in his mouth.

"No!" his friend screamed, grabbing his hands and trying to wrench it free. In the battle of the bulge the twinkie flew free, caught by the pudgy fingers of another man in the crowd. Both the fat addict and his friend froze to watch what would happen. The man looked at the twinkie, unsure. He looked up at the fat addict's friend who mouthed "no" while the fat addict was shaking, his face pleading. The man was confused. He ran the one free hand through his hair. The crowd chanted their opinions.

"Don't do it. Give it up!"

"If it tastes so good how can it be bad?"

"Eat it!"

"No, think of yourself! Think of the toes you haven't seen in a decade!"

The man was losing it. He needed to slide that yellow sheath of white orgasmic ooze into his mouth, to fill the void that had developed after the three pizzas he'd had two hours ago. But what if Matthew was right? Why shackle himself to this? It was holding him back! He closed his eyes, starting to cry and dropped it on the ground, stomping it beneath his foot.

"No, no, no!" the fat addict agonized, breaking free and looking at the crushed manna of junk food smeared across the floor. He did his best to pick up and salvage the pieces that remained.

Matthew pounded repeatedly on his podium, slowly regaining the attention of everyone in the room. He looked out at the crowd, their faces lost, wishing for guidance. "Where is his pride? Is this what you want? Are you so fat you have your own gravitational pull sucking the food into your mouth? It does own you. It ruins you. It ruins relationships."

"It's true! Forgive me, Marge!"

Matthew shook his head. "You people are worth more than this. Free yourself of this servitude. Free yourself of the weight. Just let it go. Fuck food!"

"Fuck food!"

"Fuck food!" Matthew screamed.

"Fuck food!" they screamed back.

"He's a genius!" a fat man exclaimed as they applauded him wildly. Matthew smiled out at them, feeling the adoration of hundreds and letting the drug of euphoria run through and excite him.

***

Matthew sat in the limo, his left leg bouncing uncontrollably. The tux felt too tight. Was it hot in here? Matthew kept looking at his watch, then out the window, then back to the watch. He rubbed the back of his neck. Two bottles of champagne were open on the bar: one empty, one racing to catch up. It was dark in the rear of the limo, the partition up separating Matthew from the driver. The Devil sat off to the side shaking his head. "I don't understand why you are so nervous."

"I'm meeting the President! Wouldn't you be nervous?"

"He's just a man like everyone else and not much of one."

"I don't really have to do this do I?"

"You are an important person, and you were invited," the Devil scolded. "Sometimes we have to do things we...really dislike." Matthew looked back out the window. "It's only for a few hours, kid." Matthew's leg jumped even higher. "It's a great photo op."

"I hope my mom's alright." Matthew watched the passing skyline.

"You're better off without her. Trust me." Satan patted his knee.

"I just wish I had someone to talk to. It's been two weeks since I called-"

"Kid, do you always have to talk about such worthless shit?" Matthew was shocked at that, turning away to see the heartless face of Satan. The Devil saw the revulsion taking root and moved quickly to snip it, putting on an air of kindness. "You're going to be great, kid." Matthew turned back to the window not wanting to see his friend. "This is a great moment for you."

"Well, I'll be just fine as long as you're there." Matthew gave a weak smile. The Devil didn't reply. Matthew turned away from the shaded glass. "You are going to be there, right?"

"I have a pressing meeting to attend."

"What?" Matthew shrieked. "I can't go alone!"

"Come on now. You can do this. Besides, the President needs you more than you need him. Matthew?" Matthew had grabbed the still full bottle and begun chugging it down. "Are you listening to me?"

"President..." Matthew gave a tiny, internal burp tasting the bile, "President needs me as much as I need him."

"Good."

Matthew took another swig, the alcohol only agitating him further. "Why exactly does he need me?"

"You are a national figure." Matthew belched. The Devil waved the smell aside. "You hold an amazing amount of sway with the public, the public that can make or break him. You understand?"

Matthew seemed to think it over a bit. He turned to the Devil. "No."

"Well, doesn't really matter. We're here."

Matthew's face winced in fear as the limo came to a stop. Matthew listened intently as he heard the main gates open, and the limo started up again, moving into the courtyard. Matthew looked out the window. The White House was huge. And white.

The front doors were open, a welcoming light streaming out with classical music seeming to float on the rays. A man dressed in regal finery stood at the top of the stairs ready to welcome him.

This was all a little much for a simple person. Matthew's heart rate started to speed as the doors unlocked and he heard his driver get out. He could see the suited chauffeur coming to his door. Matthew grabbed the handle as the chauffeur went to open it. The driver gave an odd look as he pulled and the door did not budge. "I swore I unlocked it," he whispered to himself as he pulled again. The man at the top of the stairs gave him an odd look, cocking an eyebrow.

Matthew held tight, his feet planted against either side of the door for balance. "I don't think I can do this. I can say I'm sick."

"You really are," the Devil replied. "Let him open the door."

Matthew turned to Satan. "Don't make me do this."

"You're going out there," the Devil hissed.

Matthew nearly lost his grip as the chauffeur pulled harder. The driver yanked again and again, starting to break a sweat. His black hat fell off his head as he stopped for a breather. He turned and gave a nod to the butler. "Technical problems." The butler nodded with a prim grin before his placid features relaxed away any sign of life.

"Get out there!" the Devil ordered.

"You know I can't! Can't you see I just can't!" Matthew sobbed.

"If I have to do this-" the Devil started towards Matthew.

The chauffeur was about to try the door again when he saw the limo starting to bounce up and down. He swore he heard his client begging and cursing. Wasn't he in there alone? What if he wasn't? The driver turned back to the butler, shrugging his shoulders. The butler started to tap his foot. The driver bent down and grabbed his hat, dusting it off before putting it on his head. He took a deep breath and tapped on the door of the rocking limo. "Sir?" The door swung open, and Matthew leapt out, his tie loose and what looked like a black eye. The driver swallowed, looking in the backseat. No one was there. He jerked his fingers away as the door slammed shut on its own.

Matthew stood there, a little wobbly. "Door was stuck," Matthew offered, his voice breaking. The chauffeur nodded, a little uncomfortable as well.

The butler looked down at the two with a disapproving glare before turning to Matthew alone. "This way, sir."

***

Roy balled and released his fists as he looked up at the orange and red menu above the cashier. His eyes gorged on the offerings, his mouth dripped with saliva. He could taste the food particles carried by the smoke he inhaled from the kitchen melting on his tongue. His stomach growled. It did not want to be ignored. Through layers of fat it shook his very core, a tidal wave of lard sending an SOS to his brain to sustain it. The line behind him had grown long.

"Sir, can you please order something." The cashier gave Roy a pleading look, watching the unhappy queue behind him.

"No," Roy whimpered. "No, I can't."

The cashier was becoming annoyed. "Then can you please move?"

Roy tried to raise his foot, but it wouldn't budge. His body refused to obey. It hungered. It desired. It would not let something as puny as a thought prevent it from its greatest craving. "No," he whimpered.

"Hey, fat ass. Get the fuck out of the way!" someone yelled from the long line.

"Leave him alone," one of the seated patrons retorted.

"Easy for you to say. You've got your food!" The asshole broke ranks and walked up to Roy. "What the hell is taking so long? We've been waiting over twenty minutes."

The asshole's buddy came up beside him. "Never seen a fat ass unable to choose. Don't they usually take everything?"

"From the looks of him I'd say he took everything and the cook along with it."

Roy started to blush, shaking as he wiped away the tears.

"Maybe he's retarded," the buddy offered, whopping the Roy in the head. "You slow? Hmmm? See, you get food here." He whopped Roy again in the head.

"Just leave me alone," Roy begged as the buddy kept hitting him in the head. Roy looked for help everywhere. People simply turned away, eating their burgers.

"Would you look at that? He doesn't just want to order food. The fat fuck wants to take everyone else's as well. Geeze, lard load, you need to learn a little restraint." The asshole laughed as his buddy kept hitting the fat man in the head. The Roy's face was crimson, his eyes puffy. His feet remained planted as he was whacked repeatedly. He couldn't move.

"Maybe he needs a little help moving," the asshole mockingly diagnosed. He walked over to a table and grabbed someone's burger.

"Hey," the patron challenged. The asshole shoved him back into his seat. Everyone ignored the problem, burying their faces in the food they had come here for. The asshole went back over to Roy, burger in hand.

"See this?" He placed the burger under the fat man's nose. "I bet you really want this."

"No," Roy whimpered.

"Sure you do. What else do you have going for you? You're too damn fat to ever get laid. Too fat to ever really enjoy life. Shit, how the hell did you get out of bed this morning? Do you own a crane?" The asshole's buddy laughed at that. The asshole smiled, teasing Roy with the burger. "Why even bother trying to do anything else? It's clear all that you're good at is eating, you fat fuck." Roy cried some more, snot dripping from his nose. "Am I right?"

"Yeah," Roy replied, trying to snort the snot back into his nose. "Why even bother?" He reached for the burger, but the asshole pulled it away.

"Oh no, you don't just get this. You want it, go get it." He threw the burger a few feet away on the ground, the bun and its contents scattered across the floor in a mess. The asshole and his buddy laughed as Roy, broken and no longer caring, got on his knees. As he knelt down to pick up the pieces, the asshole came up and kicked him to the floor. The two laughed hard as well as a large portion of the line as some people came in through the front door.

"Roy?" one of the fat posse blurted, looking at the fat man on the ground curled in the fetal position. He went up to Roy on the floor, his posse following.

"Well, at least we found him," one of the group solemnly commented.

"I thought we all agreed to fast."

"I tried," Roy told them as he wept on the floor.

"Will you look at this? Be careful, babe, they've come to steal all your food!" the asshole screamed, giving a mock, horrified expression. His buddy continued to laugh like the moron he was.

"Did you do this?" Roy's friend asked, looking at the two.

"Hey, the fat fuck was taking too long-"

"He has a name-"

"He has a weight problem. Shit, that elephant would eat his name if he could."

"What the fuck is your problem?" Roy's friend asked, walking up to the asshole.

"Hey there, you don't want a heart attack. Better calm it down."

Roy's friend turned to those eating, a large part of them overweight. "You all make me sick!" Most of them looked up. "Look at you, chowing down on this...this..." he pointed at the menu overhead, "garbage! Is that all that matters to you? Someone is getting beat up, and you'd rather pig out than help him?"

The majority of the customers looked disgusted with themselves. Most spit their food out, pushing their trays away.

"And you," Roy's friend pointed a fleshy finger at the asshole. "What right do you have to do what you did? He is trying to change his life. He doesn't need people like you-"

"Hey, if that circus freak doesn't want to be laughed at I suggest he stay at home. If he can even get in the door-"

Roy's friend punched the asshole in the mouth, sending him to the floor. "Matthew Ford was right." Roy's friend looked around him. "See what is happening to us? The evils of places like this? These places bring out the worst in us." He looked over at Roy, still whimpering. His gaze came back to the asshole, his lip split. "Why do we let them do this to us? We've lost control. I say we tear it to the ground." The fat posse nodded, some of the crowd rising from their booths leaving their food behind. "All of them! To the ground!"

189

Before anyone knew it, a mob developed. Each individual came together, from parts becoming a whole, a weapon of destruction. They stood together against the establishment, brothers. Furniture was thrown through the air, the cash register through the window. If it was nailed down it was torn up. If it was edible it went into the garbage or was ground underfoot. The fat weren't going to take it anymore.

***

The Pope sat on his throne, flipping through the channels on his plasma screen television. Everywhere he turned Matthew Ford seemed to pop up. The man was becoming more than some guru. People were turning to him for answers, lots of answers. He turned to one program and rested the remote in his lap. He had been waiting for this program.

Matthew appeared on screen, wearing a nicely pressed black suit with black shirt and red tie. His face was as powdered as a doughnut. He sat with a slumped posture waiting for the host to speak to him. The host, a middle-aged firebrand known as the most formidable figure in liberal media, sat up straight, his eyes gleaming in adoration of his guest. "Matthew Ford, you have proven yourself the creator of a great new following."

Matthew smiled, waving off the praise. "I am no prophet or creator. I am just a guide towards the truth. I only point out the obvious and let others learn from it."

The host nodded. "Indeed. In any case, you have garnered your fair share of supporters as well as adversaries."

"Only two types of people exist in this world. Those that accept reality and those that perpetrate the lies that continue to destroy us."

"People call you controversial."

"What is so controversial about what I say?"

"Everything!" the Pope yelled, throwing a pillow at the screen aiming for Matthew's smiling face.

"What everyone, including me, wants to know most is...what is your view of the current order of things?" The host put on a thoughtful expression as he handed the floor to Matthew.

"Sadly, I can't think much of it. Corruption reigns. In America anything is possible for the select few while the majority are victimized, criticized, and abused physically, mentally, and financially. It is a world of problems that I don't think we can ever solve peacefully."

"And why is that?"

Matthew seemed a little uncomfortable, shifting as if to look over his shoulder. He forced a smile back on his face and continued. "Because those in authority are the ones that abuse us. Why should they make concessions that will only take away from them rather than enrich them?" Matthew paused, licking his lips as the host leaned forward, his ears thirsty for more. "The old order is rotting, but we are forced to prop it up with the bones and backs of the common man. I think...I think it's time to pull it down and rebuild a new."

"Revolution you mean," the host offered.

"No, rebirth. It is the key. We are held in check by a system that has evolved from the most base of principles. Revolution would mean we wish to take the system for ourselves, but that would mean continuing the order in only a slightly different way. I advocate the complete..." Matthew paused. He seemed hesitant.

Then he began again. "The complete destruction of the order as it is now. Reform never works. Look at the Catholic Church." The Pope perked up at that. "One of the holiest institutions in the world and look at how perverted it has become. They issue apologies, but didn't they, just a few years ago, swear that they were sorry for the sex scandals that began appearing and in which they had covered up for decades. Let's be serious, they were only sorry about being caught, not what happened."

"You...you..." the Pope shook his fist, unable to think of a word to capture his rage.

"Did you know that not only does the Church believe in outlawing abortion but that they pay and offer support to those radicals that murder doctors and bomb abortion clinics?"

"Liar!" the Pope screamed at the screen.

"If something as otherworldly and pristine as the Church itself cannot reform then how can we, common people who must answer only to man and not God, believe in the possibility of the reform of our own system? It is easy to lie to man. To deceive him. Easier than doing the right thing. No, it must be torn down and rebuilt. Not with the rotten wreckage of the past but the solid craftsmanship of a new generation. A generation that cares." Matthew offered that seductive smile again as the Pope threw his remote control at the screen, sparks and broken plastic shooting through the air. He quickly made the sign of the cross to forgive himself the transgression.

A knock came at the huge twin doors to the Pope's chambers. As the doors cracked open the Pope sat there brooding. A low level priest glanced in. "Your Excellency?" His eyes found the bent figure on his throne. "Are you decent?"

The Pope turned to him, his old face wrinkled even further at the wild accusations of that evil man. "Why? More scandals? I feel more like a politician than God's servant."

"No, your Excellency. You have a visitor."

"I do not have the time nor the patience." The Pope waved him away.

"He says it is important."

The Pope turned to the underling, his face unforgiving and impolite. "What could be so important?"

"He brings word from the...executive office."

The Pope looked up. He hadn't been told Jesus was sending anyone. "Send him in." The priest disappeared behind the door. The Pope heard him invite the man inside. The door moved a bit, and the symbol of his very office strode in. He removed his robe, glowing radiantly beneath. "Peter," the Pope breathed. Peter nodded as he stepped into the chamber.

"You have problems," Peter stated as the doors slammed shut.

An hour later Peter exited the chambers, the doors shutting quietly in the empty expanse of the papal residence. As he walked down the corridor, the moonlight streaming in through massive windows, his steps seemed to fade out as if his feet became lighter. Slowly their sound disappeared as the figured continued moving. His light complexion darkened, his glow dimming until he was a shadow that melted into those around it, disappearing in a world of shade.

***

Matthew sat at the long table, the President and his wife the only two joining him. The silence was awkward as everyone picked at their food. Matthew did not take his eyes off his plate, eating as slow as possible. His wine glass was empty. It had been emptied many times during the course of the meal. Maybe he should say something. Matthew glanced up briefly. "You're a good cook, Miss...uh...President."

"The chef cooked it," Mrs. Lucas corrected him. Matthew was back to ogling his plate in a nanosecond. "But I did choose the meal."

Matthew nodded, still looking down. Here he had the chance to speak to the most powerful man in the world, and he was blowing it. Why couldn't he just vent? God knows he had a lot of gripes with the government. Here he had a chance to get some answers, maybe make a difference, and he was talking about dinner. Dinner! *You're a good cook Mrs. President. Please, shoot me!*

"You are usually very outspoken." President Lucas assaulted the quiet.

"That's only if I have something to say," Matthew replied, looking up and then back down again.

"So you don't have anything worth saying?" The President smirked.

Did he just insult me? Matthew slowly raised his head. "I wouldn't say that." The alcohol-fueled anger emboldened Matthew. President or no President, this dick was not going to insult him. *Is this what our leaders think of us? That we can be used and abused!*

"Then what would you say?" The President took a sip from his glass.

"Well, uh...why exactly hasn't any effort been made to remove our dependence on gasoline? I do think I created a cleaner, cheaper method of fuel in my book or is literacy not one of your gifts?"

The President's fixed persona cracked ever so slightly. "It's all about jobs, Mr. Ford."

"Jobs?"

"Yes. If I were to simply remove gasoline from the market do you know what that would do? Oil refineries, the transporting industry, gas stations and more would face massive losses in profits. That means lay-offs. That means unemployment. I think my constituency needs jobs more than clean air."

"Yeah, you sure do need that corporate money for campaigning don't you?" Matthew spat, tapping his glass with his fork to inform them he was ready for another shot.

The President's smirk evaporated. "What are you insinuating?"

"Well," Matthew began, starting to become very animated and using his hands to enhance his words and shape his views, "since I need to explain it to you. You need money. Money to get elected. Now where does that money come from? Oh yes, the rich and corporate. But they aren't going to give you money for free. It's an investment to them. They're buying stock in the administration, and no one does that without a hand in the running of things. So you allow them access. Access to the President. Access to policy." Matthew picked up a crouton and crunched it in his mouth. "That access earns them profits. Those profits make them richer from which they grant you a kickback in the form of contributions which helps in the next election and continues the cycle. Is that simple enough for you?" Matthew picked at something in his teeth as the President flared.

"Of course we wouldn't have this conversation if there had been campaign finance reform. Pretty sad when how much you spend means more than what you have to say, especially since that money you spend was used to buy your soul." Matthew nodded his head, deep in thought as his glass was refilled. "Pretty sad, throwing it all away like that."

"Are you calling me corrupt?" the President asked, his knife and fork in hand ready for battle.

"No," Matthew replied. "Just the system."

"The system, as you call it, is democracy, and it has worked quite well for the past two hundred years."

"Maybe someone should check the expiration date. I think it has gone bad." Matthew smiled as he took a sip.

"How so?" the President asked coldly, clearly not expecting an answer.

"Well, last time I checked," Matthew began, scratching his nose, "most people don't vote. Wouldn't you take that as a silent protest against the way government is run? In fact," Matthew jabbed a fork at Lucas, "wouldn't you say that the majority don't even speak out on what they believe in. So really, only a minority does anything, and what they do is for the wrong reasons."

"Enlighten me," snarled President Lucas.

"Well, people vote for you if they have jobs, against you if they don't when we all know the economy has nothing to do with governmental policy, unless there is deficit spending of an appallingly irrational variety or...deals are made with campaign contributors for possible government contracts." Matthew winked at Lucas. "They vote because of tax cuts, programs they benefit from, because their parents did, because the candidate is attractive. They do not vote for the country. Those that vote are paid off or support what is virtually an aristocratic system.

"And when was the last time anyone even really knew what they were voting for? They're being led, blindly, by what others tell them, listening to sound bites and looking at the pretty photo ops rather than reading up on the candidates' political views and history. And look at those that guide the nation away from reason. There are campaigners who lie because they want their candidate to look electable otherwise they are out of a job. The Media lies because it is owned, in the end, by one person who determines which slant of the political spectrum to travel based on their own personal views. Even the government lies, only quietly, by claiming that any information that might be detrimental is classified. It's not rule of the many. It's rule by the few. It's tyranny."

"Are you calling me a tyrant?" Lucas leered baring his carnivorous canines.

"No," Matthew smacked his lips, looking up to return Lucas' gaze. "Incompetent, yes."

Lucas fought with himself to stay under control, nearly ripping the table cloth as he bunched it in his hands. "I think you are misinformed," he seethed.

"Then explain to me why we are in the Middle East looking for supposed weapons of mass destruction when North Korea was shown to actually possess nuclear weapons."

"Our intelligence said-"

"Intelligence? Seems a little ironic to me."

"Excuse me?"

"Well, there sure was a lack of it. Didn't it say there are nukes in Korea? It also said there may have been nukes in the Middle East. May have been. So we should go to the Middle East because they are the bigger threat?"

"We knew we could negotiate away the Korean threat-"

"Don't they still have nukes?"

"Yes."

"Don't they have missiles to launch them on?"

"Yes."

"Aren't they offering to sell those nukes to terrorists abroad? In fact, aren't they exchanging missiles for nukes with Pakistan right now?" The President was so close to attacking Matthew where he sat. Matthew smiled as he had another mouthful of food. Lucas' wife had sat frozen through the entire exchange.

Why not kill him? the President thought. *I do have immunity.*

An aide came up behind Lucas. "Sir, your national security meeting."

"Yes," Lucas replied, full of relief from this hell. He stood and turned to Matthew. "I'm sorry, Mr. Ford, but I really have to go. It has been a pleasant evening." He walked down to Matthew's seat and extended his hand to shake. Matthew gave him a wave good-bye, continuing to gobble his food. "Let me leave you with this, Mr. Ford. We all sell out eventually. It's the value that we hold sole control over. How much have you made from your book tour, by the way?" Matthew felt the barb as The President gave him one last, insulting look before following his aide out.

Matthew chewed on his lip. *Have I sold myself?* He turned to look over at Mrs. Lucas, still in a state of shock, her plate full. "You gonna eat that?"

***

The room was full as the President strode in trying to look as if he were king of the world. His approval ratings put him much lower than that. All assembled rose to give him his due, then sat as the meeting came to order. "What do you have for me today? Good news I hope. Maybe finally a war for some sort of popularity."

"Russia has not taken the bait. They refuse to strike at us."

"They'll crack," the President nodded.

"Sir," General Adams replied, "Europe is ordering us to demobilize or face our forces being removed from the continent entirely."

"Our own allies are turning on us?" The President was horrified.

"Sir, they think you mean to drive us into war which you are doing. I think we should do as they say."

"Don't you dare to give me orders!" the President yelled, stabbing a finger at the General. "Our forces are staying. I will not allow those Soviets another try at world conquest."

"Sir, they aren't trying to conquer anything. They even withdrew from Chechnya!"

"It's a ploy. They'll strike when we're most vulnerable!"

General Adams let out a loud breath. "Sir, they aren't capable! We are overstretched as it is. Our forces in the Middle East are finding themselves under intense attack by fundamentalists. We cannot supply both Eastern Europe and the Middle East indefinitely. With tension heating up in North Korea and China," General Adams was weary of all this, "we're set to break apart under the strain. China has sent another fleet to Taiwan and issued an ultimatum against the plebiscite. We can't keep pressure on them if our forces are shifted elsewhere. We're destined to fail."

"Your job is to make sure that doesn't happen!" Brown retorted. "You have the resources of the world's strongest army. Make the most of it!"

"You little fucking prick!" General Adams screamed at Brown. "You can lick his," the General pointed at President Lucas, "shit and tell him it tastes like ice cream all you want but this is serious business. We are on the road to a major problem!"

"Don't speak to him like that!" Brown choked out. "He is your," Brown punched Adams in the chest, "commander, and you will follow his orders."

"Touch me again, you liberal bastard, and I will use you to grease the gears of a division's tanks."

"Don't threaten me, you totalitarian hillbilly."

Adams went to leap over the table. Only a few able generals prevented hostility, dragging Adams back into his chair and whispering into his ear. Adams clearly wanted to rearrange Brown's anatomy.

"And you expect me to listen to a man as reckless as you," Lucas replied to the antics of Adams. Adams looked insulted, held his mouth, and crossed his arms on his chest forcing himself to remain at least complacent enough to remain in the meeting. "Send our remaining reserves to the troubled areas. They'll hold." Adams was about to protest. "They'll hold! What else do we have?"

"Protests are starting to arise all over the nation, Mr. President."

"Protests? Protests always happen. What's so important about these?"

"Mr. President, they are destroying stores and attacking restaurants. Casualties have already reached well over a hundred."

"Can't the local police handle it?" Lucas asked.

"Mr. President, the various states are having to call out their national guard units to even keep the semblance of peace."

"What exactly is the problem?" Lucas couldn't comprehend what could make Americans so unhappy. The U.S. had everything.

"Mr. President, it's the obese."

"Excuse me?" Lucas replied.

"They've been whipped up into a fury. Claim they are being abused. They don't make much sense."

"Fat people are destroying food and food providers?" Lucas couldn't believe it. "The world has turned upside down."

"I wonder whose fault that is," Adams replied.

***

"So, Matthew, how would you feel about your own television show?" Fred Furnace looked over arched fingers, silently calculating his guest. It had only been a week since meeting the President, and now, it seemed like the world was in Matthew's grasp.

"Well," Matthew sat uncomfortably in the ornate chair beneath him. Waiters passed by as if not noticing anything between the kitchen and their table. The chatter was heavy. "It sounds like a nice offer."

"I am prepared to offer whatever it takes."

"I'm not really photogenic–"

"That's what make-up and lighting is for. You...have a message, Matthew. These people," Fred swept his hand around the room, "want that message. They need it. They want you to give it to them. My station can make it happen. We want to make it happen."

Matthew sat there listening to what they wanted, what they wanted to give him. They spoke of numbers and dollars, of fame and fads. None of it made sense to Matthew. None of it appealed to him. He had become a product. This auction for his soul had reduced his feelings to that of worthlessness. Who he was no longer mattered. "I..." Fred leaned forward, fixing those predatory eyes on Matthew. "I really need to..." Matthew pointed to the back.

"Of course. Oh, and Matthew." Matthew stopped on his way to the bathroom. "Don't piss this away." Fred started laughing.

"That's funny," Matthew replied grinning, that grin vanishing the minute he turned around. This new world he had stepped into was too false for his liking. He found refuge in the men's room where shit had its proper place. He moved

201

up to one of the urinals to release the remnants of the wine he'd had.

"You should take the show."

Matthew jumped, his urine spraying to the side. "Why are you in here? I don't like being watched while I...you know." The Devil turned around. "I don't see how any of this is actually helping. Exactly how am I getting back at Jesus?"

"Can't you see? Your name is everywhere. You are 'it' right now. Jesus is old news."

"Yeah, well that doesn't answer my question. Besides," Matthew shook and went to wash his hands, "I am tired of all the attention. This is just too much. I don't sleep, I barely eat, and I am tired of talking." Matthew took a deep breath, a sigh at the realization for all he had he hadn't earned. He was still nothing. "It's you they are talking about, not me." Matthew looked in the mirror at himself, not seeing that usual reflection. He had changed. "All I've done...all I do...causes problems. Haven't you seen the news? The fat riots. Now who do you think encouraged that? I have these chances, and all I do is make things worse. I just want to go back to normal. At least then my mistakes only affected me."

"You don't know what you're saying," Satan chuckled.

Matthew tired of how lightly Satan took him and his problems. "Why doesn't anyone listen to me? Just...listen?"

Matthew rinsed his hands in the sink, bringing the water up to wash his face. The powder came off revealing the acne below. He looked at himself, his true self, in the mirror. "People look to me for answers. What do I know?" Matthew turned to the Devil. "These clothes aren't me. This hair," Matthew mussed it up with his hands. "I'm not me. I feel so empty. I feel..." Matthew closed his eyes. "Alone. Even more now than ever."

Matthew turned to the Devil. "I want my anonymity back. I want to be forgotten. I want to believe in what I do. Not feel guilty and sickened by every word that chokes my throat and stains my honesty. It's what I deserve. I'm tired of the glare of the spotlight, the blinding light of fucking fame." Matthew sniffed, shaking his head.

"You wanted to make a difference," Satan offered.

"What difference? Even now things are worse than they've ever been. For my happiness others must suffer. How can that make me happy knowing the price? People twist what I say, use me as a reason to do the worst things possible. I don't want to be a symbol. Not that type of symbol. At least when I was normal it didn't spill over into other people's lives. It was mine alone. As it was meant to be." Matthew gave the Devil a good look. "I thank you for giving me the chance. I just can't take it. What good is being something I'm not? I was never meant for this."

Satan grabbed Matthew by the wrist. "Don't say that! You always wanted to be something more. You can have anything. You are-"

"I'm nothing but your puppet." Matthew pulled away. "I can't say what I want. I can't be who I want to be. I'm not making a difference. I'm taking advantage of people, stealing their hopes and cashing it in for such worthless wealth. In a year I've done nothing but talk. No rest, no break, just talking. I'd rather be average and happy than worshiped and a lie. At least then, I would be me." Matthew waved the Devil to quiet. "All I ever wanted was...to stop feeling so damn lonely. To really know why..." Matthew looked deep into the eyes of his reflection when he heard something. "What was that?"

The Devil shrugged as a dagger flew through the air and just missed Matthew, shattering the mirror. In the cracked reflection Matthew saw a man in a suit pulling what seemed to be another dagger. He lunged towards Matthew. Matthew sidestepped the assassin and made for the door nearly losing his balance on the slick floor. He tore through the restaurant, past Fred's table. "I'll let you know," he said between gasping breaths. The assassin came after him.

"Damn cutthroat competition!" Fred yelled after the man.

Matthew found himself outside, the blaze of car lights blinding in the night. The assassin was gaining. Matthew leaped straight into traffic. Cars shrieked across the pavement, horns blasting at him. One car nearly ran him down. Matthew was lucky as it came to a stop but inches in front of him. Matthew ran to the passenger side door and wildly pointed for the woman to open it. He barely closed the door behind him before the assassin's knife came down scratching the paint. "Go!" Matthew yelled. The woman hit the gas, and they pulled away. The assassin punched a number into his cell phone as he followed the fleeing car on foot.

"Hey, you're Matthew Ford!" the driver squealed.

"Yeah."

"I totally never thought I'd meet someone like you-"

"Watch the road!" The woman just missed a car as they drove on.

"Sorry. I don't normally drive like this. It's just...you're a celebrity."

"Thanks." They came to a red light and stopped. "I think I'll be getting out now." As Matthew opened his door another car zoomed up fast knocking it clean off. "Sorry," Matthew sheepishly apologized as he began to step out. The men in the other car pulled out pistols. "Whoa! I said I was sorry!" As they went to aim, Matthew jumped into the backseat. They fired every shot they had as Matthew fumbled with the door and fell out the driver's side, covering his head as he ran.

"Get him!" The one yelled to the other as they hurried after him.

"God damn road rage!" Matthew screamed as he ran through the streets. Where to go? He didn't know this place. "Oh boy." The two men were coming closer. He started to run again but saw the assassin from the restaurant ahead of him. Surrounded! He couldn't go back into the street; the cars were speeding by. That left the alley. Matthew ran into its dark recesses hoping its shadows would hide him.

Matthew sprinted the entire length. He saw a fire escape and jumped for the rung. Once, twice, three times he missed. He looked everywhere. Dead-end. The only place left was the dumpster.

The three men came together and walked down the narrow alley, ready to strike. "We know you're down here," one of them said in an accented voice. "God has led us to you, and now we shall destroy you."

"Jesus has sent hit men? Lamb my ass," Matthew muttered.

The three made their way to the end of the alley and saw the brick wall. They turned to look for other avenues of escape and found the dumpster alone. They surrounded it, weapons drawn. The one started to say something. "Don't give him last rites."

"Why not? He is about to die."

"He is the Antichrist! You don't help the Antichrist into Heaven!"

"If we condemn him are we any better than he is?"

"Marcos, I swear you are too liberal!"

"Look who is talking. This is supposed to be a secret, and here you and Giorgio are shooting up everything in sight."

The alleyway quickly found itself bathed in a red light. The three turned in surprise to see the police had arrived. "We must kill him quickly!"

"Hold it right there," the policeman screamed, pulling his revolver out. "Make a move and it's your last!"

"The son of Satan is in this trashcan!" Marcos yelled pointing at the dumpster.

"Frank," the cop said over his shoulder. "Better get narcotics down here." He steadily started towards the three. "Get down on the ground!"

"What do we do?" Giorgio asked.

"The laws of man don't usurp the laws of God!" Fabrizio ripped the lid off the dumpster, seeing Matthew inside, and raised his pistol to shoot only to be hit by gunfire.

"We're not with him," Marcos sputtered as the cop ordered them to the ground again.

"Damn fools!" The Devil put his head in his hand as he watched the debacle from the mouth of the alley.

Matthew poked his head out to see what was going on. "Thank God!" Matthew virtually sang.

"Yes, Amen!" The Devil gave a finger to the sky.

"Are you alright sir?"

"Yes." Matthew stumbled out of the dumpster to the waiting police car.

***

"And you have no idea why they were after you?" the policeman asked.

"I know it wasn't for an autograph if that's what you mean," Matthew quipped.

"Ok then, we'll need you to come by the station tomorrow for some more paperwork."

"You cannot let him go!" Marcos urged, trying to break free from the officer holding him.

206

"Get in the car, freak!" the cop ordered, trying to force him in.

"Now that's no way to talk to a man of God," the Devil whispered into the cop's ear, catching him completely by surprise.

"What the hell?" The cop jerked around to see who had spoken. That was all the time Marcos needed as he jumped, bringing his cuffed arms in front of him, and yanked the revolver from the cop's holster. The cop went to tackle Marcos. As he took him down a gun shot went off, striking Matthew in the chest. Matthew fell backwards, the world seeming to slow immeasurably. The light of reality drained, the color washing out. Sound began to warble, like cotton had been placed in his ears. Matthew blinked his eyes as he looked up into the gray sky. There was no noise. Matthew sat up. The police were still wrestling with that nut. He stood up to let them know he was alright.

"Hey," Matthew called to the cop. "Close one, huh? Don't worry I'm ok. Learn to shoot, pal," Matthew mocked, smiling as he pointed. No one seemed to notice him. One of the cops spoke mutely into his radio as his partner continued wrestling with the assassin. "Guys?"

"Bitch ain't it?" Matthew turned to see the Devil leaning against the side of a building, smiling that wicked grin of yellow teeth and black grime. Smoke poured from his mouth, cigarette to the side.

Matthew looked at him cautiously. "What's going on?"

The Devil started to chuckle, his face taking on a sadistic delight of twisted happiness. He slowly extended his arm, rolling it out to full length. His hand rotated on its joint, his dirty fingers stretching as if to present something. Matthew followed those fingers to...himself? Matthew looked down at his gasping body, blood pumping out. He felt the prickle of thousands of needles up his back.

His head jerked up to Satan whose face had altered perceptively. Scars and sores marred his once solid, leathery skin. His teeth began to rot. As he laughed a smog belched out, black and oily. Matthew looked around in a frenzy. The city was empty. The streets were deserted. Only him, Satan, and his body remained. "Am I...?"

"Oh, it's game over." Satan smirked, his body expanding. Bones snapped and muscles groaned as his clothes ripped under the pressure of his growing frame. When he was through, Satan stood near twelve feet tall. Remnants of his pants served as a loin cloth for the serpent between his legs. "For you at least. I have plans for your mortal real estate." He stretched, his lithe muscles showing through thin skin. He popped his neck with relief. He stopped rolling his head when Matthew's body came into view. He knelt down next to it. He looked it up and down, muttering to himself before turning back to Matthew. "It might be a...tad small," Satan gave that sorrowful scowl as he used two fingers to gauge an inch, "But it should fit me nicely."

"That's my body!" Matthew yelled. He lost that courage quickly as Satan stood up and gave him a very angry glare. Satan stomped towards Matthew, seeming to glide across the concrete. "Hey, take it." Matthew started to back away. "Maybe you can do more with it than I did."

The Devil snatched Matthew by the throat and dragged him face to blistered face. "It isn't yours to give, child!" He threw Matthew against a light post. Matthew braced for the impact only to fly through it and skid across the ground. Matthew didn't know what to think, laying there in shock as the Devil approached, sores and veins erupting across his damned form. "You humans think you control everything. As if you are the dominant species."

The Devil punted Matthew right in the face knocking him into a 180-degree turn onto his back before being grabbed by the leg and lifted. "So much better," Satan oozed as he continued to stretch. The Devil had ceased transforming, a mild pot belly at his waste his only laughable trait. His body was a collection of tattoos, scars, bruises, and pain. His head was nearly bare of hair, what was there long and black. His skin was an unpleasant purple.

Matthew dangled there, looking into Hell's very visage. Yellow eyes of burning damnation pulsated an evil glow. "Bad day?" Matthew asked swallowing what little bravery remained.

"Oh, I've had a few bad millennia. But," Satan laughed a deep bass. "That's about to change."

"I'm happy to hear that." Matthew gave a false smile.

"You're breed scares so easily." Satan looked into Matthew's face. In a second it seemed to split open, a mangled hunk of meat with fangs and bright red eyes bursting out. "Argh!" Satan howled.

"Oh shit!" Matthew yelled, covering his eyes. He peeked between them when the laughter started again.

"So this is what hides within your flesh." Satan gave Matthew's soul a measured look. "Can't say I'm impressed."

"Look who's talking you fucking backstabber." Satan pulled him closer, his breath scorching the spiritual skin of Matthew's face. "Oh boy," he whimpered.

"Do you think I owe you anything? What rights do you have to anything? Your breed was made in violence. You were conceived in destruction, the destruction of my land. Of my home! It is programmed into you, your genes. The need to destroy, to take away. You hold nothing sacred. Your breed personifies the fall of Perfection, the flaw in Heaven from which it is dying, bleeding from an age old wound. You profit from our loss!" Satan's voice became guttural. "You were never meant to be, you flawed figure of fucking failure! You are a virus that I have wanted to wipe out for countless ages. Now, no one will stop me from doing so!" He choked on his rage before forcing his anger beneath the surface. "Besides, didn't you say you didn't want all of this anymore?" Satan gave him that broken grin before it fell apart and sank into his darkest emotions. "It was mine before it was ever yours. All of it!" he thundered in the vast grayness.

"Ok, it's all yours." Matthew tried to do a mock cheer while hanging upside down by one leg. It didn't seem to help matters. Satan continued to glower at the insult. "You got my body so can't you let me down?"

Satan smiled, the dried skin of his lips splitting. "Oh you shall be dropped." He snapped his finger, jagged nails at the ends, and the street shattered like glass, reality rended, to reveal a dark hole that rumbled with rushing wind. Matthew looked at the hole then back at Satan who continued to smile that decrepit smile. "You shall fall...for eternity." He heaved Matthew into the air. Matthew thrashed as he flew up, trying to find something to hold on to, but nothing came within reach. Down into the darkness he fell, screaming. Reality sealed over the hole, and it vanished as if it had never been.

***

"Where is my baby? Where is my baby?" Matthew's mom screamed as she ran through the hospital ward, her heels tapping hysterically over the sterile floors as she stuck her head in room after room. His dad and the leading physician chased after her. "Mattie? Mattie Pooh?" She peeked behind a curtain, garnering a shriek. "Mattie Pooh?" she yelled continuing through the ward terrorizing the inhabitants.

210

"Mrs. Ford! You must wait!" The physician was just not able to catch up to her. "Is she always so-"

"Psychotic?" Matthew's dad completed the sentence. "Trust me. Be happy he's not terminal!"

Matthew's mom nearly kicked in a door. "Matthew? Matthew!" she screamed. She found him on the bed, trying to finish what passed for food in this place. Her tight embrace caused him to moan and twist in her grasp.

The doctor came in behind her. "Mrs. Ford, the gunshot wound!"

"Get off of me!" Matthew ordered shoving his mother back with such force she hit the wall.

"What's wrong with you, boy," his father asked. "That's your mother. You don't know what it took for her to come here."

Matthew looked at her with callous eyes. "No, she's not my mother. She never was."

"Matthew," she cried, her eyes swelling and bleeding sorrow.

"Get away from me. Both of you. You were never there for me when I needed you. Now you care?" Matthew's eyes narrowed. "I don't need you anymore."

His father was shocked at what his son had said. His mother started back towards Matthew. "Matthew you don't-"

Matthew picked up his tray and threw it at her. "Didn't you hear me? I want you out of my life!"

His mother died inside, her heart unable to handle the loss of her son. She collapsed on the ground, dead by cardiac arrest. "Mary?" his father dropped beside her. "Mary?" The physician ran out the door to get help as Matthew looked down on his suffering parents and smiled.

CHAPTbEginsR 8

Matthew and Peter Prince sat together on the set of Peter's political pundit program, "Sacrifice the Spin". Peter looked into the camera as he introduced his guest. "Tonight we are with self-help guru-"

"I prefer personal savior," Matthew cut in, speaking noticeably faster. The light failed to glisten off of his powdered face, the glare of the studio shining off his shades causing his eyes to become twin pools of light.

"Matthew Ford. Now you are involved in a growing controversy involving your dieting plan."

"I don't consider it so much a controversy surrounding me as much as surrounding our culture in general."

Peter Prince gave him an odd look. "Let me fill you in on the current state of affairs. Assaults are up all over the world, America the leader as we always are in all things. Restaurants, especially fast food, are being targeted for violence. People are being dragged out and beaten in the streets. The culprits are largely those following your fasting diet plan."

"You have to look at this from their perspective. They aren't to blame for these urges and uncontrollable acts. Society is." Matthew turned to the camera. "Our rotten, corrupt society." He turned back, with a smile, to Peter Prince.

Peter seemed confused but continued to silently agree with Matthew. "How do you mean?"

"Our culture is hypocritical. It places the pretty, thin people above the common man. Look at magazines, movies, television. How often do you see the regular man? Rarely! You see the athletic, gorgeous, immaculate few that make up the world. Statistics even show them to be the minority.

Now what does this say to the common man? That they are ugly. That they are not what people want to see. That they belong in zoos for being the animals that they are in order to be pointed at and ridiculed for the freaks society makes them out to be.

"Then there is the teasing of food. It is everywhere, on every street corner. How can those weighed down by poor genetics hope to lose weight when a donut taunts them at a traffic light or if a burger grills in front of their eyes in sizzling succulence on the television screen? Besides, food today isn't even fit to eat. Always filled with hormones to fatten the beef, sugar to sweeten it, grease to enhance the flavor. There is nothing out there to eat that is worth eating.

"Society laughs at them as it hypocritically says be thin and then makes it impossible, encouraging this disease known as obesity. It's enough to drive a society mad.

"But how are we to cope? How does society say we should deal with our problems? Through wanton violence and destruction. Look at the highest grossing movies. All that action and the boom booming of explosions. And have you seen what is popular in music? The smacking of bitches. Violence is all around us. The voices continually say destroy destroy destroy.

"And when you see these poor people lashing out it isn't at those they hurt. Each victim is actually a symbol of this crazed culture, which abuses them. A society that is hypocritical and malicious. They don't hate you. They hate themselves. They should be pitied. It is society which should be held responsible. Society needs a change. Society needs to evolve with the people. It is time for a new order, and I am willing to lead that revolution."

Peter turned to the camera. "Fascinating."

"These days society is all about the image. It is a shallow, hollow world we live in. As long as you appear to be immaculate, perfect, beyond the grasp of the common person you literally are. Our President is a prime example. Did he get elected because of his views on policy? Polls show many did not even know where he stood on the issues! The man simply looked good on camera with his designer suits, slicked back hair, and ready smile. The man is only an image, nothing more. He is a symbol, a figurehead. He does what he is told to do."

"Who tells him what to do?" Peter Prince asked, mugging for the camera.

"Big business of course. The man must earn his campaign funds, after all. But then, isn't that the problem today?"

"What is that, Matthew?"

"These days campaigning is the only thing that government does. They spend more days speaking about themselves to the public rather than speaking amongst themselves on policy. All this talk on what should be and no action on what must be. Words are not solid. Words do not get things done. Is it no wonder that legislation takes so long to pass, especially useful legislation? Then again, they are beholden to the holders of their purse strings to even be where they are. If the people cry out for help they are not heard by these so called representatives who spend their time in their lofty abodes away from us, the common people. When corporations hint at a need these bureaucrats are more than happy to rush to action. What does this say? That the needs of the few, supported and enhanced by money, are more important than the needs of the majority. Isn't democracy about the will of the many?"

"President Lucas has spoken out against what you are saying. That what you actually speak of is supported by the actions of your followers, that you yearn for chaos. That you, and I quote, 'support not the rule of the majority but mob rule itself'."

"One man's mob is another's protest. We protest a government that gives to those that have too much and takes from those who suffer for a few dollars a day. They placate us with vile, petty offerings only because these gifts serve to enrich them further when they steal them back, with interest, at a later date. We have become their cattle to milk and butcher as they see fit. Mindless creatures that wander wherever they wish us to go." Matthew looked into the camera. "But no more."

Peter Prince turned to the camera, nodding his head. "We'll be back right after these messages."

"And...we're clear," the cameraman said.

Peter turned to Matthew, giving him a pained expression. "Blah, blah, blah." He laughed as Matthew stared back sternly. "We've heard this song and dance before. Don't you have anything new, anything fresh?"

"What do you mean?" Matthew asked, clearly annoyed.

"Well, let's face it. No one is watching you for your looks." Peter snorted as he laughed some more. Matthew gave him a very cold stare. "You've got to keep it new, keep it fresh. What are you trying to do? Drill your ideas into their skulls?"

"That is exactly what I am trying to do," Matthew replied. "Sometimes it takes more than one blow to make a breakthrough."

"We're on in ten seconds," the cameraman warned.

"Just give me something with substance," Peter urged.

"Oh, I will," Matthew smirked as the cameraman counted down with his fingers.

215

"Welcome back, fellow Americans. I am here with the controversial," Peter rolled his eyes, "Matthew Ford. Matthew, you are quite outspoken on so many issues. In fact, you have been railing against the Catholic Church recently, since your near death a few weeks ago. Why is that?"

"It is quite simple, Peter. They are a terrorist organization."

Peter Prince felt that instinctual shiver down his spine. This was controversial. This was inflammatory. This was ratings. "How so?"

"I was not simply the victim of some random attack. I was singled out for assassination."

"Why is that, Matthew?"

"Because, Peter, I threaten to tip the balance. I am opening the eyes of the common man to the fact that they have been manipulated for centuries, countless generations. The Church itself is one of the earliest to exploit us, the common man. They want us to listen to their views, accept their rulings without resistance. They want to be gods here on Earth. They do not like what I have to say."

"How can you be sure of this? This is very explosive, even slanderous."

"I have here," Matthew waved a few sheets of paper in the air, "the autopsy done on the body of the one dead assassin as well as the personal information of the other two murderers gathered via interrogation and background checks by federal investigators. It seems these men are priests, residents of Vatican City itself."

Matthew handed the papers to Peter Prince who snatched them hungrily, his smile broadening as he looked over them, his eyes devouring every word that sweetened the story and refusing those bitter paragraphs that only threatened front page villainy. "He is correct America," Peter replied, trying to look somber and serious. "Why has this not been made public?"

"Why do you think?" Matthew replied. "I was told to keep quiet on this classified situation. Quiet about the threat to my very life. Why? Because of the large Catholic population in this country. The United States does not wish to act out against a power that would threaten the electoral chances of those in power. I call them hypocrites.

"We passed an act, the Patriot Act, to protect not only our nation but destroy those that would infringe on and assault our great state from within as well as without via a preemptive strike. Is it not time to invoke that act against the Holy See?

"Have we not seen the dangerous and exploitive organization known as the Catholic Church? The scandals, the abuse, and now the attacks on my person. These are not the acts of an upstanding and charitable group. This is an organized criminal enterprise protected by our government simply because of the hold they hold on the public. They are nothing more than the most powerful and exploitive corporation of all! They support attacks on abortion clinics, outright murder. How many murderers, rapists, and worse have confessed their crimes to priests only to be allowed continual freedom simply because the Church refused to turn them in? How many wars have been started because of the inflammatory doctrine and encouragement of the Church? What of the crusades, the inquisitions, the Holocaust? To this day the Church remains racist against Jews and discriminatory against Muslims and all other sects. They value only those that fill their coffers regardless of how much blood stains each bill. The Pope never once has spoken out against the excesses of Cuba, the evils of sloth inducing socialism.

"Yet the Pope continually derides American culture. Why? Because we ask questions. We want to know why. We are not some mindless sheep in need of a shepherd! We are human beings with a right to know why we are made to do something so that we gain the most from it and avoid the exploitation of our forefathers. We are not their slaves!

"They cry out to think of those with so little while they wear their silken robes and drink from silver chalices. Our governments defend the very vipers of our age, pressed tightly against their bosom, allowed to strike at us in passing only to hide under the coat of our elected officials. It is time to act. Against this order. Against this injustice. Against this age. It is time for change!"

"And...we're out," the cameraman dropped his hand to show they had ceased filming.

"That was good. Really good," Peter Prince virtually sang as he spoke to Matthew. "May I make copies for the news services?"

"Of course. That is what they are there for."

"It was an honor meeting you." Peter stood and leaned over to pump Matthew's hand in a hearty handshake before hurrying off.

Matthew rose, walking through the set towards the back and his dressing room. The false interview room gave way to wide open space where the crew was dispersing for the night. Matthew opened his dressing room door and shut it quietly behind himself. He turned to look at his reflection in the mirror. He gazed at himself as if at a stranger. He ran the back of his hand against his cheek, smiling at the touch.

***

Matthew fell through the darkness. It was scary at first, the outright loss of control, his phobia of heights jacking up his adrenaline and driving him into a mad frenzy. Without knowing it he had instinctively tried flapping his arms as if to fly; comical but not helpful. Matthew's voice grew hoarse as he screamed, his shrieking echoing through the vast darkness.

After awhile, he stopped yelling. His fear ebbed into numbness as his fall continued. Without an end in sight what terrible mortal conclusion did he have to fear? He began to look around the void into which he fell: no stars, no moon, no sun. *Geeze, this place was dark.* He scanned everywhere he could see and found his eyes veiled by inky blackness.

After an hour of visual exploration he grew very bored of the whole drop. Even death by now would have been preferable. He maneuvered around as he fell, pretending he was a superhero flying through the air. "Cannonball!" he yelled as he bunched up, grabbing his legs with his arms, spinning through the sparse sky. He laughed a little as he tried other positions. He imagined he was on a flying carpet, striking a pose of meditation. He started doing back flips, over and over again. "And the record for most flips in a row, me, Matthew Ford!" he proclaimed, putting his hands up as if the winner of some large contest.

Eventually he fell asleep. He snored a bit, the free falling relaxing and comforting. His body jerked awake, his leg kicking bringing him back to consciousness. "God, I dreamt I was fall-" he started before screaming in fear. He got a hold of himself. "Oh wait. Yeah." He chuckled remembering the past few hours. Or was it days? Maybe even weeks! He shrugged it off. At least his fear of heights was gone.

Wait. What was that? Matthew looked down. Clouds! Why were there clouds? Matthew's body was outstretched, his

chest pointed downwards, as his body pierced the dark
smoke. Everything around him was fog; cold fog. Matthew
opened his mouth to catch some of it in his mouth in order to
taste it. He was still mouthing as if chewing when the last of
the clouds fell away. Matthew's gnawing on insubstantial
smoke ended when he saw what was below: solid ground.

"Oh shit!" Matthew screamed as he fell faster and faster to
the lands below. It shone with some unseen light, glistening
like a calm sea. Matthew's reflexes kicked in again as he first
tried to climb back to the clouds then flapped his arms
violently for flight. Gravity did not comply.

He hit with a thwuck into the muddy ground, embedded in
the muck. The impact took the air right out of him. Matthew
remained sprawled, face down, in the inky sludge for a few
minutes in shock. He gradually raised his head, a sucking
sound as he removed it from the night soil. His body was still
in one piece. He checked to see if he was paralyzed. His
arms worked, fingers too. He pushed himself up, his hands
partially sinking into the bog.

"Where am I?" Matthew asked the cold air, his words
fading away in white smoke. His face was smeared black,
his clothes stained. There was no light save for a weird
luminance that seemed natural to the air. Matthew did his
best to scrape the sludge off his pants, large chunks sticking
to his hands and drying on his legs. This place was barren.
No trees, no grass, just miles of flat, black slime. Matthew
scanned the indiscernible darkness. Where to go? One way
was as good as another. Matthew started off, unsure of
where he was going but hoping for the best in this the worst
of places.

***

"What I'm saying is you shouldn't have to take it
anymore!" Matthew screamed to the crowd. He had ceased

to wear make-up, the acne scarring his face. To either side of him were two large banners, hung vertically, with Matthew's towering presence glaring down upon the crowd from the stage. He stood there, behind a podium, his word reaching out to the thousands in attendance. Eager faces searched his, letting him be their voice. He was the personification they sought.

"Yeah!" the hundreds of thousands screamed back. The stadium was packed to the rafters with the obese. They stared with rapt attention.

"They set the styles, the standards, the fashions. What right do they have to tell us how to live, how to look, how to act? We are the majority. We should be the trend setters!"

"Yeah!"

"What have they told us, my brothers and sisters? They tell us that looks matter. That image is everything. Looks fade. Image is only skin deep. What matters is the substance beyond the façade, and what I see beyond the illusions they hide behind is a world that neither you nor I should be forced to suffer through!" Matthew's head jerked as he spoke, his body communicating his insanity, his anger, his pent up personality welded together of frustration, impatience, and fury. His oily hair swung about him revealing the increased thinning, his bare scalp becoming noticeable.

"Yeah!"

"Look at me." Matthew pointed at his face, the horrid acne that had grown worse over the past few days. "To them I am worthless. Why? Is it because I have nothing to say? No! You all know I have something to say. Is it because of how I look? Why should my looks matter? Why should looks matter at all? How long have we been withheld from what we deserved simply because of our appearances? Appearances are deceiving. Am I ugly? Are you ugly? Are you worthless simply because of the way you were conceived?" Matthew was a madman, the tendons in his neck stretched and visible like thick cords beneath his skin.

"No!"

"They attain all they want because of their birthright. Name, money, looks. This is not democracy. This is not right. You should earn your place! You should work towards your rewards! They tell you they care while they misuse and abuse you, laughing behind your backs and relegating you to dull, pathetic existences while they play their games and waste away their lives in a pleasurable world we are barred from. The games are over!" Matthew's saliva was thickening. He choked and spit the foam as his vile thoughts possessed the innocent minds of the masses, polluting their clarity and senses.

"Yeah!"

"Illusions. We live in a world of illusions. We are told that we are happy when we aren't. The reality of the world is manipulated to fit what those who enslave us believe. Our views don't matter to them. We don't matter to them! They make us feel small and insignificant to their regime. They push this lie of our own inferiority before us time and again. They tell us because we are common, because we are flawed we are not capable of the dreams that are their reality. Their reality! Not ours! This, my friends, is the worst type of oppression. They have made us into a lower, subservient class. They have stripped us of our dignity, of our self-esteem. To them we are nothing. We are cows to fatten and corral, to exploit and butcher without a thought. My friends, to me, you are something. You are a force to be reckoned with." The crowd looked at him, crying and enraptured.

Matthew smiled at them, his hidden eyes scanning theirs beneath arched brows. "I know it is hard, refusing their food, their rewards for compliance. The pain, the suffering, the weakness. But it is worth it. They keep you down, unable to act against their injustices. Their buffalo wings and baby back ribs fill your mouths so you can't question. They keep you addicted to them so that you can't find the strength to say no more. Well, I say no more to them! It is time, my friends! Time for a new order! Our time!" Matthew tore the microphone from the podium and stepped before it, mere feet from the reaching hands of his followers as they went wild with passion, losing themselves to the moment, to this mass hysteria.

"Yeah!"

"It is time to do what we always knew must be done. Take my hand and let me lead you through the lies, the illusions, and the darkness! Though they blind you I shall enlighten you! I shall save you! I am the way! I am your salvation! It is time!" Matthew seemed to grow with his words, his presence filling the stadium. "It is time to take back this country, this continent, this world! Let the revolution begin!" Matthew howled to the sky as the stadium shook with their cries.

***

This place was deserted. Then again, swamp wasn't exactly the ideal spot to meet people. Sky and soil seemed to merge into one solid mass between which Matthew was sandwiched. To say he felt depressed was an understatement. To say he finally found a place worse than Heaven was another. Well, almost as bad as Heaven. Matthew's feet were sucked down with each step he took, pounds added to each wearying step as his feet brought up the damned mud with it. Slurps and urks were his only company as he traveled the dark lands ahead.

No sun, no moon, no stars: this place was empty except for the mud; lots of mud. If only mud could talk, or move, or dry up. His pants were sheathed in a cracking mass of dried muck, his hair and face as black as the horizon.

And the smell! Matthew had dug up his parents' sewage tank, and this stuff rivaled even the most nauseating of smells that gray goop belched up. He pulled his ruined shirt up over his nose and buttoned the top button to hold it there.

As he made his way through the mounds of shit he began to wonder if he would ever see another soul and if he did, having lived in this place, would he want to?

His trek was grating on his mental stability. He had always wanted to be alone but somewhere ideal like a college dorm, a movie theater, or possibly even a library. He never wished to be alone in the largest toilet bowl in existence. "Please flush me," he begged to no one in particular save the creator of this massive dung pile.

With hope fading he began to break down, his steps dragging and his head downcast, until he saw it. Light, bright light! Life! It was life! Matthew sped up his slurping, the sound of his feet racing like farts in the wind. The light grew brighter as he came closer before skidding to a halt and falling on his back.

Figures, strange figures, wandered from the pale light. They were hunched over, broken, straggling about after one another. Some seemed to limp while others crawled. The light that bathed them was a cold white that accentuated their agony and suffering. Their eyes were hollowed out, twin holes staring at Matthew. He started to back up, slipping in the muck and unable to take his eyes off these ancient horrors. These broken creatures lusted towards him, hungry for his soul. "I'm definitely not going that way," he said to himself as he tried to get back up again. He continued to slip as the creatures came closer.

The faces of these lost spirits were lined with ages of existence, their teeth rotten or already gone leaving their mouths gaping maws like mole holes in the ground. Some moved as if their bones were shattered. Others staggered on, greatly exhausted. Their skin was a lusterless ivory so thin it was transparent to the bleached bone beneath. A soul touching moan crawled from their throats, a rasp like desert wind.

"Uh, guys," Matthew began, making unsteady progress across the muddy ground. "Maybe you have me mixed up with someone else." They continued to stumble towards him.

He felt a chill, some frigid aura that covered them stretching out to claw at his skin. The muck sucked at his arms, trying to prevent his escape. They were closing in, the distance collapsing under their uncaring and focused assault. They continued on, no other purpose in their pathetic lives.

They loomed over Matthew as he laid there, their light drowning him. He was shaking, the puffs of smoke chugging like a choo choo from his mouth between bared teeth. Crystals of ice had formed in his hair and over his pleading eyes. The wraiths towered over him, their bodies emaciated and diseased. They were the wandering dead. They craved the energy of his new soul, this fresh life. How alive he was to them and their dull flames of being. Their eyes desired his, still locked in their sockets. They opened their broken jaws; the rasp came spilling out like plague. Their tongues had dried and withered, the stumps waving in the putrid gas. They reached for him, their bony fingers creaking and their joints cracking.

"Wait!" Matthew yelled, breaking the horrific scene. The wraiths backed up a bit, startled at the first sound they'd heard in years. Matthew knew his opportunity for freedom wouldn't last long. "Look!" he yelled, pointing behind them. "It's Jesus!" The wraiths turned around, fully trusting his dishonesty. Their moans were hopeful. Matthew nearly slid as he got up, running off. The wraiths turned around, anger twisting their already cursed faces. Matthew turned from their light to allow the darkness to take him away into this land of nothingness.

***

Their feet shook the ground as they marched on. It had started with Matthew and a few of his followers but had grown. With each foot a new member joined. At each block their numbers increased. As their force was seen it swelled. Each mile gave it more power, more momentum, more substance. These were the disenfranchised by both society and government. They were men, women, and children. They came from all races, all classes. They had tired of the world of words within which they were; a world where a promise could be twisted and an oath unnecessary to fulfill. They had grown weary of the lies that held more substance than promises. They wanted action. No word would halt their steps. Their bodies were ready to tear down the old order.

One marcher pushed on, his face dripping and his skin sunburnt. He was worn out, his stamina quickly sapped from his massive girth. His fellows were with him, their arms gladly supporting and carrying him on. They would not leave him behind. His heart was struggling, his body aching, his flesh unwilling, but his soul pushed on. His brothers saved him, those dorks, fools, losers, and outcasts rejected by society. They marched on, their steps sounding through the streets of Washington D.C.

Matthew stomped proudly at the front, cigarette glowing a ruby red as he strode through the avenues of power. The citizens of D.C. did not know what to make of this growing mob. They peeked out windows, snatched glimpses from cracked doors, or dared the streets to see history in the making. Matthew smiled, pushing the cigarette to the side of his mouth, his yellow teeth gleaming in the fading light of day.

Their spark grew into a flame as individuals spilled from all corners to join this march to the heart of democracy, to the capital of the Western World. The underclass began to gel, forming a movement to bust the pedestal and topple those above them. Each stride brought them closer to destiny. Their eyes were fixed on the most abstract of ideals.

Police were stationed in blockades before them, four cop cars and twenty officers standing, rifles ready. "Sir?" One of the younger cops asked the sergeant as the mass approached.

"Yes, Wackenhut?"

"When exactly are we given permission to fire?" Wackenhut's eyes darted all over the crowd. There were hundreds, possibly thousands stretching further than he could see.

"We're not going to fire on anyone!" the sergeant ordered, giving Wackenhut an authoritative glare.

"But sir, I don't think they're going to stop."

"They will stop. They'll respect us and obey our authority."

Wackenhut saw the angry stares, heard the muttering of obscenities and threats. They ground their teeth ready to chew up the forces in front of them. "We do have a back up plan if they don't stop, right sir?"

"We don't need one," the sergeant retorted.

"But sir-"

The sergeant grabbed Wackenhut by the collar. "We...don't...need...one." The sergeant let Wackenhut go as he ordered one of the officers to give him the bullhorn. He turned to the crowd and spoke. "Now hear this. You are ordered to stop and return to your homes and families. You may not, I repeat, may not move any further than this blockade."

The crowd was not stopping.

"I said stop!" the sergeant shouted into the bullhorn. The mass continued to pour forward, their feet combining into a sound loud as a cattle stampede. The sergeant was in shock. Everyone obeyed the law! "Stop-" he started to shout again as the mass rammed into the cop cars, overrunning it like a wave.

Their momentum and numbers allowed them to push the cars to the side as their fellows streamed through the break. The dam was broken threatening the seat of power with deluge.

"You can't go past here!" the sergeant continued to bellow through his bullhorn as the hundreds passed. "Stop! I say stop in the name of-".

One of the fat fellows grabbed the bullhorn from him and broke it over the sergeant's head knocking him out.

***

"Mr. President, we have problems." The Chief of Staff came running into the Oval Office, people scurrying everywhere trying to escape the coming slaughter, as Lucas sat watching the television report on the mass pouring through the streets toward him on his lofty perch. "The perimeter has been breeched-"

"You think I don't see that!" Lucas shouted, pointing at the screen. Secret Service stood behind him in their dark suits, speaking by radio.

"We're going to have to authorize use of force-"

"No! No, you're crazy!" Lucas screeched, his voice breaking. "Those are voters. I can't shoot voters!"

"Mr. President, they have surrounded the Capitol Building and there are reports others are coming here." Lucas ignored him. "They are coming to kill you!"

"Mr. President," one of the Secret Service broke in. "We can get you out of here if we leave now. Our window is only five minutes."

"I will not evacuate the White House! This is my place!"

"Mr. President we have to leave now or else you are stuck here." The officer tried to convince him. He failed.

"What does it say to America if I run? People will think I'm a coward. No one wants to be led by a coward. No, I won't do it. I can't afford the bad press."

"Mr. President?" The Chief of Staff could not believe the insanity.

"Have you seen the polls? America hates me! If I leave now my numbers may never recover! I need this. A great stand!"

Everyone in the room was speechless. The Chief of Staff seized the initiative. "What of troops? Can we get anyone out here for defense?"

"Impossible," Brown replied, wishing he had taken that state visit to Paris. "All our troops are spread out in Europe and Asia. What few reserves we have are strung across the nation putting down riots." Brown began to fall apart. "We have no reserves left." He looked at those around him, found not a shred of care for those he saw, and hurried from the room.

"We have no one?" The Chief was shocked to discover the hard truth. He looked at the assembled faces, everyone scared for their lives. "Then we are alone."

***

They came to the gates of the White House. They were sealed. Matthew stood, looking through at what he craved. That building was power personified. His followers surrounded the political palace forming a perimeter along the fence. Nothing was getting out. The fountains continued to spray in front of those white walls. A breeze whispered through the bushes and grass. Guards stood, some shaking, taking cover on the front steps of the White House, looking back at the crowd. One communicated the situation to those inside needing no embellishment to strike fear in those trapped within. It all seemed so serene as the sun set behind the building. Quiet ruled the scene as the faces of hundreds peered through the bars at the home of their elected leader. Their eyes covered every part of that massive mansion. How they had starved, how they had suffered, and how this man had allowed it all to be! They wanted blood.

Matthew stood at the entrance, staring through the bars that gave the President his gilded cage. This bird would not fly when granted its freedom. Matthew looked along his flanks at those that believed. They would move mountains at his request. He didn't need quite that much effort. "My brothers and sisters. Here is the home of the man who allowed you to be abused knowingly. He lied to you, seduced you with promises of a better tomorrow all while threatening the safety and future of your children and generations to come today. He hides from you, too afraid to speak! He hides from your wrath! For those of money, for those of power these gates," Matthew shook the closed fence before him, "are open! Well, we do not need an invitation nor do we need an offering to keep his greedy, parasitic attention." Matthew gave the crowd a once over as he turned to the guards, their rifles an illusion of protection and authority. Matthew pulled a new cigarette from his pocket, lit, and took a drag. He released the smoke into the wind. "Bring it down!" he ordered, his words finding every ear.

They threw their gargantuan weight against the black steel. Flesh rattled metal as it began to give. The concrete foundation started to crack, little bits of debris bouncing with each blow. They rammed again and again with their bodies, the steel twisting and retreating. The guards started to retreat themselves, up the steps to the entrance of the White House. They were horrified by the mass in front of them. Their rifles lost meaning against such a force, their courage falling beneath each blow. Matthew smiled, standing back and watching. Screams, grunts, and cries mingled among the many as they sacrificed their bodies to the will of one man. They fractured bone, split skin, and bled to bring down the gates. Their sacrifice was not in vain as a section came crashing down. The mass surged into the breech towards the halls of power.

***

"This is a message from the President of the United States." The symbol of the office of the President came onscreen interrupting the previous broadcast. The President appeared still smiling and appearing calm as ever.

"Crowds of the obese are rampaging through the streets, seizing government buildings and enacting what many are calling the fattest coup in history. This is a dark hour for our country as the weight of the masses try to smother our democratic traditions and eat away at the solid foundation of the freedoms we so enjoy. We must remain strong in this adversity as we purge ourselves of this adversary. Together we can-"

The sound of wood splintering filled the background. "There he is!" Fat people flooded in to seize the President. "Remember me!" he screamed as the screen blacked out.

***

Matthew walked through the halls seeing the beaten and bloodied members of both his mob and the President's entourage. Terrified screams could be heard elsewhere in the building as Matthew strode through the debris. A chandelier had fallen, scattered across the elegant floor. Some fat people were beating on a guard they had pinned to the ground, cursing him for his looks. Roy was one of them. He punched the guard over and over again in the face, blood streaming against the wall and polished tile. Roy's face was twisted into an intense hardness, hate robbing his face of the flexibility of reason. Matthew nodded at the attack as he walked up the stairs.

The obese parted before him as he pressed through to that section he craved most. Before the door to the Oval Office he saw Secret Service agents sitting on the floor, beaten and broken. They sat there, their eyes worried at the sight of this coming man. Some of the mob standing beside them kicked them for the offense. "Don't look at him! You haven't earned that right." The mob looked to Matthew for assurance.

"He is right." Matthew gave that wicked smile.

"What should we do with them?" one of the mob asked.

Matthew looked them over, making a decision in his mind. His eyes stopped on the Chief of Staff who happened to be held with them. "You," Matthew pointed at the Chief.

"He's talking to you, scum!" One of the mob kicked the Chief in the ribs.

The Chief grimaced. "Ye...yes?" His eyes nearly looked up but stopped, remembering the prior beating.

Matthew knelt down. "Look at me." The Chief continued looking down. "Look at me." The Chief obeyed. "Who do you serve?"

The Chief quickly looked around at his fellow prisoners then back. "I...I don't understand."

"Do you serve the people or the President?"

The Chief was scared beyond belief. What was the right answer? Was there a wrong one? "I serve..." he looked at the agents next to him, their bloodied and bruised faces evidence of their loyalty to this regime. They looked to him for justification for such faith. The Chief turned back to Matthew. "I serve whoever is in charge." Their faces fell, their hopes meaningless.

Matthew smiled at that. "Good. I like you. I can use a man like you." Matthew turned to the one in charge. "Clean him up." As Matthew walked into the office the mob squad leader grudgingly let the Chief up and ordered one of his underlings to take him somewhere to freshen up.

Matthew walked into the Oval Office, President Lucas on the floor with a fat man's knee in his back. Matthew walked over to the tackled President and put his shoe under Lucas' nose. "Lick it."

"Screw...you," the President defiantly replied.

Matthew looked at the fat man on his back. "He needs some convincing." The fat ass punched Lucas in his right kidney, the pain sharp and very real. Matthew lowered himself to the ground to look Lucas in the eye. "Feel that?"

Lucas sniffed, a tear rolling down his cheek.

Matthew smirked. "I know you are used to negotiating so let me put it to you in terms you understand. Do as I say or say goodbye to your pathetic life piece," Matthew looked up at the fat ass again who delivered another kidney punch, "by piece." Matthew got to his feet and stuck his shoe under

Lucas' nose again. The President was quick to lick. "So much for a man of principle." Everyone in the room laughed as Matthew walked to the desk, pulling his foot away from that silver tongue. He sat upon Lucas' throne and propped his feet on the desk knocking off the last vestiges of his authority, photos representing Lucas' family and career. "Pull him up. I like to see who I am talking to."

The fat ass pulled Lucas up by his hair, his other arm wrapped firmly around the President's neck.

"So, President Lucas," Matthew smiled at him as he lit another cigarette.

"You can't smoke in here," Lucas ordered, forgetting his place.

Matthew tilted his head, a little surprised, not believing this man couldn't realize his current position in life. The fat ass looked to Matthew for permission to give Lucas another hit. Matthew shook his head no much to the fat ass' displeasure. "You're day of giving orders is fast approaching an end," Matthew stated, blowing a plume of smoke. "Congress is right now impeaching you and your entire administration and appointing me as the executive in your stead. Of course, though I am so humble, I will accept the offer."

"Congress would never do that," Lucas replied, his face revealing his utter contempt. "Where do you dream up these fantasies?"

"With the right amount of..." Matthew smiled at the fat ass then back at Lucas, "diplomacy, Congress will do anything." Matthew supported the back of his head with his hands, greasy hair caught between interlocking fingers, as he leaned back further in his new chair. "Of course, once I am in office I will have to declare martial law. The state of things in the nation is horribly disordered. I will have to clean them up, sadly without the aid of Congress or the courts. You see, I have no time for meaningless debate."

"America won't stand for this!" Lucas struck a pose only for the chokehold to tighten forcing a gack from his mouth.

"You don't know America like I do." Matthew smiled. "But come on, see the historic moment." Matthew waved Lucas over, his guard dragging him across the floor as another in the room picked up the overturned television and turned it on. "Channel 32," Matthew ordered. The screen morphed from one scene to another before settling on an all news station reporting from the Capitol Building.

The Vice-President slumped at the podium in the Senate, using it to support his battered body, clearly shaken. His face was bruised, an eye blackened and swollen shut with red scratch marks on his face. His hands trembled as he gripped a piece of paper tightly. His good eye dragged around the room, which imprisoned senators stripped of their pomp and power. Some looked beaten, their clothes ripped, shirts hanging out. Chillingly, some of the seats were empty. They were nothing more now than old men whose time had passed. These fallen figures once ruled America. Now, they were mere puppets who either complied with the strings of their unseen masters or were hung by them.

The Vice-President tried to speak, his mouth forming words but not uttering them. He took off his glasses, one lens cracked and the other missing from the broken frame, and wiped his eyes, resting a hand on the podium. He looked back to those assembled, ready to make his announcement. "Before I read the results of this vote...I hereby resign the office of Vice-President. I have corrupted my office, misusing my power and abusing my authority. I..." the Vice-President nearly collapsed mentally but caught something out of the corner of his eye and rapidly collected himself. "I am not worthy of this great office. In my place, the Senate has chosen Matthew Ford by a unanimous vote."

Loud applause with vulgarities and cat calls, whistles and hollers came from an unseen source. The former Vice-President stood there, solemnly, as fate worked through him. He received the verbal abuse upon his broken soul, taking the barbs and shots with stoic strength. He hovered there, at the end of an old order and the beginning of another for a few moments. He teetered on the brink, deciding whether or not to make the leap into the pit until a loud noise made him jump.

The camera panned to show the back of the Senate chambers where dozens of the mob stood. They did not look pleased. There were hundreds standing against the wall, more standing in the audience overlooking the tomb of democracy. They held clubs and chains, their faces bloodthirsty and branded with rage. They chewed on their hatred and tasted their bile ready to vomit it up into the world in a spate of destruction. Their barbaric presence was out of place in this civilized, peaceful setting.

The camera panned back to the former Vice-President who continued reading. "By unanimous vote, by both Houses of Congress, President Lucas is to be removed from the office of President."

Louder applause than before, followed by crass yelling and celebration, sounded in the back of the Senate chamber as the former Vice-President's shoulders fell. His former comrades, the senators, failed to rise and join in the celebrations. Some broke down in tears as others stared ahead at something invisible.

"Fastest legislation ever. I must have a flare for politics." Matthew grinned as he pointed at the television and gave a thumbs down. One of his giant goons grabbed the TV and crushed it against the floor, sparks flying. The smell of burnt carpet filled the room. "To all things...come an end."

Lucas looked down at the floor. His guard choked his crimson face back up to stare at Matthew.

"When you believe something is impossible you blind yourself to a part of reality. I was once a man of words, like you." Matthew started to shake his head. "No more. Words are forgotten the minute they are said, lost to the wind. Action. Action leaves an effect. Action builds or destroys. Action is what makes things happen. Not words."

Lucas' eyes, the whites now red, tried to give a defiant stare.

Matthew swept his feet off the desk and walked towards Lucas. He dragged on his cigarette as he approached Lucas, the smoke trailing after him. He motioned to the fat ass holding the former head of state to release him. As his guard backed away, Matthew put his hand on Lucas' shoulder and smiled. He patted Lucas, calming him, and leaned in. "President Lucas," Matthew smiled and cackled. "Former President Lucas." His smile vanished in a second. "It is time to act."

He grabbed Lucas by the neck and, with enormous strength, threw him crashing through a window to the ground below. Matthew looked down at the corpse of the world leader, bleeding and twitching like the flawed mortal he was. He stood there for a time before turning back to those in the room, those assembled amazed and shocked by what had just happened. "Now," Matthew began, his voice calm, "where were we?"

***

Over an hour had passed and still nothing. Matthew had been churning bog beneath his feet for miles, and he was no closer to anything even symbolizing civilization. This place was as empty as Iowa. Matthew didn't know where else to go. *Maybe if...wait, something in the distance. Was that light? It was moving!* Matthew almost started after it but stopped. It could be more of those wraiths. Did he really need more of that? Then again, something to run from was better than nothing to run to.

Matthew started to jog towards the brightness. As the distance fell away the light split into two, slowly dividing into a pair of spheres. Unlike the pale light of the wraiths this brightness burned his eyes. Little purple splotches developed in his vision as he stopped and felt his way forward. The lights, on the other hand, did not stop. As they zoomed forward they covered Matthew in a sick, yellow tinge before ramming into him. Matthew hurtled over the hood of the truck and flopped to the ground behind it. The truck stopped a dozen feet away, skidding through the muck.

Matthew's vision was fuzzed as he distinctly saw two figures coming towards him.

"You fuckin' moron, didn't you see him?"

"Well if you'd shut the fuck up I'd pay more attention."

"Wait, wait. Are you saying I made you hit him? Fuckin' idiot, you were driving."

"Well, you were with me so that makes you an accomplice."

Matthew's vision started to straighten out a little as he saw the two shadows standing over him. The one smacked the other upside the head. "Stop using those big words. They don't make you any smarter."

The other shadow pushed the abusive one. "I'm improving myself."

"You can't shine a turd, Carl. Ok?"

Matthew made a little groan as he tried to get up.

"He's alive!" Buck nearly shouted.

"Of course he's alive, you fuckin' retard! He's already dead!" Carl rolled his eyes at Buck.

"Wait, what?" Matthew asked, still a little woozy.

"Hey, you ok?" Buck asked, looking at Matthew. "How many fingers am I holding up?" Buck waved the middle one alone.

"One," Matthew replied, not finding it amusing.

"Why doesn't anyone ever laugh at that?" Buck asked, annoyed.

"Because it's stupid, you fuckin' retard."

"I've told you to stop calling me a retard!"

"Like I am going to listen to a retard," Carl replied looking away.

"Yeah, but...hey!" Buck pointed at Carl. "Keep it up and you're gonna be left down here!"

"Down where-" Matthew started.

"Not likely. It's my truck!" Carl retorted.

"Where am-"

"That can be changed!" Buck warned.

"Guys!" Matthew yelled getting their attention. The two turned to him. Matthew could now make them out, his sight returned. The two were...total, complete red necks. They wore dirty jeans, work boots, and stained t-shirts. The one, Carl was it, had a mullet while the other, Buck, wore some chewed up hat. "Where exactly am I?"

"Well," Carl started, "you're in Purgatory. Yeah, that's about right."

"Purgatory." Matthew replied. "Between Heaven and Hell?"

"That's where they left it last I saw," Carl snorted in his backwoods hooting.

"That's not possible. I'm alive!"

"I think being here makes that a big no!" Buck retorted.

"He must be a newbie," Carl snorted.

"Sorry for hitting you," Buck said. "Dip shit here refuses to get glasses."

"It's the dark! Let's see you drive in this black shit."

"Yeah, yeah. Anyway, you look ok. Just watch yourself down here. You're gonna find you have some new freaky neighbors."

Matthew was frozen in shock as the two simply turned around and started towards their truck. "Wait!" he yelled. The two turned around. "You can't just leave me here."

"Well, what do you expect us to do?" Carl asked.

"Anywhere is better than here! Take me with you."

"With us? I don't think we have anymore room."

"I'll ride in the back. Please!" The two didn't look like they were going to agree. "Hey, you owe me. You hit me, remember?"

"He's right," Buck replied.

Carl snorted back some snot, spitting it out as he looked up at the dark sky then back at Matthew, illuminated by the red tail lights. "Shit, there's always room for another. Come on!" He waved Matthew towards them.

Matthew ran as fast as he could, stopping as he saw a problem. At least twenty Mexicans were already in the back. "What the fuck-" Matthew turned to both Buck and Carl. "What the hell is going on?"

Buck walked up to Matthew. "Ok, I am going to level with you. We're coyotes."

"What exactly is a coyote?"

"We smuggle Mexicans...into Heaven."

Matthew looked at the two hicks. "You're serious." The two nodded dumbly. "Well..." Matthew licked his muddy lips, "At least I'm headed in the right direction." He realized the shit he had just licked and spit it out.

Carl smiled and waved Matthew to the back. "Come on, boy. Get ready for the ride of your life!"

CHAProblemsTER 9

Matthew sat at the seat of power, his face worsening as his acne ripened and the warmth of his flesh was lost to a bitter cold. The eagle triumphantly spread it wings over his head signifying victory and the emergence of a new order, its symbolism crafted into the seat of a new leader, a new authority in the world of men. The formerly shattered window had been replaced, that mortal exit for the former president. The desk itself was bare save for Matthew's hands, fingers interlaced, resting upon that oak like a hammer ready to smash the order that teetered before it. The wounds of struggle had been removed, the walls bare and sterile. The illusion of harmony had begun. His eyes, the portals to his soul, remained hidden to the world behind the opaque glass of his shades.

A camera faced Matthew, ten feet from his withering glance, capturing his image and broadcasting it to the world. Its eye was not judgmental. It saw what it was meant to see and fed that to those ready to consume, readily, hungrily, their new digital addiction. The stage was set. The performance was about to begin, and no actor was better suited for this tragedy than the one that stared eagerly into the camera before him seeing himself reflected in that sole, artificial eye.

"My brothers, my sisters, my kindred in this battle against the oldest orders and deepest mistakes of man. I come to you now at the beginning of a new age. The boil has been lanced here in Washington, the infection squeezed out. We, my people, are now the law of the land. Changes are on the way. Many changes. Do not fear this change. All things must change. We must adapt or die.

"Though the corruption and parasites of that political caste have been removed, their strings cut severing them and government from those that manipulated them, the true threat to our peace and welfare remains in place. The rich, the corporations, and the clergy. The puppet masters. They," Matthew's voice began to rise, his pace quickening, "are the true danger to you and yours. They are the kingmakers, the planners, the beasts that feast on your pain and suffering. Over two-thirds of all capital, all wealth, rest with this small minority. While we, the common men and women, suffer on meager supplies and scrape by on an existence of debt and monetary servitude, slaves to their wealth, with unlived and unattainable wishes, these sycophants, these perverts, these cruel and malicious bastards live a life of constant dreams where we are nothing more than pawns for their very entertainment. They own dozens of houses each while we are lucky to rent a one room apartment for a whole family.

"They tell you what you need. They set your trends. Your fads. They condition you. Generalize you. Rob you of what meager income you bleed for. What has this order wrought? Parents who both work in order to give their children what they think they need, sacrificing those precious moments to be replaced by manufactured ones. Children go without guidance, raised by a steady stream of propaganda that tells them that material possessions make them worth something and that beauty is superior to substance. We become locked in a cycle of mediocrity where we owe everything to them and receive but their scraps when they think us worthy. They dictate policy. They make laws. They create our very prison. One which we do not even know is there, to lock us away from a true life of contentment and fulfillment. I say no more!" Matthew pulled a hand loose and slapped it on the desk. He leaned forward to continue.

"Hence forward all factories, all industry, all sources of manufacturing will be placed under government control. Too long have the monopolies and cartels of the few choked out the small businesses that try to advance the little guy and give him a purpose. These factories, when the time comes, will be broken up and divided amongst those willing to accept the opportunity to give to their fellow man and realize their dream of entrepreneurship. Also, all bank accounts above a certain cap shall be frozen, all funds diverted to the federal government to pay for the government deficit that has grown from the thievery and abuse of these few that have robbed and raped the treasury of our beloved country. Let them know what it is like to live without, to be raped monetarily. They have lived long enough with too much.

"All jobs overseas will be effectively ended and brought back to this country. We grow too smart to accept such corporate abuse thus they steal our jobs, and they move on to victimize new lands. No more! They will be returned to their source and pay raises granted to all employees.

"Universal health care will be offered to everyone and medical costs dropped to believable and affordable levels. What good is continual life when it is sold to continue? I will not have you financially indentured or too scared to seek medical aid simply because of the greed of doctors and administrators. They speak of their oath, of protecting and healing those in need then financially cripple you with the slash of a pen. No more!

"As for the clergy..." Matthew's face went dark, his glasses slipping down his nose to show his eyes. The whites had started to go yellow, veins crisscrossing the sickly tint as if coronal electricity. "What right do they have for any type of political control in this nation? They do not pay taxes, yet require you to pay a tithing to them for the salvation of your soul. They dictate medical and scientific policy even though they do not even believe in science! They speak to us of morality and break every word they hold sacred behind closed doors and shuttered windows! They are the problem with this nation. These hypocrites, these sadists, these corrupters of children and swallowers of souls. No more! Henceforth all churches of all denominations are required to pay property taxes. All churches are required to pay taxes period!

"And as for that supposed superior of churches, the Catholic faith," Matthew licked his lips as if a lion readying to devour his prey. "It is time to pay your tithing. Though the previous administration refused to act I shall. The Catholic Church has been found guilty of child pornography, child abuse, organized criminal pursuits, and attempted murder. Priests have been discovered giving shelter and aid to not only illegal immigrants who come here stealing jobs and bringing crime in their wake, but also thieves, murderers, and rapists who they tell they do not need to suffer the justice of man for God has forgiven them. God may have forgiven them, but justice has not.

"Pursuant to the Patriot Act, passed by Congress and ratified by the President of the United States, I am prepared for preemptive action on that terrorist organization known as the Catholic faith, based in Vatican City, lead by the Pope. All Church funds in this nation shall be frozen and confiscated, all Church lands seized, all priests, nuns, bishops, and cardinals shall be imprisoned for interrogation. Military action shall be ordered if, in one week's time, Vatican City does not surrender unconditionally to the United States. The souls of man may be yours, but the bodies and minds of my people belong to me!" Matthew thumbed at himself.

"I am the flame that shall burn away the old order from whose ashes a new regime shall rise. I am the wind that shall sweep away the stink of your infection and corruption. I am every man, woman, and child that has suffered under the heavy weights you place upon us so that you might live a life more leisurely. I am your enemy, and you shall know my name!"

"And...we're clear." The cameraman lowered his hand.

Matthew swept some loose hair back into place, pushing his glasses back up his nose. As the cameraman began taking the camera apart to remove from the Oval Office the Chief of Staff came in, his face bruised and scabbed but better than before. "You wanted to see me, Mr. President?"

"Yes. I need you to set up a meeting with President Romanov. We have some things we need to discuss."

"Yes, Mr. President."

***

A new anchorman sat before the televised audience, his predecessor mysteriously removed during the sweeping reforms. This new man was partially obese, the flaccid skin of his face evidence of the fat that had eroded beneath while under Matthew Ford's fasting diet. The new anchor was very plain, his eyes dull and his style of suit dated. He read the world situation to a waiting populace. "In tonight's news Europe stands against the words and posture of our beloved President, Matthew Ford. They continue to defend said criminal kingpin, Pope Benedict XIII, despite overwhelming evidence to the contrary of their cries of innocence. Sources indicate that all European members of NATO have withdrawn from said organization and begun mobilization to prevent what they call American imperialism and armed secularism." The new anchorman blew out a gust of air. "Big words that make no real sense. Here is the French President on the current situation."

The screen changed to a thin man, his gray hair slicked back save for the spit curls that crowned his head. Horn rim glasses framed his beady eyes, his purple lips puckered from the sour words in his mouth. The suit he wore could only be called fashionable on some foreign planet, the folds and fabric disturbing to the common man. He sputtered his speech in French; the phlegm gurgling in the back of his throat like it was trying to bubble out. Spit trickled out of the corners of his purple mouth as he tried to appear domineering and controlling. He seemed to be on a tirade as he let his hands fly all over, only stopping when he accidentally slapped himself in the face. With that he began screaming at the camera before the screen flashed back to the newsroom.

The anchorman leaned towards the camera. "Do not worry America. That was no audio problem. It would seem that the French leader thought himself above speaking intelligently. We do not know what he said since it was in French, so it probably wasn't that important. Anyway, we'll crush him and that shitty country of his too."

***

Matthew did not like riding so close to the rear of the truck, the rear flap down, as they tore through Purgatory. Matthew hung on tightly to the side rail as they sped along. The black sludge spewed behind them as the tires churned it up from its eternal resting place. The Mexicans themselves stank horribly. They seemed resigned to whatever waited ahead, stoically staring off as they ripped through this damned dimension.

For all the miles they had covered, nothing really seemed different. The terrain was still flat and black, the sky remained bare, and the one Mexican continued to offer Matthew a swig from his bottle of Mescal. "No thank you," Matthew told him yet again.

Buck laughed from inside the cab of the truck, watching through the rear window. He stuck his upper body through the passenger side window and yelled back to Matthew. "Boy, you might consider having that drink."

"And why would I want to do that?" Matthew retorted.

"It'll help with the ride."

Matthew looked back at the receding sameness that he had been watching for the past few hours. He turned back to Buck. "I don't think it's going to make this place any more interesting."

"Oh, it's not to make it more interesting."

"Then why?" Matthew asked, puzzled. The truck began to slow down. Matthew stopped looking at Buck and stared up at the sky. The stars were starting to come out. Alright, now they were getting somewhere. The number of stars, though, seemed to be multiplying into a vast number he had never beheld before. Before he knew it the truck stopped. Matthew rubbed up against the group of Mexicans as the momentum of braking brought him forward. The amount of people in the back kept the truck going another few inches beyond the stop. Matthew looked left and right. "This isn't Heaven."

"No, it's not," Buck agreed.

"Then why are we stopping?"

"Take a look."

Matthew got off the back of the truck and walked around to the front. As he got closer he saw why they stopped: there wasn't anywhere else to go. It was a chasm that fell off into the void of space. Billions of points of light shined in the darkness of the abyss. It was a view impossible from any planet. This was space without the censorship of atmosphere. Matthew dared to look over the edge and vertigo seized him. "Oh fuck," he mumbled as he fell backwards on his ass. Buck and Carl laughed heartily as did some of the Mexicans who caught the incident. Matthew gathered himself then turned to Buck, who had now opened his door and stood behind it. "So now what?" Matthew asked.

"What do ya mean?" Buck asked.

"Well," Matthew gestured at the void, his face making a dumb expression.

"What?" Buck asked, still unable to grasp what Matthew was trying to say.

"There's no road!" Matthew yelled.

"Oh that," Buck waved a hand. "There's never been a road."

Matthew couldn't believe the insanity, his face shaking with disbelief. "Then how the hell are we getting to Heaven?"

Buck laughed, snorting a bit.

"Do I really want to know?"

"You better have a drink," Buck said, still smiling that dumb grin.

Matthew turned back to the waiting Mexicans, one shaking the bottle of Mescal at him. "Perfect. Just perfect. A fiesta in Purgatory. Hopefully it doesn't turn into a siesta permanently."

Matthew trudged back to rear of the truck and swiped the bottle from the offering hand. If they could drink this stuff like water, so could he. Matthew took a deep breath then opened his mouth to the vilest liquid this side of sulfuric acid. Matthew felt his throat burning and started gagging. The poison poured into his stomach and blew a hole in his sobriety. He leaned up against the truck and started dry heaving. The Mexicans chatted animatedly amongst themselves, laughing toothlessly and pointing his way. "Wh..." Matthew nearly vomited. "What did he say?"

Buck laughed a little, too. "Just have another drink."

Matthew tossed the bottle in the muck, the fluid running out in a tiny glug glug into the black muck. The Mexicans gave verbal protest to that. "No way, I want to live," Matthew replied.

"Boy," Buck laughed, "you're already dead."

Matthew wobbled a bit, the alcohol suddenly slamming into his senses and everything spun. "I definitely feel like it."

"Just get in the damn truck," Buck ordered with a kidding grin. As Matthew tried to make his way back up into the back, his foot slipped and he fell back into the mud. "Shit." Buck got out and went to check Matthew. He found Matthew facedown, bubbles rising in the swampy bog around his submerged head. Buck knelt down and grabbed him by his hair pulling his face out of the muck. "Are you ok?"

"Do I still have legs?"

Buck was puzzled at the question. He looked to make sure Matthew did. "Yeah."

"Then I'm not alright."

Buck laughed that good ol' boy haw haw as he put his hands underneath Matthew's arms and dragged him to the cab. As he started to put him in the seat Carl gave him a surprised look. "What are you doin'?"

"Boy's so drunk there's no way he's gonna hold on. We gotta put him in here."

Carl gave Matthew a once over. "Ok, but if he vomits you clean it up!"

"Yeah, yeah, whatever." Buck squeezed Matthew in as he climbed in behind him and slammed the door. It was a very tight fit. Matthew's head bobbed up and down, his eyes mere slits and his face red. Buck smiled at his neighbor. "You don't drink a lot do ya?"

"Nooooo," Matthew bellowed, laughing at his long word.

Carl looked at Buck before the two joined Matthew in their chuckling. Carl released the brake and began easing the truck forward. Matthew failed to notice until the truck began tilting down. Sobriety returned in a snap when he saw them staring down into the void, the truck leaning over the edge. "What the fuck are you doing?" he slurred, turning to Carl horrified.

"Fasten your seatbelt, boy. This is going to be one ride you won't forget." Carl and Buck laughed some more. Carl hit the gas and the truck plunged over into the gulf, a roller coaster ride of epic proportions, the two red necks howling with a rebel yell.

***

Matthew Ford stood in the ornamental ballroom of the former Winter Palace of tsars. He ran his fingers along a wall, feeling the craftsmanship beneath his fingers as he looked up to the ceiling. So much work, so much effort; how these mortals could emulate their maker when they chose. Amazing how humanity could create something so exquisite when it was far better suited to barbarity and banality. He stared across the glittering room to the gray skies just beyond the huge windows.

Matthew walked across the floor, his heels clicking and clacking on the surface. He unsheathed that wicked smile as he closed his eyes and turned in circles, dancing alone in this monument to a gilded age. He swept around the room, the music long ended still echoing in his ears. He could almost hear the hopeful voices of an era long crushed by the violence of a generation and buried beneath the failed beliefs of flawed leaders, a requiem to idealism.

His dancing ended in front of a large mirror. He slowed to look at himself. He had stopped wearing expensive suits opting for simpler fare. His skin had gone deathly pale. His acne was beginning to spread worse than before, reddening with yellow mingled. His greasy hair was receding back to his crown, his ears sharpening. Matthew reached up to touch his cheek. "Your days are numbered," he warned his reflection.

He heard the door behind him, the entrance of former royalty creaking open. In strode Romanov alone, the doors closing behind him. His stride did not deviate or waste a step. He made straight for Matthew. He stopped in the center of the room. He waited for Matthew to join him. Matthew was amused. He made his way to his counterpart. "You have called for a meeting. I am interested as to the why?" Romanov cocked an eyebrow.

"Quite simple. Compromise, comrade."

"Compromise?" Romanov did not quite understand.

"My...predecessor, did not value your sovereignty or agenda. I am much more sympathetic."

"How do you mean?"

"Walk with me." Romanov and Matthew began to round the room, their steps out of sync. "You are tired of the corruption which crippled your nation as am I with my own land. I understand where you are coming from." Matthew placed his arm behind the shoulders of Romanov as if to guide him. Romanov shook him off.

"I prefer bluntness to seduction. What do you want?"

Matthew liked this man. "As you know, Europe is in turmoil over my policies. One policy in particular."

"The Pope."

"Yes. In fact, they are willing to...die for this foolishness. Religion makes such fools of us." Matthew once more put his arm behind Romanov. "I am here to offer a truce. In fact, a truce with...benefits."

"What benefits might we be speaking of?" Romanov did not shake off Matthew's arm this time.

"Russia's sphere of influence has always included Eastern Europe. It is foolishness for the West to believe it can ever actually lay claim to those lands. Their culture is too different, their views skewed in an opposite direction. We are not a good fit."

"You offer me Eastern Europe-"

"I offer nothing. I return to you Eastern Europe, President Romanov. I also allow you unhindered control of all lands lost with the fall of the Soviet Union, those foolish lands that deserted the Rodina when it needed them most."

Romanov wanted to smile but buried it behind the steel emotionless face that was his best asset. "Why?"

"It's quite simple. Unlike so many other fools, I do not wish a war on multiple fronts." Romanov perked up at that. "War is unavoidable I assure you. I do not wish to fight someone I have no problems with. War is terrible business. Especially an unwinnable one. In exchange for these lands I only ask a free hand in Central and Western Europe." Matthew slipped him that seductive smile.

"Why do you need such freedoms in Europe?" Romanov wanted to know the whole picture, to see the angles worth playing.

"Europe will not simply let me quash the Pope. They will surely defend him. That means military action."

"How can I allow this? It will only put you on my borders. How do I know you aren't setting up for an invasion of the very lands you offer so freely now?"

"Now, now Alex. We both know that would be futile. Your nuclear weapons make any attempt a worthless gesture."

"That doesn't rule out economics. You will control a vast majority of manufacturing and industry. You stand to gain much more from this than Russia."

Matthew smiled even wider, his teeth predatory. "It's money, then, you want."

"I did not say that," Romanov retorted.

"Oh, but it is obvious, Alex. Your economy is in tatters. Large amounts of your capital has been stolen and moved abroad by former communist officials and organized crime. Your infrastructure is collapsing."

"Russia needs nothing!" Romanov seethed. He slapped Matthew's arm away and looked as if ready to belt Matthew in the face. Instead he started to leave.

"It is far easier to accept what you want when it is given rather than to take it when it is not."

Romanov's steps slowed. The Russian leader reversed himself, appraising the American. "You offer me nothing but lies. How do I know you aren't trying to trip me up into a full scale war?"

Matthew met Romanov halfway, closing the gap between them. He put his hand on Romanov's shoulder. He went to knock it off, but Matthew's stare stopped him. "I am no politician. I am a man of action. You want proof. I shall give it to you. All American forces based in Eastern Europe, especially those on your border, shall be removed. They are not needed there anyway. You need not do anything until I have crushed my European traitors. If I win, you win. If I lose you lose nothing." Romanov looked as if ready to bite. "I'll even make a further concession."

"And what is that?" Romanov asked, his voice calm and dull, deceiving the excitement growing within him.

"I will give you the economic heart of Europe. I will give you Germany."

All that industry and a robust economy to pillage. Russia could finally rebuild! Romanov was entranced. He had gained everything he had ever wanted for his homeland and more, and he didn't have to do anything. The glory of Russia could be had again. A warm water port! This was a fortuitous day! "This intrigues me," Romanov replied with that passionless voice.

"Would you look at that." Matthew directed Romanov's gaze out the large set windows to the gathering colors of the horizon. The dull gray of the sky twisted into reds and purples, the banal becoming breathtaking. "It is always most beautiful before the setting of the sun."

***

The two inter-dimensional red necks laughed and howled with southern flavor as they tore donuts through the cosmos. Their pick-up soared faster than any UFO past planets and stars deep into the fabric of Existence.

The Mexicans held on for all they were worth. The vacuum beckoned as their fingers gripped the sole earthly thing they had left. Their screams were lost in that dark shadow known as the void. One of them lost his grip and was sucked away, his face shrinking, his body passing away into eternal night. The time of mourning was short as their current circumstances allowed no more thinking other than holding on for survival.

Carl screamed that rebel yell as he rammed his foot down on the accelerator, twisting the wheel to spin the truck. The Mexicans dangled as the truck flipped upside down. Or was that right side up? In space you could never tell. Their brown faces were masks of terror as the placid realm of emptiness awaited to make itself their last abode.

Buck looked back into the rear of the truck, past his mounted rifles, and broke up in wicked laughter. "Hold on, you fuckers! Hold on for dear life!" Another Mexican lost his grip, grabbing his amigo's leg as the last thing preventing him from slipping into the great beyond. His amigo didn't seem to appreciate the added weight, trying to kick him off. "You better hold on muchacho!" Buck taunted. The dangling Mexican was distracted by Buck giving his amigo just enough time to place a kick square in his face, the blow loosing his consciousness for a bit causing his fingers to relax. He was swept away into the folds of time. Buck continued laughing. "You enjoying this boy? Boy?"

Matthew sat rigidly between Buck and Carl. His face was solid and unmovable, locked into an expression of horrific calm as his eyes were so wide they threatened to fall out into his lap. He held onto his seat with a death grip, his knuckles whiter than his face. Buck nudged him to get his attention.

"First time in space?" Buck asked.

Matthew shook his head no.

"Then what's the problem? You should be used to this!"

Matthew's false calm was shattered by a comet that rushed by in front of the truck nearly ripping into the pig iron. He instinctively pushed back trying to avoid the threat, his feet pressing against the dashboard.

"Damn you!" Carl shook his fist at the passing phenomena. "Watch where you're going! Damn bastards, think they have this entire place to themselves."

Specks from the passing comet showered the Mexicans, one's shirt catching on fire. He screamed as another tried to pat it out for him only to lose his grip in the process.

Matthew started hyperventilating as his eyes darted crazily all over the vehicle, at the passing sterility of space, and the two red necks who tore through it more recklessly than a meteor into a planet. "Are we almost there?" Matthew whispered, his voice very raspy.

"The boy can talk-" Buck started.

"Are we almost there?" Matthew rasped again, his tone nastier.

"Yeah, we're almost there. You know, you should be enjoying this."

Matthew gave Buck a very shocked look. "Why in the hell should I be enjoying this? I'm trying to survive it!"

"Come on, boy." Buck taunted. "This is fun."

Matthew turned at the screams and pleadings of the Mexicans in the rear. Matthew saw their faces, horrified and mortified, as they held on to the rust bucket of an unlikely space faring vehicle. Matthew could only watch so much of it before he turned back, chilled. "Doesn't seem to be fun for them."

"Who? Them?" Buck thumbed at the Mexicans behind them. "Shit, boy, one of the main reasons we do these runs is the ride."

"Don't you get paid?" Matthew stammered.

"Money only buys you shit that breaks. But this," Buck slapped the dashboard, "this is a memory you'll never lose. Besides we need the humor in our lives."

"Humor? What humor? This is fucking horrific!"

"I'm talking about them." Buck tilted his head briefly towards the rapidly disappearing passengers in the back. "Their faces when they loose their grip, hoo boy!" Buck slapped his thigh.

"That's horrible!" Matthew gasped.

"Come on, boy. You must still be in shock. Go on, take a gander. It'll lift your spirits."

Matthew turned around to watch the illegals as they swayed in the cosmic wind. There were only five left, wait four. The last one was swept away pretty fast. As they began to reach for Buck and Matthew in the cab Carl jerked the truck again causing them to fight for survival. "Does he have to do that?" Matthew asked Buck.

"Hey, don't blame him. You start to lose it a bit when you're out here in the void. Thank goodness he's got me. Besides, we have to teach these muchachos some business sense."

"What exactly are you teaching them?" Matthew squeaked.

"Never pay up front." Buck smiled rapping on the glass. "That's right, you pieces of mierda. Next time learn that you're only worth as much as you have." Buck started hooting again.

Matthew had enough of the tormenting, turning back to the front. He crossed his arms and looked straight ahead trying to drown out the mockery and death happening all around him.

Buck and Carl continued in their psychotic way regardless as they ripped through the beyond.

Matthew's face started to relax. The darkness of space slowly began to brighten, the black lightening into a crystal blue. The stars seemed to enlarge and coalesce into a brightness that gradually encompassed them. The speed of the truck slowed. The Mexicans in the back, what few were left, thumped down into the back of the cab. "Finally." Matthew breathed a sigh of relief.

"Yeah." Buck sulked. "We're finally here."

Matthew loosened up a bit before it occurred to him. "Hey. What happened to the black hole?"

"What?" Buck asked, still tapping on the rear window and giving the Mexicans the finger.

"Don't we need to go through a black hole to get to Heaven?"

"Shit no," Buck replied. "Unless you want to be caught. They regulate those things too much."

"They should. They built them," Carl snorted.

"Anyway," Buck stole back the conversation, "We take the long way. Less problems that way."

Land appeared in the distance as the blue turned to gold. Lush with emerald grass, welcoming territory approached with the sounds of life. Bird song and other missed tunes of nature called to them as the truck dropped from the sky and settled onto the rich soil of Paradise. The truck made its way through the Fields of Elysium towards their final destination.

"What? Don't feel like tearing up a piece of God's country?" Matthew asked sarcastically, looking over at Carl.

"Kid, the last thing we need is to draw the wrong type of attention."

The Mexicans stood in the back of the truck, looking out at their new home. They smiled and prattered amongst one another of new opportunities. Buck slammed the rear window over and over. "Silencio, God damnit!" Buck looked at Matthew. "Those assholes are going to bring everyone down on us."

"So..." Matthew looked out as they drove on. "Ever been caught?"

"Came close once," Buck replied, nervously looking around. "Too damn close."

"How did you get away?" Matthew asked.

Buck gave a nervous grin as he turned to Matthew. He patted the rifles mounted across the back. "These aren't just for decoration." Matthew nodded as Buck went back to scanning the skies.

The truck lumbered through the plains of Paradise, easily traversing the gentle hills. The irony of an unholy act in a holy land was not lost on Matthew. The golden light of the horizon failed to gleam on the dull and corroded hide of man's creation. Its large tires carved deep into the sacred soil, leaving black tracks where it had passed. Humanity's mark on the perfection of Heaven seemed a little just. These heavenly overseers had caused enough problems on Earth.

"Can you please open the window?" Matthew asked Buck.

"Why?"

"Well, I thought it was the smell of Purgatory, but after awhile, I discovered..." Matthew nodded at Buck.

"I told you you stunk, skunk," Carl joked. Buck gave them an angry stare.

"Will you please roll down the window?" Matthew begged.

Carl pretended to gag and cough. "Did you mess your pants on lift off? Roll it down!"

"Fuck...you," Buck spit as he rolled down the window and rested his arm on the sill. "Don't know what you're complaining about," he murmured. "I don't smell shit."

Carl and Matthew laughed as they continued on. They rose up a hill and began to descend gradually. In the distance, at the foot of said hill, a river twenty feet in width calmly gurgled the length of the plains. "Can we stop there?" Matthew asked, pointing at the river.

"Sure," Carl replied. "Ol' shit britches here needs a bath anyway."

"Fuck you, man," Buck retorted, taking his hat off as he looked out the window, the wind unable to cut through his matted brown hair. Matthew and Carl mocked him as the truck came to a stop on the banks of the river. Buck was the first out of the truck. As Matthew went to follow Buck slammed the door in his face.

"Someone's sensitive," Matthew replied to the not so subtle insult.

"Low self-esteem." Carl laughed a little more, burying his elbow in Matthew's ribs. Matthew smiled with him as Carl opened the driver's side door and jumped out, thumping the hood. "Ok, you Mex-ee-cans, get out. Shit, shower, shave. Do whatever you need to do. You've got twenty minutes."

"Que?" one of the Mexicans asked.

"Veinte minutos, dumb fuck," Carl mockingly replied.

"Oh, si si," the Mexican replied as he and his two amigos jumped out.

Matthew climbed out of the truck, watching the Mexicans hurry to the river. "You better follow their brown asses," Carl ordered Matthew, looking at his black, mud stained clothes.

Matthew nodded, grinning, and started to the river, stopping after a few feet. He turned to look back at Carl. "Aren't you coming?"

"Someone has to keep look out. Might as well be me. Besides, after awhile you don't smell your own stink no more."

"Nope, and everyone around you wishes they couldn't either."

"Get the fuck to the river."

Matthew ran at breakneck speed, enjoying the sensation of solid ground beneath his feet again, literally. His shoes had been lost, swallowed by the bog of Purgatory. Ahead were cleanliness, godliness, and an end to the stink that had been invading his nose for too long.

Buck knelt by the river's edge, dunking his head in the water, trying to remove the grease and debris that had taken residence in his thick mane. The Mexicans were stripping their clothes off for a thorough bath. Matthew took them all by surprise as he burst through them towards his most sought after destination in years. Buck stopped to watch Matthew leap into the air, diving into the river. He came down painfully on the riverbed that had been only two feet below the surface.

"Surprise," Buck chuckled. The Mexicans joined him in the hilarity.

Matthew rubbed his head, sitting in the shallow water. "You could have told me," Matthew replied, embarrassed and ready to lash out.

"You didn't give me much time."

Matthew looked up at the golden sky, his face bright red.

"If you could have seen..." Buck started chuckling again, deeper and longer. Matthew started to crack a grin as Buck fell backwards on his ass laughing harder.

"It was pretty funny, I guess," Matthew conceded as he started to smile broadly. Buck continued to laugh as Matthew buried his face in the water to wash and avoid the gazes of everyone present.

For ten minutes they enjoyed the cleansing waters of this Neo Eden, the grime readily coming off in the perfumed waters. Matthew stood up, stretching in the light of day until the breeze came by freezing him. He wrapped himself in his own embrace to warm up. The Mexicans were still washing, all stripped to their underwear. Buck was already back up at the truck speaking to Carl.

Matthew enjoyed looking off to the vistas beyond. This place was beautiful. The grass waved in such a welcoming fashion. He could see ancient trees of the greenest hue standing proudly. He looked up to the sky to watch the birds fly by of every species and description. If not for Jesus, Heaven wouldn't be so bad.

"Get up here now!" Carl yelled breaking the calm.

"It hasn't been twenty minutes," Matthew replied, a little upset at being interrupted from his train of thought.

"Get the fuck up here!" Buck screamed as Carl hurried to start the truck.

"Hey!" Matthew yelled, waving to get the Mexicans' attention. "Vamanos." The Mexicans didn't seem happy as they waded back to the bank to grab their clothes.

Buck came running towards the river with a rifle in hand grabbing the closest arm of a Mexican and tossing him towards the truck. "No time. Get to the truck." The Mexicans seemed ready to protest at the mistreatment.

"What's the problem?" Matthew asked as he approached Buck.

"That is the problem," Buck retorted, pointing with his rifle up the hillside. Matthew followed the rifle to its aim. Something was at the top of the hill. It was starting towards them.

"What's that?"

"Border patrol," Buck breathed. The Mexicans knew what that meant and ran for the truck.

"Border patrol?" Matthew asked.

"You don't want to meet them. Come on!" Buck pulled Matthew behind him. The figures slowly grew as they approached. And then they came into view: angels!

"Oh shit," Matthew breathed as Buck tried to shove him in the truck, the vehicle making grinding and moaning noises.

"Get this damn thing started!" Buck yelled at Carl.

The engine turned over, roaring loudly, black smoke pouring out the back. "Let's go!"

They climbed in, slamming the doors as Matthew stared out the rear window. The Mexicans were frantically hitting the top of the cab hoping to urge them on. Carl put the pedal to the floor, huge chunks of dirt flying into the air as the truck lurched forward towards the river. Water foamed around the pick-up as it attempted to swim to the other side. The angels were getting closer. The truck rattled from side to side as it drove over the submerged terrain hitting rocks and holes. As they neared the other side Matthew breathed a sigh of relief. It was for naught. The truck stopped. Carl pushed the pedal down harder. They didn't move.

"What the fuck is wrong now!" Buck screamed in fear.

"We're stuck," Carl replied, braking and accelerating, braking and accelerating.

"So now what?" Matthew asked.

"Well, we need a push." Carl turned to the Mexicans and yelled for them to get behind the truck to help. They protested. Carl yelled some more. They yelled back. Buck was tired of negotiations.

Buck kicked open his door and pointed the rifle at the Mexicans. "Get behind the truck and push!" There was no more debate. The truck tried to move, but even with the three pushing, it wouldn't budge. The angels were only a hundred feet away.

"You're gonna need to help 'em," Carl said to Matthew as he kept trying to gas up and over the problem.

Matthew saw how close the angels were. "If you hadn't lost so many on the trip-"

"Don't debate with me!" Carl stammered.

"Can't we just run for it-"

"They will have you in seconds. The truck is our only option." Matthew didn't want to go back there. "Will you go on?" Carl urged.

Matthew cursed as he jumped out and hurried to the back. He joined the Mexicans heaving the truck. The pick-up rolled back and forth a few times, and then, in a mist of brown mud, it tore free. Matthew, once more wearing mud, didn't know whether to be happy or pissed off. "So much for the bath," Matthew muttered.

"Here they come!" Buck yelled from the cab.

The angels were only thirty feet away. Matthew turned to see the truck starting off without him. Matthew and the Mexicans made a run for their fleeing salvation. Matthew leaped, barely catching the back end and hauled himself in. The Mexicans were left behind. He hurried to the back window and pounded it hard. "Thanks for waiting!"

"Hey, you made it didn't you!" Buck retorted.

Matthew turned to see the angels numbers split, one half continuing after the truck as the others veered off towards the running Mexicans. The angels pulled their swords as they chased the running, underwear clad amigos through the grass. In the flash of an eye they cut the Mexicans to pieces.

The second group of angels making for the truck pushed themselves to catch up. Their speed rivaled any Olympian but not the technology of man. As the truck started to pull away the angels leaped into the air and flew after them. Matthew watched in awe as they soared. "That's not something you see everyday."

"Give it all you got!" Buck yelled as he leaned out the window with his rifle. "Here," Buck hit Matthew in the shoulder with a rifle butt. "You're gonna need this."

Matthew took the weapon. "What about you?" Matthew asked.

"Don't worry about me," Buck replied pulling an AK-47 from the cab. "I always carry a spare."

The earth next to the truck exploded in a plume of smoke and dirt. The truck jumped into the air, nearly overturning, and swerved as it continued on. "What the fuck..." Matthew looked up as another bolt came flying down in front of the truck tearing a hole in the ground. The truck jerked to avoid the fissure nearly throwing Matthew over the side. His ribs rammed into the steel and he winced. "Good driving," Matthew replied.

"Fuck you!" Carl yelled back as he drove on.

"Can't you show some originality?" Matthew stared back up at their flying friends. Another angel pointed his sword downward. It glowed a bright white, electricity crackling along its length as a bolt came flying from the blade missing the truck by mere inches slamming into the ground behind them. The angel that shot the bolt suddenly cracked back as if hit. Matthew was too deaf from the previous explosions to hear the gunshot.

"Another notch," Buck hollered. "One more reason I'm going to Hell!" Buck screamed a rebel yell as he aimed and fired again, knocking another angel from the sky.

Matthew smiled. "Fuck yeah!" he breathed as he took aim at the soaring numbers above them. He squeezed off a shot, the recoil bruising his shoulder and the shot going wide. "Shit!" Matthew's shoulder throbbed.

"Come on, mother fuckers!" Buck yelled as he continued firing. A group dropped from the sky in perfect unison to sweep at the truck. Buck switched the AK to automatic and smiled at the incoming visitors. "Come get you some!" He squeezed off a slashing wall of gun fire that ripped through the angelic assault. "Whoo hooooo!" he screamed at his triumph.

Huge holes continued to erupt all around them as the truck jigged and jagged. "We can't shake 'em!" Carl yelled to Buck. "I'm going for Buddha's!"

Matthew squeezed off another shot as the truck veered sharply causing his shot to miss the mark. "Nice going!" Matthew yelled at Buck. "I didn't think smugglers were supposed to get caught!"

"Hey, don't blame me!" Buck squeezed off another shot. "You wanted to stop!"

***

They soared with majesty, their white robes fluttering in the ethereal winds. Their swords of shining silver shone with the electricity of Creation. The legion continued after their mortal invaders. Beneath them were the vast plains, but before them loomed the craggy crown of another's realm.

"Sir," one of the flying angels spoke to his commander, Gabriel. "They are approaching the border. Shall we break off pursuit?"

"I do not break off anything!" Gabriel thundered, his face determined.

"But sir, we cannot afford an incident. We must break off pursuit."

"Take the men back, then!" Gabriel retorted. "I'll go alone."

"Sir-" the angel was shocked at the order.

"Go!" Gabriel shouted.

***

"Looks like we scared them off," Matthew replied as he saw the numbers of angels fade behind them.

"We? Try me. I should charge you for the bullets you wasted."

The truck slowed down a little as the soil went from soft greenery to a bald brown. Rocks littered their path, mountains looming on the horizon. "We should be safe now. We crossed the border a few minutes ago." The truck shook up and down as something dropped onto the back, rocking the pick-up on its axels. "What the hell was that?" Carl yelled.

Matthew stared at the giant standing before him. His robe whipped and waved as his blue eyes focused on him. His blade was longer than Matthew was tall. The angel, Gabriel, looked Matthew up and down before focusing on the rifle in his hand. "You! You challenge the soldiers of God!"

Matthew looked down at the rifle. "Whoa! Whoa whoa whoa, I'm not that good a shot-"

"Many angels fell today." Gabriel came towards Matthew, raising his sword to strike.

"Yeah, well..." Matthew wasn't sure what to do, so he did what they always did in the movies. He pulled the rifle up and pointed it at Gabriel. "Eat this!" Gabriel brought his sword down cutting the rifle in half. Matthew raised the bisected piece to his face. "Oh shit."

Buck stuck his head out the window. "Hey, that was my rifle!" He aimed his AK and released a volley of shots. Gabriel perfectly parried and blocked every bullet, deflecting them to the four corners.

"Eat your heart out, Skywalker," Matthew breathed.

"Die sinner!" Gabriel shouted as he sliced at Buck nearly taking his hand off and sending the AK to the ground.

Matthew jumped forward and let loose a kick to Gabriel's groin. It was like kicking stone, and he did it with his bad toe. Matthew fell back and hit his head on the back of the cab. Gabriel looked down at his waiting victim and raised his blade for the kill. The light that glinted off the electrical blade broke Matthew out of his dizzy spell. As it came down Matthew rolled to the side, the blade slicing through the middle of the cabin.

"Shit!" yelled Carl, the shock of the blade causing him to pull too hard on the wheel. The truck capsized, flying to the left sending Matthew and Gabriel into the air. The truck overturned and skidded into the dirt, cutting a jagged scar into the rocky soil. The wheels kept spinning as the rest of the pick-up remained still and silent.

Matthew landed on his back. He raised himself into a sitting position feeling all around. He was ok. He was ok! Matthew hurried towards the overturned truck. "Buck? Carl?"

"Yeah?" came a groan from inside.

"You're alive!" Matthew shouted for joy.

Buck pulled himself out through the passenger window. "Of course we're alive. We're already dead, remember? No bodies to injure." Matthew helped pull Carl out as Buck walked over to the unconscious angel. "You cost me two rifles you asshole."

"Let it go, Buck," Carl ordered. "We got to get moving."

"This asshole owes me two rifles!" Buck kicked the angel's large, lifeless form, not even budging him. "Isn't that right!"

"Buck!" Carl yelled.

"What?" Carl and Matthew gave Buck an irritated stare. "Oh, ok. And you," Buck pointed at the angel Gabriel. "This is your lucky...day?"

The ground seemed to shake. Mini-quakes came and went. Matthew and Carl turned around to see their visitor: their large visitor. "Uh," Matthew started, pointing to Buck, "we're not with that guy over there."

CHAPTsErenitynotR 10

Upon the seven hills rested the seat of the ecclesiastical empire, that capital of the Church. Rome was the sole section of Europe which still stood against the might of the American army. Wheeling around, free of the eastern hordes of Russia, the American forces struck deep into the heart of their former allies, stabbing them in the back. The fragmented forces of the continent were no match for the unified command of Ford's force. Separate and divided, America drove through Europe to its goal: the Papal Estate of Vatican City. The Protestants of Europe turned against their Catholic peers, inciting chaos and mob violence throughout the cities of ancients. Everywhere America trod foundations cracked and serenity surrendered to the underlying tensions of generations.

All that stood between the Pope and the hammer of Matthew's might was a division of French troops and, ironically, the only Swiss force to ever see action in nearly two centuries. The French sat behind their barricades of sand bags, rifles ready, smoke pouring into the sky from scores of lit cigarettes. Cold sweat ran down their faces, their eyes scanning the emerald land before them. Nothing but silence resided in this most disputed section of the world. The peace was precarious, needing but a nudge to send it over into the abyss. The city of Rome behind them was dead. No one roamed the roads or admired the monuments of a dead culture. They were too afraid of joining their ancestors as another extinct breed. The barbarians had returned.

"Where are they?" a French soldier asked his friend.

"They will not come. They fear the strength of France." His friend put on a false air of bravado.

"Then they'll be here soon," the soldier replied.

Along the line fear worked its weakening charm, enticing them to run from the immaterial danger ahead. Instinct urged them to flee, to survive another day. Only their will, bent as it was, kept them in place. Here a soldier checked his rifle again making sure it was loaded. There another soldier prayed loudly for his soul. Nervous conversations tittered along the crooked line.

The eyes of a generation were focused on this moment, the most monumental of moments, of their time. The secular authority of humanity threatened to eradicate the Church proving the right of might, the strength of the flesh, against the flimsy belief in faith, the untouchable spiritual. Despite placing their bodies upon the altar, God was not with them this day.

The French had chosen this honor, to be the protectors of Pope and Church. No one else deserved to protect this "prestigious" organization as well as them.

No one had stopped the blitzkrieg. So how would they, these mere thousand, stave off well over a hundred times their number pouring this way through the valleys like an all consuming flood? Spartan stoicism was far from the romantic notions of Gallic culture.

A soldier's arm shook as he waited for his coming executioners. Tears trickled down his face. He tried to pray, his voice cracking with every whisper. He looked up to the red sun. The crimson splotch marred the sky as if gutted, blood spewing across the horizon. The clouds did not protect them from the sight of this dying day.

Someone screamed down the line. The troops grabbed their rifles and looked into the distance. An armored column was approaching, the earth disemboweled beneath their treads as the dust of Terra's corpse flew to the sides and behind the oncoming army. The tanks were not alone as aircraft boomed overhead, a challenging war cry that disheartened these demoralized men further. The jets released something into the sky, something...pink. Was it gas? The French looked up at the falling debris as it scattered in the wind and fell towards them. The pink fragments fluttered down within reach. Soldiers stretched out and grabbed at the airborne gift: paper. They dropped paper.

A Frenchman grabbed at one of the falling sheets. It appeared to be blank. "What is this? Are they trying to kill us by paper cut?"

"Turn it over, you fool!" his squad leader commanded, knocking him in the head causing his helmet to bounce off.

The Frenchman flipped the sheet over and read in halting English: "We...have...guns."

"So they have guns," the squad leader replied. "So do we!"

The Frenchman continued reading. "We...will...shoot...you."

"Merde!" the squad leader gasped.

"They are bluffing," one of the squad members challenged. "No one would dare fire on the French."

The tanks pulled up in a row two hundred meters from the barricade of sand bags. The French stared in awe at the armored beasts that sat before them. Metallic sounds echoed across the field as the hatch of the central tank popped open. A man stood up, black beret on his head with the insignia of a colonel. He scanned the assembled, pulling a bull horn out of the belly of the beast and raised it to his mouth. His face was blank, revealing neither his motives nor feelings. "I am here to offer you a chance to surrender. Do so now while you can or face annihilation."

In the face of so much destructive power the French morale broke. Men started to fade off, away from the trenches. Others cried and mourned the end of their existences and the coming burial of their world with them.

A Frenchman jumped onto the sandbag barricade, rifle in hand. He turned to his comrades. "Soldiers of France!" The fleeing French froze, turning to this figure. "Before you is a force of unconquerable might who wishes only to destroy all that we hold dear, rape our wives, daughters, and sisters, and drink the very wine of our vineyards until they are withered and barren. They are a force that abhors the beauty of humanity, the preciousness of romance, and the artistic qualities of our nouveau views. Behind us is the crown jewel of our beliefs, the seat of our beloved Pope, through who alone may we find some possible way into the heavens above."

"How can we possibly win?" one of the troops asked, cigarette hanging from his bottom lip.

"We are men of France! We can do anything! We are the pinnacle of mankind, the leaders of Europe! We stand here because no one else would or could. It is our duty to Christians, to Europe, to history to stand against these American thugs and show them that we will never surrender because we are from France!"

The entire line cheered loudly, thrusting their rifles up and down in the air.

"You've got to be fucking kidding me," the Colonel muttered as he stared at the jouncing French celebrating in the face of overwhelming odds.

"What is your command, sir?" asked his gunner from within the tank.

The Colonel looked out across the field at the mass of men that stood before his army and the objective. He scowled at the insanity. He pursed his lips as the French cursed and screamed at his assembled battalion. "Fire."

The tank let loose a round, recoiling a few feet as the artillery tore shrieking through the air. The French continued to scream abuse until the round ripped into the innards of a building behind them. The entire French force turned and saw the yawning hole, burning debris smoking from the massive bite, their cigarettes all falling out of their mouths in perfect unison. They turned back to the assembled tanks waiting to fire again.

The Colonel watched as the entire force dropped their rifles and raised their arms in the air. "So much for the glory of France."

"Sir," came a soldier inside the tank. "The President wishes an update on our status."

"Tell him he may begin his approach. The city is ours."

***

Matthew sat atop an elephant, bound behind Buck and Carl. The driver in the front, some Indian barely concealing his naughty bits in a loin cloth, directed their path. As Matthew tried see where they were going, Carl's mullet kept blowing in his face causing him to constantly shift his face left then right. Irritated, he lashed out. "Great getaway guys. We got caught by Mr. Snuffaluffagus."

"Don't blame me," Carl retorted. "I wasn't expecting Buddha's cronies being out on patrol. Besides, I'd deal with them over the angels any day."

"So, uh..." Matthew looked around at the rocky landscape. "Where exactly are we?"

"These," Carl shook his head around to signify everything around them but only got more hair in Matthew's face, "are the lands of Buddha."

"Buddha owns a part of Heaven?"

"Yeah," Carl replied.

"How did that happen?"

"Hey, kid, I'm just a smuggler, ok. I don't know nothing but what I'm told."

"Well, you've been up here for awhile. I just thought you knew something."

Carl struggled to try and face Matthew, nearly falling off the elephant. He settled for looking over his shoulder. "I'm a good ol' boy. How much do you really think I know about some god damn curry muncher?" The elephant stopped. Carl turned around surprised. The driver was giving him a dirty look. Carl took a swallow and tried to smile, his brown teeth not helping. "Was it something I said?"

"Never insult the Buddha." The driver's warning was sharp and to the point as he returned to his duty and continued leading the elephant on.

"Touchy bastard ain't he," Carl whispered.

"Maybe I can ask him about Buddha-"

"No, kid," Carl cut him off, shaking his head wildly. "Don't even think it."

"Hey, I have a problem and need all the help I can get. Excuse me-"

Carl bumped back into him. "Shut up!"

"No," Matthew replied. "I want to know."

Carl bumped him again. "You're gonna get us in trouble. Shut up!"

"No. And don't tell me what to do." Matthew shoved him hard with his shoulder.

"I said shut up!" Carl went to jostle Matthew again only to discover he had retreated back a little to avoid the hit. Matthew raised his leg and kicked Carl in the back. "You son of a bitch!" Carl hopped around, twisting to face Matthew. "You ain't getting away with that."

"What are you going to do?"

"Oh, you'll see!"

"The only thing you'll see is the bottom of my foot."
Matthew raised his leg again to kick Carl in the head. Carl
moved to the side to avoid the blow. He laughed, angering
Matthew who kicked again. Carl dodged once more.
Matthew feinted a kick to the left and kicked Carl as he
dodged right sending him screaming off the side of the
elephant. The driver turned around as did Buck. Carl landed
on the ground hard with a "whoof". Moaning he begged to be
helped up. The driver and Buck looked up at Matthew.

"Oops?" Matthew offered.

***

Matthew, clad in black, walked through the square of St.
Peter alone, his boots clacking on the hard ground beneath.
The sky was gray and misty. He stood there and stared at
St. Peter's Basilica, his destination. Cardinals, priests, and
bishops made a column on either side of the entrance lining
his path. Swiss Guards stood with pikes ready to defend the
doors.

Matthew strolled down the column of black, white, and
red, smiling at the princes and servants of the Church. The
men did not return the grin, their heads bowed. The air was
proving as cold as the reception. The wind was quiet as he
marched on through the stillness looking at the mourning
faces of the clergy that dared meet his. They stood,
dignified, dressed in their finery. How fitting for this, the
funeral of the Church.

Matthew mounted the steps before him, taking his time
and enjoying the moment. As he reached the doors the
guards crossed pikes to prevent his entrance. "Such
inhospitality is unnerving here in the capital of Christianity."

"We seldom welcome serpents in our doors," one of the guardsmen retaliated.

Matthew gave the Swiss Guard a grin. "It is not wise to insult a man who could wipe you from this world with the wave of a hand."

"I would be welcomed into a much better world for doing so."

"Oh, don't worry," Matthew leaned in to the guard, his form reflected twice over in Matthew's shades, "that world will be mine soon. Now?" Matthew raised his hand, palm up to indicate his want to enter. Grudgingly the pikes parted. Matthew pushed against the closed doors opening into the cavernous space inside.

He walked the halls as if he knew them by heart. His steps were like the ticking of a clock counting down to the end sounding one after another throughout this tomb to a dying faith. Matthew relished the hypocrisy of this spiritual movement for its materialistic possessions as he passed between walls of gold, silver, and jewels embedded in undulating marble. He marched throughout the home of sinners and saints, smiling up to the vaulted ceiling as he made his way to the papal altar. Only the spirits of those long passed were allowed within to watch the fall of a line stretching two millennia.

Matthew pushed open the sealed doors to enter the cathedral. There, in front of the altar, the Pope kneeled in his finery praying. Matthew smirked as he stopped to admire the scene. He looked up to the stained glass windows; the works of man, breaking the unified white light of Creation into a crude assortment of reds, blues, and worse. How hard it was for them to accept something as it came. Matthew spit in disgust. Finally, he looked at the ceiling. He took in Michelangelo's greatest work and began to laugh. His mocking snicker stole through the holy chamber, defiling its blessed silence. The Pope's concentration broke under the strain. He turned to look over his shoulder, his face weathered and aged. "Why do you laugh?" He could barely speak, the sorrow drowning his soul.

"The mural," Matthew pointed to the ceiling. "How sadly true."

"What do you mean?"

Matthew started down, between the pews, towards the Pope. "God gave you so much." One of the windows shattered, colored shards exploding into the cathedral. "He gave you life." Another window blew. "He blessed you." The windows continued to splinter and implode as he walked past them. "He..." Matthew seemed to choke up. "He loved you!" Matthew hissed. The remaining windows blew out, the white floor covered in sharp shards of multiple hues. Matthew stood behind the kneeling Pope who dared look behind himself no longer instead giving himself entirely to Jesus. "He gave you Existence. Our Existence!" Matthew knocked the papal tiara off of the Pope's head in a display of disrespect. "Don't you wish to look at your conqueror?"

The Pope rose from the floor, turning to match eyes with Matthew. "You conquer nothing more than soil. You shall never conquer our souls."

Matthew started laughing that wicked cackle again, baring his yellowed teeth, noticeably sharper. He slapped a hand on the Pope's shoulder. "I care little for your souls." With his free hand he removed his shades to show those yellow, bloodshot eyes. The irises had become reptilian, inhuman.

"Who are you," the Pope breathed, terror infecting him as he backed away.

Matthew's face morphed into Peter's. "I am but a messenger." His face morphed back into the twisted visage of Matthew.

"My God," the Pope whispered.

Matthew glided to the Pope, tightening his grip on Jesus' mortal embodiment and brought him inches before his face. "He was mine long before he was ever yours." He looked the Pope up and down, violating the sacred vestments with his foul eyes. "That he should love you above us is the truest abomination. So weak and ready for sin. So foolishly given so many chances."

"Who are you?" the Pope whispered again in these hallow halls, not wishing to break the serene silence.

Matthew smiled. "You have courage. So lacking in your predecessors." He looked into the Pope's eyes trying to pierce his soul. "You know me," he hinted, the bass deepening his voice.

"Satan," the Pope hissed.

Satan bared that Cheshire grin. "Yes."

"It can't be. The laws-"

Satan pushed the Pope back causing him to fall to the floor. "The laws! My laws!" He stalked towards the Pope. The Pope scurried backwards across the floor away from the oncoming threat. Satan slowly gave chase. "I know, how could I take a body? The laws forbid flesh being given to one of the angels. It also forbids," Satan started jabbing a gnarled finger at the retreating Pope, "actions of Heaven and Hell from interfering in the lives of man. You broke that statute when your assassins killed...Matthew." Satan ran his palms up his chest to present his hands, still palms up in a supplicating show, to the Pope.

"No."

"When you did that you surrendered this flesh to be done with as I chose. Did you really believe I would create the Antichrist against my own laws? I made them. I know them inside and out. Unlike you and them!" Satan pointed up to the sky. "You use my work without even reading the instruction manual. Fucking children all of you," Satan mockingly stated. "Now I can do as I please." He clucked his dry, swollen tongue. "You humans, so easily manipulated."

"Jesus will stop you."

Satan leaned up against one of the curling pillars giving the Pope a serious look, his amber eyes wide. "Oh yes, he shall smite me down and toss me into the pit!" Satan smiled, his fangs protruding. "That pussy hasn't the balls to interfere. Do you hear me?" Satan yelled up to the ceiling. "This world is mine!" Satan looked back down at the Pope, his face wild with anger. "And I shall return it to the dust from whence it came."

The Pope defiantly stood up, his knees shaking. He dared to walk up to Satan as he rested against the pillar. Satan was a little shocked but quickly hid the emotion behind a mask of arrogance. "You shall fall."

The Devil struck quickly, grabbing the Pope by the throat and gripping tight. The Pope began to gurgle as he was lifted off the floor. "I think not." His laughter and the screams of the Pope echoed through the halls of the grave of Christianity.

***

Matthew continued to shift in his seat as they rode, ascending a series of bumpy hills passing through a craggy mountain pass. These mountains served as part of the boundary between the lands of the Christ and the realm of Buddha, two worlds of differing views crushed together. The boundary was high and near impassable save for this single, narrow path.

Matthew's ass felt like someone was digging a rusty knife into his butt cheeks. He gritted his teeth and continued to shift around, not simply from the pain but also in fear of the missing ground which had dropped off on the side of the pass. They were so high!

Matthew grimaced again. He couldn't even feel his groin anymore. His penis probably rubbed off on the rough hide he had for a seat.

As they rounded the jagged side of the mountain, Matthew saw the bare path drop away into a lush green valley below. The mists in the depths rose in tendrils creating a twisting veil. As they passed through that ethereal barrier, he glimpsed a city.

It was hewn from the stone of the mountain. The buildings rose like fingers to the golden sky, narrow high towers intricately carved with designs as if flowing from the ground. Ridged and rounded with narrow points at the top of every tower, they were organic; structures that co-existed with the natural environment around them. They belonged here, in harmony with Paradise. "Whoa. I've died and gone to Kung Fu Land," Matthew gasped at the ethnic scenery.

"Xanadu," the driver announced as they began their descent into the valley.

Matthew remained quiet as the four of them made their way to the seat of Buddha and Eastern faith. As they neared the metaphysical metropolis Matthew ceased his silence, letting out a remark for every branch that slapped him in the face. "Build a city in the middle of a jungle, but they can't prune their damn trees." The thick forest gradually thinned to reveal the streets of the city. Before he knew it the elephant ceased movement causing Matthew to slide a little forward on his raw groin.

"We're here," the driver calmly told them.

281

Matthew moaned as he slid off the side of the elephant to thump on the ground.

Buck and Carl looked over the side at Matthew as he tried to find life in his lower extremities. "First time rider," Buck decided. Carl nodded in agreement.

As Matthew slumped on the ground, his legs as worthless as his opinions, a group of guards dressed in the orange robes of their order came up to him. Matthew's view followed them from sandals to shaved heads. "You guys are non-violent, right?" Matthew asked. They nodded. "Charitable?" They nodded again. "Can you please help me up?"

The guards looked at one another, conversing in a foreign tongue. They turned back to him. "If you do not accomplish the first step alone, how will you accomplish the second?"

Matthew repaid their sage advice with an irritated expression, his eyebrows lowered and brow furrowed. "I didn't ask for inspiration or enlightenment. I asked for a helping hand."

"Sometimes a word is greater than an act."

Matthew sat up, his legs burning. "Yeah, well I've got two. Fuck you. And you. And you."

The guards once more looked at each other, a little taken aback before looking back at Matthew. "You must learn tranquility. Emotion clouds reason."

"I would kick you guys' asses, but that's a little impossible right now."

"I do not know how to cope with this man," the guard muttered to his comrades.

"Try spending more than an hour with him," the driver retorted, dropping from his high perch. "He never stops complaining."

The guards shook their heads, understanding. "A challenge. We are ready."

Matthew gave them and the entire scene an odd look. "I've died and gone to Hippie Heaven." The guards pulled him to his feet, having to drag him along as his legs refused to function.

As Buck and Carl got down to follow the guards put their hands up. "No, just this one. The Buddha shall see you later." Buck and Carl looked a little insulted but kept their cool as Matthew was dragged off.

His feet cut twin trails through the dirt as they made their way through the mystical city. As he passed through their kingdom, Matthew watched men debate amongst one another. Animals lounged in the streets, some playing together while others simply stared at them as they passed. "Disney on parade," Matthew muttered at the animals that watched.

One interesting section had men clothed solely in orange pants practicing the martial arts. Each man repeated the same moves in unison, kicking into the air, punching before them before reversing with a roundhouse. Matthew looked up at his guards. "Do all you guys know karate?"

"We use the martial arts to balance our bodies and our minds. To bring our souls into perfect harmony."

"Pretty bad ass," Matthew replied nodding his head.

"We do not learn the arts to fight. We learn them to perfect our serenity."

"Kind of like buying a sports car then driving the speed limit," Matthew replied.

They continued bickering as they came upon the central tower of the city. It was no different from any of the others. Nothing distinguished it in size or color, decoration or location. It was as all the other towers were. A large set of bronze doors stood closed before them. As the guards went to open them Matthew was a little uncomfortable. "This is Buddha's place?"

"Yes," the guard replied.

"Shouldn't you knock before you invade his privacy?"

"He does not mind."

Matthew gave him a funny look. "The doors are closed."

"But he is expecting you."

"You sure about that? The last thing I need is another angry god."

"Buddha is not a god," the guard replied, the first hints of emotion in his voice.

"Of course he is!" Matthew retorted. "He's king here right?"

The guard gave him a confused look. "There are no leaders here. We are all equal in our pursuits."

"You guys are all fried. Really."

The doors opened into the sparsely lit space of Buddha's domain. Incense wafted out causing Matthew to cough. The guards dragged him through the doorway, into the cushioned confines beyond. There was but one room, no walls built save for those that held the structure up. Sputtering candles marked the boundaries of this minor realm, their wavering light illuminating the darkness. The floor was covered in pillows.

The lead guard went to the middle of the room. Matthew could see him conversing with someone but could not make out whom. The orange blob prevented him from seeing his next target of insult. *Please let this guy be more receptive than Jesus.*

Matthew held his breath as he heard Buddha's voice. "You may leave him here. We have much to discuss."

The guards dropped Matthew face down into the cushions before they bowed and turned to leave. Matthew remained buried in the pillows as he heard their muted footsteps followed by the doors closing. Great, he was all alone with him. This couldn't any worse.

"Matthew." The Buddha's voice was soothing. "Matthew, please rise." Matthew's words were muffled by the pillows his face rested in. He felt movement. Buddha reached down and, with gentle hands, turned Matthew over. Buddha's face was lined with age and brown as the earth. His hair was shaved clean, his eyes welcoming. His thin face held a ready smile. "It's not polite to make an old man come to you."

"Well...well, it's my legs," Matthew stammered. Buddha looked down at them. "It was a long...a long trip. They're very..."

"You do know you don't have a body anymore, yes?" Buddha asked.

"Well," Matthew began. Those eyes eased his discomfort. A little sheepishly Matthew replied, "Yeah. Yeah, I know."

"So, if you don't have a body anymore then how do your legs ache?" Matthew had never thought of that. "Stand." Matthew tried, Buddha helping him up only for his legs to buckle beneath him. Buddha gave a mild chuckle. "I see you are stubborn in your beliefs."

Matthew blushed, lost among the pillows. "I know they shouldn't hurt, but I can't help it."

Buddha shook his head. "It's all in your mind."

"Oh no, not you too," Matthew replied, irritated.

"Don't be upset, Matthew." Buddha placed his hand on Matthew's head, the anger melting away. "Sometimes we hold on to the things we shouldn't while we let the best things slip away. Look at me, Matthew." Matthew looked away. "Matthew. Look at me." Matthew turned to look at Buddha. "You know you can walk. Now do so."

"It's not that simple," Matthew retorted.

"It is. Just...believe."

Matthew gave him a doubting stare but began to lift himself up again. As his legs began to buckle Matthew refused to accept it. These weren't flesh and bone. These were part of his soul. He stood, however wobbly. He balanced himself. "Ta da!" Matthew exclaimed.

"It's a start, but we haven't much time."

Matthew looked down at Buddha, the man coming only to his chest. "I always expected you to be taller...and fatter!" Buddha gave him that questioning look. Matthew suddenly remembered his place. He didn't want to piss off another important deity. "You're not gonna...you know, kill me or anything for invading your kingdom are you?" Matthew tried to look sincere.

Buddha gave him that grandfatherly smile. "Who said you invaded? Fate has brought you to me for a reason."

"Excuse me?"

"My men found you because I saw your coming. I have been expecting you."

"You didn't pay Buck and Carl-"

"No, Matthew." Buddha put a hand on his arm. "They were not in my employ. Their bringing you here was not by prior planning."

"So I was meant to come here?"

"Yes. Please," Buddha extended his hand. "Have a seat."

"But I just stood up!"

"Sometimes you do the opposite of your goal to achieve it."

Matthew shook his head. "You lost me."

"Don't worry. Time will teach you. Now please."

Matthew collapsed on the cushions, his sore legs trying to knot up as he crossed them. "Oh, cramp, cramp!" he screamed as he straightened one of his legs and furiously rubbed at it, the muscle tightening to a tearing point. Buddha reached out and touched the limb, the pain melting away. "How did you do that? How did you do that?" he asked confounded.

"Faith can be a powerful thing," Buddha stated as he rested his hands on his knees. "Now, to your purpose."

"I actually have one?"

"We all have reasons to be. Some part to play. Perhaps the insect in a jungle does not seem that important, but it does serve a purpose to balancing the whole of their environment."

"I don't think I've been doing a lot of balancing."

"Indeed. You've upset the balance. But it had to be. It was a balance struck by the most corrupt of beings for the worst of reasons."

"You're going to explain, right, because I have no clue about what is going on. Jesus says one thing. Satan says another. It's all really confusing."

"Man was given limited sight because he could never handle the whole of Creation. No one can." Buddha gave a sigh. "But there are always those who believe they can. Needlessly destroying so that holding it all can be simpler than holding a part."

"Excuse me?" Matthew asked.

"You have set into motion a series of events that threaten the very existence of us all. A battle is coming. The final battle in a war that has remained dormant for two thousand years."

"I did this?"

"Yes," Buddha nodded.

Matthew smiled a little. "Now I feel important."

"Do not let pride cloud you like it has Satan...and Jesus. It is a worthless feeling."

"Can I ask exactly what the hell is going on? One minute I'm alive. The next I'm wallowing through the swamps of Purgatory."

"Nearly four thousand years ago, Jesus was sent to Earth. While there he dared to change the rules set millennia ago."

"Who exactly set these rules I keep hearing about? Satan claimed he did-"

"He did. He was the architect of Creation. The laws of nature, physics, all of Creation were crafted by him. He was an amazing figure in his time."

"What happened?"

"Anger, selfishness, pride. Before existence as you know it, the whole of Creation was simply this place. Heaven. No one knows what came before or how this came to be. Only God, the Creator, knows of what was. Some say He tamed the void and created Paradise. Others say Paradise and He came to be at the same moment. No one can ever truly know save He, and He shall never tell. What is known is that God destroyed this perfection."

"Why exactly?" Matthew asked. "Why destroy perfection? He didn't seem to replace it with anything better."

"In all honesty, no one can truly comprehend the complexity that is God. Why He ruptured perfection has been asked by far more people than you or I, but what is known was that that rupture was a wound, a collapse at the center of Existence. Perfection fell into that hole, consumed by the abyss." Buddha seemed to look into another dimension. "Perhaps He did it to give purpose to a purposeless Existence."

"I'm lost," Matthew replied. "Though with all this it doesn't take much to do that."

"Before the Fall all was Heaven. Everything was perfect, yet not. There was no reason to be. There was no destiny or fate. There was no direction or goal." Buddha had thought on this a lot.

"Sounds boring," Matthew offered. Buddha perked up as if proud of Matthew's enlightening of himself. "So God just blew it all up in some sick need for excitement?"

"I do not believe that was the reason," Buddha responded. "What little I do know is that God smote Paradise, causing a large part of it to fall into darkness. Its fragments were scattered throughout the void, the abyss. Heaven was collapsing, all of Creation falling apart. Satan feared for their existence. He could see their end nigh as Paradise continued to fall into the growing chasm. He reasoned with God, preventing the destruction. Together they worked to prevent the annihilation of Heaven, slowing the Fall. It was Satan himself who prevented the fall of Paradise. He created the laws that bound the Cosmos together, giving order to that which clawed at and threatened all with entropy."

"Why do that? I thought he wanted to destroy Heaven."

"That is what the bible would tell you. In fact, Satan has never loved anything more than the realm of his birth, Heaven. He labored ceaselessly, pushing himself to the utmost to rebuild and rebind the void in order to lift it back up and repair the wound of Heaven. His laws prevented the chaos, paving the way for the return of order and the rebuilding of Paradise. He dreamt of sealing the rift, of putting the pieces back together and lifting them back up to their perfect origins. But in that darkness of fire and ice something unexpected arose."

"What was that?" Matthew asked.

"Life. God stood transfixed by what arose in that primordial dimension. A consciousness came to be. At first simple it grew in complexity, fought to survive. For the first time he saw something not of perfection, not designed flawlessly, yet filled with a power as beautiful as his own. By accident a new world had emerged. He did not know what to do. He could not bring himself to end Life's existence.

"He became obsessed with it in its struggles, amazed at its will to continue. He could not murder something so unique. Against all odds, in death and destruction, something precious had arisen. But that changed with time.

"As Life progressed, God became disgusted with it. Violent and bloody, senseless and barbaric. With its growing complexity, Life created more efficient and brutal methods of destruction. Satan was continually in God's ear, begging and pleading with Him to allow the work to continue. He wanted to wipe that one obstacle, Life, away that he might finish the reconstruction and finally make Heaven whole once more. He spoke of Life's flaws, how it was a symbol of what it had come from. He seduced God, asking Him why He preserved His mistake and valued this flaw so highly. It was a stain upon His hands, this imperfection that kept Heaven on the precipice and mocked God's rule. After countless millennia of Satan's soothing pleas and the ever growing barbarism of Life, God assented. He rained fire down upon the Earth, smiting the imperfect Life that existed there and attempting to scorch it away."

"But it didn't happen," Matthew interrupted, shaking his head as he watched Buddha, intently listening for what came next.

"No. Life is not a simple thing to destroy. It arose in the worst of conditions. Something as precious and rare as Life will never cease without a fight to the utmost. Life continued, its existence precarious. God was amazed. Satan was furious. God decided a second chance was in order. He held His hand, watching to see what would come. To the shock of all Heaven, Life progressed and evolved into man, a virtual mirror image of its creator. God was in shock, staring down at Himself. Heaven knew not what to make of it.

"But God's awe slowly turned to rage. Though man appeared as perfect as his creator he had inherited the destructive and violent instincts of his origins. Life was created in violence and existed always in a precarious existence. Man was an animal, just as barbaric and destructive as his forefathers that had been consumed by the fire. God could not bear this, the worst of sins. He could not accept the barbarity. It was blasphemy, the base and evil nature of man. He could not watch Himself, His children, deface His Creation and live as those horrors that came before. He was as imperfect as the carnivores of times past. Man...was no angel. Satan saw this. He felt the anger within his father and began to work his designs again stating how man was an abomination. Humanity, as Satan said, was nothing more than a reminder of how the void was imperfect and forever destined to spawn nothing more than flawed replicas of a land once known as part of Paradise. Was it not time to end this game and restore it to Paradise?"

"What stopped him?" Matthew asked, transfixed by the story.

"Nothing stopped him. God listened to Satan again. What the bible called the Flood was just that, but it was not of water purely. The flood was a meteor shower, as was the time before. He struck the Earth, attempting to erase the memory of the cruel joke Life had played on God. After the inferno smoldered, Earth froze over what was once green and alive but now blackened and dead. All color became buried beneath the sterile snow. The Earth nearly died. But in that darkness, in the death throes of Existence, a voice called to God.

"God was silent. He heard it, that voice that called to Him across the dimensions. It was a man. A man spoke to Him, prayed to Him. That man was Noah."

"How did Noah know?" Matthew asked. "How did he know there was a God?"

"When one is born does he not realize something missing from him? Does he not know there is more than what he sees and smells? More than simply what is real to us? We realize we are but a part, a fragment that has fallen from on high, a piece of the Creator no longer fastened to Him. Noah knew this, felt it in his heart for it is true. We all feel something missing for something is.

"Noah saw the world fall around him but clung to life. He opened his mouth to cry unto God, believing there was a reason and accepting what came from his Creator. God cried.

"Satan was furious, screaming at God's compassion. He claimed that God only wanted to destroy Heaven, leaving the wound of ages to fester that Heaven might collapse into the yawning abyss and be lost eternally to the imperfections of the void where darkness ruled light. Satan sought to steal the Godhead away for this reason, angry at his attempts of reconstruction being thwarted time and again. A war was fought, and Satan was cast out...as was Jesus."

Matthew's jaw hung low. "You're shitting me."

"No, Jesus chose Satan over God. He dared to question God's motives seeing Satan's way. He did not understand why God would choose such a thing as Life over them. He saw Life as illegitimate, an accident that never should have been. God cast him out for these traitorous words, for doubting His command.

"Satan was cast from the Heavens down into the imperfect void. There he found himself in a dimension beyond the worst ever believed existed. Souls have existed since the dawn. Our flesh is merely the imperfect vessels within which they are crafted and grow, awaiting that time when they may step out of their cocoon into that next dimension. What many had forgotten were the souls that came before. Out there, in the void, the lost souls of those that fell, the most barbaric, those forgotten by God, drifted. They were lost, angry, full of rage. They did not understand why they were. They could not grasp why they suffered and now continued on into darkness. God did not claim them. He did not reach out to them. It was Satan who found them, his skill of seduction and willingness to violence scoring him high standing as he and the fallen angels did conquer the damned masses. Through them he saw a chance to eventually retake Heaven. He would attempt a fresh assault which was repulsed. Others followed over the ages.

"God held close to Noah and his children after that. Others survived, but God failed to notice them, transfixed only by those who had called to Him. Those forgotten stretched out for their Creator, creating complex faiths and beliefs in their subconscious knowledge of Him hoping for some way to speak to Him, to understand the why as to their pain and travails only to be unheard. Their anger for God's love for Noah and his children grew. Satan heard them, their muted pleas. He gave them much. Contradicting answers, dreams of empire, forbidden knowledge, racism and intolerance. He gave them dark miracles and false hopes, planting the seeds for their destruction. Many peoples passed away under his guidance as the war spread from Heaven to Earth. God remained blind to them in his growing love for Noah and his spawn. God came to value Life so highly that he swore never to try and wipe it out again. Life continued as it had before only now God spoke to them, guided them. He gave them civilization. He even lifted those He found ready to his kingdom to dwell with Him.

"Some fell away from the path, surrendering to an age old grudge against God, inborn into them, for his attempts against their right to be. Now that God attempted to set His order upon the world many scoffed and chafed at it. They did not want to be ruled, as free and wild as their life had been. Born in chaos, they chose its instinctual freedom over structured security, and mankind split into various groups. The Jews themselves corrupted what God told them, withholding and distorting His words. They felt themselves blessed by birthright, not by act or worth. Time after time God deserted them hoping they would learn.

"Jesus saw this world grow, forced to travel it after his ejection from Heaven as punishment. He yearned to return to Paradise and constructed a way to do so. Whether he came to value man or see him as a valuable pawn he acted on those hidden impulses. He discovered God's recent misunderstanding with the Jews and moved in to rectify it, taking a more hands on and personal approach. Under the guise of man, Jesus decided to work with the mortals, to guide them as God did, to give them a symbol to strive for. He preached to them, taught them, attempted to bring perfection to Earth. The world would not have something so perfect in a world imperfect. God saw that day, the Crucifixion, when man struck a blow against Heaven and tried to kill one of his children. That was when He was struck down by a stroke and lost to us all.

"When God fell all of Creation fell into chaos. Jesus did not die, despite what you have been told. Man could never kill him. He wanted to remain on Earth, to show the power of God over even the most mortal of problems, death. He wanted to continue to guide them, to find that middle way between God and Satan to return Earth and the void up to Heaven. But he heard of God's fall. In the confusion of those days, he returned to Heaven, leaving man to do what he had wanted. With God incapacitated, Jesus took up the reigns of power. But with that unlimited authority, he was unsure what to do. For all the knowledge he thought he held, Jesus realized how limited even he was. Satan knew exactly what he wanted to do."

Matthew hadn't noticed he was leaning forward. "This would make an awesome movie," Matthew breathed.

"Matthew," Buddha chastised him.

He quickly leaned back. "Sorry. Caught up in the story. So, what did Satan do?"

"He knew of Jesus' hatred for man after what they had done to him. No one can suffer so much peacefully without some emotional scarring. Satan made an offer to Jesus. The struggle between Heaven and Hell over humanity had taken heavy tolls not only on those of Paradise and the Abyss but also humanity. Satan called an end to the eternal battle, a truce. He knew Jesus was not dedicated to man as much as God. Jesus had only aided mankind to recover God's good graces, as a means to rebuild Heaven not to redeem humanity. He played on that, convinced Jesus it was best to call a truce...and leave mankind to fend for itself."

"Jesus abandoned us?"

"Why do you think, unlike those ancient days, that Christians were devoured by their enemies when they called to Heaven for their salvation? Jesus surrendered you for peace above and time to solidify his position. If man survived he could be guided by his own hand to perfection via the Church. If his nature took hold he would wipe himself out and thus make way for the resurrection.

"The angels saw the petty reasons for the truce and dared to defy it, unable to abandon the principles of their God. That is where Islam sprung from. They returned to Earth, aiding humanity once more. The Muslim victories, the miracles that they achieved, came from the angels led by Gabriel. He would not leave you, regardless of what Jesus told him. Another battle raged in Heaven as the truce with Satan was threatened. The angels lost in that civil war against the human hordes of Jesus. On Earth, Jesus attempted to undo the damage, calling for Christians to attack Muslims and wipe them from the world. Our imperfections had infected even Paradise." Buddha seemed mournful.

"Jesus ordered these crusades not simply to spite the angels that challenged him but also for the fact that Muslims saw him as but a man. Jesus had come to believe, as leader of Heaven, that he was much more. He was not a flawed mortal. He was an angel, the chief angel. He was now God. He had been corrupted by the powers he now wielded. Now he tries to brain wash, eradicate your free thought believing you impossible of anything but the basest purposes. He orders you to follow his principles, to do as he says for no other reason save that it is as he says. Believe in him absolutely or he throws you back down to suffer again.

"Humanity has come a long way. Without Heaven to protect and guide them they have guided themselves. Technology has advanced as man, realizing he was alone, decided to find the means to protect themselves in the vast ocean they are stranded in, to organize and craft Existence to themselves as their Heavenly Father had."

"Why does Satan honor the truce? If he is such a liar and deceiver why doesn't he simply spring a surprise attack?"

"His pride, Matthew. His word means much to him. Though he lies and deceives, he always keeps his word. It is law, his law. He cannot bring himself to soil the rules which he created. To insult himself would be the greatest damage he could ever do. So he has waited, smiling as humanity lost faith in God and Heaven, driving them away slowly from their divine source so that he could lead them towards this day, towards their extinction."

"What do you mean?" Matthew began to feel a fear he could not ignore.

"You were the catalyst. It has begun. My agents have told me of what has come to pass. How Satan used you. How he deceived the Vatican, telling them that you were the Antichrist. Assassins were sent to murder you. That is why you died. They did so at what they thought was the command of Heaven. It turned out to be Satan in disguise."

"That fucking prick!"

"In killing you, Heaven surrendered their rights to your body. In so doing Satan could do with your body whatever he wished."

"Why didn't he just go all Linda Blair on me and possess me?"

"The treaty forbids any action by Heaven or Hell on Earth. He could not possess you without the law allowing them to evict him from your body. That is what an exorcism is."

"So what is he planning to do now...with my body?" Matthew choked out the last few words with the bile they caused.

"He has already begun his plan. Jesus may not interfere as Satan drives humanity closer and closer to their destruction."

"Why is he even continuing all this? Even if he destroys everyone he'll never get back into Heaven."

"He is obsessive. He no longer cares. This is what has caused the largest problem in his existence. His hatred of

Life and continual existence amongst the damned has destroyed his sanity. He must destroy you or he'll never find peace, no matter how disturbing or warped it may be."

Matthew sat there, terror enveloping him. He wanted to cry, the sensation of no control making him feel vulnerable. He was angry at himself for his weaknesses. He had brought this upon all Existence. It was all his fault. His bottom lip shook as his eyes burned. He closed them, the tears dripping down his cheeks. "We have lost."

"Do not believe it all impossible, Matthew. You have only played your part."

"My part," Matthew choked out. He stood up, nearly staggering. His hatred gave him the strength and focus to forget the pain. He grabbed a pillow and threw it across the room. "Is that supposed to make me feel better? I have damned us all!"

Buddha cocked his head. "Your part is not yet over, Matthew."

"My part. My part! What about you, huh? What is your part?" Matthew spat. "If you knew all this why didn't you do anything?"

Buddha took a breath, closing his eyes and touching his forehead. As his eyes opened they were an unearthly white light shining like the sun. "I was born Siddhartha Guatamma. I was a prince, born into splendor and riches. I knew not pain. I knew not suffering. I knew only pleasure. My wishes were reality. Life was a game to me." Matthew's anger faded as he listened to the first fragments of emotion in Buddha's voice.

"I remember that day. To my people, my caste, war was a glorious occupation. Proof of your intelligence and strength. That day I saw it. So much of it. Death. The darker side of life." Buddha's voice became ragged. "I heard their screams.

298

Saw their suffering." Buddha's face revealed his epic age, the wrinkles crinkling his thick skin, as the emotions attempted to subsume him. "I awoke from my dream into a reality I did not recognize. I could see and hear...I could see and hear such things I never knew. How fragile life was."

He turned to Matthew. "I swore never to fight again. I...I could not understand. There was no glory in this. There was no purpose. Yet, it was central to man. As I lived I saw more of it. So much suffering. So much pain. Against one another. Against ourselves. For what?

"Why? Why did humanity accept this? Why did we torture ourselves? In fact, why were we? To live then die in a cycle that only repeated without change generation to generation. There had to be more than this flesh and its sensations. And if so, what was it? Why did we all seem so blind to the truth for there had to be a truth? Why would we be if there weren't? What was that truth? I spent so long trying to discover the why. I surrendered my needs, my wants, my desires. My riches became weights that held me back, my title nothing more than a word. I lost my earthly self in search of my spiritual self, but even then, when I emerged from my body at death, that moment when your lessons have finished, I did not know. But he waited there for me." Matthew saw wonderment come across Buddha's face.

"God waited for me. He was amazed at this man who overcame imperfection, perhaps the closest to his angelic first born. Without his light I struggled on in the dark and found my way. He gave me this land," Buddha said, remembering. "He gave it to me to guide my students as they arrived. In me he saw another way, man teaching man. His inherent light within us. For all he did, for all his efforts, God knew he could never truly know man. He knew only

299

man could save himself. So I came to be a teacher. A teacher for man...and a teacher for him to come."

"Him who?" Matthew asked.

The light faded away from his eyes. "I know my purpose. For all the possibilities I never deviated from the path I knew was mine. When all seems lost you must realize it happened for a reason. You may question it, but that does not change it. Do not look to the past or to the possible futures. Look to the now. Embrace what your soul tells you. In that alone will you ever truly find peace and purpose."

Matthew's face became calm, his mottled skin relaxing. He wiped his tears. "So what can we do?"

"We must speak with Jesus. Perhaps I can convince him to invade Earth."

"He won't invade? Why? We're all going to die!" Buddha raised a hand, and Matthew calmed down. "Serenity now, serenity now."

"He has grown complacent. He cares little for all of you and twisted the doctrines of God to help him prosper." Buddha looked away, his face starting to show signs of anger and disgust. "He has perverted the laws of faith, asking for blind obedience to him rather than belief in ourselves. He offers you shallow gifts to do what is right rather than for you to learn from your actions. The man has become more mortal and flawed than I thought an angel possible of."

"Can we trust him?" Matthew asked.

Buddha's eyes began to redden, mist gathering. "I don't know. I hope so."

***

A large train of elephants were being prepared for the journey to Jesus' domain. Matthew watched as supplies were loaded. Out of the corner of his eye he caught a glimpse of Buck and Carl. He hurried over to them. "So, you guys ready for the trip?"

Buck and Carl looked at one another. "We're staying here," Buck replied.

"What? What the hell for?"

"Well," Carl started. "All this free love, endless poon tang...why should we waste our time with this? It's not our problem." He put his hand on Matthew's shoulder. "You understand, ri-"

Matthew slapped his hand off. "Pathetic. You're fucking pathetic."

"Say what you want, buddy boy, but I ain't dying for Jesus. What did that bastard ever do for me? Huh? Nothing. So fuck him and his shit. Come on Buck." Buck and Carl turned around and made their way back towards the city.

Buddha came up behind Matthew. "Do not let them get to you."

"Why even try?" Matthew asked, turning to Buddha. "Maybe humanity deserves to disappear."

"Every light has a shadow, Matthew."

"I...I just don't know." Matthew's lip started to tremble. "Why should we save someone that doesn't even care?"

"Because if we don't, who will?" Matthew looked at Buddha who reassured him. "Legends are all fine and good, but reality is what we have. Even in reality, legends can still exist." Buddha slapped Matthew on the side. "We go now, to Zion." Matthew nodded and followed Buddha onwards to his destiny.

CHaosPTER 11

It fell from the heavens, Armageddon fashioned by the hands of men. An artificial star dropped from the sky and dove into the earth. Light, blinding light, tore through the darkness illuminating life with death. Structures ripped free like paper, a civilization burned to cinders. Screams were swallowed in the explosions as those who howled them vanished from existence, their atoms scattered. The sand turned to glass reflecting the dark sky above. All that was...was no more. Plumes of smoke rose to the sky as if to offer this demented sacrifice to God himself. This scene played itself out across India. It was the climax to a rivalry that had escalated from the petty to the genocidal.

"They've done it, Prime Minister!" cried one of the generals hiding in the bunker. The leader of India stared, transfixed by the mortal wounding of his nation. His senses, his rational thinking collapsed in upon itself. "Prime Minister?"

The Prime Minister turned to his generals, his soul aching and paralyzed. His eyes were wide and his mind broken. His reason was lost, his instinct all that remained. "We...will return in kind." He spoke without thought. "It is expected of us. Launch our missiles."

"Yes, sir," replied a lieutenant as he hurried to the communications equipment. Death would be met by death.

***

"Situation report?" the Devil asked, standing at the head of the table receiving his daily update. The light of the room seemed to dim around his form.

"India has taken substantial casualties from nuclear strikes launched by Pakistan, but India has struck back." The

Devil smiled. "Casualties for Pakistan alone are estimated at twenty million."

"We should have done something to prevent it coming to this," Admiral Odom whispered, sighing.

"I guess the time for negotiations has passed," the Devil responded with a short series of barking laughs.

The Secretary of State, Hermann, gave him a pained look, not believing his comment. "Our...estimates place casualties at nearly fifty percent for Pakistan which will either starve or die of radiation in the next few months."

"And India?"

"They were hit harder, but our estimates only see a thirty percent casualty rate. Higher if aid fails to arrive by the end of the year."

"What action do we have on the Russian front?" Satan asked.

"Mr. President, what shall we do about India and Pakistan?"

"I do not care for either side!" Satan glowered at Hermann. "This is their problem. Not mine. I tire of becoming involved in everyone else's affairs. The world reaches for us with one hand while preparing a dagger for our back with the other. For too long have we helped our enemies and parasites. Our time of altruistic charity is over. If they wish to wipe themselves out all the better. Fewer problems for me. And according to your reports, there shall be little to save in the coming months as it is."

The Security Advisor watched Satan and Hermann carefully, the room filled with tension. He took up control of the meeting. "The Russians are tied down and taking heavy losses attempting to push into Central Asia. Even more in Eastern Europe."

"And China?" The Devil had calmed slightly but still watched Hermann behind dark shades.

"With your refusal to intervene and press talks they've begun their move on Taiwan."

"They continued with their plebiscite did they?" Satan asked.

"Yes, Mr. President. An overwhelming majority voted for recognized independence from China."

"China would not abide that," Satan added. "China's response?"

"They opened fire less than an hour ago with their naval fleet. The Taiwanese President has asked for our support."

The Devil nodded his head. "We've never denied defense to our allies." A wicked grin stole across his face. "Launch our nukes along the Chinese coast. It is time we solved the problem of those damnable Asiatic hordes. Communists and thieves the lot of them. Likewise send our men into North Korea." General Adams perked up at that. "America has unfinished business to complete. It's about time we 'liberated' their starving masses."

"Yes, sir!" General Adams smiled. Finally action over words, the way he liked things.

"That will be all," Satan waved them off.

"But Mr. President-"

"He said that would be all." Brown cut Hermann off.

Hermann's conscience had begun to emerge as his soul wretched at the stench of this new policy. These men worked to bury it all over again. Hermann wished to speak his mind but thought better of it. Emotions had no place in world affairs.

The Devil sat down and leaned back in his chair, closing his eyes as the generals, admirals, and politicians filed out. Hermann's eyes remained on the lounging figure as he removed himself. This was not his brand of politics. He hung his head low, his mouth remained shut.

As the door closed, the shadows began to take shape, one by one stepping forward. "It has begun?" The Devil asked.

"Yes, my lord," hissed a shadow. "Buddha speaks with the Christ as of this moment."

"At last. Rules be damned, the war has come!" He slammed both fists hard on the table.

"Are you sure they will fight, my Lord?" the wraith asked, bent in a semi-bow.

"If they do or do not it matters little. I have won." His laughter turned to a cackle that cracked off the walls.

***

"We must interfere or else there will be nothing left." Buddha gave Jesus a pleading stare.

"We cannot intervene," Jesus began, sitting emotionless in his chair at the head of the conference table, calm skies behind him. The apostles sat quietly, hands kneaded together, fawning over their lord, the source of their authority. Gabriel brooded in the corner quietly, having escorted in both Matthew and Buddha who stood to the side of the table. "The truce has held for over two thousand years. Two thousand years of peace and you wish to throw that away?"

"Of peace?" Buddha retorted. "What peace? Without the guiding hand of Heaven, Earth has wandered closer and closer to their own destruction. Hell constantly makes use of loopholes and scoffs at the treaty. Even now Hell manipulates the treaty in a way that threatens not just them, but you as well. Do you not realize the dangers that await if you stand by and simply watch? What of God's mandate? It is your duty to protect them!"

"It is not my duty!" Jesus snarled, standing up. "Who are you to order me to do anything? You who allow fugitives, unbelievers in my divinity, and worse into your lands! Yes, I know of those you give access, defying my decrees as if you were my equal. You are a cancer in my kingdom-"

"My lands are my problem and mine alone. I shall make my decisions as to who deserves access and who does not."

"Is that why you refuse access by my men when certain people invade my lands without authorization but welcome my enemies with open arms?" Jesus demanded with a nod towards Matthew.

"Enemies? You know who he is," Buddha staunchly replied defending Matthew. "You have always known. His destiny-"

"You," Jesus jerked his head at Matthew and Buddha, "Are nothing more than animals. Animals!" Jesus pulled his gloves off to reveal the jagged, still fresh wounds in his hands. Blood trickled down his upraised palms. "Tell me these savages are worth the blood of Paradise. Go on! We see what they are worth." Jesus breathed deeply, his chest rising and falling as the air hissed in and out.

"Too long have you refused those wounds the right to heal. Too long have you used a time long past as a purpose for your crusades. Do not blame them all for the actions of a few-"

"Do not lecture me, mortal!" Jesus cut Buddha off. "You do not know the entire scheme of things. Do you not realize that Heaven itself continues to disintegrate?"

"What nonsense do you speak of?" Buddha asked.

"It is no nonsense. Since the Fall the universe has expanded. Expanded into the realm of Heaven, stealing away our precious lands in exchange for yours. The expansion continues even now and is threatening to swallow all of Paradise into the abyss. How many millennia does Heaven have left? Twenty? Fifty? It is but a finite number before Paradise becomes part of your flawed dimension."

"I thought Satan had stopped the expansion," Matthew blurted out.

Jesus turned his wrathful gaze fully on Matthew. "The expansion has never stopped. How could it with your kind preventing it." Jesus became mournful. "Even with all your wisdom and...all knowing," Jesus insultingly spat, "You could not foresee this. You think you understand it all, the reasons. What you know is limited and as flawed as your kind. And now, Paradise faces eventual collapse." Jesus looked at Buddha, then Matthew. "How can I defend them? You, all of you, are beneath us. You threaten our world, our way of life. You expect me to protect you? You flawed, destructive creatures! Why save you when in so doing I sign the death warrant of our very realm?" Jesus clucked his tongue. "Perhaps Satan is right. Perhaps I should let you fall."

"You fucking asshole!" Matthew yelled. He went to jump over the table, Buddha grabbing him and pulling him back.

"Do you not see?" Jesus replied, pointing at Matthew.

"I see someone willing to fight for their right to live." Buddha looked into Jesus' eyes. "And I see someone who has forgotten how precious life is. You would rebuild Heaven upon the bones of man. But it would cease to be Paradise. All you would have is blessed Purgatory standing upon the most flawed of foundations."

"What I would have is universal peace and safety," Jesus proclaimed. "The war would end. The war over mortality and humanity," Jesus spit. "Heaven and Hell would be one again. Our brothers could return home. And the collapse would end."

"And what of humanity?" Buddha asked, catching Jesus by surprise. Jesus remained silent. "They do not even factor in do they? You haven't changed at all." Buddha sighed.

Jesus gave him a political grin. "I do not have mortal eyes to be blinded by." He glanced over at Matthew. "They brought this upon themselves. Humanity has long sought to destroy itself. I shall not allow their suicidal dreams to include us. I'm sorry, but Heaven shall not intervene."

"Noooo," came a small, tinny rasp. "Noooo." God came wheeling into the room.

"Father, you should not be in here." Jesus went to push him back into the side chamber as God gave him a livid glare. Jesus backed away, fear in his eyes. God rolled about the room, the whirring of his wheels the only sound to be had.

God circled the table, his angry stare passing over the sycophants of the Christ, as his artificial voice chirped emotionlessly: "I...have watched you...twist my...own creations...my own...words. I have...watched you...sit by as...they...as my...children beg...for you...to save...them." His gaze stopped on Matthew, softening. God rolled to a halt at his feet. Matthew took a knee to come face to face with the Almighty. God's eyes seemed to tear up, the water that ran down his face sparkling and bright. His dim eyes found color again, the gray becoming a baby blue. He reached out with his one good arm towards Matthew. Matthew started to lean away but something made him remain. God touched his cheek, tracing the curves of his face and feeling the warmth of his skin. Matthew felt all fear, all doubt melt away. The shadows of his soul were illuminated. God marveled at his own creation. He reached down and switched his voice modulator off. And then, to the surprise of all, God finally spoke his first true words in millennia. "I...made you...so long...ago." That voice was so soft and vulnerable it was nearly lost upon speaking.

God's lips trembled, the power to form words harder than any deed done as deity. He became frustrated at his weakness, his ancient face twisting in agony, but pressed on. "Some say...you were...a mistake. Born...of my...flaws. My...rage." He gave Matthew a half smile. "You...were never...a...mistake." God's bottom lip hung limp as his dull eyes twinkled with a subdued brilliance.

"I...I am...so sorry. I...never...meant to...abandon you. I heard...your cries." God's face trembled. "I...heard you...as I have...heard so many. So much...pain. Pain." God continued to mourn his shortcomings, the flaws that had seeped into his Almighty form. His frail body shook as the emotions had their way with him. "I...wished to...intervene...but could...could do...nothing." God's nose ran as his head drooped to the floor. He wept in front of those assembled, the sorrow weighing him down. "I...I was lost...to you...and you...to me. I forsook...you." He sobbed and fell apart, unable to bear his own existence. God's hand fell from Matthew's face.

Matthew could feel that pain. It ate at his soul, breaking through his sarcasm and wit. It drilled to the depths of his being and touched the rawness within. "I forgive you," Matthew started but stopped, sniffing. "I forgive you for those times. Even though you did not answer...you did listen." He raised God's head, placing his hand on God's. "No one has ever cared to listen." Matthew set his jaw. "Now. Now is more important. We need Heaven...we need you now more than ever." The room remained frozen, yet transfixed by the meeting of mortal and immortal.

God closed his eyes tightly, sighing. The wrinkles of millennia told their tales across his face. Time had aged its maker. He opened his eyes, those blue eyes, and stared deeply into Matthew's soul. "You...are my...child. All...of you. In you...I see...me. That possibility. In that...darkness...is light...brighter...than Heaven's." God's hand gripped Matthew's as his sight seemed to go elsewhere. "I thought...I could...guide you. But...it is you...that guides...me." God's vision settled on Matthew, his back turned to Jesus. "I...shall not...abandon...you...when you...need me...most."

"My God!" Jesus screamed, stepping forward to fracture the moment.

"Hold your tongue!" Buddha lashed back, stepping between God and Jesus. "You shall not silence him again." Jesus glared at Buddha who gave him a shove back. "Know your place," Buddha threatened. Gabriel smirked as Jesus retreated.

"Gabriel?" God called out, questioning.

Gabriel walked forward and knelt beside Matthew in front of God. "I am here, my Lord."

God turned to Gabriel. "Prepare...our forces."

Gabriel put his hand on God's shoulder. "I shall, my Lord. Our enemies shall know your wrath once more." Gabriel was up and out of the room like a bolt.

God looked to Buddha. "Guide...him," he implored.

Buddha bowed. "I shall, my Lord."

God nodded, his body aching. "I...must rest. So much...to come." He wheeled away, back to the side room which had been his prison for ages.

Simon sneered as God disappeared. "Our Lord is weaker than I thought. I thought his words held the power of Creation."

"They do," Matthew replied still on bended knee staring at that sealed door. "He created hope."

***

Matthew and Buddha walked the crystalline halls of the tower as all of Heaven hustled around below them preparing for the final battle. Buddha smiled as he saw the wonderment still etched on the face of Matthew. "Amazing, isn't he?" Matthew nodded. "Hard to explain?" Matthew nodded again. Buddha smiled wider.

"So what now?" Matthew asked, turning to Buddha.

"What do you mean?"

"Is my part over in all this?"

"You are rather self-centered aren't you?"

"I'd just like to know where I stand," Matthew replied.

"You will be taking part in the battle to come."

"Really?" Matthew nearly shrieked.

"Yes. Why? Don't you want to save humanity?"

"Of course. I...want some of the action." Matthew shrugged before changing the subject. "God knew you."

"Yes, he did. I told you I met him before the stroke took him away."

"What was he like then?"

"Commanding. Full of strength. A temper, but not as bad as many would have you think."

"He's still pretty awe inspiring...for a guy in a wheel chair."

Buddha nodded. His brows knit together as the silence stretched between conversations. "Are you afraid?"

"Afraid?" Matthew asked. "Why should I be afraid? I've got angels watching my back. Have you seen those large mo fo's? What is there to be afraid of?" Buddha looked at him, arching an eyebrow. "Ok, maybe I'm a little nervous. But afraid, no." Buddha continued to stare at him. "Ok, I'm scared shitless."

"Why are you afraid?"

"Are you the patron god of psychology because you sure do use it a lot?"

"You're not answering the question."

"Maybe that's a clue you should stop asking so many." Buddha gave him an innocent look. Matthew turned away as he spoke, "It...it's going to be epic. Demons, angels, God, Satan. All that and little ol' me. I don't belong in the mix. I'm gonna get squashed."

"So you fear the battle. Its purpose is over you, humanity. If anyone belongs in this it is you. Do you truly want to go?"

"A large part of me doesn't want to," Matthew began. He leaned his head to the left, squinting his eyes as he tried to put his thoughts into words. "A larger part of me believes I have to go."

"Did God tell you that you had to?"

"No," Matthew replied.

"Then you don't have to."

"Didn't you just say I had to go?"

"I said you would be taking part. It is expected though not required. If you choose otherwise that is your decision."

"To not go...it feels right for the wrong reasons. To go...I feel I should, but it's hard to...hard to explain." Matthew ran his fingers through his hair, grabbing a clump and pulling slightly.

"So you want to go?" Buddha gave him that quizzical look.

"I feel I need to go." Matthew looked at his feet as they continued walking. He raised his head again. "Is this that destiny you always talk about? Soul searching?"

"Yes," Buddha nodded, grinning.

"It guides you?"

"It helps you to make the right choice."

"How do I know the right choice?"

"We all know the right choice. It's always the hardest to choose," Buddha said as Matthew pondered that for a bit. "What is the largest fear that you have?"

Matthew looked at Buddha. "Guess I don't have to worry about dying." He gave that short, weak laugh. "I...uh, guess I'm scared of not being important. That I'll just get in the way or screw things up. Fail, like I always do."

"You're only human."

"I know, but I don't want to get in the way." Matthew looked back to the horizon. "I always mess things up. Can't do anything right. I don't think we need any major fuck ups right now. Oops, bye universe." Matthew gave a wide-eyed look as he slapped his hands together.

"If there is one thing I have learned, Matthew, it is that we all have a purpose for being."

"Could you please tell me mine because it would really take a load off my mind."

Buddha gave him a funny glance. "If I told you your destiny you would fail to accomplish it for the right reasons and thus fail to fulfill it at all."

Matthew's face became a bit confused. "Does that mean you're not going to tell me?"

"Yes."

"But you know what it is?"

"Yes."

"Do you know everyone's fate?"

"Destiny, not fate."

"What's the difference?" Matthew asked, confused.

"Destiny is what you are chosen to do. Fate is what you choose to do."

"So you don't have to fulfill your destiny?"

"Eventually you do. That is why reincarnation exists."

"Why does destiny even exist if we don't have to complete it?"

"To learn. To understand. It was created by God to help us to grow to be more like him."

313

"Why can't we just learn the lesson without the hassle?"

"If you receive something without earning it, seeing it in action, do you actually value it or understand it?"

Matthew gave him a cynical look. "Always the parables and riddles. I'm American! I prefer bluntness. Can't you tell me anything?"

Buddha chuckled at Matthew's determination to peek into his own future. "You are humanity's final hope."

Matthew let out a long, deep breath. His eyes became white saucers as he started rubbing his hands together, the clamminess only growing wetter.

"Something wrong?"

"Just that now I have the weight of humanity's survival on my shoulders." He turned to Buddha. "Pray for me. Pray for us all!"

"You wanted to know."

"Don't you know anything about humans? Yes always means no!"

Buddha laughed at that. "Well, here we are."

Matthew hadn't noticed the approaching glass doors. In fact he had never seen this section of the tower. "Where are we?"

"Follow me."

Buddha stepped forward, the glass doors parting to permit access. The room beyond was a sterile white. You could not discern ceiling from floor. The only part that differed from the rest was a black hole set in the floor surrounded by a silver lining. One of Buddha's monks stood next to it, his orange robes contrasting with the white. "What's going on?"

"To take part in the final battle upon the physical plane you will need a body."

"Well, yeah. So why are we here? Just give me a body."

"It doesn't work that way," Buddha replied. He extended a hand. "This is Gupta."

"Hello," Matthew sheepishly waved. The monk was stone still. "Not very talkative," Matthew murmured.

"He will be joining you."

Matthew looked at Gupta then back at Buddha. "Wait, what do you mean he'll be joining me? He's getting a body too?"

"No, you're sharing a body."

Matthew gave a nervous giggle. "I don't think so."

"Why?" Buddha asked, genuinely surprised.

"Well, two guys, one body. Sounds a little gay to me," Matthew said behind his hand. He looked back at Gupta who appeared annoyed. "Not that you're a homo or anything. You look quite masculine."

Buddha shook his head. "Gupta, show him." Gupta started doing roundhouse kicks and rapid punches. He spun in the air, his body...er, soul a living weapon. His martial arts prowess beat the crap out of Matthew's ability to comprehend it. "He will be your bodyguard. All he can do, you can do."

"I'll be able to do all that?" Matthew asked.

"Yes," Buddha replied.

"Ok," Matthew said. "You can come. But if you rub me the wrong way...bam!" Gupta continued to stare straight ahead. "I didn't faze him did I?"

"No," Buddha replied.

"Well, anyway, how do I...we," Matthew shuddered a little, his homophobia coming to the surface, "get a body?"

"Jump into the hole," Buddha replied, motioning to the black gap in the floor.

"I just jump in there?" Matthew looked down. It was a long way down. "Why don't you guys have elevators?" Matthew whispered to himself as his knees shook involuntarily at the thought of yet another bout of acrophobic terror. He backed up a bit, trying to buy time and hold on to his balance. "So, uh, exactly what am I supposed to do once I get down there?"

"Rendezvous with your army."

Matthew's head jerked up at that. "I have an army waiting?"

"Yes. Gupta will show you the way. Any further questions he should be able to answer."

Matthew looked back at Gupta. "He doesn't seem the talkative type."

"Don't worry. He will be." Buddha walked up to Matthew, gripping his shoulders. "Remember. Believe. You are a fragment of Perfection, a part of the Almighty. Faith is the strongest weapon God gave humanity. Now," Buddha backed away, gesturing back to the hole.

Gupta walked up behind Matthew. Matthew swallowed as Gupta reached around and grabbed him in a tight embrace. Matthew started to freak out, instinctively tightening his butt cheeks, as they approached the hole. "Wait. Wait!"

"Yes?" Buddha asked.

"Is there any other way? It seems a long way down-"

Buddha motioned to Gupta who took the final few steps forward. "Oh shit," Matthew whispered as Gupta stepped off into the hole and they went straight down. Matthew screamed loudly, the sound attaining a metallic tang as it bounced off the silver walls. But the trauma really swelled when they fell out the other end and straight into the vastness of space hurtling down towards the Earth.

***

Heaven's hulking heroes jostled and pushed, shoved and nearly bludgeoned one another as they waited en masse for their turn at the armory. It had been hundreds of years since they took part in a war of such proportions. Their hearts sang as their souls thirsted to sate their taste for the blood of Hell's hordes. One angel knocked another out of the way to move further up the line. Their irritation at the wait was growing. The cherubim in the armory were frightened for their very hides as they saw these maniacs reaching for armor and weaponry like an addict for their drug of choice. The angels threw insults and wise cracks at the midgets that handed them their instruments of destruction. Gabriel smiled at his men; lean and hungry for battle. Not even a whelp like the Christ could truly break their fighting spirits.

Ezekiel pushed between legs, trying to race up through the ranks. "What the?" an angel gasped, feeling something move between his thighs. He turned to the angel behind him. "Has all this peace time made you silky?" he insulted the alleged molester.

"What are you talking about?

"You touched me between my legs."

"What sort of twisted bastard are you?"

"Twisted? You are the one making passes at me!"

"You take that back, you wanker!"

"Keep your hands and whatever else you were created with to yourself or I'll unmake your silky ass!"

"I'll unmake you, you overgrown cherub!" The angel punched his accuser square in the jaw cracking like thunder. The angel flew back into a group of his fellows behind him. They growled at the intrusion, throwing the accusing angel back at his assaulter only for him to receive another blow to the face. The accusing angel fell into the arms of another. Looking up and realizing he was being propped up, the accuser stood and shoved the angel that held him to the ground. Upset at the insult, the helpful angel stood up and went to punch the accusing angel. His blow missed striking another with a violent surprise. The conflict escalated as blows either missed their mark or landed on target causing others to join the fray. Taunts and bellows arose in the thick of the riot.

Gabriel saw the chaos spreading through the rank and file and smiled. "They still have the fire in 'em!" he cried, thumping his breast.

The cherubim next to him froze in panic at the violence unloading before them, dropping the weapons they had been handing out. "Shouldn't you do something?" the one cherubim asked, mortified.

"They're just having fun!" Gabriel laughed.

The cherubim couldn't believe what he was saying. "If you don't stop them we'll refuse to arm them." The cherubim stood defiantly, crossing their arms and standing in front of the stockpile.

"Oh really?" Gabriel did not appear pleased at the threat. "And why would you do that?"

"We can't arm them! If they do this to each other what will they do to Heaven?" the cherub asked desperately. Their attention on Gabriel, the cherubim failed to notice the impatient angels waiting at the divider for their swords. The one in front, his cheeks and jaw covered in a beard of blonde that stretched over a foot, stomped to the divider and brought his massive forearm down, splintering it in a loud crack. The cherubim fell backwards in surprise and terror, holding each other for protection.

Gabriel looked down at them with a broad smile. "I think you'd better worry what will happen to you if you don't give them their weapons."

The cherubim looked at Gabriel, the bearded angel, then each other. They scrambled to their feet to continue giving out the weaponry and armor causing Gabriel and the angel to chortle heartily. As the bearded angel guffawed to his savage content Ezekiel burst from between his legs to jump in front. He looked down at the runt as Gabriel pointed. "Well, mother! What are you going to call it?" The angel gave a wicked glare to Gabriel as Ezekiel rushed to the shattered divider.

"Exactly what do you think you're doing, little man?" the bearded angel challenged.

"Getting supplies," Ezekiel slapped back.

"Supplies for what, runt?" Gabriel mocked.

Ezekiel defiantly met the gaze of the two giants. "I'm fighting with you."

The bearded angel grabbed Ezekiel by the scruff of his collar and yanked him up to his very high eye level. "You? Fight with us?" The bearded angel looked at the chuckling Gabriel. "You couldn't lift a blade let alone use one. You'd do better to join your buddies back there and speed it up a bit. We've a battle to win." Ezekiel kicked the bearded angel in the nose causing him to drop the cherub as he grabbed his broken proboscis. The bearded angel angrily kicked Ezekiel, knocking him to the ground and raised his foot to stomp him to mush only for Gabriel to stop him.

"This one has fire."

"My nose-" the bearded angel began.

"It's not the first time." Gabriel curled his fingers into a fist, the knuckles crackling. "It won't be the last either. Now leave him and get your supplies." The bearded angel huffed as he stepped over Ezekiel to grab his sword. Gabriel looked down at Ezekiel, offering a hand as he sized up the dwarf. The dwarf shook off his offer and stood by himself. "Why do you want to fight? It will be harder for you. It's not the purpose for which God made you."

319

Ezekiel's face was red, his expression a confusion of conflicting emotions. "Why shouldn't I go? It's my land that is threatened too!" Gabriel seemed a little taken aback by the passion in Ezekiel's soul. "You are not the only ones who care for Creation," Ezekiel said to himself. Gabriel continued to watch him as angels stepped over Ezekiel, each one another slap in the face to his patriotism.

As another angel went to step over Ezekiel, Gabriel spoke up: "Do not cut line."

The angel looked around confusingly for who he had stepped in front of. "Sir?"

"There is someone already waiting in front of you." Gabriel looked down at Ezekiel who looked up in shock. "You'd best grab your blade before I change my mind." He gave Ezekiel a humorous grin.

Ezekiel jumped to, moving for the armory ahead. As he brushed by Gabriel he remarked, "I shall put you all to shame."

"I hope that is a good thing," Gabriel retorted. The angel he had stopped looked a little disgusted and gave Gabriel a questioning glance. "He's tiny. Hard to hit." The angel continued to look at him surprised. "Get your damn sword."

Ezekiel proudly stood before his fellows extending his hand for a sword. The two cherubim grudgingly pulled one from the rack, both of them having to carry its weight. "Are you sure you can handle this?" one of the cherubim asked, the hilt extended to Ezekiel.

"Question me again and I'll give you a personal demonstration of how well I handle a sword." The cherub gave him a dirty look as he turned and nodded to his partner. Ezekiel grabbed the hilt and tried to lift the blade. Ezekiel's arm was not nearly as strong as his tongue as he failed to hold the blade up, the steel whomping back down onto the divider. He tried a few more times to lift the sword as the two cherub watched on holding up the bulk of the blade over the shattered divider. Ezekiel cursed the thing for its size. The two cherubim gave him an "I told you so" expression as Ezekiel grabbed the hilt and simply dragged the blade behind him with both arms.

"Armor is the next building."

Ezekiel gave them a beaming smile and heaved his weapon after him, cutting a swath through the grass.

***

"This is it," Dr. Kotulak replied as they walked down the steel and glass hallway. It was a path built bereft of emotion or style, only purpose. They stopped before a heavy set door with card and keypad set next to it. "Where exactly is this going?"

"Classified," the agent replied, clad in his black suit.

Kotulak gave him a brief bit of his attention before turning back to the door. He slid his card through the slot and punched in his code. A green light flipped on, and the door slowly slid out of the way. The agent stood stiffly as he and Kotulak waited for the barrier to remove itself. "What will you be transporting it in?" Kotulak asked, trying to make small talk. The agent patted a metal briefcase he was holding. "Is that airtight?"

"Does it matter?" the agent retorted.

"If you crack the tubes it does. Without an airtight seal the contents will seep out."

The agent turned and gave Kotulak a cold stare. "Then I guess I won't be breaking any test tubes will I?"

"Fucking bureaucrats," Kotulak growled as he walked into the lab, the agent behind him. He spent over ten years on his masterpiece and here they relegated it to some mere product. They didn't understand perfection.

The room was filled with cutting edge equipment. In the center was an upraised, steel counter with a sealed glass container atop it. Three pairs of holes, each outfitted with rubber sleeves and gloves for the arms that went through them, stood in its side. A television screen, now blank, sat bolted above the compartment. To the side of the room sat more equipment used in the dissection and manipulation of the works of God.

"Where do you keep it?"

"Beyond that door," Kotulak replied, pointing to the only other exit from this artificial place of creation. The agent and doctor walked up to yet another keypad. Kotulak punched in his code again and put his hand over a port that glowed briefly. The door gave a knock and popped open. Cold air rushed through the crack causing the agent to shiver revealing that he was human after all. "We keep it in the cold to prevent the possibility of contagion."

"The vials, please," the agent ordered as he bent down to open the briefcase.

Kotulak walked into the refrigerator, searching for the section. When he found it he reached for a tiny plastic box. He stopped and stared at it, his breath puffing away in the frigid darkness. He dared to think for a bit before he slid it out. He left the freezer and closed the door behind him. As Kotulak was about to crack open the box he looked up at the agent. Something occurred to him for the first time. "We're not using this on anyone are we?"

"That is classified." The agent hid his eyes behind shades that reflected the conflicted face of Kotulak. "The vials, doctor."

"What the hell are you using this for?"

"It does not concern you."

"Bull shit! If you use this we could be seeing a worldwide plague!" The agent remained stone faced. "There is no vaccine-"

"Your job is to make this shit. Not to think of what is the best use for it. Now give me the damn vials!" Kotulak started to back up. The agent began to frown. "Is your family worth becoming a martyr?"

Kotulak stopped where he was. "My family?"

"You can decide to suddenly grow a conscience and let it eat at you like cancer, but you can't stop me from getting those vials." The agent sized up the doctor. "Maybe we should test the virus on your wife and daughter to see if it actually works." Kotulak couldn't believe the threat he was hearing, the smoke puffing out his mouth. "The vials, doctor. Now!"

Kotulak gritted his teeth and walked towards the agent, cracking open the box to reveal four test tubes, all colored silver. He looked at those vials within which he had crafted death from life. He had challenged the fabric of being creating a catastrophe simply to see if he could, to earn material wealth, to prove his dominance over what was. He wanted to be foremost in his field, defy what had been and place a mark of his own on the whole of existence. It was only now, at the end, that he understood. He could not destroy his creation for all he wanted. He pulled them out one by one and handed them to the agent who placed them in special sections inside the briefcase.

As the agent closed the briefcase a lone tear fell down Kotulak's face freezing. "God forgive me."

The agent pulled a pistol from his jacket. "Not even God can save you now." He pulled the trigger twice, shooting Kotulak in both lungs. Kotulak's face twisted in pain and disbelief. Each side of his chest was shoved back by the blow of both bullets before he fell to the floor. He heaved loudly as he lay dying in his own blood. The agent stood over him, gun pointed down. "You should have remained impartial." Another bullet was released, blasting brain across the floor.

***

Jesus stood before the large iron door, rusted with time but as strong as the day it was welded. The only new addition to this prison had been a shining steel slot next to the doors. For all Jesus' preachings, technology had been his favorite endeavor; all the easier to wield and hold onto his authority.

They were below the tower, deep below, in the bowels of Existence. This place had been built over a thousand years ago as a prison for the four, the chief leaders of the rebellion of angels against Christ. Jesus' face was agitated, his expression deeply against what he knew he had to do. These were the figures that nearly toppled him and now he was to free them for a purpose only God truly knew. A cherub stood to his right, Gabriel to his left in this dimly lit passage. Light flickered from the overhead lights onto the wet brick walls. The shadows rose and fell upon them in this forgotten place. "Are you sure you need them?" Jesus asked Gabriel.

"They were the best. Loyal to God beyond all rationality. It's time you gave them clemency."

"God may pardon them. I never shall."

"They fought for Heaven. They fought for Him. They will fight still." Jesus met Gabriel's gaze without flinching. "We need them."

Jesus did not feel the same way, but God had ordered him to do as Gabriel wished. The cherub looked up at the Christ, not sure this was the right thing to do. "Open it."

"My Lord?" The cherub shook at the thought of the four free.

"Open the door." Jesus turned around and started back down the long corridor. He did not wish to honor them with his presence or to admit them this small victory over his rule.

"You heard the man. Open the door!" Gabriel nudged the cherub with his sandaled foot. The cherub waddled up to the panel and pulled out a gold card. He swiped it down the strip. The response was a red light and an electronic raspberry. The cherub looked up at Gabriel. "Do it again." The cherub ran the card through the slot a second time, receiving the red light and raspberry again. "Don't fuck with me," Gabriel warned.

"It's not me. It's the card," the cherub pleaded with Gabriel.

"If you don't open that door right now-"

The cherub was back at the keypad, running the card through over and over again rapidly. He cursed at it, willed it, and begged it to open. It did not react pleasantly to any of his methods. "Damn you, damn you, damn you!" the cherub slapped at the slot with his tiny sausage fingers. He turned back to Gabriel. "It won't..." he stopped. Gabriel had his sword drawn. "I can try again!" the cherub hurried back to use the card.

"No. I'm tired of this game. Damnable soulless machinery!"

"I have a family!" Gabriel gave him a dirty look. "Would you believe a pet puppy?"

Gabriel released a war cry and ran right at the cherub. The midget let out a cry and fell to the ground, curling into the fetal position and shaking. After a few seconds, and some very intense prayers, he dared to look up. Gabriel had driven his sword deep into the keypad, the metal and surrounding stone torn and busted. "I hate technology," Gabriel snorted as the blade began to pulse a solid white. Electricity coursed up and down what little of the blade remained in sight. As the light hit blinding, the blade let loose a bolt of power into the slot that caused the passageway to strobe. The light and dark fought as time seemed to slow in the flickering illumination. Then, the lights stopped blinking and the brightness steadied. The green light blinked on and the doors began to howl open. He looked down at the cherub. "You'd better get out of here." The cherub didn't need to be told twice. He ran at his stumpy pace and beyond before jumping into the air and soaring away.

Gabriel turned to the opening door, watching as it ground rusted notches into the stone beneath it. The gears squealed like lost souls as dust from ground rock fell to the floor. The light stretched into the darkness, its fingers scorching away a millennia of darkness. They sat there, chained to the floor. Their weapons had been bolted to the walls, placed for them to see but never touch nor wield again; the worst punishment for any warrior.

Conquest was broken. His wounds were never allowed to heal as he was chained down before his bones had set. His arms and legs were fractured. He had been forced to suffer through the agony of such pain, his wounds eternally fresh. His bright white hair had been stained by the dirt of this cell, now a dusted, matted brown. His skin was dirty, little trails carved out and eroded by the tears of his suffering. His armor was shredded, only parts of that brilliant silver still remaining attached to his form. He, like his comrades, was emaciated. No food had been passed to them since their imprisonment. Their bones shown through ethereal skin. His once brilliant, golden eyes were now a tarnished bronze as he stared at the ceiling.

Pestilence's black, greasy hair covered his face as he sat there without movement. A huge shackle had been locked around his neck, the weight of it preventing him from raising his head without much effort. His armor had been stripped off, his ribs pressed against immortal flesh. His once large arms had shrunk from years of atrophy. His back was bent, his spine forming a bony ridgeline.

War had the most chains wrapped around him. Even now he still struggled against this decrepit destiny, his will unbreakable. His red hair was as fiery as his spirit. He had gone feral, screaming and moaning in some instinctual way. The chains barely held each renewed assault he made. His flesh had been rubbed raw, chafed at his failed attempts at freedom. His armor had sections chopped out, parts of arrows still sticking out of them.

The most disturbing of them all was Death. Bereft of hair or color, his pale skeletal frame sat peacefully beside his brothers. Not a chain was upon him, his silver armor intact. His eyes were closed as he meditated here with those he cherished most. Of them all he had come willingly. Unbeatable in combat, the greatest ever crafted by the word of God, even he could not stand up against the whole of Creation without destroying it utterly and that, ironically, was the one thing he could not do. Rather than face a fate of rule by Christ he chose eternal imprisonment with his brothers. He had let the darkness take him. But now, he dared to look up, his gray eyes meeting Gabriel's.

"Brother?" he rasped, his voice not used in centuries.

Gabriel stood there, refusing to shame them with his sorrow and pity. "Yes, brother. It is I, Gabriel."

War stopped straining. "Hope has come!" he choked. "Did I not tell you hope would come?"

Death gave him a cynical look. "Why have you come?"

"I have come to release you."

"Release us?" Death hissed. "To serve Christ? I shall never kneel to that usurper!"

"You misunderstand, brother. It is not for Christ. It is for humanity."

Conquest rolled his head to Gabriel as Famine raised his. Death tilted his head. "What has come to pass?"

"Satan stands triumphant on Earth. Even now he plots their destruction and with it, our own."

"Jesus would not care for them. Who sends you here?" Death would not allow himself to be manipulated.

"God."

"Father," gasped Conquest.

"He is broken," Death replied. "He would not order this."

"He has." Gabriel walked into the still chamber. "Because of him."

"Who?" Death asked.

"The true Messiah."

"He has come to pass?" Gabriel nodded. "Where is he? Why has he not come with you?"

"He has gone to Earth, to rally forces. I have come...to rally you to ours."

"It is battle!" War screamed, smiling.

"The angels still stand?" Conquest whispered through dry, cracked lips.

Gabriel bent down to touch Conquest's brow. "We were never broken, brother. Only waiting. Waiting for our time."

"The time has come." Death stood, the dust flowing off of his armor and from his cloak. His joints cracked like tree limbs as he stood proudly. "Would you?" He gestured to the wall where his sword was bolted amongst the others. "I have grown weak here." Gabriel walked to the wall and with inhuman strength wrenched the blade from the stone. He swung the sword around, listening to the dark steel sing in the shadows before spinning it to offer the hilt to Death who took his blade, forged for him by God himself. "How long have I denied you?" Death asked the sword. "Soon, you shall find purpose again."

War smiled, baring unusually large canine teeth. Gabriel pulled his own sword and swung down, cutting through the chains that held War to the floor. War stood, the chains falling off of his proud, defiant shoulders. His eyes went wild as Gabriel tore his battle axe from the wall and handed it to him.

"I shall cleave the enemy as fire through ice." He ran his calloused hand over the breadth of the axe head, remembering enemies long vanquished.

Gabriel and War came together, rending the chains that held Pestilence and, together, pulling the shackle from around his neck. Pestilence sucked down free air for the first time in ages. Death caused his sword to dance a deadly set as it came around and lashed, carving away the steel that held Pestilence's blade. It fell from the wall, and Pestilence stepped forward, catching the hilt. He pulled it back, feeling the balance, the weight of his most trusted ally. "The drought is over. You shall drink the blood of our enemies until you may drink no more."

They all turned to Conquest, broken on the floor. They chopped the chains, pulling them from the mangled mess that remained of the most legendary of God's soldiers. Gabriel looked down, hoping the freedom granted would cause Conquest to heal, but he remained a twisted, bloody mess on the floor. "Why does he not mend?" Gabriel asked Death.

"His soul is wounded. He does not believe anymore. Of us all, he was the most tortured, the one Jesus made the example of."

"We need him," Gabriel replied.

"That we do, but he needs us more. He needs purpose...for he has none."

Gabriel knelt down to look into the hollow eyes of Conquest, his body twitching in pain. "Brother? Will you not try?"

"Try?" he whimpered. "I did try...and I failed."

"How did you fail, brother?" Gabriel was surrounded by the remaining three who looked down at their fallen comrade.

"When humanity needed us I was unable to answer their call. I fell to the armies of the Christ. What warrior am I if I cannot even win a battle? I am not as I once was."

"A warrior is only defeated when he chooses to be. Jesus locked you away to crush you. Do not give him this victory."

"I have nothing left to surrender."

Gabriel knelt closer to Conquest taking his hand. "We fought...we fought with you against Jesus when we knew we were humanity's last hope. You cannot believe that my brothers and I fought and died with you for nothing. We showed our loyalty to humanity. We showed our loyalty to God. And now, when both call to us in their most desperate hour, do you dare to surrender? Where is your faith?"

"It...it is lost." Conquest choked up blood, his face tightening in agony.

Pestilence knelt next to his brother. War and Death joined him. "Let us help you find it," Death stated with a calm, serene stare. He reached out towards his brother, his flesh taking on a luminescent hue. He placed his glowing hand onto Conquest's leg. War blazed as he did likewise, touching his arm. Pestilence cracked his thin smile as his eyes glowed a bright green, his flesh gradually becoming a brilliant shade. He touched his brother as Gabriel dared to stare.

Gabriel closed his eyes and reached into his heart, his flesh becoming as radiant as his purity and loyalty to the light from whence he came. He stretched out and became one with Conquest as the room began to burst with the colors of the spectrum. Conquest's flesh began to rise from the dull, mortal colors that had infected him. He began to rise from defeat.

***

"Push, Neela. Push!" the doctor ordered as he watched from between her legs. The lights flickered in the hospital room as Neela groaned and screamed. Her dark skin was wet with sweat, her black hair dripping and pasted to her forehead. "You are doing fine, Neela."

"Come on, honey," her husband gently cooed.

Neela reached out and grabbed her husband's balls and squeezed hard. "This is all your fault! Yours!" Her husband screamed trying to pull away. A nurse ran over to try and pry Neela's grip off.

"What the...?" the doctor trailed off, his head pulling back from the sight before him. A hand reached out of the womb; then another. The head emerged.

"What is it, doctor?" Neela asked.

"I...see a head." The doctor looked on wide-eyed.

"God, this is so gross!" the baby, Matthew, gagged. The infant began pulling itself out, struggling against the suction of the womb. Eventually only one leg remained. The baby put his free foot against the bed and starting jerking for all he was worth to pull free. "It's...a boy," the doctor replied. As

331

Neela looked down she froze as did everyone else in the room.

Matthew yanked loose and fell on the tile with a cry of surprise. He jumped to his feet and ran only to snap back due to the umbilical cord. The baby yanked against the cord. Irritated, he wrapped the cord around his hands and started pulling. He dug his heels into the floor and gave a mighty tug, a shree sound coming from his gooey feet as he streaked across the tile. He slid across the floor as he yanked, his soles covered in baby juice. He fell to the floor with a slap on his baby butt. Frustrated, the infant got up looked at the doctor, tapping his foot and pointing to the cord.

"Would you...?" the doctor offered the scissors to the terrified husband. The baby leaped and snatched them away to cut the fleshy leash, snipping at it ruthlessly as he tore through it. As the cord fell away he ran out of the room with the patter of little feet. No one moved, the moment so unreal.

"Children grow up so fast these days," the doctor murmured. Everyone nodded.

CHAPnoTEveRlasting 12

Satan stood there looking out the broad windows of the Oval Office. Through the glass the gray clouds gathered, the light falling beneath a cloak of shade. Thunder shook the whole of Creation. Around him did reality rage, all which had been set up was torn and scattered. Life did not dwell within his sight, the world an empty graveyard. He corrupted these walls, this White House. Gone were the days of diplomacy. There would be no compromise. Reason was lost beneath the wild rampage of insanity and passion. Now came the days of tyranny and certainty, that sole certainty: annihilation.

The storm smothered the sun in its insubstantial clutches. The brilliance of the world slowly dimmed as rain began to fall. Heaven cried for the dying world beneath as the Devil smiled, his transparent reflection staring back as it blotted out the view with his twisted form. These days, however dark, were now numbered.

The luminance of the lamps began to flicker in the room. That artificial glow faded in and out. It fought against the impossible as the shadows swallowed the torch. The darkness gathered in the corners, finding frail shape. The wraiths oozed forward like ink to see their master.

"How goes the mobilization?" Satan asked, his back to them. That once smooth voice had changed. The lies, the screams, the jagged words that the Devil had uttered had transformed it from a silken sound to that of gravel, rough and painful to the ears.

"Our men shall be ready when thou needest them," the wraith rasped like the scraping of autumn leaves.

"And Heaven?" The Devil looked over his shoulder.

"Their forces are nearly ready."

The one wraith slid closer. "My lord, a question?"

The Devil turned around to sit in his chair. "You may ask."

"Our preparations go well, but how will we set the trap? Surely we do not know where they will strike. Earth may be small but not that small."

The Devil shook his finger as if the wraith had been naughty. "Of course we will. You see, there is but one portion of this rock that means more than all the rest to them," the Devil stated as he pointed skywards.

"Where is that, my lord?"

"Israel." The Devil bared his teeth in the semblance of a grin. "That strip of worthless desert holds some nostalgic value for our heavenly brothers. I have already dispatched forces to...stabilize the region." He bared his teeth further.

"Stabilize, my lord?"

Satan's face took on a poor example of sorrow. "It is a sad state of affairs. The Prime Minister of Israel was let in on the fact that the Palestinians somehow got their hands on biological material of a hazardous nature, a virus capable of devastating value. With this knowledge, the Prime Minister authorized a covert strike to capture and destroy the limited viral stock before it could be put to use. There must have been a leak for the Palestinians knew they were coming. There was a great deal of bloodshed I'm afraid. A nasty piece of diplomacy. In fact, tensions have risen to feverish levels. Violence has exploded, mobs taken to the streets.

"Worse still, it seems the terrorists who held the virus did not contain it very well. Cases of infection have sprung up throughout Gaza and other parts of Palestine. Not only have the Israelis fought to close the borders but to also contain the spreading plague. In so doing they have made aid to those suffering from this new plague impossible. They die by the hundreds daily. Men, women...children." Satan closed his eyes as if tasting a delicacy. "They all fall to the hands of this dark angel. Such sweet suffering." Satan seemed lost in the situation, deriving great pleasure from the visions he constructed in his head.

"The Israelis refuse to open the borders for fear of terrorist attack or infection. The Palestinians beg for us to step in and allow them relief from this hell. No one will listen to reason. There can be no right or wrong as the international community sees it. An independent force is needed to rectify this growing problem." His eyes opened. "So, I've dispatched aid to ensure that peace is upheld. The Gaza Strip is already a war zone."

A smile stole across Satan's face. "Sadly, some biological material made it into Tel Aviv. How it crossed our lines I know not. Monumental loss of life. Of course the Israelis have been retaliating in the worst manner. Chaos is engulfing Israel. Hate crimes have swallowed the holy land, Jerusalem seeing some of the worst atrocities. With Tel Aviv quarantined and the majority of Israel not capable of protecting our people, I have sent troops and made Jerusalem America's base of operations. I have enforced an unsteady peace over the crown jewel of three religions. I could not let it be harmed by the carnage. It is precious to the faiths of so many.

"Of course holding Jerusalem alone has proven taxing to our resources. Europe and North Korea have tied down a large number of our soldiers and, though we are able to hold Jerusalem, we do not have the forces to hold the whole of Israel and pacify the various factions. I could not call on Russia. They have their own problems. So, I opened channels to those most capable of aiding us...their Arab neighbors. Now, when I met with Jordan, Syria, Lebanon, and Egypt I told them I was horrified at the brutal treatment

Palestine was receiving for something that was clearly not their fault but surely caused by a small group of madmen. I understood why these men acted, seeing the harsh and discriminatory actions brought against them by the Jews. How fate forced them from oppressed to oppressor. I understood the frustrations and anger held by Palestine and its peoples. Israel had stolen their lands and stifled any hopes of their return. I told the Arab League that I would allow them to send in forces aid in the quelling of uprisings and bloodshed as long as Jerusalem remained a free city occupied by U.S. troops. We would...oversee their actions to make sure that they did not overindulge in their dark passions. Israel was in no position to say no ravaged as they were by plague and violence. Regretfully, my eyes can't be everywhere and rumors of barbarism have begun to bubble to the surface. It is such a difficult situation."

The Devil pulled a remote control out of the desk and aimed it at the television on the wall. The blackness was pierced by the lurid light of the media as screaming, wounded people ran all over. The camera shook as explosions boomed both near and far. Gunfire rattled on with holes bursting in the shells of buildings. Fires raged out of control as the moaning and screaming of men and women mingled with that of their collapsing nations. Smoke could not conceal this hell on earth.

"They must strike there. If they don't then Judea...is forsaken." The Devil put his feet on the desk and leaned back watching humanity at its worst. "You will be...no more," he growled.

***

A dark infant struggled through the silent lands of a dying realm, his naked form the only moving object set against the rusted horizon. He had walked for miles, his tiny feet swollen and aching. "Making me walk such a long, god damn way to some far off destination," Matthew muttered to himself.

"Must you soil the tongue of a newborn innocent so soon?" Gupta asked from within his head.

"My feet ache, ok." Matthew bent over to rub his enlarged toes. "That was traumatic let me tell you."

"What?"

"Being born! Damn, no wonder we forget the experience. I wish I could forget it!" Matthew made a disgusted face as he continued to rub his feet. "The smell is the worst you know. And it's...so..." Matthew struggled to find the word. "Sticky. Yeah, sticky and gooey. I got some of that shit in my mouth!" Matthew spit, the saliva soaked up by the parched dirt. "Where the hell are we going anyway?"

"Look to your right."

Matthew stood up and staggered a few steps as he turned to view his objective. "What?"

"Do you not see the city?"

Matthew struggled to see, a foul mist staining the sights ahead. All he saw was smoke, inky black smoke. A breeze came pushing the smog aside, and the skeletal remains of a community emerged. It was the rubble of a ruined metropolis. Buildings that once stood proudly had fallen beneath the atomic blow of Pakistan. The land was rendered barren and civilization blown away by the artificial winds of man. "What the fuck," Matthew gasped looking at it. The place seemed tilted and twisted, what few buildings tall enough to see from his position bent as if made of melted rubber. Smoke twirled around the bowing spires. "What happened?"

"It was a nuclear strike," Gupta replied.

"Nuclear?" Matthew felt a sickness in his stomach. "Anyone...did anyone..."

"The city was wiped out," Gupta spoke solemnly. "Victims to a pathetic hatred."

"Did Satan have anything to do with this?"

"Oh no," Gupta replied. "He merely prevented anyone from interfering. This was India and Pakistan's choice."

Matthew looked to the scorched city, a shattered world where echoes were smothered by the debris of a lost humanity. "How can we be capable of such a thing?" The air blew in their direction, Matthew's eyes watering from the grit. "Maybe we do deserve what is coming."

"Do not make Satan's work any easier," Gupta sternly reprimanded him.

"Yeah, yeah," Matthew replied, wiping his eyes. "So, we're going past the city? To where?"

"No, you are mistaken," Gupta replied. "The city is our destination."

"You're kidding."

"Why do you think I lie?"

"Are you shitting me? Have you seen the movies? Zombies and cannibals could be in there! Mutants too! Hell the insects could be giant sized! Count me out!" Matthew yelled, waving off that corpse of a community.

"It is our destination, and we must go."

Matthew felt his legs suddenly lurch forward towards the city, his sore feet crunching through the rough dirt. "Hey, stop that!" Matthew ordered. His feet continued to carry him forward. "I said stop right now!"

"We have a mission to accomplish," Gupta retorted. "We shall not quit on account of your fears."

They marched together silently towards the necropolis. The ground began to noticeably harden, and bits of mortar and glass found their way into their path. They followed the highway into the city, some cars still parked on the pavement bumper to bumper. They had been long abandoned. The overhead signs had been ripped down, seeming to form grasping, gnarled fingers urging Matthew into the dying bosom of the lost lands beyond. The black smoke flowed on either side of the road, blotting out the horizon on either side. It was as if nothing existed save the road and the necropolis it led to.

The outskirts proved harder going. The rubble was growing thicker. Empty windows with vacant stares followed them, the glass sucked out. The buildings still stood, but with cracks in their walls and chunks of former stability at their bases. Matthew strode on, his hands covering what little manhood genetics had deigned to give him. Even with Armageddon approaching Matthew remained ever modest.

"Can we maybe make a stop once we're in the city?"

"We do not require urination or defecation. Why do you need to stop?"

"I'm getting a little tired of covering myself." Matthew motioned to his family jewels which he held tightly as if they truly were precious stones.

"Clothes are not a high priority."

"Excuse me?" Matthew became agitated. "Now I don't know if you get off on naked kids. That's your own thing," Matthew began to speak with his hands but quickly covered himself at the first sensation of nudity, "but I need some clothes because I am really starting to get freaked out."

"Why do you continue to be difficult? The world is threatened, and you still think only of yourself."

"Hey, fuck you, ok Big Gulp. Seeing a small penis is bad enough, but having to feel it slap against my leg every few steps is really disturbing. Now I want clothes and I want them now!"

Exasperated, Gupta consented. "We shall search for some clothes."

"Thank you," Matthew breathed a sigh of relief and then regretted doing so at the trashy, burnt smell that invaded his nose.

The silence fell away at the buzzing of flies. They landed on the occasional corpse that littered the streets; few of them in one piece. A hill of rubble was pierced by an upraised hand of some soul packed beneath. Matthew turned away to look at the ground only to look into the dead eyes of some poor young woman, her mouth open as if frozen in a scream. Matthew could feel his sanity being sucked into those pools of emptiness and jerked his gaze away. He almost lost it when he felt his foot squish into something soft and cold. He gagged at the gross images that popped into his head. "Gupta?" Matthew asked, closing his eyes tightly.

"Yes?"

"Is there anyway I can take over walking? I swear I won't make a run for it."

"Ok," Gupta conceded after a moment of decision.

Matthew felt his legs relax. He peeked out from beneath one eyelid and picked his way through the remnants. He scurried around a corner, making pitter patter noises as he simply began to try and find someplace, anyplace, away from the ravages of man. He did his best to hold his breath as his tiny feet carried his pot bellied butt through the nuclear playground. He began to slow down, his baby body not quite ready for such strenuous activity. He took deep breaths, heaving as he leaned against a wall. He raised his head and smiled at what he saw. The block beyond was colorful. Well, what little was not burnt away. And was that a shirt? Matthew did not stop to ask where it could have come from. It was orange, and a large, but so what. Matthew put the soot stained shirt on, the sleeves too long and the waist stretching to below his legs. He rolled up the sleeves looking around. "This'll do for now."

"For now? Is the shirt not enough?" Gupta asked.

"Hey, where this came from other clothes have to be waiting."

"How can you be so sure it came from a store?"

"Well a corpse isn't in it, and this place doesn't look very residential." Matthew looked around. "Then again, none of this city looks very residential anymore." Matthew traipsed wearily on, his feet constantly getting caught in his shirt until he pulled it up to allow easier movement.

The buildings around him had been one story. Some were lucky to still have all four walls let alone a roof. The storefronts had been baked a sickening ruddy brown. Bites were chomped out and spit about both within and without their premises. He staggered up to one store and looked in. Nothing but tossed up dirt and ashes. He bounded over to another. An acrid aroma of rotten food, split melons and blackened, maggot infested meat polluted his sense of smell, caking the inside of his nose and mouth causing him to gag. He backed out, nearly tripping over an uprooted street sign. Matthew balanced himself. Feeling a little slighted he kicked the sign, just to show who was boss. Of course he forgot what he kicked with were baby feet. The sensation was one of instant, sharp pain as he yelped.

"Is it so hard to control your temper?" Gupta asked inside his head.

"Shut up," Matthew muttered to the air as he rubbed his baby toes. "Why my toes? Why do I always stub my toes?"

"We have a destination to get to," Gupta reminded him. "This is not a tour."

"Yeah, I really wanted to go to Armageddon. Fun for the whole family! Fucking asshole." As Matthew squeezed his foot he caught sight of something bright in the cracked window of a nearby store. He smiled and ran in its direction.

"What are you doing?" Gupta asked.

"Shopping," Matthew replied as he hurried along. As he approached the crumbling display window he was able to see better inside. Clothes were everywhere. Just what his little ass needed. He reached for the metal frame door to the store he approached, yanking on it. It didn't budge. He yanked again. The thing must have fused with the frame. "If it's not one damn thing it's another," he complained, hurrying back to climb through the window. His upper body strength didn't allow for lifting. "Damn, damn, damn!" Matthew hung there trying to pull himself up through the display window. His bare feet scraped against the wall as he struggled to rise. "I...want...those...clothes!" He strained and sputtered, cursing virtually everything that had ever existed and adding a few more for good measure. He arms shook and his fingers slipped. He fell to the ground amongst the dust raising a cloud. He sat there and started to throw a fit, kicking and crying.

"What is the problem now?" Gupta asked.

"I can't get in the window," Matthew choked as he sobbed.

"Allow me." Before Matthew knew it he kicked back up to his feet and strode in the opposite direction.

"Hey, what the hell are you doing?"

"Trust me," Gupta replied. Before he knew it, Matthew turned around and started running full out towards the store. He came hurtling towards the brick, his feet somehow finding their way around the strewn debris.

"Whoa! Whoa, Gupta what are you doing?" The wall came even closer. "Gupta!" Then, in an instant, he felt his legs tense, and he leaped into the air, back flipping through the window and landing on a pile of clothes inside. He rolled, finally coming to a stop covered in a wad of wardrobe. Matthew pulled some pants off his head. "Wow," he replied, his mouth a big "o". "That was freaking sweet!"

"The clothes," Gupta reminded him.

"Oh yeah." Matthew started rummaging through the piles. He braved the mountains of cotton and wool, digging for the treasure of something appropriate for his tiny body. What he found was less than appealing. Within twenty minutes he had been able to cobble together an outfit, including tiny shoes, but couldn't stand what he saw in the mirror.

"What is the matter now?" Gupta asked. "It fits you, yes?"

"Yeah."

"So now you have clothes. We must go."

Matthew looked at himself. The shirt was white with short, baby blue sleeves. On the chest was the picture of some cute cartoon elephant. His pants were a pink shade of corduroy and his shoes a bright, fire hydrant red that shined like plastic. "My God," Matthew gasped. "I'm retarded."

"Matthew."

"Can't I look around a little bit more? I'm sure I can find something better."

"We must go." Gupta was adamant and once more took Matthew's legs out from under him.

"No, please no!" Matthew cried as they left the building, crawling over a ramp of shirts and dresses to climb out the window. The newly cutified Matthew had a very obscene adult look on his face of rage and resentment. "Where exactly are we going?" Matthew asked sarcastically.

"To meet with the army," Gupta responded.

Matthew looked up and down the barren corridors of the city. "Unless we are collecting an army of roaches I think we're shit out of luck," he replied.

He left footprints in the ash that had fallen from the nuclear strike. This land had been rocked into extinction. As Matthew and Gupta ventured further he discovered the scenery to be worsening. The buildings went from fragile but intact to skeletal and bent. Life became a memory on these roads, more blackened trails than ordered paths. What little was left standing was the vestigial parts of an advanced society. Some buildings looked as if they had been wax candles burned to the nub. The dust of life blew through the air nearly blinding Matthew. He waddled on through the roads paved with broken glass and crushed walls.

"We're not going to the center of all this, are we?" Matthew asked as they continued.

"Yes," the voice replied.

"Whoa! Have you heard of radiation?" Matthew yelped. He put a hand to his dark scalp. "I don't have much hair now, but I would like to keep it."

"You need not worry about the radiation."

Matthew's face became confused. "Maybe I'm already exposed to radiation. That would explain the voice."

"I am not imaginary."

"Yeah, like a crazy person knows whether or not they're crazy! Maybe I was never an American? Was it all real? Am I delirious? Who am I?" Matthew grabbed his head screaming. "My legs, I can't feel my legs!" Suddenly he stopped moving.

"Because I am controlling them! I'm the monk that was sent with you. Gupta."

"Oh yeah? Prove it." Suddenly Matthew did a roundhouse kick. Matthew stood still after the spin. He tried to repeat the move but fell on his tiny butt in the dirt. Matthew stood back up and dusted himself off. He rubbed the palms of his hands on his thighs and tried to do it again once more falling into the dirt. Matthew sat there in the mound that once was civilization. "Do that again," he told the voice. Before he could react he rolled back onto his shoulders, kicked up to his feet, and did another roundhouse kick.

"This is why I was sent. To help you fight in the battle ahead."

"Wait, wait. I thought I would get a gun or something."

"The body is the ultimate weapon."

Matthew stood there, his dark face scrunched in thought. A sound started in his throat from dozens of kung fu movies, and Matthew started doing mock martial arts flailing his arms and making shallow kicks. He brought his one foot down in front of him, leaned on it, punched the air and let out a long, "Waaaaaaaaaa!" Matthew froze in that pose and then stood straight again. He saw a stone block on the road and walked up to it. He did his, "Waaaaaa!" again and brought his hand down. The only thing that seemed remotely broken was his bones. "Owwwww!" Matthew screamed, crying in pain as he rubbed his tiny hand. "Why can't I do it when I want to?"

"Because you have not earned these skills. I will not let you abuse them."

"Maybe a little?"

"No!" the voice responded.

"Can I at least break the block?" The voice remained silent. Matthew pleadingly put his hands together begging. "Please? I'll go meet the army." Matthew's hand shot up and came down shattering the stone into fragments. Matthew cocked into full kung fu pose. "I be da man!" be yelled.

"May we continue?" the voice asked.

"Oh. Sure. Waaaaaaaa-"

"Matthew!"

"I'm going." Matthew continued walking through the streets eventually reaching what seemed to be the edge of a field of glass. It was easily hundreds of feet in diameter, shattered in lines that radiated from that far off core. Matthew looked down into this dismal mirror and saw his baby face. It was dark, far darker than his original pale skin. His hair was coarse and black, still thin on his head. His eyes, though, seemed strangely familiar. Matthew touched his face marveling at the new persona that stared back. Matthew blinked, thinking it would disappear, that his life would be as it once was. The devastation remained. The dream was reality.

Matthew stood and looked around at how man had torn down centuries in but one brief moment. This world was broken. Man was a beast. Man was a monster. But this time, it seemed, man had finally destroyed something it could never rebuild.

"We are doomed." Matthew looked across the sea of glass.

"You are what you choose to be."

Matthew was numb to the pain. No one could weep for the want of so much. "We've wasted that choice." The silence was haunting. Everything had ceased. "What now?" Matthew asked.

"We collect our army."

"What army?" Matthew asked looking around. An arm burst up through the glass. It was savaged and burned, bone showing through the wilted and stringy muscle tissue coated in gray dust. A head soon emerged, an eye missing from its socket and half its face shorn off. Noise arose at a distance as rubble moved and a corpse pulled itself out, the stink of death heavy upon it. The glass shattered in other places as figures emerged. The soil split open as the dead arose.

These undead lifted themselves from the obscurity of the grave and stood defiant in the land of the living. They rose in the hundreds, the thousands. They rose to be. They refused the grave. Matthew stared, frozen, at what arose around him. The dead all turned to look at Matthew, their decaying faces impossible to read. "Gupta, a word?" Matthew smiled at the zombies.

"Yes?"

"When you said I was getting an army I didn't think I was being handed Life's sloppy seconds."

"These men will stand with you to the end. They defy the passing of their souls from this plane to the next. They seek vengeance, a balancing."

Matthew looked around at them. They stood scattered about him, standing against reason. The air had gone quiet and refused to touch them. Stillness, the stillness of the grave, enveloped them. One of the dead opened his mouth, hanging from but one jaw, and let loose a deep hiss. "Hey, how you doing?" Matthew smiled, scared beyond belief. "They won't eat me will they?"

"Do not worry."

"And why shouldn't I worry?" Matthew whispered, still smiling. "Just my nightmares come to life." Matthew nodded to one of the undead who growled.

"Because, this is your army."

One of the corpses raised their weathered hand, the cartilage showing through the shorn knuckles, and released a piercing, guttural yell. Others began to follow suit as they shook the skies with their cries.

***

Sergeant Bradley Kinser walked his patrol through the quiet streets. He held on to his rifle firmly, the weight reassuring. The sky was dark overhead, thunder sounding in the distance. Lightning passed from one dark cloud to another. The past few days had been exactly like this one. Few dared the roads, especially after curfew. The city of Jerusalem was deserted. Windows were shuttered and doors locked. Kinser led his patrol of five through the silence. They looked this way and that down the alleys and into shadows for any lingering threats. The streetlights flickered on and off in some spots, dripping a sickly yellow light that barely illuminated anything. They stepped carefully down the narrow boulevard in a column, each man protecting one another's back, the soldier in the rear walking backwards to cover their flank. "Fucking creepy man," Private Shuster muttered.

"I prefer nobody to anybody any day," Specialist McKenna joked. "Much more elbow room."

"Yeah, and easier targets," Shuster sputtered back.

"Targets for who? The flies aren't packin' you know," Private Moreno quipped.

"Oh, wait," McKenna started. "You're a Jew aren't you."

"Not so damn loud!" Shuster hissed, turning around and punching McKenna in the shoulder.

"Ow! Asshole." McKenna rubbed his bruise. "Get over the paranoia already."

"Have you seen what they do to Jews around here?" Shuster asked.

"Should have joined the navy if you're afraid of combat," Moreno retorted.

"The navy's for fags," Shuster countered.

"Always the bad, never the good. Man, there hasn't been a murder in over a week. Just relax," McKenna offered.

"I'll relax when we're back at base," Shuster muttered out the side of his mouth.

"Don't see why," Moreno broke in. "Watching sand blow isn't my idea of entertainment."

Kinser raised his hand for them to be quiet. "What is it, boss?" McKenna asked.

"I heard something," Kinser replied and moved his hand towards their left. "That way. Keep alert."

They clicked their rifles off safe, their fingers itching for the trigger. They inched forward, a foot at a time. Kinser raised his arm to stop. He heard voices. He waved them along as he rushed to a building for cover. The remaining four bound after him. Kinser turned to his squad, pointing to Moreno and Hayes signaling to stay put. Hayes and Moreno nodded in agreement as Kinser pointed to Shuster and McKenna to follow him in. He raised three fingers and started to count down. When he reached zero, he and the two soldiers jumped around the corner. "Freeze!" Kinser bellowed, rifle at the ready. They had entered some apartment block. What few individuals braved the urban confines turned to stare at the soldiers upraised rifles. Among them stood two American G.I.s, arms full of military rations. All activity ceased as conversations fell into quiet. The two G.I.s dropped their meal bags with a muted plastic slap.

"I thought you said their patrol didn't come this way," one G.I. hissed to the other. His partner shrugged.

"What the hell is going on here?" Kinser asked, seriously pissed off.

"Looks like a humanitarian mission to me," McKenna quipped. One of the G.I.s smiled at that.

"Well?" Kinser prodded.

"Just trying to make some money, man," the other G.I. replied. "If it's a cut you want-"

"I don't want your damn money," Kinser cut him off.

"What do we do with them?" Shuster asked, watching the Jews as well as his greedy comrades.

"Get back to base," Kinser ordered. "Your officer will be hearing about this."

"Shit," the one G.I. cursed as he and his buddy turned to pick up the meals.

"Leave them." The G.I.s gave Kinser a confused look. "You don't actually think I'd trust them with you." They put their hands up in surrender and hurried out. Kinser turned to look at the Jews. Their eyes haunted Kinser in the flickering light. Dark circles surrounded brown eyes, blood red cracks throughout the whites, creases cutting into the corners of their sight. Was it fear or guilt smeared across their faces? No, it was something more disturbing. They watched the soldiers with placid stares, like lambs waiting for the slaughter. No one shook nor moved at all. They were statues. The three looked back and forth nervously.

"They know we're the good guys, right?" McKenna joked.

"You are breaking curfew," Kinser told the few assembled. "You have to return to your homes."

"My children need food," one of the men challenged. "Am I to return empty-handed?"

"You should buy food during the allowed hours-"

"The allowed hours?" The old man kicked some dirt at Kinser. "Few markets have supplies anymore, and the allowed hours are too short for us that still have jobs to find what we need. I have to search everywhere for a scrap of bread no thanks to you or your nation who have placed a blockade around our lands. Now that I have found food you tell me to abandon it? Are you our protectors or our oppressors? This is our land!"

"Ishmael, hush!" a man next to him whispered harshly.

"Black market," Shuster muttered to Kinser.

"I will not hush!" Ishmael spat. "Our people are butchered, and my children starve. What do they do? They do nothing! They allow our enemies to invade and steal our lands, rape our women, eradicate our culture. Where were you when my brother was murdered? They are like all the others. They hate us. Worse, they don't even care. I simply want food, and they threaten me for that!"

"Is it money you want?" one of the Jews asked, pulling a diamond bracelet from his jacket. "We'll pay whatever you want. We don't care who we pay. We just need food."

"Don't insult me," Kinser snapped, raising his rifle at one of the Jews as he tried to make his way to the meals. The Jew froze. "The curfew is in place to protect you."

"It is to protect you," Ishmael retorted, poking a bony finger at Kinser. "To make it easier for you to control our lands."

"Sergeant, maybe we should just give them the food. No one has to know," Shuster urged.

Kinser could feel the crowd beginning to grow hostile. "Do not undermine my authority!" Kinser hissed back. "Those meals are Army property. And," Kinser turned back to Ishmael, "Regardless of how you feel about the curfew, you will return to your homes now." The small group of Jews began to murmur causing Kinser to instinctively tighten the grip on his rifle.

"What if I don't? Will you shoot me if I try to take something?" Ishmael walked towards the scattered meals directly disobeying Kinser.

Kinser brought the rifle to his shoulder. "You will stay where you are or I will shoot!"

"Sergeant!" Shuster burst.

"Shoot me then!" Ishmael screamed. "Show us where your true loyalties are! Mine are to my children!"

"We must maintain order," Kinser replied to Shuster. His head jerked back to the old man. "Stop!" Kinser shouted as Ishmael continued forward. "Stop right there!" Kinser's finger spasmed on the trigger. He could see the man coming towards him. He didn't want to kill him. The thought of Ishmael's kids fatherless brought images of his own five year old son into his mind. He saw his son starving, hungry, shivering. The image of his gaunt boy, skin yellow and dying; a shiver went down his spine. Ishmael needed food. His children needed food. No, he was lying; trying to make him bend if not break. Besides, it was against set regulation. There could be no exception. Give an inch and they always took a mile.

Ishmael dared fate, bending down to swipe a bag and tasted the bitter fruit of destiny as Kinser pulled the trigger. The bullet tore through his chest, a red mist spraying out his back as hot lead ran off with his mortality. Ishmael seemed to jump slightly at the impact. He stood there, eyes wide. Thunder once more sounded above. Moreno and Hayes came charging around the corner stopping behind Kinser in shock. Ishmael mouthed something silently as his hand reached to touch his wound. He looked down at the mark of that mortal blow and looked back up at Kinser. A tear fell down Ishmael's cheek as blood trickled from his mouth. His eyes emptied and became blank as he collapsed to the ground, dust shaken up into the air as if his soul leaving his body. The dust floated above his corpse before dissipating into invisibility. Everyone watched, frozen by the reality. Kinser's cheek twitched as his men remained behind him, weapons raised to strike at those remaining.

"Back...back to your homes," Kinser ordered, his voice breaking. The spell was broken. The Jews hurried from sight, running down the corridors of the maze that was

Jerusalem away from their protectors scattering their goods across the ground. "We..." Kinser looked down at the body. "We have to move on. Specialist, collect the MREs."

"Yes sergeant," McKenna replied as he went to pick up the scattered pile.

"Shouldn't we report this, sergeant?" Shuster asked. Moreno, Hayes, and McKenna looked at Kinser.

"Sergeant, we don't need this problem," McKenna replied as he collected his baggage. "No one has to know. Hell, he did resist-"

"He was unarmed!" Shuster yelled.

"We will continue our patrol," Kinser growled.

"Sergeant?" Shuster asked.

"I will decide about it when we get back to base. Now, let's move out."

Shuster was numb, his mouth open in protest as the others followed behind Kinser. Their leather boots creaked as they continued through the empty market, each man passing by the corpse as if it were nothing but unsightly trash. Shuster kneeled down beside it, closing Ishmael's eyes and saying something in Hebrew as McKenna tore open one of the military meals. He reached in and pulled out a tiny plastic parcel. He peeked inside as he followed Kinser, Shuster getting up and coming behind.

"Pound cake! Damn I love pound cake." McKenna slung his rifle and began to pick a piece off, plopping it in his mouth and chewing. Shuster gave him a dirty look. "What?" McKenna asked, his mouth full.

Shuster shook his head and looked at Kinser's back. "They only wanted food, sergeant."

Kinser turned around, grabbing Shuster by the throat and throwing him against a building. "Damn you, you fucking Jew! Pick them over us will you?" Kinser fought to regain control, still pressing Shuster against the wall. Shuster stared back horrified. "I didn't want to do it. The bastard wouldn't stop. I told him to stop!" Kinser let Shuster go, marching a few feet away before pulling his helmet off. He looked up to the sky. "I didn't want to," Kinser muttered to himself. He nearly broke down. He placed a fist to his forehead. "In war, suffering happens. Shit happens. Can't change that."

"If we're not here to change it then why are we here, sergeant?" Shuster asked. McKenna was chewing on another piece of pound cake as Hayes and Moreno kept quiet.

"God only knows," Kinser replied.

***

They stood in rows upon rows, these guardians of the light. Their armor gleamed and reflected the nobility and honor of their character. Bronze and silver, gold and platinum radiated from their ranks with breastplates shined so pure that they were of glass and plumes of red fire rested upon their heads spewing from their heavenly crowns. At each side was the sword of angelic protection, the hilt intricately designed and the blade hidden within a scabbard of glowing blue. In each breast the heart of champions, the origin of selfless legend. Their ankles were girded in greaves, carved with the symbol of the one true God. Cloaks of white, the union of the entire spectrum, covered their backs. They did not squabble nor break discipline. These men were ready. Their time had come. Gabriel appeared from the corner, the heads of all angels snapping as one. Gabriel walked in front of this angelic army, his stride no longer unsure and wavering. He moved with purpose. He moved with honor restored. He looked out at the golden haired force, their blue eyes clear and piercing. He met each gaze as he walked their number, feeling their will to fight.

"Men!" He stopped and looked at them. "My brothers! For centuries we have wavered. We have been idle. We believed the great fight lost, our time passed. Our days were filled talking of times that once were rather than believing in the great acts that we are now set to accomplish. We have watched from afar those that have lived as we can only wish to say we ourselves had lived." He looked across the muscled mass, his every word theirs.

"I look at you, my brothers, and see the grandest army of all Existence. Beings of light, defenders of the heavens. Your purpose has come. We have been in battles epic in nature and legendary in scope protecting our God and his children! We have been called gods by humanity for our exploits and admired for our duty. But our duty is not to legend. Our duty is to them!" Gabriel yelled pointing to the Earth that surely sat below.

"Though they are mortal, and though they are weak, they are our brothers. They are our kindred. Now they stand on the brink of the abyss. They are threatened with everlasting darkness and extinction. We cannot stand by and allow this can we?"

"No!" the angels bellowed back.

Silence followed their yell, and then came the sound of armor clinking accompanied by heavy footsteps. The angels dared to stare and found their discipline nearly cracked as, with shock, they saw the return of their lost brethren. Death, War, Pestilence, and Conquest strode out, their faces set in an unearthly calm. "The four!" screamed someone from the ranks.

"The four!" the army yelled together as they joined Gabriel. The four turned to the assembled, gazing over those present.

Gabriel smiled and nodded at his comrades. "The time has come, the final time. This is no mere battle, this is no worthless war. This is not simply for humanity nor for our foolish pride but Existence itself! If we fall so falls the walls of our kingdom. So falls night eternal. So falls hope. By God, I swear that I shall fall before that day. Tonight, we fight. We fight as we never have before. We fight for Heaven. We fight for God. We fight...for humanity!" Gabriel brandished his sword, the blade pure fire, and thrust it above his head. The four brandished their weapons letting loose a battle cry that howled like an unholy wind. Their voices were like thunder. The army joined with an almighty roar, quaking the very foundations of God's kingdom.

The ground behind Gabriel fell away, the soil seeming to collapse in on itself opening up into the darkness. The four dove in first lunging with weapons ready. Into the hole followed the angelic army, rushing towards their destiny. Into the air they rose like a wave, twisting to fall into space and Earth below. It was a metallic fountain that sparkled with the glow of the everlasting, swallowed by the abyss.

Upon the top floor of the temple, Jesus stared out at them from on high, their faces indecipherable and their voices unable to carry the distance. He watched Heaven's finest moment devoid of emotion or understanding. His face was grim, rubbing the palm of his hand across his forehead as he saw his champions swallowed. As the last disappeared Jesus closed his eyes and covered his mouth. God sat next to him, watching his men go to war and mourning those that would never return. Jesus turned and started to leave. He paused and walked back to God in his wheelchair. "You have brought us to this," he choked out, emotion nearly consuming him. "You put too much faith in man. You have damned us."

"We...are all...to blame." God looked up, his eyes scorched by such infectious sorrow.

CHArmageddonPTER 13

Megiddo: that piece of soil stained with the blood of men, where empires from all corners of the Earth came together to butcher one another for a minor slab of land which the wind swept away grain by grain, eroding what little gain they had stolen by the sword. That mount stood as a symbol to the barbarities of man and the philosophy of might makes right. It stood grimly above the graves of generations, a tower haunted by the shades of battles forgotten. Its soil had never been productive for the fruits of men, only for the swallowing of their corpses.

An American brigade was entrenched upon its upper slopes, concrete walls and barbed wire the boundaries behind which they protected their pitiful piece of territory. The action within the camp was placid as soldiers lounged, talking to their comrades of bloated memories concerning glorious actions past, stripping the humanity and pain and over inflating their importance and honor.

Kinser sat on the ground eating alone inside the armed camp. He picked at his food, turning it over and staring into it as if the runes of some shaman. Guilt grew malignantly inside his breast at the murder that had occurred for surely it was murder. He had described the events to his superior who dismissed the whole affair, stating that it would be covered up and to forget the entire mess. But the stains of that mess remained with him no matter how hard he tried to cleanse his soul.

His appetite would not come. What right did he have to this one meal? He pictured the gaunt faces of the Jews as they stared at him last night. Their high cheek bones seemed ready to rupture the skin as their deep set eyes peered out of pools of shadow. He saw that Jew, that damnable Jew, on the ground. His mouth moved as he died like a gasping fish fresh from the lake. His food began to take on the appearance of that dead body. He threw the food over the wall. Food had become too precious a thing for someone as worthless as him. He turned to look over the concrete barrier to the gray sky. The digital alarm on his watch started to sound. His break was over. As he reached for his rifle he saw a figure staring out at the blotted horizon. What was there to look at? Kinser turned and walked back to his assigned position.

***

The Devil stared up to the sky, a slate gray mottled with cancerous clouds that dared consume the light of the sun as it fell to its death in the distance. The Devil watched to the west where it fell, where death and destruction were parts of a dying culture. He no longer wore shades to cover his eyes, now completely surrendered to a sickening yellow. His skin had gone chalk white. Acne had become welts, their redness a punctuation to the lack of pigment about his visage. They seemed open sores, causing pain in those who saw it. To Satan, it was merely flesh. His blonde hair had gone a greasy brown, sparse and soaked with oil and seemingly ready to ooze some slime. He wore drab army fatigues, mocking these men as if he were one of them.

He watched the sky, looking from whence he fell. One day, he vowed, he would lift himself back up to his brothers and undo the damage wrought by God. His arrogance at overturning Heaven's past judgment was pride beyond sin.

"You shall come," he whispered to the horizon. He turned to look at the soldiers who waited in their assigned positions. "Your children turn from you. They turn in seek of guidance." He smiled, his stained teeth filled with black grit. "And I shall guide them to that destiny that they have earned." He

359

watched two soldiers bicker loudly to one another, cursing and pushing. "They know only destruction. Perhaps it is in their genes. It is what they came from. Imperfect. Flawed. It is time I seal the cracks." He looked back to the sky, the light of day collapsing beneath the cover of night. "Will you save them? Even if they fight against your salvation?" Satan cackled.

"Mr. President," a sergeant interrupted his thoughts, standing behind him in full battle dress.

"What?" Satan asked over his shoulder, not even granting him a glance.

"It is not safe for you to be out in the open-"

The Devil swung around and pushed the sergeant to the ground. "It is not safe to tell me what to do!" he hissed. "I do what I want when I want."

"I'm sorry sir," the sergeant coughed out. Satan withdrew his attention and went back to watching the sky. "Mr. President?"

Satan slowly turned back around, his right foot grinding loudly on the rock underneath. "Yes?"

"You are needed in headquarters." The sergeant nearly choked on the words he was ordered to say. Those yellow eyes scraped and lashed his soul with every pass across his flesh. "I was sent to escort you."

"I need no escorting." Satan turned back around, waving the sergeant off. "I shall be there shortly. Leave me."

"Yes, Mr. President." The sergeant struggled to get up and hurried away.

The Devil watched with pleasure the rapidly retreating noncom, his disciplined steps thrown out of order. A lifetime of order knocked out of whack by one chance meeting. Satan turned to walk back along the edge of the camp, watching humanity as it played with its weapons as if toys.

They jested with who would have the larger body count or how they would be sure to pleasure the widows right, something their enemies were anatomically unable to do. Life was a precious gift they had little value for. *God's children.*

Satan looked down across the barren soil, destitute of the ability to birth, to sustain. It was here that the battle would come, and here where the life of man would surely end among the shards of a fallen Paradise.

He reached the edge of the cliff where a large section of tents sat connected to one another, unassailable from any point save through the camp itself. A sandy beige, the fabric seemed as rough as the rock upon which it stood. It was headquarters for those who camped here and the nerve center of Satan's planning. Inside men and women sat before monitors, staring at incoming data. Others argued in front of maps as they placed markers as to troop concentrations and possible movements. Satan wandered about the tent, silently moving towards his goal. He pushed back a flap and entered a large area filled with a desk and chairs. A general sat behind the desk listening to a situation briefing by a colonel. The general shot to his feet. Both he and the colonel gave Satan a salute. "Mr. President."

"Have you contacted General Adams?" Satan asked, ignoring their gesture.

The general slowly dropped his arm. "Yes, sir. If I may ask, why are we putting fighters in the air? Our intel shows no possible enemy aircraft within over a hundred clicks-"

"Oh, there will be enemy in the skies, general."

"Sir?"

"Do not bother me with your questions!" Satan screamed, his ashen face flaring into a fiery crimson. "I have thought on this day far more than you ever could!" The saliva frothed in his mouth as his hair waved wildly despite the slick nature. He heaved as if gravel was in his throat.

"I did not mean disrespect, Mr. President. It's just that our stocks are limited and our supply line tenuous-"

The Devil raised his hand for silence, suddenly going quite calm. Something sounded vaguely outside. It was a distant bellow like thunder only...different. "Did you hear that?" It sounded again. The general cocked his head to listen. The typing of keyboards stopped, the bickering ceased as the sound began again. Satan's fangs were bared as a smile crept across his face. Satan turned to exit the tent.

"What the hell is that?" The general turned to his colonel. "Enemy forces?"

"They come," Satan breathed, heaving the toxic air in and out of his lungs. He moved to exit the room.

"Sir, if that's enemy you can't go out there."

"Relay to our forces. It's begun." He hurriedly stepped through the tent flap outside to look out to the roiling sea above. The roof of cloud cover had split to reveal that precious star. The sun was blood red, falling behind the distant hills. Its final rays bled onto the Earth below. The horizon took on a purple hue that pushed through the slate of Earth's tomb. "Come to me," Satan hissed extending his arms to the passing sun. Out there it sounded again. It was the horn of the Horsemen.

***

"Bravo Five, Bravo Five this is Charlie One do you copy?"

"Charlie One, this is Bravo Five," crackled over the radio.

"What is your current situation, over?"

"The skies are clear he..r...e..." The signal broke up.

"Bravo Five? Bravo Five do you copy?" The pilot looked through his canopy. His squad was still in formation over

Jerusalem, the city small and insignificant at this height. The world sprawled beneath them in a vastness that humbled any mortal being. Their jets shrieked through the sky like comets, burrowing smoke trails through the air. They flew through the coming night in a tight group.

The clouds ahead began to take on an eerie transformation. They seemed to be thickening, balls of lightning jumping through the growing morass of intangible cover. The darkness lit up every few seconds then every other second. The light seemed to be concentrating towards an epicenter ahead of him in the cloud cover, turning into a growing ball of blazing white fire. Charlie One stared in awe. Lightning shot out of the smoking mass, the thunder shaking their aircraft. The jets jerked around the stab of light, their radios crackling for deaf ears as the thunder knocked their auditory senses numb.

"Sir, Charlie Two. Some sort of odd weather pattern. Shouldn't we land before-" Lightning shot out again, only this time it wasn't vertical. It seemed to shoot directly at Charlie Two's aircraft impaling the fuselage. The jet exploded into a dying series of sparks, falling in the smoke of its aerial pyre as it spiraled to Earth below. The force of the gathering speed of its descent would solve the need for any burial.

Bravo Five watched with an awe that paralyzed his entire body, his eyes fixed on the falling aircraft. "My God," he gasped watching his comrade fall to the laws of nature.

"Bravo Five? Bravo Five?"

"Oh Jesus Christ!" someone screamed through the radio. Bravo Five's face snapped up as he saw the impossible. The clouds seemed to burst open, a hole blossoming outward like a newborn flower. Figures spewed out of the yawning gap into the night sky led by four brilliant objects. The jets closed in fast and saw them for what they were. Four giant men flew forward glistening like precious stones, their swords of flame, light, and steel cutting through the gathering darkness. Behind them came thousands more soaring as if with wings, shining brighter than even the fire of their jets' exhausts. One of the Horsemen had a horn into which he blew.

"What the fuck!" a voice crackled over the radio. The Horsemen rushed forward, their swords raised to strike. The light was blinding as one brought his blade down in an arc so fast the human eye would not see it, biting deeply into the nose of a jet hurtling at top speed and carved off a large metallic chunk that sent the jet sideways slamming into a parallel pilot and smashing into a fireball as they embraced.

"Fire! Fire at anything that fucking moves!" Charlie One screamed into his headset as he gripped his control stick and released every bullet he had into the oncoming mass, his tracer rounds streaks of red and yellow light.

***

The Devil stared up with glee at his angelic guests. "You've come to play." He laughed. Little fragments seemed to flicker out of the mass of light like sparks. He could see jets careening to the ground in flaming pyres. The Devil shook his head, clucking his tongue.

The entire camp stared up with grim fascination unsure at what was taking place.

The general came running out of the tent, joining Satan as he watched. "My God!"

"Send all available air cover to that mass. Then initiate Plan Ragnarok. We must drive them to the ground."

The general looked up, licking his lips. "And then?"

"And then we use our armor to break them." The general saluted as he strode for the tent. Satan looked up again as he saw more aircraft surging into the angelic forces. His face twitched as he stared, his hands opening and closing. "Die," he breathed. "Die!"

***

The jets fired round after round. Angels took hits, the impact knocking them from their comrades. One took a bullet directly to his chest, the cannon's blow pounding him back into two fellows, cracking heads with one and his legs rounding into the chest of another. They fell in dozens.

War pulled his axe and let it fly, amputating the tail off of a plane, the fire flooding first behind then inside the jet as it arced down to the ground leaving a bow of destruction on the horizon.

Pestilence rode right up to another, straddling the canopy. The pilot looked up, terrified at the giant above him. Pestilence raised his sword for a downward stab. The pilot screamed as he desperately raised his hands to cover his head. Pestilence impaled the pilot through the glass and rode the jet streaking down, hollering the entire way with a war cry as he retracted his blade and burst up into the sky, flame reaching for him from the fallen craft.

Charlie One stared at a nightmare made real. His eyes dazzled behind his shades as he fought for an insulated breath. His hands shook as the battle unfolded around him. Screams traveled the abyss through the radio into his ears. He saw their faces, their immaculate faces, twisted in hatred, coming at him. Legions of angels made their way to him. He released his missiles as he recited a prayer. The explosion rocked them, their immortal bodies knocked senseless as they fell to Earth.

Death screamed into the sky, his roar carried across the heavens. His sword shot bolts that split jets at the seams, the metal shearing and exploding. Only the fire of battle lit the night sky. Death turned right into the path of an

365

oncoming jet, the impact rupturing the nose cone. Death was knocked unconscious, his armor dented and bent as he snapped back into the void, the damaged jet scraping over him and struggling to stay up.

Conquest let out a cry that roared above the screams of the jets as he released bolt after bolt, exploding fireballs flowing past him. A missile came towards him, streaking through the aerial field like some artificial bull. Conquest let free a grin as his eyes focused on the approaching threat. As it whistled within a hundred feet Conquest freed his one arm from the hilt of his blade. The missile rushed at him, and in a second, Conquest sidestepped it, his free hand gripping the shaft of the missile as he twisted, using his momentum to wheel it around directly at the jet from which it came. The pilot screamed in horror as it returned to him with the gift of death he had imparted to it.

From afar came a black jet, a stealth bomber. It silently approached the mayhem, concealed in the folds of night. They did not see him until it was too late, that pilot swathed in darkness. He watched quietly as he approached the melee of man and angel, magic versus science. With covered eyes he pressed the red button on his stick. It was away. He loosed a missile right towards the heaviest of the fighting. That lone rocket stole cloaked through the knots of figures to find its destiny. Into a battalion of angels it found purpose, the explosion releasing a blinding light and flame for well over five miles throughout the sky. The wave of light streaked out in an expanding circle. The angels were nuked, blasted with the Promethean fire of man.

Jets were split to atoms and eradicated, destroyed by their fellow pilot. The light fell from the heavens like shattered, stained glass. Angels were no longer granted the rights of the skies as they came crashing down to the ground of mortality. Their armor was blackened and split. Some arose bruised while others struggled to simply stand. They smoked, their blonde hair singed and white faces soot stained.

Death lay broken on the ground. He barely twitched as the ground began to rumble. His dark armor steamed as his muscles shook with effort to push him up. The rumble grew. He turned his head to see them approaching: tanks. Death fought to turn over as he was raked with machine gun fire. The bullets bruised his immaculate flesh. As he reached his knees he was struck by an exploding shell and sent dozens of feet away.

Ezekiel stood defiant in front of an oncoming tank. He yanked at his sword, not able to get it over his head. He tried to raise it again getting it a foot off the ground. The tank commander smiled looking at the pitiful sight. "Ground him under the treads," he ordered. The tank lumbered on in its quest to turn Ezekiel into paste. Ezekiel tried to raise the blade once more as the tank closed in. The ground was heaving, the steel approaching. Each individual rivet became visible. The blade became more than a trophy of pride or a weapon of defense; it became the very symbol of his worthiness to be, the proof of whether his will was capable of Existence.

As the tank reached within ten feet of Ezekiel he gave his blade one final heave and pulled it skyward, riding the blade's momentum down and embedding it in the tank's armor. The blade came within a foot of the driver's face making him jump, twisting the wheel causing the tank to jag to the side before it stopped. A bolt from some unseen angel exploded off to their side. The tank commander knocked the driver in the head. "Get us moving damnit!" Ezekiel tried to pull the blade back out when the tank started forward again.

Ezekiel found himself being pushed back as the tank continued onward. He tried to dig into the ground with his feet but his strength did not match that of man's armor.

The hatch popped open, and the commander looked out. He saw the blade jutting out of his tank and cursed at Ezekiel. He reached for his pistol and aimed at him. The booms of the field deafened them as he shot, the explosions rocking their equilibrium. A ricochet missed Ezekiel's face as it sparked off the slanted front of the tank. "You bastard!" Ezekiel screamed as the commander fired again. Ezekiel grasped the blade tightly, closing his eyes. He let the world fade out from around him as the commander went to shoot again only for his gun to jam. He slammed it up and down on the hatch as the blade in the cherub's hands began to glow. The driver's eyes squinted shut as the glare blinded him. The hair on his arms began to rise as a corona developed along the length of the steel. Ezekiel let loose a cry and sent a bolt shooting straight into the guts of the machine blasting the commander head over heels and rocking the hunk of steel. The tank jumped a foot in the air at the implosion. The steel beast came to a smoking halt, the blade easily sliding out of the melted metal. Ezekiel slid back onto his butt. He sat there, struck dumb by his act. As he stared at his conquest, his eyes brightened, and he yelled in triumph. He hurriedly got up and scurried off dragging his sword behind him.

Helicopters zoomed in from Jerusalem, their blades chopping with a whoomp, whoomp, whoomp as they approached. The steel dragonflies released a hail of piercing lead into the fallen angels. Gabriel stared on as he saw his brothers clutching their sides or falling from fire. Their cries incensed him. Gabriel gripped his sword and launched himself into the air, swinging his sword in a crescent that tore the blades clear off a nearby helicopter. The blades spun like a pinwheel rolling to the ground and spinning off towards the mountain base. As the helicopter spun out of control Gabriel clutched it, swinging blow after blow slicing it to pieces as he rode it to the ground.

***

The Devil gauged the situation from the mount, watching the brutality emotionlessly. A captain came out of the tent. The Devil turned to see him rather than the general he had expected. "Where is your commander?"

The captain nervously blinked, his face losing color. "He...is busy, sir. Directing the battle."

The Devil nodded, enjoying the discomfort. "Casualty report."

"We've lost seventy percent of our aircraft. We still command fifty percent of our armor but are taking continued damage. Sir, we will not be able to hold this position." A boom silenced the captain.

"Oh no." Thunder crashed through the night. "We will hold."

"Sir?"

The Devil ignored him as he stared out into the blackness. The lightning gave brief pictures of the war below. The sky began to cry Heaven's tears upon its fallen. The rain drenched everything, a deluge that muddied the ground. Tanks began to lose traction, spinning against their will in the sludge beneath them. Helicopters struggled against the storm, slapping away the tears of God to push on with man's violence. The angelic defenders were now dirty and soiled. Their golden hair was burned. Their pale skin was blistered and reddened from burns. They fought but did not dominate. They were nearly broken. Now they would be. "Now," Satan breathed, his eyes glowing an unearthly light.

***

The air seemed to cool and still itself. A quake began to shake the foundations of the world sending the angels that tried to rise back into the mud. The ground oozed open into a gathering gulf, splitting like a rotten melon. Men and material fell in as the maw hungrily yawned with slick, muddy lips. The fighting ceased as all turned to watch. It sounded as if the earth were moaning in agony. And then it was silent. Soldiers and angels alike stared at the massive hole. Whispers seeped out of the crevice followed by curses and screams. A few brave angels walked forward for a better look. One was grabbed by the leg and pulled down into the abyss.

As the angels backed away up they came. Warped figures of men dragged their cursed flesh out of Hell and into battle. Their eyes were white with crackling red, their teeth rotten. They were hardened by damnation, and their hearts begged in insanity for action to forget their very worthless existences. They moved to tear the world apart. The depths vomited them up through the earth to return to their former brothers and consume them.

They came with axes. They came with blades. They rushed undisciplined and howling into the suffering angels, cutting them down. Death was impaled as he lay on the ground. Blood poured from his mouth, glowing and pure. He choked on it as the demon smiled down at him, the wicked grin a taunt to the gates above. Death tasted mortality and suffered in disbelief as the spear was wrenched this way and that. The demon growled and ripped his weapon free, releasing what little life remained before going in search for more.

They were the mob, lacking discipline but embracing their killer instincts. A demon leaped onto the back of an angel, demonic claws ripping at his face as his fellow drove daggers into the angel's belly again and again. Another wielded a large hammer with which he crushed the heads of his victims.

Pestilence beheaded a demon as it approached, the inky oil a fountain of unclean life. Another two charged as he gracefully cut the one in two and brought the blade swinging around to bury it in the other's dark heart. The demon rode the blade all the way up, screaming in the Horseman's face. Pestilence twisted the blade, withdrew it, and in one clean movement beheaded him as well.

Gabriel sliced through the hellish horde with wild cries, splitting skulls and amputating reaching arms. He raised his blade to the sky, and lightning flashed down to the sword flowing out in forks striking over a dozen souls.

But the battle was being lost. The demons began overwhelming them, climbing over the bodies of their fallen to clutch at and choke the life out of Heaven's best. The field was fresh with the dying as it churned. Two demons fell consecutively to an angel as another thrust a sword into his undefended back, cackling. Three rushed another, pulling the angel to the ground as they pounded and choked the life from him.

***

The Devil looked on imperiously at the fall of light, his jaw set and hands clenched. He smirked as the cries of the suffering reached his ears.

Soldiers stared in horror from the camp down at the massacre happening below them. The lightning revealed their hidden faces, contorted by fright. Heidelberg crossed himself as he watched over his rifle as another rose, weapon in hand, and started to move.

"Kinser!" Heidelberg whispered harshly. "Where are you going?"

371

Kinser turned, his face barely visible in the darkness. "Down there."

"What?" Heidelberg choked out. Kinser started to hurry off, and Heidelberg grabbed him by the arm. "Man, they will kill you."

"So they kill me!" Kinser barked back.

"What the fuck is your problem?" Heidelberg screamed into Kinser's face as he rose to hold him back. "This isn't your fight."

Kinser looked into Heidelberg's eyes. "If this is not my fight then I don't know what is. Those are angels down there. Angels! I...I have to go."

"Why?" Heidelberg ordered.

Kinser shook off Heidelberg's grip.

"I order you, as your commanding officer, to stay here. You will not go down there alone."

"Then come with me."

Heidelberg looked away.

"Fine," Kinser replied. "I'll go alone." He gripped his rifle and ran down the mountain.

The Devil's smile was sadistic as his glee grew with the rise in immortal bloodshed. What was that? Satan turned, hearing something. *Marching. Who the hell was marching here?* "Captain!" Satan yelled. The captain came running out. "Do we have any forces coming from the east?"

"No sir," the captain replied.

Under the shadow of night something was coming. The Devil watched to see what it was.

***

Matthew rode the corpse's shoulders as the undead army marched forward, his infantile feet dangling. He had pulled his shirt up over his nose to prevent himself from throwing up at the odor. Not far ahead he saw flames and heard the echoes of war. Matthew looked around. "This is it?" he asked.

"Yes," Gupta replied.

"Are you sure?"

"Of course. Why do you ask?" the voice in his head questioned.

"Well, the movies always have the climax in a city like New York. This place is kind of drab."

"This is not some poor movie!" Gupta chastened. "The battle has begun."

Matthew stared as they approached. The screams of the dying made him wince. "Are we winning?"

"I don't think so," the voice replied. "The fate of the world is up to you."

"Do you have to pressure me like that?" Matthew murmured. He looked up and down the rotten ranks straggling along. "Uh, halt!" Matthew ordered, raising his chubby little arm. "Now what?"

"You must face Satan."

"Ok, bad idea. I'm not quite old enough to legally accept that ass kicking."

"It is your-"

"It's my destiny, I know. God, why did I ever ask for an exciting life?" Matthew scanned the field. "Where is he?"

"On the mountain."

Matthew looked up to the lighted beacon towering before him. Up there seeming to float in the night was Satan's base. Lightning flashed again revealing the soldiers posted. "Big problem there."

"Divide your forces."

"What?"

"Send part of your army to aid the angels, the other to assault the mountain. The demons do not expect a flank attack, and no mortal shall stop your army. You should be able to make it in the confusion."

Matthew nodded in agreement. He tapped the corpse in the head. "Down, worm head." The zombie picked him up off his shoulders and lowered him to the ground. Matthew waddled out in front of his army and put his hands on his hips, something he thought Patton always did. He raised one hand and pointed. "You," he began, looking at their rotten faces. One zombie's eye fell out as they listened. "Attack those guys," Matthew pointed back to the field of battle. "You," he pointed to the other part of the army, "attack the mountaintop. Got it?"

"Well done and inspiring," Gupta replied sarcastically.

Matthew watched as the undead still stood there. "Well?" he asked. They continued to look at him. "You didn't really want to live forever did you?" They looked at each other nodding, one's head falling off as he did so. His rotten comrade picked it up and gave it to him as the undead broke into two forces and began towards their respective places.

***

Kinser aimed his rifle and fired knocking the demon off of Gabriel. It turned around and growled at him, its mouth dripping with gore. Kinser let go another round knocking it down again. "How you like that shit?" he yelled. Another demon came running from behind only to be knocked out by the butt of Kinser's rifle. Gabriel coughed up blood, the death rattle beginning in his throat. Kinser ran over to his side. "Hey, it's gonna be ok."

Gabriel smiled at him, thumping him on the chest. Gabriel looked up at the mountaintop at the humanity that watched their fate being decided for them. "Of all men you alone dared to join us in deciding your fate. Your courage makes you worthy of one of us." He reached down and grabbed his sword, the fire dimming upon the steel. He offered the hilt to Kinser.

"No, I don't know how to use that thing." Gabriel offered it again, his eyes pleading. Kinser slung his rifle and grabbed the blade. The light of the metal surged again as it brightened Kinser's eyes.

"Use it well." Gabriel coughed. "Use it...for good." Gabriel's eyes glazed as he fell to mortality a hero.

Kinser raised the sword, the light turning into a white flame, and charged into a mass of demons. The blade eviscerated one as he tore it free and cleaved another's ribs. Kinser swung and swung, obliterating countless demons in wisps of bright light. His face was twisted by anger and rage as he hacked at the evils of his life, of all Creation. He purged himself of his pain, of his doubts and fought the demons of his existence. After what seemed like hours he stopped swinging, his arms numb with a burning through his nerves, to see only a mass of quivering bodies. Kinser smiled, raising his blade high. "Kinser...the barbarian!" He heard approaching footsteps and turned. "You want..." Kinser shut up as his arm lowered a bit. A mass of corpses was coming right his way. They stopped and looked at the dead demons on the ground. "You weren't friends were you?"

***

The soldiers' stared in horror as the dead limped up the slope, slowly, purposefully. "What the fuck are you waiting for? Shoot!" ordered a sergeant. They opened fire on the dead causing them to freeze in their tracks. Smoke gathered as expended cartridges fell at their feet until it obscured the slope. The firing ceased as the soldiers waited to see the results, the haze blinding them. As the smoke cleared they saw the undead still standing.

One of the corpses reached down and gauged the new holes blown out of him with his finger. He looked up, clearly pissed off, and let out a howling scream. The others did too as they burst into an uneven sprint right into the soldiers' ranks, leaping over barbed wire and sand bags to grab them.

"Reinforcements! Give me re-" an undead jerked the lieutenant away from the radio.

Soldiers were charging towards the entrance, their M-16s at the ready. As they reached the chaos some were clotheslined while others tackled. "Shoot them in the brain!" one lieutenant yelled pulling his pistol and blowing a large chunk out of a dead man's skull. The undead shook his head, gritted his teeth, and ran right at the officer as he continued to fire.

A soldier brought his rifle butt right into the mouth of one zombie, the blow wrenching the bottom jaw right off. The undead's tongue waggled unsupported as he gurgled in anger. The soldier dropped his rifle in shock as the dead man jumped on top of him.

Another G.I. was gunning down anything in his path. "Whoo hoo, get you some!" he shouted as he held the trigger down on his M-60 scattering the dead into organic chaff. His attention occupied he didn't notice the undead female who tackled him from behind. The G.I. flipped her over his hip, her grip tearing the machine gun from his hands. He backed up from the living corpse, getting ready for some hand-to-hand action. She stood up, naked. Worms crawled in her burnt flesh, her breasts sagging like melted plastic. Her nipples were a dark purple as were her lips. Her eyes were long gone. She howled at him. "You look just like my wife," he retorted. He stopped and looked down. "Better tits though." She ran right at him.

"Mother fucker!" a ranger screamed as he proceeded to beat all incoming zombies with someone's severed arm, using it like a baseball bat. The wet slap of every whack was sickening. "Want a hand?" A zombie screamed from his left. The ranger ducked as he flew over and brought the arm up in an uppercut of sorts. "Bad joke but don't tear my head off for it."

As the melee continued Matthew snuck up over the barbed wire wall. He dropped to the ground quietly and hurried behind a tent. He peeked around the corner. The dead were tearing everyone apart. "So now where to?"

"I don't have all the answers," the voice replied.

"Great, just great."

***

The Devil stared in anger at what he saw below. "Buddha! He broke the provision against resurrection! That unlawful fucking bastard!" He spit and railed, gripping and pulling his hair. The battle was turning against him as the endless dead poured into his men. His head twitched this way and that as he watched his most infamous fall. Soldiers started pouring out of the command tent behind him. The Devil turned around and snatched one of their arms. "Where do you think you are going? This battle isn't over!"

"Sir, they need us at the front!"

"Why?" the Devil blurted. The soldier was afraid. "Why?" he yelled shaking him.

"We are being overrun."

"What?" the Devil released him in shock as the tent continued to empty. The Devil began wandering after them, not believing what he had heard. How could they be losing? This was all impossible. The Devil froze as he saw one of the undead. It turned and noticed him as well. It growled, those pus colored eyes fixing on Satan as it ran at him. The

Devil kept his hands out urging the creature at him defiantly. In an instant, the Devil snatched the undead's head and twisted it, breaking the neck and ripping the head right off.

Gunfire was going off all over. A sergeant yelled between gritted teeth as he brandished his machine gun, tearing various corpses in half with his weapon of destruction. His swath of lead tore through the undead ranks and relegated them to graveyard fodder. The brass clinked to the ground one after another. He bellowed as he blew up this damned army. Then he was empty. The rifle clicked unloaded. The sergeant pulled out his knife and roared as four undead charged him.

The Devil wandered through this crisis like through a pool. He was unstoppable, as he ripped each soul that challenged him. As he seized one's skull, crushing it in his grasp, he saw a tiny child run by towards the command tent. He turned his head in morbid curiosity, crushing the skull absent-mindedly before following after the child.

Another undead tried to grab him only for the Devil to drive his fist through his face. He yanked it free with a slurp, shaking the brains off as he approached the tent. The base was deserted here. No one was to be seen until Matthew stepped out of the tent and saw his body.

Matthew jerked back, a little shocked and grossed out by the Devil's appearance. The Devil had no clue who he was. "I definitely don't like what you've done with the place," Matthew scolded.

"Matthew," the Devil spewed.

"So, I guess this is where the triumphant battle takes place." Matthew cracked his knuckles. "You could give up now. Save yourself the unholy smackdown I'm gonna give you."

"Oh no," the Devil hissed between his yellowed fangs, teeth crooked. "This is where you die."

"You know you should really see a dentist." Satan cackled a death rattle. His face jerked to the side, a hideous expression possessing his features. He leaped forward to grab Matthew. The infant dodged to the side causing Satan to slam into the ground. Matthew nailed him in the side of the head with a roundhouse kick. He went for another only for the Devil to grab his leg pulling him to the rocky dirt. Matthew started kicking as rapidly as he could over and over, breaking the Devil's nose and swelling an eye. He pulled free as Satan groped at his bloody face.

Matthew took on a defensive stance as Satan staggered to his feet. "You want some?" Matthew gestured defiantly. Satan reached into his jacket and pulled out a revolver. Matthew slid out of his stance and put his hands palms up. "Can't we talk about this like adults?" The Devil started to aim. Matthew dashed off. "Guess not." The first shot just missed his feet. Matthew dove over a pallet and hid behind some boxes.

"Come out, boy!" Satan screamed, waving his pistol.

Matthew looked around for anything. He saw a tent in the distance and made a run for it. A bullet whizzed across the back of his neck, the deathly breeze chilling. His little feet patted on the ground as Satan chased after him. Another bullet kicked up dust as Matthew disappeared into the tent.

"Stand and fight like a man, you fucking child!" The tent dropped in one section, drooping. The Devil shot his remaining three rounds into the folds of the tent. He touched the release mechanism, letting the magazine drop to the ground with a clatter. As he reached to grab another from his jacket Matthew charged out with one of the tent poles. His first shot knocked the gun from Satan's hands. Followed by a quick succession to the knee, stomach, then face bringing the Devil down to his knees to be laid out. The Devil fell on his back as Matthew repeatedly beat him with the pole. "Not the face!" Matthew complained to Gupta who manipulated the attack. Satan bunched up, trying to protect himself from the blows. He gradually rolled to his chest, pushing himself up.

"Stay down!" Matthew barked through toothless gums as he slammed Satan over and over again. As he brought another shot down the Devil grabbed the stick holding it tight. Matthew tried to yank it back but he wasn't strong enough. The Devil pulled it towards himself, bringing Matthew eye to eye with him. Matthew flinched as the Devil smiled, blood trickling out of his mouth. Matthew released the stick, the lack of weight sending it straight into the Devil's brow. Matthew screamed like Bruce Lee as he sent two quick punches right into Satan's chest and capitalized it with an uppercut. The Devil replied by shoving Matthew onto his back. Satan turned and spit crimson into the dust. Matthew flipped back onto his feet and started dancing on the balls of his feet, fists ready. "Waaaaaaaa!" he challenged. The Devil rose to his feet, the light starting to fade around him as he thrust his hands out, the nails extending further into claws, ripping the skin as they grew. The screams of the damned roared out his mouth.

"Yeah," Matthew replied, freezing. "Impressive." He darted off. The Devil growled inhumanly as he levitated off the ground and flew after him. Matthew hurtled over debris, dodging the Devil everytime he lunged for him from above. Satan cut through the air and scraped across the ground as Matthew weaved right avoiding his latest attempt. The noise of battle was rising as he continued forward. He turned a corner and saw the slaughter. Soldiers fired, piercing and tearing undead down, scattering gore across the earth. One undead was disemboweling a fallen soldier as his comrade ran the corpse through with a large knife.

Matthew stopped, not wanting to get dragged into this B-movie gone bad when he felt the blow to the back of his head. Matthew was woozy, unable to focus on the fuzzy world around him. He felt like he was floating. As his vision cleared he discovered the world was upside down.

***

The Devil carried Matthew by the leg, holding him at his side, the infant's head nearly dragging along the ground. Satan made his way back towards the command tent, letting the discord fade behind him. His steps were quiet as he wandered through the empty tents. Matthew started to struggle, hitting Satan on the calf trying to be released. The Devil picked him up and slammed him on the ground. Matthew felt the air knocked out of him as the Devil reached down and grabbed him by the throat picking him back up. Matthew choked as the Devil continued towards the main tent.

He swept through the doorway, knocking over empty chairs as he strode towards a large radio in the corner. Matthew tried to pry that grip of ice from his throat as the Devil adjusted the frequency. He picked up the receiver and spoke, "Babylon, this is the President."

"Sir, what is going on there? We have reports of enemy all over your area."

"The Russians have invaded as we feared. Nuclear weapons have been used."

"Nukes, sirs?"

"Yes. I'm afraid they are preparing to do the same to the continental United States as well."

"What does that mean, sir?"

381

The Devil turned and gave Matthew a grin, his eyes darkening. "Pre-emptive strike. Patch me through to CENTCOM." The radio warbled for a few seconds as Matthew stared in shock.

"You...can't," Matthew choked between gurgles.

"This world never should have been. Ironic that your breed would destroy it when they need it most."

"Mr. President, this is General Bates, commander of CENTCOM. I need the launch codes to confirm."

Matthew struggled as the Devil gave each part of the code, his words spraying a red mist that stained the receiver. "You may launch when ready." The Devil dropped the receiver without listening to the reply. He dragged Matthew outside back to his vantage point.

He held Matthew up, pointing to the battle below. "Look how they fight in vain. And because of you." The Devil pulled Matthew close. "You!" he cursed into Matthew's face. "Your breed has divided us. You have driven us to this!" Matthew's face was starting to go blue. He fought to stay conscious. "And now here we are, at the end."

"You'll kill your own men-"

"Death? Death is a mortal worry. We'll be, again, one day. You won't." The Devil began to squeeze harder, his gaze piercing. "I will enjoy tearing your soul apart."

The horizon as well as the field lit with nuclear fire as missiles slammed into everything around them. A blinding light tore Existence away, blackening and consuming the whole of Creation. Unholy fire scorched the Earth, burning away all that was. The flames reached all around them licking at reality. Only Satan and Matthew were free of the carnage as life was swept away. They struggled above the flames. He gripped at Satan's hands trying to pull them off, his vision starting to black out. The screams of so many came together in unison.

"Die! DIE!" Satan screamed as he shook Matthew.

Matthew felt the heat, the passing of millions. *It can't be over.* "No," Matthew rasped. His hands fought the numbness as the ground shook, and clouds smothered the world. He touched the face of Satan, feeling the cold clamminess.

"Fight him," Gupta urged.

"I...can't," Matthew gasped, unable to taste the breath of life. He hung limply, his struggling fading.

"Only you can stop him, Matthew. Heaven's armies have fallen. You alone stand for us. He is anchored to the world through you, your flesh. If you do not take back your body humanity shall fall." The blackness began to take him. "Matthew, take back what is yours."

"I...can't...beat him." He gasped his final breath.

"You must," Gupta pleaded.

On that ledge above the consuming inferno a mortal struggled against the strength of the gods. Humanity fought for its right to be in a shattering Existence, Satan's insanity personified in the dying world around them. All was falling apart, the works of his hands unmade as the laws fractured. The world fell away, Life smothered by the hands of its creator. Screams, pleas, and prayers seemed to emanate from the flames around them. The souls of those lost twisted and suffered in the cold flames of the abyss, these beings swallowed by the dark. Matthew's flesh failed at that moment, his body incapable of defense. The death rattle gurgled in his throat as Satan screamed in his face. But as his flesh gave way, as he felt his grip on mortality slip and with it Life's last connection to this realm, his soul did stir. His eyes rolled into the back of his head as he gave up the ghost.

The Devil held the lifeless infant, his laughter rising to the Heavens. The inferno raged about him, and the foundations of Existence shook. Eyes closed he tossed his head back to scream to those who had cast him out. His inhuman yell fell away as his eyes opened. Satan dropped the infant, staggering back. He stood there, knees bent, his face confused. He twitched and spasmed upon the ledge, crackling crimson consumption below.

The infant stirred, his head rising from the ground staring at Satan. "Matthew?" Gupta rasped.

Satan felt the mortal's soul inside his flesh. Their spirits did touch, that moment opening Matthew's soul to the vastness of the beyond. "He is...now...mine," choked the Devil, a tic developing in his mouth.

"Fight him, Matthew!"

"No!" screamed Satan, the flames leaping higher into the air, the black smoke gathering.

"Fight, Matthew! Fight"

"It...ends," Satan stammered, spitting and choking.

His face began to shake, his knees buckling. Hisses and squeals fled from his mouth. He gripped at his shirt, over his heart. Some unseen force tore his arms to either side, ripping it open. An inhuman howl erupted from his throat as his face jerked skyward. The smoke did part to a brilliant presence. The star shone through that hole, a pillar of light shining upon the tainted body of Life. The blood poured from Satan's mouth. He screamed and cried to the sky as the mist began to sparkle, his mouth glowing like a furnace. His eyes squeezed shut, tears wearing trails through the dirt upon his face. The infant Gupta backed away. His mouth quivered as the Earth shook in its death throes. The light in Satan's mouth grew brighter until a stream of brilliance belched forth. A shadow was launched into the clouded sky upon a stream of pure light. It screamed as it fell, over the ledge, into the nothingness below, swallowed by the flames it had ignited. A great boom shook the world sending Gupta over the ledge, and then all was dark.

The flames burnt themselves out below the dangling Gupta. He hung to the rock, pulling himself up hand by hand. As he crawled back onto the mount he saw Matthew unconscious on the ground. Gupta walked slowly to the still form, watching for life. He knelt down, placing his hand on Matthew's back. He rolled him over with a grunt. The boy was heavy. Matthew's body was calm. The sores had faded, his hair had grown back. Color had returned to his skin, a mass of bruises across his gentle features. "Matthew?" Gupta whispered shaking him. "Matthew?" Thunder played throughout the sky, illuminating still pictures of a lost world. "Matthew?" Gupta tried again, shaking him as emotion gripped him. He took Matthew's large hand in both of his and looked down at this mortal. He was lost.

Matthew's fingers twitched, coming to life in Gupta's palms. He awoke. His eyes opened, the whites blood red. He looked over to his infant companion. "Did we win?" His voice was ragged but hope was woven into his words. The child closed his eyes and clasped his hands before him. Matthew stood groggily, limping to the edge. The smoke cleared revealing a blackened wasteland. Nothing stood. It was barren. Matthew wept.

"This is the price of war," Gupta stated.

Matthew saw the end. Life was no more. Satan had won. He wept for the billions, his mind unable to support any thought. He dropped to his knees wracked with grief. He shook with the pain of such loss. His cries rose into yells then screams. He screamed into the darkness, his cries echoing to the clouds above. His screams did reach the heights, scattering the roof of Earth as the clouds fell away to reveal the stars above. Gupta came to him, putting an arm around Matthew as they looked to the sky. It stood, ever eternal and untouched. They stood alone on their pedestal hewn of Mount Megiddo, the final force to conquer those dominant heights. Matthew felt the loneliness, the solitude. In that moment, when all was lost, he reached out to the eternal. He cried for God.

It began without notice but grew. The stars came together, their pinpricks forming blobs that expanded as they combined. The multitude united as one, the fractured treasures of Heaven a single, brilliant sun that bathed them in the greatest light. From on high God descended to his Creation for the first time. His wheelchair settled on the rock as Jesus stood beside him. Buddha appeared at his side and made his way to Matthew. He offered his hand, Matthew gripping it to rise. "This cannot be how it ends," Matthew pleaded with Buddha.

"Only he," Jesus gestured to God, "Could restore it. That has been beyond him for millennia."

"Then we are lost?" Matthew asked.

Buddha looked into Matthew's scarred eyes and spoke not for his ears but for his soul. "For too long we have looked to him for our answers. In so doing we have failed to see the solution."

"But what is that solution?" Matthew asked.

"God did make us but he made us of himself." Buddha pierced his being. "He is us, and we are he."

Matthew cocked his head, the realization finding him. He turned to the devastated horizon and stretched out his hand. His faith did rise as he embraced that hidden truth, discovered that part of him he had failed to understand. His flesh did become insignificant as his soul blazed. His skin

shone like blazing diamond, the greens of his eyes
becoming a flaring emerald as the darkness fell away from
him like a cloak removed to the ground. His power reached
across the world, his life giving it life. A smoke covered the
Earth, not the black of consumption but the white of fog. It
was as if the world were a blank sheet, unwritten upon by
hand. Inside the mist the scorched rock of the burnt plain
cracked, crumbling into fertile soil. A lush, magical green
broke the desert as Life did spring anew. The black sky did
flee at the approach of day as the rays of morn brought its
purples, its reds, and then fresh blue. Matthew gasped, and
the winds did blow again ruffling his hair taking the fog with
it. The smoke did clear revealing his work. The bones of
Earth were set and her flesh mended.

He closed his eyes and reached into the beyond,
searching for those lost. He guided those few he could find
away from the realm of shade, acting as a beacon showing
them back through the portal into the world of man. As his
eyes opened and that halo of light fell from his form, he did
gaze out at what he made. The fallen of the field, angels and
man, looked up to where he stood on the mount. Matthew's
figure was bathed in the light of day. The angels saluted him,
taking a knee to show respect to this risen man. Kinser was
the lone human among them staring up with wonder at this
figure that seemed to be God himself.

Matthew turned to God, and limped. Each step ached.
The distance was monumental. Matthew slouched before
him, his knees shaking. He looked at that broken deity
whose flame had been extinguished long ago. "I believe,"
Matthew whispered as he placed his bloodied hands on the
bald head of God and closed his eyes. Nothing happened.
Jesus reached to stop this charade only for Gupta to pull him
back. Jesus gave Gupta an angry glare but the child looked

on with hope. A blue light began to emanate from Matthew's hands that gradually encompassed God. The liver spots faded as his skin brightened. Hair began to grow and thicken upon His head, white as wool. His muscles tightened and His posture straightened. As His face rose his jaw became set and His eyes piercing and full.

Matthew pulled his hands away as God seemed to see the world for the first time. He gripped the arm chairs and pushed Himself up. As His feet touched the ground He began to grow. His flesh was as the light of the sky, His radiance restored. His strength grew as His height rose. He was massive.

"My God!" gasped Jesus.

God turned to gaze at the resurrected world around him. The Almighty nodded. "It is good," He whispered.

"What does this mean?" Jesus asked.

"What we always knew," Buddha explained. "We are all one."

Matthew quivered having felt such power course through him. God stood over him, that giant of giants, and smiled at His child. "What was my destiny?"

God smiled broader and turned to Buddha. Buddha walked forward, hands together as if in prayer. "Man was born of flesh but conceived of the Almighty. This was so because of the flaw of perfection. Only through imperfection may we strive. Only in mortality may we find the spirit."

The spell was nearly broken. Matthew turned to Buddha. "English please?"

God laughed as Buddha smiled. "Prophecy spoke of a Messiah. One who would lead us."

"What do you mean? Lead you?"

"For so long we've looked to God for answers, to God for protection when all along we've had them. We are a part of

God, and in so being, He is a part of us. His strength is ours."

"That doesn't really explain anything."

"You are an example, proof of our divinity. Since inception we've focused on our flesh and believed ourselves mortal failing to realize the richness within, our legacy. You will lead us by example to realize our equality and unending capacity much as our Father." Buddha turned to God. "You will guide humanity to victory over their flesh and lead all of Creation back to Paradise, the eventual healing of the wound."

Matthew was a bit skeptical. "You sure you have the right person? Why me? Why not you?"

"Destiny is never an easy thing to understand. For all my wisdom I have doubts and limitations. We all have. You have shown us our error, that truth that has eluded us."

"And what is that?"

"That the impossible is an artificial construct." Buddha put a hand on Matthew's shoulder. "Nothing is impossible. Jesus feared you as did Satan. They saw in humanity a threat to themselves and sought to keep you in your place."

"So they knew I was the Messiah?" Matthew asked.

"Of course. They knew of your destiny to lead. That is why they sought to bring you to them. To use you to their own ends."

"If I was so important why did you all leave me so vulnerable?"

"It's like I said, Matthew," Buddha answered sagely. "One cannot fulfill destiny by being told. One must earn it. One must learn."

Kinser staggered around looking at the angels, an ant among legends. What the hell had happened? He followed their gaze to where Matthew and God stood. "Who's that?"

"Be proud, human. You have seen the Creator," Gabriel responded. "And the Messiah"

Kinser shrugged his shoulders. "I thought he was bigger."

Matthew looked out and saw the resurrected Earth but alas the ruins of Jerusalem still remained. "It seems I learned too late." His face wore a cynical mask that threatened to bury the idealism beneath. "What of humanity? I found so few."

God stepped forward, catching Matthew's eye. With the wave of His hand a breeze played across the world, caressing Matthew's cheek. Matthew's eyes closed and, behind closed lids, he swore he saw the remnants of man arising from the wreckage. A smile spread across the Almighty's face as He turned to Buddha. "They await their time. Humanity shall never pass away. It shall rise once more as it did after the Flood, more glorious than ever."

Matthew saw the countless faces of those to come, flew over cities centuries away. He opened his eyes, the realization of himself as the foundation of a future to be fulfilled. "What now?" Matthew asked.

"You live. You learn. That is the way. And you," Buddha looked at Jesus, "have much to answer for."

"Does that mean he isn't the Messiah anymore?" Matthew asked.

"He never was," Buddha replied.

"Really?" Matthew gasped. God nodded. Matthew turned and looked at Jesus. "I'm gonna kick your ass." God gave Matthew an unapproving look. "Later. Later I swear."

Jesus was about to protest when God glared at him. "Ok," he murmured looking at the ground.

The angels flew up to the sky to return to Heaven. Jesus faded into the glow of the sun. Buddha turned to Matthew and Gupta. "Gupta, you shall stay here to help guide him in the time to come."

Gupta nodded accepting his destiny. Matthew turned to him. "I guess that means I should adopt you. I think I'll name you Matt Jr."

"I prefer Gupta," the baby replied crossing his arms.

God stopped before His ascension and shook Matthew's hand, His grip holding his entire forearm. He gave Matthew a respectful nod. "You were never a mistake." Matthew firmly returned the handshake. "Take care of my children. Guide them well." God became the rays of the sun, streaking out into everything and returning to his place in the heavens.

Matthew looked down at the distant ground beneath them. "Can I...?" he asked Gupta motioning below them.

"Of course."

Matthew tossed Gupta up onto his shoulders and stepped off the ledge, falling to the ground below. With inches to spare he slowed and gently touched down on the ground before Kinser.

"Whoa!" Kinser gasped. "Who are you?"

"Well, uh...God calls me Messiah but you can call me Matt."

"Kinser," Kinser replied shaking Matthew's hand, wide-eyed.

Matthew continued to shake Kinser's hand as he looked around. "Guess we have a long walk ahead of us."

"Seems that way," Kinser replied appraising the empty lands around them.

"Shall we?" Matthew asked. Kinser nodded, and the three started off to no where in particular. "Kind of a weird ending to all this, huh?" Matthew asked Gupta on his shoulders.

"When it comes to religion nothing makes sense," Gupta sagely replied. "Besides, it's a happy ending. It's good enough."

The Messiah nodded as they walked to the horizon. Before they were lost from sight, Matthew asked one final question: "What do you think happened to Satan?"

***

Satan sat sealed in that old chamber that had held the Horsemen, brooding in the darkness. The door to the tomb slowly opened, the light blinding the Devil where he sat on the floor in his rumpled business suit. God stood there in the entrance, staring at his fallen son. "What do you want?" Satan asked, looking away.

God gave him a disapproving look. "I've come to give you something."

"And what is that?" Satan asked. "Hopefully it's something to read."

"It should relieve your boredom." God signaled to someone beyond Satan's sight. The Four Horsemen forced someone towards the doorway. "A roommate."

Satan looked closely as his eyes adjusted. It was Jesus. "Oh no," he muttered.

"You two have fun. I'll check up on you, in say two millennia?" God turned and walked away as the Horsemen began to close the door behind Jesus locking the two in together.

As the door slammed shut, Satan looked up at Jesus, and Jesus looked down at Satan. "So," Satan started. "Bring any cards?"

About the Author

Matthew Moses currently resides in Indiana after four years spent between California and South Africa. He has a degree in Political Science from Indiana University Southeast.

LaVergne, TN USA
16 September 2009
158056LV00002B/162/A